# THE
# GERMAN
# DAUGHTER

# THE GERMAN DAUGHTER

Marius Gabriel

embla
books

First published in Great Britain in 2024 by

Bonnier Books UK Limited
4th Floor, Victoria House, Bloomsbury Square, London, WC1B 4DA
Owned by Bonnier Books
Sveavägen 56, Stockholm, Sweden

A CIP catalogue record for this book is available from the British Library.

ISBN: 9781471416415

This book is typeset using Atomik ePublisher.

Embla Books is an imprint of Bonnier Books UK.
www.bonnierbooks.co.uk

*For Emma and Sabrina*

# PROLOGUE

*Oslo, Norway, 1945*

Now that the war had ended, she lived a hidden, solitary life. She'd even given birth on her own – or had tried to. Her screams had drawn the old woman from upstairs, who'd hobbled down uninvited, and had sullenly helped her through her labour. With the air of someone doing a repugnant task, the old woman had cut the cord and thrust the sticky baby into Liv's arms, then left. Neither of them had said a word to one another through the whole process. The old woman had not returned since.

She was left alone with the baby. She'd never expected that she would have to take care of it. Now there was no option. She was stuck with it.

She preferred to think of the baby as *it*. But it was a girl. She'd hoped for a boy. Like a lot of things lately, that hadn't worked out.

After the birth, she and the baby slept for a few hours in the bloodstained tangle of the bed. They were both exhausted. The baby was the first to wake. She stirred and whimpered, which brought Liv out of her deep, black sleep. For a long time, she stared at the strange, red, crumpled creature she had brought into the world. She didn't want it. She didn't want any of it.

The baby started to cry. The effect on her body was instantaneous. Her womb contracted in a spasm. She'd dreaded having to do this, but again, there was no option. She lifted the baby and put it to her breast.

Frustratingly, it didn't seem to know what to do. It kept crying, a jagged torment that enraged her. 'Come on,' she hissed to the squirming, blind creature. 'Stupid thing! Come on! Stupid, stupid thing!'

Angrily, she squeezed a little milk into the screaming, toothless mouth. The baby's bleary eyes opened in surprise. It made a comical face, exploring the taste with its tongue, forgetting to cry. It smacked its lips. At last, it began to suck, violently and clumsily, on the tender flesh.

The first minutes were agony. She endured them with clenched teeth, sweat beading her face and trickling down her neck. She was ready to weep for the life she had lost, and the misery she now faced.

There was, at least, some relief in feeling the milk slowly draining. The unbearable, swollen feeling was subsiding. She was appalled by the voracity of the baby. It drank so greedily that it choked on the milk, spluttering and coughing. Liv took advantage of the pause to transfer it to the other breast. It set to work again, and the slow relief of pressure on that side was her reward.

She was still exhausted from labour. She let her head loll back, her eyes closing. A dreamy lassitude spread through her body. Strangely, suckling the infant brought a kind of peace. And then sleep.

At three in the morning, the baby woke up. Exhausted, she forced herself to heat some water on the Primus stove, and washed the infant and her own weary person as best she could. She dressed the baby in the tiny suit someone had knitted for it. That made it look more human.

She was trapped here with this burden. She had no choice but to make the best of it. She propped herself up on the pillows to suckle.

This time, feeding went much better. They both knew what to do now. The relief brought new sensations, better ones. A kind of contentment. A kind of acceptance of the sacrifice she was making for this demanding little stranger who had come out of her body.

In the soft light, she studied the curve of the baby's cheek. Somehow, its face had filled out in the past hours. It looked more babylike. Less alarmingly alien.

Her eyes drifted to the miniature hands that opened and closed as they lay on her breast. She noted the perfect, tiny nails. Did they have half-moons, like her own nails? It was too dim to see.

The baby's ears were perfect, too. Like seashells freshly washed ashore from the great, wide ocean. Her hair was fine and golden. And the skin that had looked almost reptilian at first was now soft and downy.

Liv felt a flush of pride. Whatever terrible mistakes she had made, she had at least produced a fine-looking child.

The next few times, breastfeeding became a pleasure. And then something more complex. It was still painful, but now Liv didn't mind the pain. She had learned to bypass it somehow. It was a fair exchange for the other feelings that came. Feelings that were like none she'd known before. A kind of bliss that insulated her from all the pain in her life. A richness that went beyond the material wealth she had lost.

The baby changed, almost from hour to hour. She became beautiful. As the days passed, Liv learned to take joy in her daughter. There was something new. A relationship. Feeding her, washing her, simply staring at her, filled every inch of Liv's world. She had even begun to call the baby by the name she'd chosen for her, whispering it as she dreamily suckled.

Now she knew that the milk that flowed from her was a painful miracle, something magical. No, not magical. It was divine.

That was an odd word for a woman who had been secular since her own childhood. But then, everything around Liv, and inside Liv, had changed. She was not the same anymore.

But there was a growing problem.

Although the baby had her milk, Liv herself was running out of food.

There had been some food in the room, stores that Liv had brought with her when she'd arrived in Oslo, but they were gone now, and she knew she would have to go out soon. The danger was all around, but she couldn't starve to death in this bare room, especially since she now had the baby.

She would have to face the world.

As she gathered her hair in a scarf, she noted that her hands had started to tremble. The bliss of motherhood had become a sick dread in her stomach.

She wrapped the baby in a blanket and cradled it in the crook of her left arm. The infant was sleepy, her eyelids heavy, her round cheeks flushed. Liv let herself out of the room and quietly descended the dark stairs. At the last moment, her nerve almost failed her. She peered through the dirty glass in the door of the building, seeing the blurred figures of passers-by outside. Her heart started to beat more heavily. Overcoming her fear was difficult. Only hunger could have driven her into those streets.

Then, as so often in her life, her pride ignited. Why should she cower from these people, whom she despised? They were beneath her contempt. The fear was burned away in an instant. She drew herself up straight and pulled the scarf off her hair, shaking the golden waves loose. Let them look at her, let them hate her. She welcomed their hate.

Liv emerged boldly, holding her child, not deigning to look

up or down the street. This was a rough part of Oslo, near the docks, some of it still bearing the scars of war. It had never been a good neighbourhood at the best of times. Now it was bleak and forbidding.

The shops were a ten-minute walk away. She set off, her head high, her back straight. She had money, enough to last a few weeks. After that – well, she would have to make shift. She no longer had the advantages she'd once enjoyed as her sovereign right. But she would survive, as she had always survived. She would survive for her baby.

She'd heard that there was no longer meat in the shops in Oslo. She would buy what there was, dried fish if it came to that, though she had always detested the stuff. Some vegetables too, if there were any to be had. If there was no bread, she would buy flour and potatoes, and make *lomper* on the little hotplate in her room. She was hungry enough for the thought of hot potato pancakes to bring the saliva gushing into her mouth. Producing milk for the baby made Liv ravenous.

She quickened her pace, past the oily water that lapped at the docks, past the warehouses where dirty children hunted for scraps that they could eat or sell. The war had left hunger in its wake.

At first, she ignored the footsteps behind her. When they persisted, she turned to look. It was a shabby little woman, who stopped, looking frightened at having been noticed. There was something familiar about the woman's pinched face, though Liv couldn't place her yet. Liv stared hotly at the little woman until she turned aside and hurried away like a frightened mouse.

Liv knew that people were staring at her, but that no longer frightened her. Her figure, her beauty, her clothes, her bearing, all marked her out. Of course, the mob loathed such people – those who were born to rule.

It was not easy to rule. It meant daring to rise above

narrow-minded morality. It meant grasping at what was noble and beautiful, even when grubby priests and threadbare officials forbade it. It meant being brave. It meant being defiant when all seemed lost.

She could see the shops at the end of the street – and saw the lines of people queuing up outside. She cursed inwardly. She hated queuing for anything. It was degrading to do so. She would have turned back if she hadn't needed food so desperately.

She heard a murmur of voices behind her, and looked over her shoulder. Exasperatingly, the shabby little woman was back. And now she was not alone. She had brought two other women with her, drab like herself, with the same pinched faces and the same hungry eyes. Liv glared at them. But this time, the shabby little woman did not recoil from Liv's fierce gaze. She stared back defiantly.

'It's her,' she said to her companions. 'I knew it. It's her!'

And now Liv recognised who she was – one of the cleaning women from Jorundarholt. A housemaid who had scrubbed her floors. The woman's name still escaped her, but Liv remembered her as a snivelling creature whose servility hid sulkiness.

'Get away from me,' Liv hissed. She clutched the baby tightly to her bosom and stamped her foot. The woman flinched, but did not flee. 'How dare you follow me?' Liv demanded.

'How dare you show your face in the street?' the shabby woman retorted.

'You should be hanging from that lamp-post!' one of the others said in a hoarse voice, her red-rimmed eyes filled with hate. 'Along with that brat in your arms!' The three of them inched closer, their numbers making them insolent.

It was beneath Liv to squabble with such trash in the street. But she was in a quandary. She could hardly go to the shops with these three harridans in tow. They would cause a scene. She had to get away from them. She would have to go back home, hungry as she was, and try again later, perhaps in the twilight, when she would not be so easily recognised.

She crossed the street and walked back quickly the way she had come.

But the three women followed her. They imagined that they had put her to flight, and that made them bolder. She could hear them jeering, throwing accusations, insults. And to Liv's horror, they were attracting others. Two more women had attached themselves, asking what was going on. She heard the shabby woman excitedly telling them who Liv was, what she had done. There were cries of anger and indignation.

And worse still, the idle men who sauntered on the street corners were taking their hands out of their pockets and joining the mob, their deeper voices adding menace to the chorus.

The women Liv could deal with. The men were another thing altogether. For the first time, it occurred to her that she was in danger.

And going back to her lodgings would show them where she lived. Her hiding place would be discovered. She would no longer have a refuge.

Her only hope was somehow to elude them now and creep back home under cover of darkness.

Her heart began to race. She hoisted her baby against her shoulder, cupping its heavy, downy head in her other hand, and broke into a run.

Her followers were taken by surprise. She managed to round the corner before they gave chase. Then they came after her.

The sudden jolting upset the sleepy baby, who started to scream. She stumbled, almost falling, already out of breath.

The thudding feet of her pursuers grew closer behind her. She heard their voices – many voices now – howling like dogs. Their tone was savage.

They caught her easily. A man's hand grasped her hair, yanking her head back, painfully checking her headlong flight. Women's hands tore the baby from her arms.

'Got you!'

'What shall we do to her?' a man's rough voice demanded.

'Take her down the alley!' Liv recognised the excited squeal of the shabby little woman who had started it all. 'Down there!'

'Give me back my baby,' Liv said. She had suddenly realised how much she loved her child. She hadn't known that until this moment. She was astonished at how calm her own voice sounded, despite her desperation. 'Please!'

'Your baby's going in the water,' a man hooted, 'and so are you, when we've finished with you.'

Liv was silent. She'd already made up her mind to say nothing, no matter what they did to her. So long as they gave her baby back. Nothing else mattered. She would endure anything.

They dragged her into the alley, right down to the end, where the weeds grew out of the cracked paving and the boarded-up windows shut their eyes to the world.

'Look at her clothes,' the shabby woman screeched. 'Did you ever?'

'I've always wanted a jacket like that,' another woman said. 'Take it off her.'

'I'll have her skirt.'

'I want her shoes.'

'Look at that jewellery! We can sell that!'

'Strip her naked. Let's see what she's made of.'

'Don't tear anything! I want her underwear.'

The care they took to not damage her clothes was in strange contrast to the brutality of stripping her naked in front of the grinning men. Eager fingers unfastened her buttons, pulled down her zippers, removed her underthings. She couldn't see her baby anymore. A woman had taken her to the back of the crowd, which now numbered some two dozen. But she could hear the infant screaming. The sound brought the milk from her breasts. Her resolve to be stoical disintegrated.

'Give her back to me!' she begged, holding out her arms. 'Please give me my baby!'

They ignored her pleas. When she was completely naked, they crowded around her, the men whistling, the women arguing over her clothes and jewellery.

Someone offered the shabby little woman Liv's gold bangle, which had been twisted off her wrist. 'I don't want anything she's touched,' the shabby woman said. 'All I want is this.' She stepped forward and slapped Liv across the face. The blow was hard and expertly delivered. Caught off-balance, Liv fell onto the cobble stones at the feet of the mob, her knees bleeding.

The shabby little woman turned to the men, who had stopped laughing. 'Well?' she demanded. 'What are you waiting for? Do it to her.'

# CHAPTER ONE

# AGNES

*England, 1968*

'You're so damned perfect,' Bill Dawlish said, making it an accusation, not a compliment.

'I don't think I'm perfect at all,' Agnes retorted. 'I'm very conscious of my imperfections.'

'They're not visible from where I'm sitting.' Bill wiped beer froth off his moustache, staring at her hard. The two emotions he seemed to feel for her were lust and resentment.

He was gulping his first lunchtime pint, determined to get in a second, and possibly a third, before they were due back at the office. The pub was crowded with Fleet Street journalists from various newspapers, noisily engaged in the same pursuit. The heavy lunchtime drinking (especially on Fridays) was something Agnes had never taken to, even after three years on 'The Street'. She was the only person here without a beer in one hand and a cigarette in the other. The small glass of ginger ale in front of her was more for show than anything else, and would still be half-full by the time they left.

Agnes was grateful that Bill Dawlish had finally stopped trying to get her to go to bed with him. He was a handsome man.

The fact (which he had regularly pointed out) that she didn't have a boyfriend marked her in his eyes as a wasted resource, and worse, a virgin. There were no virgins on Fleet Street, something else he had regularly pointed out; and he was ready and willing to relieve her of the burden of her maidenhood. The result of her many firm though politely worded refusals was this lingering sense of injury on his part. 'Nobody should be as perfect as you,' he went on. 'You're an embarrassment to the rest of us.'

Agnes looked around the smoke-filled pub. The regulars here were predominantly male, middle-aged and admittedly flawed in various ways. Some of them were, however, the most distinguished journalists of the day, and she rather wished she had one of those as her lunchtime companion, instead of Bill Dawlish. But Bill clung to her like a limpet, apparently on the principle that if he couldn't have her, he'd make sure that nobody else would, either. He was very hard to get rid of. But when she'd first joined the *Evening News*, Bill had been one of the few who'd made an effort to show her the ropes – even if his only motivation was getting her into bed – and she was grateful for that early help.

'Look,' she said, 'there's Jill Tweedie sitting over there.'

Bill grunted. 'Another women's libber jumping on the bandwagon.'

'Oh, she's much more than that. She's so clever and witty.'

'Not to me. Come on. It's Friday. I'll get you a glass of wine.'

'Don't want any wine, thank you.' But he ignored that.

While Bill went off to the bar, she nursed her ginger ale, watching Jill Tweedie, who was in animated conversation with a pair of colleagues. With her unruly shock of hair and intelligent face, she seemed the freest person here. She represented many of the things Agnes aspired to be – sophisticated, wry, funny, clever, a feminist. But Agnes was a long way off being any of those things. Next to Jill Tweedie, she felt very young and inexperienced. She wondered if she had the courage to go over and introduce herself, and decided that she was too shy. Bill returned with another pint and a glass of white wine for her, plonking the drink belligerently in front of her.

'Going back up to your stately home this evening?' he demanded.

'It's not a stately home.'

'It's statelier than *my* home. I mean, you don't *need* to work, do you?'

This was another theme which, if left unchecked, would lead to the accusation that she wasn't a real journalist, was she? And why was she playing at a job when others were unemployed?

'Of course I need to work,' she said briskly. 'I'm not a rich woman.'

'You will be when that grandfather of yours dies.'

'That's a very nasty thing to say. And besides, everyone should work, rich or poor.'

'Isn't work awfully *nasty* too?' He smiled derisively. 'Oh, wait. You believe in the nobility of labour, don't you? One of our new class of wealthy, titled socialists.'

'You know very well I don't have a title and I'm not a socialist. What's put you in such an unpleasant mood?'

He drained half of his pint in one go, and wiped his mouth. 'The fact of you being such an offensively blonde, teetotal, blue-eyed, touch-me-not virgin.'

'Are we back to that again?'

'I've been on the job five years longer than you. And *I've* never had a pat on the head and been told I'm a clever boy. It's not fair.'

So that was it. Bill had overheard their editor, Kennard Coleridge, praising her that morning for a piece she'd written. She felt a bit sorry for Bill. 'Well, I'm the new girl, like you said. I need encouragement. You've got far more experience, so you don't need any. You've made it, Bill.'

He brightened a bit at that. 'I know a thing or two, I suppose.'

'Of course you do!'

Which set Bill off boasting about his coups and scoops. She'd heard the stories before, and she listened with half an ear, nodding and smiling admiringly at the right places, trying not to glaze over.

At last, Bill wound up his stories, managed to get a third pint down his throat, and looked at his watch. 'Come on. Time to get back to the salt mines. Four more hours and it's the weekend.'

They pushed through the crowd towards the door, Bill leading the way, Agnes following behind. Unexpectedly, she found herself face to face with Jill Tweedie, who was carrying some drinks from the bar. Their eyes met.

'You're Agnes Tolliver, aren't you?' Jill Tweedie said.

Agnes felt herself flush. 'Yes.'

'I liked your piece about Bernadette Devlin.'

'Oh! Thank you!'

'It needed saying.' Jill glanced over her shoulder at Bill, who had paused at the door, and was glowering. 'You don't need to massage his ego, you know. You're way better than he is.' She smiled and moved on. The exchange was over. Still blushing, Agnes made her way out into the street.

'What was she saying to you?' Bill demanded.

Neither of the subjects that had been so briefly discussed would please Bill, so Agnes temporised. 'Just hello.'

'Something about me?' he asked suspiciously. 'I know she doesn't like me. Did she say something nasty about me?'

'Just hello,' Agnes said firmly. If she was to stop massaging Bill Dawlish's ego, then she might as well start now. She set off briskly towards the office.

It was high summer, and the sun was still warm later that afternoon as she shut up the little bedsit in Victoria where she spent the week, and set off for the country.

Driving down to Gloucestershire, Agnes thought about Bill Dawlish's accusations. He knew very little about her, and had made a lot of assumptions. The assumptions were wrong – and yet not a million miles from the truth. She'd had a lot of luck in her life. Things might have turned out very differently for her.

She'd been born at the end of the war, and had been only a few months old when both her parents had been killed by a German V2 rocket, one of Hitler's dying thrusts at his hated enemy. She might have died with them, in the rubble of their house. She might have grown up in a succession of orphanages and foster homes, with uncertain prospects for happiness. Instead, she had survived, and been taken in by her grandfather, who had given her all the love she had needed.

And while it wasn't true that her grandfather was titled, he was inordinately proud of belonging to a family which went back to William the Conqueror, one of the oldest families in England. He would explain with great relish that the name 'Tolliver' came from the Norman French 'Taillefer,' meaning 'iron-cutter,' and had been bestowed on one of William's knights, who had cut an armoured English king in half at the Battle of Hastings.

Bill's accusation that her grandfather was rich was also a half-truth. The Tollivers had once been wealthy, but taxes and inflation had whittled down the estate since the war, and no matter what the appearances were, Barbar was not wealthy. Far from being left a pile of money when he died, she would be lucky to inherit anything more than debts. And the prospect of his death was a source of perpetual terror to her now that he was growing older and frailer. She had no one else. She would be heartbroken by his departure, and she did not know how she would face it.

As for being a touch-me-not virgin – it was true that she'd been born in late September, making her star sign Virgo. Her social life (and thus any possible sex life) were very restricted by her spending every weekend in the country with her grandfather. But she would far rather spend the weekends with Barbar than in the sort of Saturday night fumbling and groping and Sunday morning regrets that had been her experience thus far.

Trundling along leafy country lanes, she had reached the turnoff to Dowdeswell Hall. She'd told Bill it was not a stately home, and it really wasn't; it wasn't anything like big enough or historical enough or stately enough to qualify. But it was very pretty. It was one of the loveliest houses in that part of Gloucestershire, and as she drove through the gates, her heart, as always, soared.

Dowdeswell was a Queen Anne house built of Cotswold sandstone, which had mellowed over two hundred and fifty years to the colour of old gold. It stood not far from St Michael's parish church, in whose churchyard generations of Tollivers lay at rest, including her own parents, who shared a headstone, as they had shared their death. The house was approached through an avenue of magnificent elms, believed to be as old as the house. They were so large that their crowns met over the road, making a green tunnel, which opened out at the last minute to reveal Dowdeswell Hall, bathed in sunlight.

In her mind, the house was always bathed in sunlight. Though there must have been grey days, and plenty of them over her twenty-three years of life, her memory obliterated these, and here it was always high summer.

Agnes parked her powder-blue Mini next to Barbar's venerable Rolls Royce, a 1930 Phantom the size of a battleship, that had belonged to his father before him. Her little Mini looked as though it would fit in the cavernous trunk.

She lugged her weekend bag through the garden of nodding roses to the arched, oak front door, which opened before she reached it. Dowdeswell had once been run by a staff of a dozen, but now only Mrs Cawthorne was left to look after Barbar. Her husband did the gardening. They were both frail and white-haired, but they'd stuck by Barbar through thick and thin. Mrs Cawthorne reached for Agnes's bag. 'He's not been himself,' she greeted Agnes.

'What do you mean?' Agnes asked in alarm. 'You mean he's unwell?'

'He's not himself,' the housekeeper repeated flatly. 'Grumpy and bad-tempered.'

'That's not like him.'

'No, it isn't. He wouldn't let me tidy his study, and it's in an awful mess, papers and dust everywhere.'

'Why didn't you call me?'

'Didn't want to alarm you. Doctor says it's just his age.'

'Doctor? Has he had the doctor?'

'I called Dr Dobbie. He popped round. Your grandfather wasn't very pleased to see him. But Doctor says his heart and lungs are fine. Just his age.' She nodded in the direction of the conservatory. 'He's in there with his geraniums. I'm off now, Miss Tolliver. He's all yours until Monday morning.'

Agnes hurried through the house to the conservatory. Her grandfather was potting geraniums, wearing his usual shabby old cardigan and Panama hat. He turned as Agnes came in, and for a moment the vacant look in his eyes frightened her. It was as though he didn't know who she was.

'Barbar?' She'd called him that from her infancy – her baby attempt to say the word 'grandpa'.

He smiled at last. 'Hello, sweetheart,' he said, dusting loam off his hands. 'Welcome home.'

She kissed his cool, dry cheek. 'Have you been sick, Barbar?'

'Never better. Come and have a cup of tea, and tell me all about London.' He led the way to the kitchen, shuffling in his carpet slippers.

Agnes studied her grandfather over a cup of tea. He appeared much the same as always – on the surface, that was. There was no sign of the grumpiness Mrs Cawthorne had talked about.

'Never mind my week,' she said. 'Tell me why Mrs Cawthorne was so worried about you.'

'What do you mean, my dear?'

'She said she had to call the doctor.'

He frowned. 'I have no idea why she saw fit to summon the poor man away from his proper duties. Silly nonsense. Wasting everyone's time.'

'But what did he say?' she pressed.

'That I was good for another fifty years.' He waved his brown, veined hand, dismissing the topic. 'Game of chess?'

'If you like.' They usually played two or three games on a weekend, but this time, Agnes had the feeling he was steering her away from a topic he wanted to avoid.

They went out into the garden, and set up the board under the parasol on the lawn. They played in silence for a while. They knew each other's games well. They had been playing chess since her childhood, a ritual that was conducted amicably but seriously. Barbar had once been a county chess champion, and she had learned to play well under his tuition. There had been a time when he would sacrifice a queen or two castles to make the games more even, but that hadn't been necessary for years. Agnes could give him a good match, and sometimes managed to draw or even win.

She noticed that Barbar was moving the carved chess pieces, which were smooth with use, unusually slowly and carefully. There was something off about him. Mrs Cawthorne was right. You couldn't quite put your finger on it, but the phrase 'not himself' was apt. It was as though Barbar were somehow impersonating himself, putting on a brave show of being Wing Commander Louis Tolliver, DFC.

He had been staring at the board for ten minutes without moving his knight, which she had threatened with a pawn, although the position wasn't at all complicated. At last, Agnes prompted him. 'It's your move, Barbar.'

He blinked. 'Oh? Is it?' But he still didn't move the knight.

'Perhaps you're too tired for chess?' she suggested gently.

'I suppose I am a little tired.'

'What's made you so tired?' she asked.

'To tell you the truth, I've been doing a spot of writing.'

'Writing? Your memoirs?'

'Just a letter.' A smile that was like a wince crossed his gaunt face. 'I suppose it's an attempt at a confession. One which is rather difficult to write.'

'A confession! What have you got to confess, venerable ancestor?' she asked. 'Youthful indiscretions?'

'Something like that.' He carefully picked up the knight at last, and moved it out of harm's way. 'A plea for forgiveness, perhaps.'

'Whose forgiveness?'

'Someone who has made me feel deeply ashamed.'

'You're frightening me.' She pushed a bishop forward, resuming her attack. 'I've known you all my life, and I've never seen you do one shameful thing.'

'You've known me for twenty-three years, my dear. But I was fifty-four when you were born. Time enough to do shameful things.'

She glanced up with a smile, thinking he was making a joke. But his face was grey, and he looked ill. 'I think that's enough chess,' she said, alarmed. 'You need a nap.'

She saw the unmistakeable relief in his eyes. 'All right. Will you accept a draw?'

'Absolutely not. I'm thrashing you.'

'We'll see about that, young lady.' He smiled a little crookedly as they laid the board aside. Then he lay back in the deckchair, tilting his Panama over his eyes.

Leaving Barbar dozing in the garden, Agnes went into her

grandfather's study to see if she could do something about the mess Mrs Cawthorne had complained of. The blinds were drawn, casting everything in a yellow gloom. She pulled them up, letting in the evening sun. Clouds of dust motes swirled in the air. Books and papers were indeed piled up on every available surface. With a sigh, Agnes realised there wasn't much either she or Mrs Cawthorne could do. Barbar was always researching some aspect of the war he'd played such a distinguished part in. He had a system, chaotic as it seemed, and only he knew where everything went. Rearranging things would not be welcome.

She'd noticed a sharp smell of burning paper in the room when she'd come in, and now she noticed that there were some charred pages in the fireplace. If he'd been writing a letter, then he'd decided to burn it, unposted.

Part of a single sheet remained, covered in Barbar's stylish Edwardian handwriting. He always used a fountain pen with dark blue ink. Curious, she knelt to take it out of the ashes. This must be the 'confession' he'd mentioned. As she glanced along the lines, her own name caught her eye. Puzzled, she took the black-edged fragment to the window to read it more closely.

What she read stunned her so much that for a long time, she stood immobile, staring into space with unseeing eyes.

At last, feeling numb, Agnes went back out to the garden to talk to Barbar, and wake him up, if necessary. He was still in his deckchair, but she saw at once that something was wrong. His hat had fallen off, and lay on the grass beside him. One arm was hanging limply down.

Her heart lurching, Agnes ran over to her grandfather. '*Barbar!*'

Barbar's face shocked her. His eyes were half-open and rolled back in his head, his jaw hanging slackly, showing that his lips and tongue were blue, as though he'd been drinking his own fountain pen ink. She knew at once that he was dead. She put her arms around his lean shoulders and laid her head on his still-warm chest, sobbing as though her heart would break.

Dr Dobbie finished writing and pocketed his pen. He blotted the paper carefully. 'I've put "natural causes",' he said, handing her the death certificate, 'which will satisfy the coroner. But to be accurate, it was a heart attack. His third.'

'His third! I thought he was so healthy!'

'He was an old man, Agnes.'

She nodded dully. Barbar had been old, but he'd made her feel protected. She no longer had that comfort. 'Why didn't anybody tell me?'

'He didn't want attention of any kind. He hated fuss.' Dr Dobbie snapped his Gladstone bag shut. 'He refused all the treatment I offered,' he said sadly. He was an old-fashioned doctor who exuded a smell of iodine, tweed and the carbolic soap he washed his hands with. He'd come as soon as Agnes had telephoned him. His face was sombre. 'Your grandfather was a quiet man, but he had a will of iron. I respected his wishes. Would you like me to stay until the hearse gets here?'

'No, it's all right. Mrs Cawthorne will be here soon.'

Dobbie touched her shoulder. 'I know this will be hard for you. Your grandfather was a wonderful man.'

'But he wasn't my grandfather.'

The doctor raised his eyebrows. 'You're Giles and Elspeth's daughter.'

'No. I found a letter he wrote today. Or part of one. It makes it clear that I came from somewhere else.'

He looked at her face curiously, as though there was something he wanted to say, but couldn't find the right words. 'Well,' he said slowly, 'it doesn't make any difference now, does it? You were devoted to each other, even if you were adopted.'

'Yes,' she replied, 'we were.' But Barbar's letter hadn't suggested adoption. It had suggested something much darker.

'You're in shock,' Dobbie said sympathetically. 'I can give you something to take.'

Agnes shook her head. 'I'll manage.'

After he'd left, she shrank into herself. Her world had been shaken to pieces – and then the pieces had been turned upside down. If she wasn't Barbar's granddaughter, then who was she?

She'd never felt like this before – stunned, angry, and deeply, deeply lonely. Barbar had died with his secret.

Perhaps his secret had killed him.

Mrs Cawthorne arrived back from the village as the evening shadows were lengthening. The first thing she did, seeing Agnes's shaken state, was to make a pot of strong tea. They drank it together in the kitchen.

'He was only seventy-seven,' she said. 'It's no age, is it?' She didn't say anything more until they'd drunk their tea. Then they went to see Barbar's body. Mrs Cawthorne started crying. 'Look at the state of him,' she said, mopping her eyes with her apron. 'He always went around looking like a tramp.'

Agnes was crying, too. She looked through blurred eyes at Barbar's darned cardigan, the worn knees of his corduroy trousers, his shabby carpet slippers. 'He can't go out like that,' she said, pulling herself together. 'They'll want his best suit. Shirt, tie, shoes, all that.'

'I'll get everything. You stay with him.' Red-eyed, she went upstairs to Barbar's bedroom, leaving Agnes with Barbar's body.

They'd laid him out on the scuffed leather couch in his study, his arms crossed on his chest. Dr Dobbie had closed his eyes and mouth, but his cheeks and eyes were already sunken. Agnes brushed the silvery lock of hair back from his brow. His skin was cooling already. The loss of this old man, whom she'd loved so much, trusted so implicitly, had left a huge hole in her life. Yet he was a stranger to her now – and not just because death had altered his face.

She'd known no other guardian for twenty-three years, and the words on that torn sheet of paper shouldn't really – as Dr Dobbie had said – have made any difference. But they had. Because everything he'd told her had been a lie.

He'd lied to her all her life, deliberately and elaborately, and now he'd left her bereft. He was beyond reach. She couldn't ask him why he'd done any of it. She couldn't reproach him, and he couldn't explain. Being angry with Barbar wasn't a logical response to his death. But she *was* angry. Angry with him for lying to her, angry with him for dying and orphaning her yet again. Angry because they'd never finished their last game of chess. Angry because he hadn't told her how sick he was, so she'd had no chance to prepare for this bereavement.

Angry because he'd never told her who she really was.

In their last conversation, he'd spoken of 'an attempt at a confession'. Of a 'plea for forgiveness'. It hadn't been a plea for *her* forgiveness, that was clear. He'd talked about someone who had made him feel 'deeply ashamed'. None of it made any sense, but it all made her profoundly uneasy. She had to get to the bottom of this, because whatever Barbar had felt guilty about had clearly concerned her very closely.

Mrs Cawthorne came down the stairs with Barbar's dark suit neatly folded in her arms. Laid on it was a row of medals. 'Do you want him buried with these?'

Agnes touched the colourful ribbons of Barbar's 'gongs', which he'd been awarded for bravery, but never wore, not even on Remembrance Day. He seemed to care nothing for them, and whenever she'd asked him about them, he'd replied wryly that others had deserved them more. 'He never wore them while he was alive. I don't think he'd want them on his chest for eternity.'

'We can pin them on a nice velvet cushion for the service.' Mrs Cawthorne examined the tarnished clasps. 'I'll give them a polish before the funeral. You can show them to your children one day. Tell them what kind of man their great-grandfather was.'

Agnes winced at that. 'I found something odd in his fireplace,' she began hesitantly.

'Well, I told you he wouldn't let me clean in his study.'

'I don't mean dust. I mean part of a letter he'd burned.'

'I don't know anything about that,' Mrs Cawthorne said. Agnes thought her tone sounded defensive. Mrs Cawthorne blew her nose, avoiding Agnes's eyes. 'I don't go around reading people's letters.'

'Of course you don't. But he wrote something very strange. I wanted to ask you about it—'

'No use asking *me*,' she snapped, cutting off what Agnes was saying. 'I don't involve myself in your personal affairs. I never have done, and I never will.' Her tone had grown from defensive to angry. Her eyes were redder than ever, her cheeks flushed. 'So don't ask *me*.'

Agnes was taken aback by the vehemence of the housekeeper's reply. She knew that Mr and Mrs Cawthorne had been with Barbar since before she was born, and were utterly loyal to him. Yet the way she was responding now made Agnes suddenly feel like an outsider, as though she had committed some grave solecism in asking about the letter.

A knock at the door heralded the arrival of Fletcher and Marshall, the funeral directors, all in black, wearing Homburg hats. They proffered unctuous condolences. With lugubrious professionalism, they took charge of Barbar, loading the deceased, as they called him, into a coffin and wheeling it out to their gleaming hearse, which was pulled up alongside Agnes's Mini and Barbar's Rolls.

'If you could drop by the premises tomorrow, Miss Tolliver,' Fletcher said in a hushed voice, 'we can discuss all the arrangements.'

Agnes nodded. That use of her name had sounded odd in her ears, for the first time in her life. Was she really Agnes Tolliver?

And if she was not Agnes Tolliver, then who was she?

# CHAPTER TWO

# KAROLINA

*East Berlin, 1968*

Karolina had to take the long way home from the factory every day. The short way went close to the Wall at one point. They would know – the secret police, the Stasi – because they watched her. She'd been warned that if she was seen within two hundred metres of the Wall ever again, she'd go straight back to jail. And she would rather die than go back to Stauberg, the women's prison at Hoheneck, where she'd been sent at nineteen.

She carried the scars from those three years in Stauberg. Physical scars. Mental scars that brought her awake at night, choking and sweating.

And worst of all, the jagged, invisible scar that zigzagged right across her life.

The scar that had stopped her finishing her university degree, even though she had been scoring the best grades in her year since she was five. It had stopped her from getting any work except the most mind-numbing factory jobs, and invariably on the night shifts. (She'd given up applying for anything better, because the Stasi followed her everywhere, and after each job interview – no matter how promising – they dropped by the prospective employer to explain exactly why Karolina Schmidt was unemployable.)

It prevented her from living in any of the nicer parts of East Berlin, from having a television, from going to summer camp, from associating with other young people, from just about anything that made life bearable. In fact, everything was intended to make life *un*bearable.

And all because, at the age of nineteen, she'd made a stupid attempt to get over the Wall to the West.

It had been little more than high spirits. A teenage prank, an escapade, a *Bubenstreich*. But what had really sent them crazy was how far she'd managed to get on her escapade. They'd caught her right on the edge of the Death Strip. Another few steps and she'd have been blown to pieces by a mine, or shredded by machine-gun fire. They wouldn't believe that she'd climbed the concrete barricade, crawled under the electric fences, avoided the dogs, crossed the spike mats and been undetected by the guards in the watchtowers, all by herself. They were convinced that she was part of a secret capitalist escape organisation. And the fact that she wasn't – and couldn't give them the information they tried to prise out of her – was why things had gone so badly for her.

Of course, she'd been walking a tightrope since birth.

The Wall escapade had just furnished them with the truth they'd suspected all along, that she was tainted, born bad. The German Democratic Republic had done its best for her, despite her shameful origins. It had given her a place in an orphanage, paid for by her hard-working fellow-citizens. It had raised her according to the purest communist principles, shaped her to be an industrious member of the proletariat, obedient to authority, fed by the ideology of Marx and Lenin. It had tried to inculcate in her the socialist awareness that was so essential to becoming a contributing member of a healthy society. The

State had done everything for her. It had been mother, father, mentor, guardian.

And in return, she had tried very hard to be perfect.

Of course, the State had never allowed her to forget her shameful origins.

She was reminded of them daily, and reminded of how grateful a degraded orphan should be to suckle at the breasts of the State.

And that was perhaps why the long, rigorous process of socialist education had begun to falter in her mid-teens, leading to small acts of rebellion, then more serious contraventions – listening to degenerate Western music, wearing deviant clothing, expressing seditious opinions – and finally, the most unforgivable offence in the book, trying to escape from the workers' paradise to the corrupt cesspool of the West.

She was an experiment that had failed.

It was summer, and the sky was already light. The morning sun was attempting to shed some glamour on the rows of grim apartment blocks, built by the Soviets among the ruins of an industrial neighbourhood that had been bombed to rubble by the Allies in 1945. The golden light only made the buildings seem to hunch down, becoming even uglier, darker and bleaker. They'd assigned her a tiny apartment in this district, where vacant bombsites still grew harvests of highly toxic fireweed. An object lesson, no doubt, in the inherent violence of the capitalist system. The Stasi were not subtle in their object lessons.

As she approached the block where she lived, the repairman of the building, old Herr Möller, was trudging the other way, going to his allotment. He was carrying his oddly-shaped spade over his shoulder. He didn't even turn his head to look at her as they passed each other – to acknowledge her in the street would be observed and noted – but out of the side of his mouth he muttered, 'They're waiting for you.'

Karolina's heart sank. There was no question who *they* were. Her steps faltered for a moment, and she was on the point of turning around and going back. But there was nowhere to go. And avoiding the Stasi would betray that Herr Möller had warned her. And he was her only friend. She shouldered her knapsack, took a deep breath, and walked on.

They were indeed waiting for her inside her apartment. They'd let themselves in, of course. There was no privacy where the Stasi were concerned. There were two of them, as always, middle-aged men who would be anonymous but for their impregnable self-assurance.

The fatter of the two did the talking. 'J.O. 832, shut the door and empty your knapsack.'

Karolina obeyed. The contents of her knapsack did not amount to much: a neatly folded plastic raincoat, the dog-eared Thomas Mann novel she was reading, and an apple.

The fat Stasi man picked up the copy of *Buddenbrooks*. 'Why are you reading bourgeois literature?'

'Thomas Mann is not banned.'

'That is not what I asked.'

'Thomas Mann won the Nobel Prize,' she replied quietly, 'and his works were burned by the Nazis. That should reassure you.'

'The cover depicts a bourgeois family,' the man pointed out.

'That's because it's about a bourgeois family. But it's not a bourgeois novel.'

'Only a bourgeois would write about the bourgeoisie,' he retorted. 'Or want to read about them.'

She knew better than to argue about literature with a Stasi thug, so she said nothing.

He turned to the apple. 'Where did you get this fruit?'

'From the factory canteen.'

'And you brought it home?'

'Yes.'

He pointed to the bowl of identical apples on her kitchen bench. 'And all these – from the canteen?'

'Yes.'

His eyes gleamed triumphantly. 'You admit that you have been systematically stealing fruit!'

'We are allowed one apple a day,' she replied. 'So I take one apple a day. It's not stealing.'

'Canteen food must be consumed in the canteen,' he shot back. 'To take it away is stealing!'

'That's not logical.'

The other man, who had been lounging in her only armchair, uncoiled himself languidly. 'As a matter of interest, why do you bring the fruit home?'

'Because it brightens the place up.'

He bared sharp teeth in a derisive grin. 'You are full of bourgeois ideas, J.O. 832. Food is not a decoration.'

They enjoyed calling her that. It stood for Juvenile Offender Number 832, the number she'd had in prison – even though she was now twenty-seven. They hoped to rile her. But losing her temper with these men would not be wise. 'They won't be wasted. I'll eat them when they're ripe.'

'What else do you bring home from the factory? Tools? Materials you can sell?'

Karolina had seen the opened cupboards, her things scattered on the floor. 'You've searched the place already,' she said quietly. 'You found nothing. That answers your question.'

'We'll decide when our questions are answered,' the fat one snapped. 'You will never be trusted again.'

'Do they trust *you*?' she asked.

The two men stared at her grimly. 'What?'

'They always send you in pairs. Not alone. It must be so that each of you can watch the other. So I guess they don't trust you, either.'

There was a moment's silence. Then the thin one spoke. 'Are

you still in touch with the secret organisation which helped you escape?'

'I didn't escape. You caught me. If there had been a secret organisation, I'd be drinking champagne in the West by now.'

'You never change,' he said contemptuously. 'You are a criminal through and through. Society should rid itself of cancers like you. One day it will. And I'll be here to see it.'

'I have nothing left to lose,' she replied.

'You think so? That shows a failure of imagination, Juvenile Offender 832.'

They took all the apples.

They also took the potatoes and onions that Herr Möller had grown on his allotment and given her.

And her copy of *Buddenbrooks*. She regretted everything, but the loss of the book brought tears perilously close. Finding another copy would be hard.

They'd punctiliously noted the confiscations on squares of flimsy government paper, which they handed to her as they left – *five pieces of stolen fruit, six potatoes, eight onions, one bourgeois novel*. It was ludicrous. The whole visit had been absurd, farcical. But not the kind of farce that made you laugh. These calls were intended to grind her down, until she learned to obey. Or perhaps until she threw herself into a canal with her pockets full of cobblestones.

After they'd left, she tidied the mess they'd made, and tried to get the smell of them out of her apartment. But her only window opened onto a stairwell, and rather than letting the smell out, let in a miasma of boiled cabbage and drains.

She took the confiscation slips to her toilet, which was screened only by a strip of curtain she'd put up. She was about to flush them away, when she noticed that she was running low on toilet paper. So she kept them. She would have a use for them.

\* \* \*

It was the weekend. Saturday was family day at the public swimming pool four streets away from her apartment. It would be very crowded, but she never missed it, not least because on family day, they offered soap and shampoo in the showers. The Soviet architects who'd designed her housing block had decided that one bathroom was adequate for each floor of six apartments. Using the communal bathroom on her floor was something she avoided. It was not only dirty, but the men who hung around there could be troublesome. She'd had two unpleasant experiences, fighting off unwanted attentions.

So without going to bed, she packed her bathing suit and a towel in her knapsack, and set off. Berlin was stifling in the summer, but the early mornings were a gift, with light breezes ruffling the young leaves, shedding dappled light on the sidewalks. She missed the weight of the novel in her knapsack. Thomas Mann novels were thick and comforting, and she had been looking forward to reading on the grass after a shower and a swim. It had left a hole in her morning. She couldn't afford a new copy, and second-hand ones were hard to obtain.

People were already queuing at the pool. Karolina swam winter and summer, unless the water froze. She preferred the winter. Prison had left her with a deep distaste for crowds. But there was no option.

Being composed of German socialists, the queues were orderly, and eventually she got in. She went straight to the showers, and was lucky enough to find one that had just been vacated. She soaped her lean body luxuriously and washed her short, blonde hair, using the detergent from the dispenser.

By the time she got to the pool, it was crowded with parents and their children, jumping and screaming. Staying close to the edge, she swam cautiously, stretching limbs cramped by a night hunched over a factory line, trying to avoid the watchful eyes of the pool superintendents. If she was caught swimming, she would be told to leave. Swimming was forbidden on family day. Only jumping and screaming were allowed.

An hour in the water took some of the weariness out of her body, and some of the anger out of her mind, although there was always a residue of both in her soul. The grass was crowded, so she went to sit on the wooden tiers overlooking the pool. The sun was hot, and she started to feel drowsy. She would go home to sleep soon.

By now, the blue of the pool had almost vanished under a solid mass of bodies. The administration issued white rubber swimming caps, which were obligatory for everybody, and the effect was rather strange.

'It looks like a sea of ping pong balls.'

She turned her head to see who had spoken. A young man of about her own age had sat on the bench beside her. She saw smooth, tanned shoulders and a muscular belly before she looked away again. She didn't answer. She didn't speak to strangers at the swimming baths, or anywhere else.

'Too crowded for you to swim today,' he went on. 'I like to watch you swim when the pool isn't full of kids. Your style is absolutely flawless. You could be a champion.'

She said nothing. She had been a junior champion until her crime against the State. After that, of course, it was all over. She'd been banned from competitive swimming forever. Which had hardly mattered, after three years in prison.

'I like to watch you, whatever you do,' he went on. 'You're so beautiful. You have a perfect body.'

By now fully awake, Karolina stood up, gathering her towel, preparing to leave.

'You don't need to worry about me,' he said gently. 'I'm queer.'

Now she couldn't help looking at him. He was staring up at her from under a sun-bleached fringe, a bronzed, handsome boy with green eyes. 'You shouldn't say that,' she muttered. 'People can hear you.'

'We've been decriminalised. Officially. Of course, it hasn't stopped the Stasi from spying on me and harassing me. And they still beat me up now and then.'

'I'm sorry.'

'I'm used to it. As long as they don't break my Grecian nose.' He crossed his legs. 'Don't go. Let's talk a bit.'

'Not a good idea.'

'Why? Because I'm a deviant?'

'It's not that.'

'Well, at least tell me your name.'

Poised to flee, she hesitated. 'Karolina.'

He nodded. 'My name is Rafael. Don't mind me watching you. There's something very special about you. So beautiful, yet always alone. Alert, like a gazelle, but you never look at anyone. You stand out from everyone else, but you're invisible.'

'You're looking right at me.'

'But you don't want to be seen. Which is strange in someone who looks like you. If I were straight, I'd be so in love with you.' He smiled. 'Matter of fact, I think I'm in love with you anyway. In a theoretical way. Sit down for two minutes. We'll make each other look normal.'

'I'm not normal.' But for some reason, she sat back down anyway.

He looked into her face with dreamy eyes. 'You could be on the cover of *Vogue*. If you got those broken teeth fixed.'

Instinctively, she covered her mouth with her hand. One of her front teeth had been broken and another chipped by a club in Stauberg, and she hated it when people noticed.

'Don't do that,' he said. 'I didn't mean to upset you. How did it happen, by the way?'

Karolina lowered her hand slowly. Something about this boy held her. 'A guard at Stauberg did it.'

His expression changed. 'What did you do to earn a holiday in Stauberg?'

'I tried to get over the Wall. When I was nineteen.'

He leaned forward, his elbows on his knees, clasped hands supporting his chin. 'Aha. A serious deviant, then. Even worse than me. That explains a lot.'

'We shouldn't be talking to each other.'

'We shouldn't. But we are.'

'Two Stasi were waiting for me when I got back from night shift this morning. They're probably watching me now.'

'I doubt it. They'd stand out here, wouldn't they? Everyone in bathing costumes, and two men in raincoats? Don't worry about it. So. What did they want?'

'They keep hammering at me to tell them about some vast underground organisation that supposedly helped me escape. They refuse to accept that I did it all on my own.'

'And did you? Do it all on your own?'

'Of course. What would I know about underground organisations? I was just a kid.'

'You were stupid to even try.'

She made a face at him. 'I know that. I was a stupid kid. They confiscated a bowl of apples. And the copy of *Buddenbrooks* I was reading.'

'Thomas Mann?'

'They said it was a bourgeois novel.'

'Snap. They say homosexuality is a bourgeois perversion. It's hard to believe that such stupid men run the country, isn't it?' He nodded in the direction of the pool. 'I suppose that's the explanation. A whole people with heads as empty as ping pong balls.'

Talking to him was making her nervous. 'I have to go.'

'I want to see you again. We should be friends.'

'Did the Stasi put you up to that idea, too?'

He grinned. 'You think like a true deviant. Luckily, the answer is no. I'm the urban spaceman, baby. Will you be back here tomorrow?'

'No.'

'When, then?' he coaxed. 'So I don't have to hang around here waiting for you to turn up.'

She answered reluctantly. 'Tuesday morning.'

'I'll try and be here. Look out for me.'

She hurried down the benches without saying goodbye. There was a hot molten lump in her chest. Talking to a boy of her own age – and about such subjects – was a very unusual experience for her. 'Stupid, stupid, stupid,' she whispered to herself as she made for the changing rooms. He was probably a Stasi plant. And if he wasn't, that was even worse.

Yet she felt so distracted by the encounter that when she went back into the showers to rinse off the chlorine, she forgot to draw the curtain; and when she turned, a group of children were standing there, staring open-mouthed at the scars on her buttocks from the beatings at Stauberg.

She drew the curtain quickly. Invisible. Rafael had been right. That's all she wanted to be.

Invisible.

# CHAPTER THREE

## AGNES

*England, 1968*

Agnes's sense of loss was profound. But after that first acute access of grief, when she'd found Barbar dead on the lawn, the loss had settled into a dull ache. Barbar had always been there, since before she could remember. Remoter than a father, less tender than a mother, he'd nevertheless sustained her, guided her, nurtured her.

She'd been around five years old when she'd first started wondering why other children had a mum and dad, and she only had Barbar. It was then, for the first time, that he'd taken her to the grave in St Michael's churchyard. She'd only just started learning to read, and Barbar had taken her hand and traced her small finger along the chiselled letters that read *Giles and Elspeth Tolliver*, and had explained that they were her mother and father.

He'd explained that Giles and Elspeth Tolliver were buried in the ground under the stone, and that they were his son and his son's wife. Being Barbar, he'd also explained that one day, he would have to go under the ground, too – and that so, in time, would little Agnes.

'Going into the ground is a wonderful thing,' he'd said confidentially. 'It ties us to the earth. We're English, and we'll always be part of England. But being buried in England makes you the most English of all. Some people are lost at sea, and some people are burned up in fire. People who go into the English earth are the luckiest people of all.'

Young as she was, that had given her an insight into Barbar's mind, into his beliefs, his patriotism. In time, it had become part of her, too. Her upbringing had been a love affair with Englishness. Barbar had taken her to everything that was quintessentially English: Glyndebourne, Wimbledon, the Henley regatta, Royal Ascot, the Chelsea Flower Show – and of course, Gilbert and Sullivan, where she would always remember Barbar singing lustily along with *H.M.S. Pinafore*:

*But in spite of all temptations*
*To belong to other nations*
*He remains an Englishman*
*He re-he-mains an Eng-lish-man!*

That was one of his favourite verses. Another, which he would quote in quieter moods, was Wilfred Owen's

*Red lips are not so red*
*As the stained stones kissed by the English dead.*

Those particular lines of Owen's were about as much as he ever said about the war.

But as far as parents went, she was left only with the black and white photographs that stood on the piano in the drawing room at Dowdeswell – the piano that was never played, because only her mother Elspeth had known how to play. And Elspeth Tolliver was now part of England forever, her musical hands stilled, clasped on her bosom for eternity, deep in the English earth.

Barbar's funeral was a muted affair. Agnes had been surprised that so few people – especially from Barbar's RAF circle – had attended. But then, it was almost a quarter of a century since the war had ended. And Barbar had been a very private man, with very few friends, an Englishman who'd kept to his castle. He'd lived among his memories of the war, but had never been one for reunions or commemorations with other ex-servicemen. He didn't like the drinking that went with such occasions. Barbar was a teetotaller. There wasn't a bottle of alcohol any-where in the house. The war was a subject for serious research, not reminiscences or idle conversation. Like his medals, his memories were kept in a drawer, never spoken of or paraded in front of others.

The medals themselves, pinned onto a velvet cushion, had lain on his coffin during the service at St Michael's. She and Mrs Cawthorne had polished them to brilliance, and after it was over, a shabby little man whom she didn't know had sidled up to her and had offered to buy them. A few elderly men had proffered their condolences.

And then Barbar had been laid to rest in the churchyard, beside his son and daughter-in-law. Her parents. Except that they weren't. The day that Barbar had traced her finger along the letters chiselled on the gravestone had been a charade.

They'd prepared a reception at Dowdeswell Hall, with sand-wiches and cake, but in the event, only a handful attended. After an hour, they too melted away, and Agnes was left with Barbar's solicitor, Mr Nethercott.

Mr Nethercott cultivated a benevolently Pickwickian manner, underwritten by a plump chin and curly white hair. 'I will read you the will in a moment,' he said. 'But before I do, I want to explain, in layman's terms, what it amounts to. With your kind indulgence, of course.'

They were sitting in Barbar's study, on either side of the great oak desk. The sun was blazing outside, but in here it was, as always, cool and dark. Through the leaded panes, she could see Mrs Cawthorne's husband Alfred, mowing the lawn. The thick glass diamonds made his distant figure shrink and grow, as if by magic. 'Please go ahead.'

'Your grandfather was as frugal as he could be throughout his life, and over the past ten years, he tried to take every precaution to ensure that his estate passed down to you intact. I have to say that the current tax laws are . . .' – his pale blue eyes glinted with righteous indignation for a moment – '*savage* would not be too harsh a term, I believe. You should have been left a wealthy young woman. That, alas, will not happen. But you do inherit the house.'

'I see.'

He looked around the study. 'This is a beautiful old place, Miss Tolliver. You're very privileged to have it – and all the treasures in it. There are a couple of van Dycks, as I remember. It was built to raise generations in. I trust that it will not be too long before we see the hallway of Dowdeswell Hall strewn with confetti. And not too long after that, that we hear the patter of little feet.'

'You have a way with words, Mr Nethercott,' Agnes said dryly.

He smiled slightly. 'You are a pithy young journalist, and I am a wordy old lawyer. Now, shall I read the will?'

'Before you do, can I ask you something?'

'Of course.'

She leaned forward. 'What do you know about my birth?'

His eyes opened wide. 'Your birth? Surely you know all about that?'

'I thought I did. It seems that I didn't.'

'You're the daughter of Wing Commander Tolliver's son Giles, of course. He and his wife Elspeth were both killed by a German V2 rocket when you were only a few months old.'

'That's the story. But the day that he died, my grandfather wrote something that flatly contradicts everything you've just said. It suggests that the circumstances of my birth were quite different.'

'I'm very sorry,' Mr Nethercott said cautiously, 'but I know nothing about that. Your grandfather never discussed any such matter with me.'

Agnes took the charred scrap of paper out of the file she'd carefully kept it in. 'This was in that fireplace over there. Part of a letter he'd written, but decided to burn.'

He frowned. 'I see.'

She read: "*Getting the child into the country was easier than I had expected. My friends were of great assistance to me in this. Once I had brought her home, I realised I had not even named her. I decided to call her Agnes Elizabeth, after my mother. I had her baptised in St Michael's. She slept through the whole performance, as beautiful as an angel.*" She laid the scrap of paper down. 'I wasn't even born in this country, Mr Nethercott. He must have picked me up somewhere abroad during his war service.'

Mr Nethercott scratched his cheek. 'That means nothing to me, I'm afraid.'

'Well, it means a great deal to *me*. He'd been hiding something from me all my life.'

Mr Nethercott drew back. 'If you're implying that your grandfather did something underhand or dishonourable—'

'My birth certificate was issued fourteen months after my parents' death.'

'Good heavens, is that what's worrying you? It was the last year of the war, you know. Chaos. Absolute hell. Families displaced, London full of refugees, whole streets of people being slaughtered by Hitler's bombs. Hundreds unaccounted for. Nothing at all strange about a delay getting your birth registered!'

'They were killed by a bomb that struck their shelter. I survived. A baby. How's that possible?'

'Well—'

'My grandfather knew a lot of important people. He obviously got someone to lie for him on the official record.'

'Look, there's no need to worry about anything,' he said confidentially. 'Your birth certificate is completely valid. Registered at Somerset House. Nobody can challenge it.'

'Except that everything on that birth certificate is false. Probably including the date of my birth – which means I don't even know my real birthday! Or how old I really am!'

Mr Nethercott cleared his throat cautiously. 'The official records are full of . . .' – he balked at the word *lies* – 'errors large and small.'

'You mean I could be anybody's daughter.'

'As far as the world is concerned, you are Agnes Elizabeth Tolliver. Whatever his reasons for writing those words might have been, it is clear that he never intended the letter to be read. And if we are to respect his final wishes, then the best thing you can do is to put that scrap back in the fire and forget all about it.'

'I can't do that, Mr Nethercott. And not just for my own curiosity. Writing that letter made him ill. The strain quite possibly killed him.'

He drew back. 'That's putting it very dramatically.'

'I don't think it is. I played chess with him an hour before he died. He was depressed and agitated. And he told me he was writing a confession. That he was ashamed of something he had done. I believe the stress killed him.'

'It is 1968,' Nethercott said. 'The world has changed enormously since 1945. You should be looking to the future, not the past. Most *definitely* not the past. You have your whole life ahead of you, Miss Tolliver. Don't go raking among the ashes for things that were intended to be burned.'

Something about the way he spoke stopped her from arguing any further. If he knew anything, he was not going to give it away, and she had to accept that. 'So you're not going to help,' she replied flatly.

'I'm afraid I don't know how to.' He stared back at her as though daring her to challenge him. 'Now, if you'll permit me, may we return to the will?'

The frustrating conversation with Mr Nethercott left Agnes with the conviction that if she was to get at the truth, she needed to find it for herself. Nobody, clearly, was going to give it to her. Mrs Cawthorne had shut her down in a way that brooked no further enquiries; and Mr Nethercott had slid away from direct questions with a lawyer's practised ease. She had to take things into her own hands. But where was she going to start?

It took her an aimless day to come to the conclusion that if Barbar was writing to someone, he might just have received a letter prior to that. A letter from the person he was writing back to.

The *Evening News* had given her compassionate leave to deal with Barbar's funeral and the aftermath, and it would soon come to an end. She didn't have much time before she would have to be away from Dowdeswell for another five days. She began to systematically go through her grandfather's correspondence.

There was a lot of it. Although Barbar had not enjoyed the company of others, he'd been a prolific correspondent with archivists and other academics. The old red concertina folder where he filed his letters was stuffed full of mail from regimental historians and universities all over the world, including Oxford and Cambridge. Most of the letters were dry questions and answers on the topics that interested him, especially the war in the Scandinavian countries, where he'd served. She sifted through it all for hours without finding anything relevant.

'What are you doing?'

The sharp question made Agnes look up. Mrs Cawthorne had come in, and was standing with her hands on her hips. Her lined face was set. 'I'm going through my grandfather's correspondence,' Agnes replied.

'What for?' Mrs Cawthorne demanded with clear hostility.

'I told you – there's something I want to clear up.'

'Something *you* want to clear up! It's all *you*, isn't it, Miss Tolliver? He's barely cold in his grave, and you're digging through his things already!'

Agnes was so taken aback by the vehemence with which Mrs Cawthorne spoke, that for a moment she was open-mouthed. 'I loved my grandfather,' she said at last. 'I just want to understand—'

'You didn't know him like I did,' Mrs Cawthorne said in a shaky voice. And Agnes saw that her cheeks were now wet with tears. 'He was a good man. A good, good man. Everything he did, he did out of the kindness of his heart!'

'I know that.'

'Then let him be. If you really loved him, you would let him rest. And don't go digging in his papers like – like a hyena.'

With that, she hurried out of the room, leaving Agnes dumbstruck.

She sat in the silent, empty room for a long while, the housekeeper's words ringing in her ears. For the second time in a few days, Mrs Cawthorne had made her feel like an outsider, a stranger who was neither loved nor wanted. It was a terrible feeling, as though the past twenty-three years had all been a sham, empty of meaning. Was that how Barbar had seen her, behind the appearance of love? An interloper? An intruder? Perhaps not even English?

Then, without thinking about it, she lifted the red leather blotter on Barbar's desk and looked under it.

And lying there was an envelope that hadn't been filed in the concertina folder with the others. And unlike the others, which were mostly typewritten, this one was addressed by hand, in handwriting so strange and spiky that it was a wonder the post office had been able to decipher the address. Barbar's name had been spelled wrong, with one 'l' instead of two.

She picked it up. To her intense disappointment, the envelope had been slit open, but there was no letter inside. He had hidden – or perhaps destroyed – the contents. But turning it over, there was a bonus on the back – a return address, in Norway.

There was no way of telling who the sender was. There was no name. There was only a box number, a street name – Kittelsen 157 – and a town, Berlevåg. She hurried to pull Barbar's battered old atlas off the shelf, but looked through it in vain for any mention of Berlevåg. Disappointed, she reflected that there were far better atlases at the office. She would have to consult them when she got back to work tomorrow.

She stayed in Barbar's study, thinking about Mrs Cawthorne's unaccountable hostility, and looking into the empty envelope, as though she might have missed something that would solve the mystery.

The research library at the *Evening News* offices held a hefty atlas. It revealed that Berlevåg was a small seaport in Finnmark, Norway, clinging to the jagged roof of continental Europe. You couldn't get much further north without landing in the Barents Sea, or further east without finding yourself in Russia. Murmansk was only half an inch away on the map.

Who would have written to Barbar from such an icy, obscure, remote place?

Consulting the multi-volume *History of the Second World War*, she learned that Berlevåg might be remote, but it was not obscure. And it had endured a torrid war. Occupied by the Germans, who had built an airfield there, it had been heavily bombed by the Russians for months on end. When the Germans had finally been driven out, they had dragged the inhabitants with them, and burned the town to the ground.

The inhabitants had returned after the war, and had rebuilt their town. There were no trees in Berlevåg (why no trees?), so they had dug the wooden planks out of the German airfield, and had used those to build their houses, a peculiarly Nordic version of beating swords into ploughshares.

Enlightening though these details were, they didn't help Agnes guess who Barbar's mystery correspondent might be. But they were highly suggestive. Going all the way to Berlevåg to find an anonymous person was a very long shot. She decided on a compromise.

When she got back to her Victoria digs that evening, she wrote a brief letter.

*23rd June 1968*

*I regret to inform you that my grandfather, Wing Commander Louis Tolliver, passed away suddenly last week. I believe that he may have been preparing to write to you when he died, as I found your envelope, but no letter, on his desk. I would welcome any information that you can give me.*

*    Yours faithfully,*
*    Agnes Tolliver*

She posted the letter the next morning. And having cast her bread upon the waters, she got down to resuming life without Barbar.

# CHAPTER FOUR

## KAROLINA

*East Berlin, 1968*

He was waiting for her at the swimming pool on Tuesday morning, as he'd promised, sitting in the same place on the stands, wearing only a striped Speedo. Among the largely pale and unhealthy bodies, he stood out, golden and lithe. He didn't acknowledge her, but Karolina felt his eyes on her as she swam.

It was another hot day, the sun already high in a cloudless heaven. The pool was emptier today, and they'd strung out the lanes of floats, so she was able to extend herself fully, swimming laps in each of the four strokes in turn until her muscles burned with the exertion.

What was his interest in her? It wasn't sexual, by his own admission. And if he wanted the company of other 'deviants' he must surely be able to find that?

Still, it was undeniably flattering to have the interest of a creature as beautiful as Rafael. Even his name was beautiful. She wondered whether he had chosen it himself, having begun life as plain Otto or Heinrich.

As she cut through the water, she remembered lesbian women she'd known at Stauberg, both warders and inmates. Some had been tender and kind, others had been brutes. But they stuck together against the system, and she had envied their solidarity. Did the same apply to men? She had so little experience of men, either straight or gay, that she didn't know. Men were not drawn to women who had the toxic presence of the Stasi hanging around them. And if they didn't notice at first, the Stasi soon paid them a visit to explain. Apart from the times she'd had to fight off amorous advances in the bathroom in her apartment block, her sexual life was a void.

She hauled herself out of the pool at last, water streaming down her body, which felt taut after the exercise. Wrapping her towel around her waist, she climbed up the tiers to sit near – but not beside – Rafael.

He gave her a luminous smile. 'You slice through the water like a battleship.'

She frowned. 'I look like a battleship to you?'

'A cruiser, then. A corvette. I don't know the military terms. Something slim, fast and dangerous.'

'I used to be fast. Now I just swim until I'm tired. You don't go into the water?'

'Sometimes. I'm like a cat. I don't like to get wet. Unless there's a good reason.'

'Such as?'

'A fish to catch.' He reached into the shopping bag at his feet. She noticed it was green and gold, from Harrods in London. Plastic bags were prized in the DDR, communist East Germany. One from Harrods was both an inaccessible luxury and a potent status symbol, suggesting foreign travel. She wondered how he had got it. 'This is for you.'

He was holding out a book. It was a copy of *Buddenbrooks*, new, or nearly new. Her eyes widened. 'You bought that for me?'

'Bought, but not with money.'

She stopped herself with an effort from reaching out for it. 'What do you mean?'

'I did a rich man a favour. In the back of his car, as it happens.'
When she still hesitated, he said, 'Take it. Don't worry, I didn't
get any on it.'

'Any what?'

'You really are an innocent,' he said dryly. 'Aren't you, Karolina?'

'Oh. That.'

'Yes, that. It's the currency we use in the bourgeois deviant
world.'

'What do you want for it?'

'Nothing.'

She didn't believe him, but she couldn't resist any longer,
and took the book at last. It was heavy and glossy, and though
it wasn't quite new, it had obviously never been read. 'It's very
kind of you,' she said awkwardly. 'Thank you.'

'I don't read much myself. Certainly nothing as long as
that. Books are for people who live in their heads. You live in
your head, don't you? You're a dreamer. Not of this world. You
don't even know you're beautiful.' He reached into the Harrods
bag and took out a bottle of Skol suntan lotion, yet another
unobtainable luxury. He dribbled the amber-coloured oil gener-
ously on his chest and rubbed it luxuriously over his belly and
thighs, making himself even more golden and gleaming. She
watched him enviously. 'Take your towel off and turn around,'
he commanded. 'I'll do your back.'

This was turning into a very surprising morning. Karolina
obeyed. He flipped off the shoulder straps of her bathing
costume in an oddly intimate gesture. She had to hold the
cups to prevent them falling off her breasts. She felt his warm
palms smoothing the lotion over her shoulders and down her
spine. Luxury enveloped her. The pleasure of being touched
was a half-forgotten delight, the exotic scent (was it orange
blossom? Jasmine?) was intoxicating. It was almost like escaping from Berlin for a few moments, and being transported
to some freer, more glamorous location.

He was good at this, more of a massage than a coat of sun oil, his thumbs finding the knots of tension in her neck, pushing up, down, around, until her head hung forward, heavy as a rose in the rain.

'There,' he said, capping the bottle again, 'now you won't burn that flawless skin.'

She was glad he couldn't see the scars lower down. She felt drugged. 'It smells so wonderful,' she murmured.

He smiled with slightly scornful pity. 'It's just Skol. Wait till you smell Chanel or Dior.'

'This is good enough for me.' She tried to pull her shoulder straps back but he stopped her.

'Don't do that, you'll get tan lines. And Skol is certainly not good enough for you. You deserve the best. I think I'll have to take your education in hand.' He tilted his head and narrowed his eyes, appraising her. 'You could do really well, you know.'

'Do well?'

'With men. Or women, for that matter. Make a lot of money.'

She was incredulous. 'Are you telling me to become a prostitute?'

'Just saying you would do well,' he said with a sparkle in his pale green eyes. 'You're not only beautiful. You have that touch-me-not thing going on. Ice maiden. Virgin goddess. Everybody wants that.'

'How long do you think I would stay a virgin goddess,' she asked ironically, 'if I had sex in the back of a car every time I wanted a book?'

'You're not very grateful,' he retorted.

'I didn't ask you to do it.'

'I did it because I like you.'

'Did you like the man in the car?'

'Well enough to do what I did. And he's a good contact. He can get all kinds of nice things.'

'So you're a rent boy?'

He grinned, showing straight, white teeth. 'You're a piece of work. Where did you learn a term like "rent boy"?'

'I've been in prison,' she reminded him.

'It's a terrible thing to call someone. I'm not a rent boy.'

'What are you, then?'

'I'm the urban spaceman.'

'What does that mean?'

'You don't know the pop song?'

'I don't listen to decadent Western music anymore.'

'You need to start again.' He put the bottle of Skol back in the Harrods bag, and handed it to her. 'Keep it. Use it every time you go in the sun. The hot weather is here. You have to take care of your skin.' He rose to his feet. The striped Speedo (yet another status symbol) was stretched by its contents, and was cut so low that the curly hair at the lean base of his belly showed. She looked away quickly.

'I don't want all these presents,' she said.

'What's wrong with them?'

'They frighten me.'

'Karolina, you can't go through life being frightened.' He gestured at the book he'd given her. 'I put my address in *Buddenbrooks*. Come to my place on Saturday night. Not too early. I'll play you "The Urban Spaceman". We'll have a few drinks. Talk about life. Okay?'

'I can't.'

'You can. You will. I'll have another big, square, thick book for you by then.' He gave her a mocking, American-style salute. 'See ya.'

She watched him leave, feeling the familiar nausea rising from her belly to the back of her throat. Her own early-warning system. But his words echoed in her mind. *You can't go through life being frightened*. They resonated with her. Being frightened was part of life in the DDR, sucking the joy out of your lungs, sapping the energy in your blood. But she'd had enough. She couldn't go on like this.

Nevertheless, she wrapped Rafael's gifts carefully in her towel before leaving the pool. Walking down the street swinging a Harrods bag would attract the kind of attention she just didn't need.

His invitation, too, resonated in her mind all week, and not altogether comfortably. He'd written the address on a slip of paper, put between the pages of *Buddenbrooks*. The house was in Pankow, a very different part of Berlin from her own, near Schloss Schönhausen, a walled-off Baroque palace used as a guesthouse for visiting heads of state (communist states, of course) and Communist Party dignitaries. It was not the kind of neighbourhood Karolina frequented.

Going there would be asking for trouble. If she was followed by the Stasi, they would almost certainly stop her and want to know where she was going. That would be bad news for everyone concerned. She decided firmly that she would ignore the summons. She didn't trust Rafael. He was, in any case, far too arrogant to be any kind of friend.

She slept most of Saturday, weary after a week at the factory, and surfaced in the evening. She made herself a cup of Mona instant coffee, the cheapest chicory blend, but one of the few indulgences she looked forward to, and settled down to read the last chapters of *Buddenbrooks*. She was a voracious reader, very fast, with a retentive memory. The story of the decline of the Buddenbrooks family, written in Mann's detached, ironic prose, was fascinating. If she were ever to write a book, she had decided, she would write like Thomas Mann, cool and dry. But the idea that she would ever write a book was so unlikely that she didn't let the fantasy settle in her mind.

The sun set late, past nine thirty in the evening, and the darkness swam into Berlin, warm and muggy. She turned the last page of the book with a sigh, leaving the Buddenbrooks with their entirely bourgeois conviction that there would be a grand reunion for them all in heaven.

Perhaps it was because she herself had no family, not a single relative in the world, that she had enjoyed *Buddenbrooks* so much. Reading it had made her feel part of something, for a while, at least – and not just a loose pebble rolled along the margins of life's river. Her isolation was something she had never become used to. Loneliness was the most effective weapon in the Stasi arsenal. It crushed you, in a way that beatings and prison couldn't.

She decided to make herself a fried egg, and then go to sleep. Sleeping at night, in the darkness, was another indulgence she looked forward to. Night shift robbed her of that simple pleasure. Having to sleep away the daylight hours was yet another of the refinements that the Stasi inflicted on her.

She was standing at the stove when she heard the knock at the door. Her heart sank. The police, at this time on a Saturday night? But when she cautiously opened the door, a young man in a paint-stained T-shirt was standing on her mat.

'Ready?' he demanded, speaking around the cigarette in his mouth.

'Ready for what?'

He squinted through the curl of smoke. 'I'm Jonas. Your driver. Rafael sent me to pick you up.'

'I'm not going anywhere,' she said, her voice rising.

He glanced at his watch. 'Come on, hurry up. I haven't got all night.'

She felt an almost physical pressure, pushing her to do something she didn't want to do. Rafael was really impossible. Sending a car for her? Really! Did he think these things impressed her? Did he think he could buy her with a bottle of sun lotion and a ride in a car? Yet the showing off was oddly touching. And a car ride was a novelty that intrigued her. Against her better judgement, she shrugged. 'Okay. But I have to dress. You wait outside.' She shut the door in his face.

There wasn't much of a selection in her slender wardrobe. She didn't earn enough money for clothing. Her best summer outfit was a simple yellow frock and plain sandals, and she chose these. She brushed her short, blonde hair into some kind of order, and was ready.

She'd expected the car to be a smoke-spewing Trabant, like most of the cars in East Berlin, but it turned out to be a Wartburg, quite sleek and stylish-looking, on the outside, at least. The inside was a hideous melange of orange vinyl and black plastic, with mottled nylon carpet. But it still smelled new, and she stroked the faux-leather upholstery of the back seat appreciatively while Jonas drove.

He looked over his shoulder and saw what she was doing. 'This is the 353,' he said proudly. 'The new model. The police drive these. And important government people. Very limited access for the proletariat.'

'Does it belong to Rafael?' she asked.

'Yes.'

She was sceptical. 'Really?'

'Let's just say he can use it any time he wants,' he replied, 'which comes to the same thing, know what I mean?'

She didn't ask any more questions, but stared out of the window. They were cruising through a suburb of wide avenues. The scars of war had been assiduously erased here. The streetlights all worked. Gleaming cars were parked under spreading trees, and handsome villas stood in large gardens. There was more than a whiff of capitalist decadence in Pankow, but of course, the elite of the socialist state had special privileges; all animals were equal, but some were more equal than others.

Jonas stopped in front of a substantial apartment block, built around the turn of the century. Entering it, one left both war and socialism behind. He led her through a marble foyer, where a guard sat stolidly behind a granite desk, to a mirrored elevator, where her own expressionless reflection stared back at her.

The apartment was on the top floor of the building. It was crowded with people, loud music playing, plenty of alcohol being served. She also caught the whiff of marijuana smoke as Jonas steered her through the crowd. It took her back to being eighteen, before her fall, when life had been very different.

Rafael was sitting on a sofa at the back of the apartment, which was less crowded than the rest of the flat. He was in a grey silk shirt that looked Thai or Indonesian, open at the chest to show off his tan. Beside him on the sofa was a formally dressed woman wearing dark glasses, her gleaming black hair swept up into a fashionable beehive. Rafael rose to greet Karolina with a kiss on each cheek, as though they were already old friends. She held herself stiffly away from him, but he ignored that, taking her arm. 'Why haven't you got a drink? What do you like? Gin? We have Beefeater and Gordon's. Or Johnnie Walker, if you want whisky.'

The list of Western drinks was yet another sign of privilege. She let him put a neat whisky into her hand, and looked around. The apartment was furnished in a heavy yet comfortable style, and there were further signs of luxury to be seen, including a glimpse of smart new appliances through the open kitchen door, and the sort of antique lamps and ornaments which had long since disappeared from the black market.

'You like the place?' he asked.

'Very nice. Is it yours?'

He laughed. 'It's a little middle-aged for me, don't you think? It's not my style. But it's big, and the owner lets me use it whenever I want.'

'Like the car.'

'Exactly. Like the car.' He drank, watching her face over the rim of his glass. 'You don't miss much, do you?'

'You seem to have generous friends.'

'I'm lucky that way.'

'So where *do* you live?' she asked.

'Here and there,' he shrugged.

'That's a bit vague.'

'I don't think it's good to be stuck in one place. But I want you to meet Hedwig.'

Without rising from the sofa, the woman with the beehive hairdo held out a cool, white hand. 'You are very pretty,' she said. She took off her dark glasses to study Karolina, revealing that she was older than she had first seemed, perhaps in her late forties. Her dark eyes were hard. 'Yes, very pretty. Who is your father?'

'I don't know.'

'You don't know? And your mother?'

'I don't know that, either.'

'Then what is your background?'

There was something about this woman that reminded Karolina of others she had known throughout her short life, people with power, people with authority, who expected swift and truthful answers, people whom it was dangerous to annoy. She had answered such questions so many times that the words came automatically to her lips. 'I was a war baby. The Russians found me with some other children in the woods in East Prussia. They took care of me. I grew up in an orphanage here in Berlin.'

The woman with the beehive nodded slowly. 'So. You are a wolf child.'

That word – *Wolfskind* – was one which Karolina hated. It implied something less than human, feral, regressive. But she didn't show any emotion. 'Yes, I was a wolf child.'

'Interesting,' the woman named Hedwig said. 'You seem quite normal.'

There was nothing Karolina could say to that comment. She tasted the whisky Rafael had given her. It was unaccustomedly heady, burning her lips.

The woman asked, 'And you made no effort to find out who your parents were, or what happened to them?'

'It's forbidden,' she replied quietly.

'Perhaps just as well, eh?'

'Perhaps,' Karolina agreed neutrally.

Hedwig gave a brief laugh, showing bad teeth. She was heavily made-up, with cosmetics that Karolina knew were expensive. Everything these people had was *very limited access for the proletariat*, as Jonas had put it. She was starting to feel that familiar nausea rising in her gullet again, the nausea that warned her something bad was coming. But she knew better than to let that show.

Hedwig rose. 'Let's go somewhere private, Rafael.'

They led Karolina to a back bedroom, shutting the door. The noise of the party was muffled. The room's heavy flock wallpaper and monstrous furniture had striven for opulence, but succeeded only in being oppressive. There was a stereo set against one wall, and Rafael switched it on. 'This is the song I wanted you to hear. "I'm The Urban Spaceman".'

Karolina listened to the bouncy track, which seemed to be made for children. Hedwig had produced a hand-rolled cigarette, which she lit using a gold Dunhill lighter. The rich smell of marijuana filled the room. She sucked the smoke deep into her lungs, then passed the joint to Karolina. Karolina shook her head.

'Don't be silly,' Rafael chided her. 'It's top-grade stuff from Albania. Take it.'

'No thanks.'

'Take it!'

Against her will, Karolina took the joint and drew on it briefly. It was far stronger than anything she'd had as a teenager, and she felt an instant ballooning in her brain. Without thinking, she took another hit. She'd forgotten what it was like to get stoned, why she'd done it in the first place: because nothing mattered anymore. Pain and fear went away. You floated above your troubles, disassociated.

They smoked in silence for a while, passing the joint around. She realised she was very stoned. The bouncy music took on a new meaning. It was ironic, detached. Like Thomas Mann's writing. The song was about nothing meaning anything, about an urban spaceman who didn't feel pleasure or pain, a being floating beyond earth's pull, a man who didn't exist.

When the joint got down to the sticky end, Rafael extinguished it carefully and put it in a little plastic bag.

'Sit down,' Hedwig commanded Karolina, pointing to the bed. Karolina obeyed, feeling as though she were moving through oil. 'Listen to me. I have work for you.'

'What work?' Karolina heard herself ask.

'Good work. Very good. Everything you've dreamed of. Far better than you deserve. You'll make money. Have luxuries. Nice clothes, nice things to eat. Get out of the Democratic Republic. Travel abroad.'

'What are you talking about?'

'You'll go to Bonn. You'll have a nice apartment there. You'll meet men. Important men. High-ranking officials from the West. Sometimes they'll be women. It doesn't matter, it turns out the same. You'll bring them back to your apartment and have sex with them. We'll have cameras in the apartment, and everything will be filmed. You understand?'

Karolina's mouth had gone dry as chalk. 'I can't do that.'

The woman rode on like a tank. 'Afterwards, you never need to see them again. We take over. We'll use the film to make them give us information we need. Or we tell the wives, the husbands, the employers.'

She'd been wrong, being stoned didn't lift you out of the horror. It just made the horror more sickening, more overwhelming. She felt that she was going to vomit, but her stomach was tight, as though concrete had been pumped into it. 'No.'

'Do not refuse,' Hedwig said with quiet menace. 'You will regret it, I promise you.' She pointed to the little bag that Rafael was holding. 'We have hard evidence that you are using illegal drugs. We've developed a chemical test now. It's infallible. We'll drive you down to the nearest police station and take your blood. You'll go back to jail, for fifteen years this time. By the time you get out, you'll be a worn-out old woman.'

Rafael sat on the bed next to her. 'You and I are the same, Karolina. We have nothing except youth and beauty. We have to make them work for us.'

She turned her head to look at him. 'Is that what *you* do?' she asked thickly. 'Blackmail foreigners for them?'

He smiled. 'Of course. I'm gorgeous, and they can't resist. You'll be the same, because you're just as gorgeous. It's a wonderful life in the West. I love it. So will you. We can even see each other out there. Like Hedwig says, you can have everything you dream of. Including freedom.'

'Freedom? Being a whore for the Stasi?'

Hedwig stooped quickly and slapped Karolina across the mouth. The balloon in Karolina's brain exploded into a jumble of jagged pieces. She tasted blood. 'Don't be insolent,' Hedwig rasped. 'It's time you repaid the State for what you've cost it.' Her voice was harsh, her face suddenly coarse under the greasy layers of make-up. Her pouchy eyes bored into Karolina's. 'You came into this world out of a degradation which even now brings shame. Your mother dropped you like the sow she was, and went her way. You roamed the woods with others like you, eating carrion, stealing from decent people, filthy, covered in lice, no better than an animal. Even the Russian women refused to take you. Nobody wanted you. And only because you were a German, *we* took you in. We gave you everything. And how did you repay us? By disobedience and treachery. You are a piece of human garbage that has floated around the world all your life, ungrateful, seditious, contributing nothing to the State that nurtured you. Well, all that ends now. You serve us – or we will flush you down the lavatory like the piece of shit you are.'

Karolina felt that she had turned to stone, unable to speak, or even breathe.

Hedwig turned to Rafael. 'See that she understands.'

'I will,' he nodded.

Hedwig put her dark glasses back on, and stalked out of the hideous bedroom, slamming the door behind her.

Karolina finally found tears. She bent over double and sobbed, covering her face with her hands.

Rafael let her cry for a while, then spoke gently. 'She means it. They'll destroy you if you don't cooperate. I've seen them do it. It's not pretty. Hey. Don't cry like that. It's not so bad, trust me. The secret is to take what they offer and make it work for you.'

'You betrayed me,' Karolina said in a broken voice.

He ignored that. 'It's not difficult. You won't be sent in unprepared. They'll get you ready. You'll be given all the right clothes, cosmetics, accessories. Like a princess. You'd like that, wouldn't you?'

'Shut up.'

'They'll train you. There's a special school. They have experts who'll show you everything you have to do. How to attract attention without being obvious. How to get the targets to come to you. They'll teach you exactly what men like in bed, what women like. You'll work for ten years, maybe fifteen, until you're too well known, or your looks go. After that, you'll come back to some quiet town in the East. They'll find you a quiet job and you'll live a quiet life. It'll all be behind you. You could even get married and have a couple of kids of your own. Nobody will ever know what you've been.'

'Leave me alone!'

He put his hand on her shoulder and squeezed. 'There's just one thing you have to accept, Karolina. You can't get out of this. They've chosen you. The sooner you realise that, the better. You can't fight and you can't escape. So you might as well enjoy the ride.'

She shook his hand off. 'Leave me alone!'

'I've got another book for you, like I promised. *The Magic Mountain*. It's huge. You'll be reading it for days.'

She couldn't stop crying, so he gave up trying to comfort her, rose from the bed and put the record on again, about the urban spaceman who felt no pleasure and suffered no pain because he didn't exist.

# CHAPTER FIVE

## AGNES

*England, 1968*

Agnes hadn't really been expecting a reply from Norway, but one came at the end of August. The postboy left it on her desk at the *Evening News*. She recognised the spiky handwriting at once, and quickly slit the envelope open, with her heart beating faster.

Inside was a sheet of paper with one line of writing on it. It read:

*I am able to give you the information you seek if*
*you come to me.*

There was no signature. Nothing to identify the writer, beyond the same address in Berlevåg on the back of the envelope.

Agnes stared at the letter blankly. Who was the writer? Why did this person think he knew what information she was seeking? She felt a twinge of unease in her stomach. It was like standing at a locked door with the key in your hand, yet not knowing what might lie behind the door.

Bill Dawlish interrupted her thoughts, arriving at her desk

with his jacket slung over his shoulder. 'It's nearly one. You coming to the pub?'

'I'll skip it today, thanks.'

He frowned. 'Why?'

'I need to think.'

'Do your thinking over a pint. Stimulate the grey cells. Works for me.' He craned his neck, and before she could fold the letter, he'd read it. 'What's all this, then? "The information you seek?" A secret source? Don't try and scoop me again!'

'It's not work. It's personal.'

'"*Come to me*",' he read from the letter in a theatrical voice, crooking his fingers in a grasping movement. 'Very dramatic. Who is this person?'

'I don't know.'

'And what's it all about?'

'I don't know that either.'

He stared at her speculatively. 'Well, you look like you've lost a shilling and found sixpence. Come to the pub and tell Uncle Bill all about it.'

For once, she felt that she needed a lunchtime drink. And although Bill could be irritating, he was also intelligent, and she needed someone to bounce ideas off.

Sitting in a corner of the pub, she gave him a very brief version of what had led up to this.

He listened intently. 'So you think your grandfather may have stolen you from your cradle, like some wicked fairy king?'

'Well, something strange went on, that's for sure.'

'And this weird correspondent of yours in Norway?'

'Whoever it is, I'm going to meet him.'

'All the way to this Godforsaken place—'

'Berlevåg,' she supplied. 'Yes.'

'Finnmark is the edge of the known universe. It's a long way to go on a wild goose chase.'

'It might not be a wild goose chase.'

Bill cocked his head on one side. 'Why do you think that?'

'Because I've been looking into my grandfather's war service. And the last place he was posted was Norway.'

He raised his eyebrows. 'Go on.'

'He was in the occupation force. The RAF put him in charge of disarming and disbanding the German Luftwaffe. He was there until the autumn of 1945.'

'Doing what, exactly?'

'As far as I can tell, decommissioning any aircraft and installations left behind by the Nazis. Demilitarising airfields. Destroying remaining bombs and ammunition. Getting rid of war stuff. Mopping up, you could say.'

'And you think you were one of the things he mopped up?'

'Could be. That's what I need to ask this person.'

He drained his pint. 'Well, I'll say this for you, young Agnes. You lead an exciting life. So you're not the last flower of an ancient English family, after all? Does this mean you'll be my girlfriend now?'

'No. And it's not something to laugh about. I don't know *what* I am.'

Bill saw the danger signs in her eyes. 'Sorry. Shouldn't have been flippant. Apologies.' He went to the bar and came back with two fresh drinks. 'So. When are you setting off for Finnmark?'

'As soon as possible.'

'What about the job?'

'I'll ask for unpaid leave.'

'For how long?'

Agnes had already drunk half her second glass of wine. Her head was swimming slightly. She would be lighting a cigarette next, she thought wryly, and completing her entry into the alcohol- and nicotine-guzzling ranks of Fleet Street journalism. 'As long as it takes,' she said boldly.

'You might get the sack.'

'This is more important to me.'

'You mean it, don't you?' Bill leaned forward, lowering his voice. 'You're on the threshold of a brilliant career, Agnes. Top marks from Kennard Coleridge, pat on the back from Jill Tweedie. You don't want to throw it all away.'

She drank the rest of her wine. 'Bill, people are hiding something from me. About who I am, where I came from. They know, and they won't tell me. That makes me feel . . .' She searched for a word. 'Lost.'

'Why lost?'

'Because everything I knew about myself has melted away. And it keeps melting away, more and more every day. I was always told that my parents were killed when I was a baby. I used to go and put daisy chains on their grave every day, for God's sake. But they weren't my parents, after all. So I've *really* lost them now. I've lost Barbar. And whoever my real parents were, I've lost *them*, too. So I'm drifting. I don't want to go on like this. I need to anchor myself to something, to some people who have my blood. So I can look at myself in the mirror and know who is looking back at me.'

Bill was moved by her obvious emotion. 'Look,' he said gently, 'if they're hiding something from you, then possibly that's because it's something not very nice.'

'I know that.'

'Then wouldn't you be better off not knowing?'

'No. Whatever it is, I need to understand it.' She paused. 'Whatever it is, this person – Mr Come-To-Me – knows the full details. So I am going to ask Kennard Coleridge for a leave of absence to find them out.'

'And when you come back, you won't be lost anymore?'

'I don't know about that,' she admitted. 'But at least I won't be living a lie.'

Her interview with Kennard Coleridge was brief and not very comfortable.

'You've already had a week off for compassionate reasons,' he pointed out sharply, 'and now you're requesting indefinite leave to pursue some deep family mystery – which you won't tell me anything about?'

'Yes,' she said unhappily. 'That's about it.'

'Well,' the distinguished editor said, clearly not pleased, 'I can't stop you going off. But I also can't guarantee that you'll have a job when you get back.'

'I understand. But when I do get back,' she offered, 'I might have a human-interest article for you.'

'We're a London newspaper,' he said witheringly, 'not a gossip magazine.'

'Yes, Mr Coleridge.'

'Off you go then,' he said, returning to the copy he was blue pencilling. 'And whatever you get up to, for God's sake be careful.'

'Yes, Mr Coleridge.'

She had already started booking her journey to Berlevåg. It was not an easy place to reach, and the trip would be a long one. She would get the train from King's Cross to Newcastle-upon-Tyne. From there, she would take the North Sea Ferry to Stavanger, then go by train to Oslo. From Oslo, she would take a flight to Kirkenes, and from Kirkenes she would go by bus to Berlevåg. The whole journey would take at least three days, perhaps four.

She was feeling butterflies in her stomach at the thought of it. She hadn't ever travelled outside Britain in her life up until now. The holidays she had taken with Barbar had all been within the United Kingdom, to beaches in Yorkshire, the Welsh hills, or the Scottish Highlands. She would have to get a passport. Looking at the map of Norway didn't help much, either. Even on the map, it looked an awfully long way, studded with foreign names she couldn't even begin to pronounce. The outside world was going to be a very new experience.

But her determination was increasing, the more she thought about it. Whatever Barbar had got up to in Norway, whatever he had tried to hide from her, couldn't hurt him now. He was beyond all that. As for herself, she was prepared for whatever she would find out. She was not afraid of the truth, in whatever form it came.

A turbulent sky in South Shields should have warned Agnes that the ferry trip to Stavanger was going to be gruelling. She had never been seasick before, but now she began to understand why travellers dreaded it. From the moment they left the River Tyne and entered the mountainous grey-green swells of the North Sea, the rolling of the ferry filled her with deathly nausea. It was a twenty-eight-hour passage, and she was prostrated in her cabin from first to last.

By the time they docked in Stavanger the next day, she barely had the strength to close her suitcase. She staggered ashore to find herself in a quaintly pretty seaside town, set at the end of a spectacular fjord under clear, pale summer skies. She had been planning to go straight to the railway station to buy her ticket for Oslo, but there was no way she could face any more travelling in her present condition. She needed a night to recover.

She got on a bus which took her from the ferry terminal into town. She dragged her suitcase past picturesque rows of brightly painted wooden houses to the first guesthouse she saw. Checking in hazily, she was led to a cosy, tiny room, evidently made for gnomes, where she collapsed on the bed, deeply grateful that it wasn't moving, and went out like a light.

She woke many hours later, feeling weak but hungry. She hadn't eaten anything for thirty-six hours; in fact, nourishment had been passing in the opposite direction. She needed food, despite the danger of further affliction. She went out into the warm, sea-scented evening air. The feeling of being in a foreign country enveloped her with visions of blue water, high mountains, and charming timber houses. She wandered as though in a dream down pretty streets until she found a restaurant she liked the look of. She went in, and was led to a table by the window. She scanned the menu without understanding a word. When the bearded waiter came, he addressed her with a smile. She replied awkwardly, 'I'm sorry, I don't speak Norwegian. Do you speak English?'

'Oh, I was sure you must be Norwegian. You look very Norwegian. We don't have a menu in English. What would you like?'

'Anything but fish.'

He was surprised. 'You don't like fish?'

'Sorry, no.'

'Then you are definitely not Norwegian. You came on this morning's ferry?'

'Yes,' she said, reflecting that she must look awful for him to guess that.

He nodded sympathetically. 'How about meatballs and mashed potato? That will settle your stomach.'

She agreed gratefully.

She got back to her room at 11p.m., weighed down by the meal she'd eaten, but feeling better internally. She had to close the double set of curtains before getting into bed. The sky was still light, even though September had arrived. She'd already travelled a fair way north from London. And she would travel a long way further north before she had reached her destination.

The Stavanger train took her to Oslo the next morning, and a bus from the railway station went straight to Fornebu airport. The terminal was a spectacularly beautiful modern structure, a world away from the quaint chalets of Stavanger. There were two flights a day to Kirkenes, and she got a ticket on the later one, leaving at 4 p.m. With her seat secured, she went upstairs to the lounge, where panoramic windows offered a view of the apron.

She ordered a coffee and a slice of apple pie, and watched the planes taking off and landing. She had a long flight ahead of her, and from Kirkenes it was a bus ride to Berlevåg, and a meeting with destiny. At least, she hoped it would be a meeting with destiny. This would be a very long and expensive journey for nothing if it didn't answer her questions.

It didn't escape her that she was surrounded by tall, blonde, blue-eyed women and men, not unlike herself. She thought about the waiter's remark last night – *you look very Norwegian*. Since reading that fatal scrap of Barbar's letter, her feelings about herself had undergone a steady process of change. Or perhaps it was better to say development, because she'd never really had feelings about herself before. She'd simply accepted that she was who she'd been told she was. It had never required much processing. She'd gone through twenty-three years like a toy train on tracks, stopping at the right stations, hitting all the marks, easily achieving all the goals that were expected of her.

She was now a lot more emotionally fragile. A waiter's casual remark could fill her with anxiety and uncertainty. Seeing her reflection could stop her in her tracks, wondering who she was looking at. She'd always felt that people liked her; she no longer had that certainty, because she no longer had confidence in who she was. Perhaps she was odd, unwelcome, different from others. Bill Dawlish had teased her about being 'perfect'. Was that an ironic way of saying she was somehow unnatural?

Her self-esteem was going fuzzy at the edges. In fact, it was starting to crumble. And she hated that feeling. She found herself looking at her hands. They were slim and graceful. Barbar had always told her that she had inherited her mother's hands. Well, that must be a lie, because the woman who lay in St Michael's churchyard was not her mother. She'd inherited her hands from someone else altogether.

So many fabrications! Barbar had built a mountain of lies

for her. Stories about her parents, boasts about her ancestors and her family's ancient pedigree, all false. All made up.

It was hard to forgive.

For all the kindness Barbar had shown her, it would have been better if he'd just told her the truth, whatever that was – rather than create a whole identity for her that was one day, inevitably, going to collapse like a house of cards. He probably hoped she would never find out, but he should have anticipated how much damage the eventual revelation might do to her.

The plate glass windows of the café shimmered each time a plane roared off the runway. This was going to be her first flight. She felt renewed queasiness at the prospect. People said flying was exhilarating, but to Agnes, the prospect was more frightening than anything else. How those huge tubes of metal got off the ground, and stayed off the ground, was beyond her. She hoped flying wasn't going to produce results similar to the North Sea crossing. What if one of those dozens of windows cracked? And what if an engine failed?

In the event, her plane turned out to be a DC-7 with four reassuringly large propeller engines. It was an old-fashioned-looking beast, even to her untrained eyes; she knew that jets were the modern thing. The interior was somewhat shabby, with worn carpeting between scuffed blue seats. She'd been given a window seat right over the wing, because the booking clerk had told her that was the safest part of the airplane. She had a good view of two of the engines. If anything went wrong, she'd be the first to know.

Take-off was terrifying. The aircraft shuddered as the howling propellers dragged it sluggishly along the runway, faster and faster. Rattling, thudding and thumping noises were horribly distressful to delicate nerves. Incredibly, some passengers were reading, talking, even laughing, as though death were not staring them all in the face. She wanted to shut her eyes tight, but she knew that her duty was to watch the engines and report any misbehaviour to the stewards and stewardesses. This was worse than the ferry. Was it too late to beg to be let off? Yes, because the DC-7 was already hauling itself into the air, and climbing into the blue. The die had been cast, and there was no turning back.

A couple of hours into the flight, the cabin crew laid the little tables with white linen and served a meal which, to Agnes's dismay, consisted of fish. She ate the vegetables and then stared out of the window. The amazing view above the clouds had not palled on her yet. A piercingly blue sky above made the mountains of cumulus below the plane dazzling. It was strange to think that below the white clouds, it would be overcast.

The sun was very low over the cloudscape when the plane began its descent towards Kirkenes. Going through the clouds was alarmingly bumpy, water streaming across the little window, and then they emerged into a darkened, wild landscape where, Agnes saw with some surprise, there were considerable amounts of snow on higher ground. Of course, Kirkenes was well above the Arctic Circle; the little town was set between two huge, grey fjords that were flecked with lumps of – was that *ice*? The landing was even more alarming, the DC-7 veering from side to side in heavy rain and wind; and emerging from the warm cocoon of the cabin was a shock. It was bitterly cold as they hurried across the tarmac to the terminal, hunched against the lashing rain. In her ignorance, Agnes realised, she hadn't packed anything like enough warm clothing. She would have to try to find some more suitable things somehow.

The terminal, bearing the proud boast, 'Høybuktmoen International Airport', was a simple, basic building not much warmer than the outside world. Rain drummed on the metal roof and the panels creaked in the wind. There was a café, and most of the passengers made a beeline for it, demanding coffee and aquavit. Agnes bought the same as everyone else.

Not being much of a drinker, she poured the generous glass of aquavit into her sweet, black coffee, and drank it like that. It helped warm her insides and prepare her for the next leg.

The bus to Berlevåg would not leave until the next morning. She had booked a hotel in Kirkenes for the night. A short taxi ride took her into the town, which was clustered around the harbour, where fishing boats were packed together on the dark sea. She bought a cheese sandwich by way of dinner. Tired and made drowsy by the aquavit, she went straight to bed.

The bus ride to Berlevåg the next morning took her through a bleak but majestic landscape of wooded hills in autumn colours, descending to dramatic coastal roads that wound around silvery inlets and fjords. The rain was clearing. Agnes was now very tense. Days of travel – and considerable expense – were coming to a climax. For several hours in the half-empty bus, she had time to reflect on the wisdom of what she was doing. A bit late for that, of course!

She was a long way from home, a very long way. The sense of what she was doing was no longer as clear to her. Was she going to reach a dead end in Berlevåg? And if she did, was she going to pursue her quest, at the possible cost of her job? Her savings? Her peace of mind?

She kept thinking back to the scrap of letter she'd salvaged from Barbar's fireplace. Had she misread it? Misunderstood what it meant? But then she remembered the words of her mysterious correspondent in Berlevåg: *I am able to give you the information you seek if you come to me.*

That must mean, surely, that there was something to be known?

Her thoughts were interrupted by an old man, who leaned over the back of his seat and pointed out of the window. '*Vi har kommet til Barentshavet,*' he said.

'Sorry, I don't understand,' she apologised.

'The Barents Sea,' he said in accented English. 'Good fish. Many, many.' She followed his knobbly, pointing finger. A massive, rocky headland stood stark against a Prussian blue sea. They had reached the swathe of the Arctic Ocean that Norway shared with Russia. She smiled and nodded her thanks. He looked like a retired trawlerman.

The road now took them along the shoreline. The clouds had all but cleared away, and the autumn sun was bright. They stopped occasionally at houses dotted along the road, where passengers got off, dwellings so isolated that Agnes wondered how people could live in such lonely spots. Groups of reindeer were grazing peacefully by the side of the road. Otherwise, the landscape was barren, almost lunar. This was a part of the world, Agnes thought, where the Creator had started running out of ideas – but not colours. The palette was vivid. What vegetation there was glowed an almost fluorescent green against the slate-grey rocks and mountains, and the water was the deepest blue she had ever seen.

And at last, they came to Berlevåg, a cluster of wooden houses painted in simple primary colours at the very edge of the sea. A little church was perched on a hill overlooking the village. The harbour was filled with fishing boats of all sizes; more boats than houses. Hundreds of white gulls wheeled in noisy circles over the boats or perched on the roofs of the warehouses in long lines. Across the sound was a lighthouse, glowing orange in the sun. By now there were only a handful of people left on the bus, all of whom got off. One of them was the gnarled old fisherman who had pointed out the Barents Sea. Agnes showed him the address. 'Can you tell me where this is, please?'

The old man squinted at the paper. '*Christiansen?*' he said, sounding incredulous.

'I don't know who it is. I only know the address.'

His filmy hazel eyes peered at her through a web of wrinkles and bushy eyebrows. '*Dette er Christiansens hus,*' he said, as though warning her about something. 'Christiansen house. You go?'

'Yes,' Agnes said.

He stared at her for an uncomfortably long time. He suddenly seemed unfriendly, his expression closed. He pointed up the hill, past the little church. '*Der oppe. Et hvitt hus.*'

'Sorry – '

'White,' he snapped. 'White house.' Without another word, he shouldered his duffel bag and walked off.

She set off up the hill. The road was packed earth. On each side, Arctic poppies were still blooming, yellow, white and orange. The church, with its sharp steeple and slate roof, was shut and silent. She passed a few houses, made of wood, and recalled that the village had been burned by the Nazis, and rebuilt using boards from the Luftwaffe runway. None of the houses were white, all had been gaily painted. Seagulls swooped over her head, rapacious eyes alert for any scraps she might have. Their cries were oddly like desperate calls for help.

Halfway to the top of the hill, she reached the last house in the village, standing all on its own, with no neighbours. It was bone-white, with a grey, corrugated roof. There were no curtains at the dark squares of the windows. The garden was neat and austere, cordoned off by a white picket fence. There were no flowers. She stood staring at the house for a while, her heart thudding. It seemed permeated by a sense of loneliness, of isolation from the rest of the town. It seemed to say, 'Pass by, there is nothing to see here.'

She opened the gate at last and climbed the steps to the front door. She knocked, wondering if she was going to get any answer.

After a while, she heard footsteps from within. The lock rattled and the door opened. The woman in the doorway was in her mid-forties, wearing jeans and a white T-shirt. She was tall, slim and athletic looking. Her blonde hair was tied back severely, no make-up on her even, regular features. Her eyes, the blue of cornflowers, met Agnes's calmly.

'So,' she said. 'You came.'

Agnes's throat was dry. She found her voice somehow. 'Are you the person who wrote to me?'

'Of course.'

'You're Christiansen?'

'My name is Liv Christiansen.'

The woman's face was somehow familiar, but not because Agnes had ever seen it before. It was familiar like something in a dream. Agnes felt the world spinning around her. Almost too dizzy to stand, she whispered, 'Who are you?'

'You are looking at me,' the woman said with a touch of dryness. 'I think you know who I am.'

# CHAPTER SIX

## LIV

*Norway, 1968*

I was born here in Berlevåg. You've already seen how remote it is. Today, tourists come to see it, and say it is picturesque. But in those days, it was beyond the edge of civilisation. I grew up exiled from the rest of the world. There was nothing but the sea and the wind.

I hated it.

Even as a girl, I knew that I was different from the people I grew up among. I despised them all. They had no ideas beyond their own fishing boats. From childhood, I knew that the God they worshipped didn't exist. They prayed to Him for fish. They were so banal! So self-righteous! Above all, so *dull*. As a teenager, my life stretched before me without a glimmer of hope. I was deeply unhappy.

I yearned for something greater. I wanted to be a part of something significant. I didn't know exactly what. But I knew I would recognise it when it came.

Even when my uncle took me behind the breakwater on my fifteenth birthday, the experience was crushing in its banality. I could have fought him. I could have got away easily. But I was so bored that I let it happen just to experience something new.

The light dawned on me in the cinema, a year later, when I was sixteen years old.

We used to take the cart to Kirkenes to sell fish, and sometimes we saw a film in the *kino* there. This film was from Germany, and it was called *Triumph of the Will*. It was about the Nazi rally in Nuremberg in 1934.

I remember people in the audience sitting silent with awe. Only at the end, some men started shouting, 'Nazi propaganda!'

Oh, yes. It was propaganda, all right. The most powerful propaganda ever made. And created by a woman, Leni Riefenstahl. You will find this hard to believe, but at sixteen, I didn't even know what the word 'propaganda' meant. I had no idea that it meant corrupting the minds of the young and innocent. But that was exactly what it did.

At that time, I was profoundly ignorant of the world. My imagination was a blank. *Triumph of the Will* was a brush thick with paint, which filled every corner of the canvas. It was the greatest thing I had ever seen – this majestic spectacle of seven hundred thousand young men and women, marching in unison. A mass movement of energy, health and beauty. Young people with a purpose in life! Young people seizing the future in their hands! And there was a name for this wonderful new race: Aryans!

They were blonde and tall, their muscles gleamed in the sun. Their hair was like gold. Their eyes were clear as crystal. And they were brave, unafraid to break free from the rotten old life. They marched in flawless ranks, shoulder to shoulder, thigh to thigh. They were forging a new future, with purpose and will. They were supermen and superwomen. I felt an intense sexual arousal – I am not ashamed to admit that. It was the first time I had known such feelings.

What a revelation!

You ask me now how I could have been so gullible. Did I not know about the persecution of the Jews in this same Germany? Had I not heard of Dachau? Had I not read that the Nazis savagely crushed all opposition? Did I not hear the drums of war, beating already?

All I can tell you is that I was a very uninformed, isolated young girl in those early years of the 1930s – and that I, like so many others, fell prey to an indoctrination machine much, much more powerful than I. I was caught like a fly in a vast web.

On the ride home, lying in the back of the cart, staring up at the stars, I felt an inexpressible yearning fill my heart. Then I had a revelation. It struck me like a thunderbolt that *I was* an Aryan.

Yes! I had everything in common with those young German Nazis, and nothing in common with my family or my neighbours.

At last, everything became clear. I couldn't breathe. I couldn't speak. For the first time in my life, *I knew who I was.* My identity was forged. I looked like them, blonde and strong. I thought like them, with scorn for the old conventions. I was one of them.

I saw *Triumph of the Will* three more times before it left the theatre. And each time, the message became clearer to me. I dreamed of the day I could join the National Socialist Movement and fulfil my destiny.

Now I knew why I had always felt that I was different from other people. Now I learned to love myself, to respect myself. I was conscious of carrying something precious within me. The seed of new life, that must not be wasted. I was the custodian of it, until its time came to bloom. It was what I had to give to the Movement.

From that moment, the years seemed to fly past. In 1936, Hitler put his troops in the Rhineland. After that, he began demanding the Sudetenland, even though the British tried to stop him. It was like a mighty river in flood, carrying all the old rubbish away.

I was beautiful, then. I turned heads wherever I went. All the boys in the village were after me. After school, they would roll up their sleeves and fight each other with bare knuckles for the honour of walking with me. What fools! As if I would give the time of day to those clods! I felt nothing but contempt. When I saw their bloody noses, I thought only that their blood was inferior to mine. I was proud of being an Aryan, fiercely proud. I was their queen, and they were my vassals.

I told my father I wanted to go to Germany. He was astonished.

'Are you mad? Do you think you are a Nazi, now?'

'Yes!' I told him. 'I am an Aryan and a Nazi!'

'That ridiculous film has addled your brains. You have no idea what the Nazis really are. They are not the glamour-boys you seem to have fallen in love with. They are brutes with horsewhips!'

'I don't believe you!'

'There is no money to send you to Germany, whatever you believe,' he replied angrily. 'You had better think of finding a husband with money, who will put up with your airs and graces!'

And of course, I already had proposals of marriage aplenty, even at sixteen. Every bachelor in the district wanted me. They brought flowers, chocolates, gifts. Men came from miles around to ask my father for my hand. And he tried to sell me, like a cow at a cattle auction. 'Marry this one, he has his own boat! Marry that one, he has plenty of money!'

I told him, 'They all stink of fish! How can you tell me to marry some crab-catcher I can never love?'

I refused to let them marry me off. I sent all the suitors away with a flea in their ear. They were bitterly offended because my father had foolishly encouraged them. And, as is the way with these things, I was the one whom they abused. They called me a coquette, and many uglier words. I gained a bad reputation as a woman who lured men only to humiliate them.

'That Christiansen girl,' they said, 'she thinks she is too good for us.'

My father was horrible to me. He threatened to turn me out of the house. He wanted me off his hands. My mother was the same. They said I was lazy, vain, didn't pull my weight. I would not cook or clean. I brought in no money. They ran out of patience with me. But I refused to be sold.

My father said, 'If you're too good for the village, then go! Take yourself to the Nazis and see how you like it!'

But of course he didn't mean it. He thought the Nazis were monsters, and he would never give me the money to go.

I couldn't make anybody understand what had happened inside me. I became, if anything, more alone than ever. By 1939, the whole of Norway was trembling. They were terrified of a German invasion. I mocked my father's fears. I told him. 'You won't let me go to them, so perhaps they will come to me!'

When the Germans occupied Norway in 1940, I knew that my time had arrived at last.

I said to my father, 'Now you will see how they shake up this dusty old house that is Norway! They will chase out the rats and open the windows to the fresh air!'

He slapped my face and called me a traitor.

I saw my first real-life Nazis at last. They came to Berlevåg to build an airfield. Everybody kept out of their way, except those they forced to work for them. But I went up to them, unafraid, and gave them smiles and flowers. They used to invite me for a drink at the tavern. Of course, I always went!

I could feel everyone staring at me with hatred – a Norwegian girl, laughing and drinking with German soldiers! You could see how my fellow countrymen loathed me. But my heart was full of joy. Ah, those Germans in their uniforms! They were charming, and yet awe-inspiring. It was as though they strode in the clouds, and I had risen up to be with them.

Yes, I flirted with them all. With Heinrich, the blond fighter pilot, with Fritz and Otto, who were twins, and always made me laugh. I knew that none of them could be the man I was waiting for. But I had fun with them all.

One night, when I came home, my father was waiting for me. He had been drinking, and he was in a rage.

'How can you bring such shame on our family?' he shouted. 'You have become the Nazis' whore!'

He took off his belt and he beat me, this time seriously. He cut my legs and bruised my arms. When the German officers saw my face, they went to speak to him.

After that, my family were afraid of me. They stopped insulting me. They tiptoed around me, I can tell you! They watched me as mice watch a cat. What a wonderful feeling that was!

Of course, there were other girls who thought like me. Some fell into the arms of the first Germans they saw. It happened. Nobody wants to believe it. Today, no woman boasts of that. They would as soon say they slept with the Devil. But at that time – yes, of course it happened. And the inevitable consequence ensued. That was how I found out about the programme. From a girl who knew a girl who was pregnant by a German officer. Her family threw her out, but the Germans took her in. She had the best of everything. A beautiful place to live. Luxury. The best food, new clothes. They treated her like a princess. And when her time came, the best medical care, the best doctors and midwives. Nothing was too good for her or her baby.

And so she escaped from disgrace. More than that, she slipped from her dreary life into a glamorous new world. She became a darling of the conquerors instead of a vassal. From a caterpillar to a butterfly. I pricked up my ears at that. I asked my new friends, the German officers, about it. They told me the programme went much further. They called it *Lebensborn*.

Do you speak any German? Well, it means the Fountain of Life. It was a plan of Himmler's to mate SS officers with Aryan women. People say it was a Nazi plan to breed a master race. I suppose it was.

I saw at once that this was my path to greatness. A glittering stairway to a better life, a life that had real meaning.

I see by your expression you think the idea repugnant. And yet, as a result, here you are, a beautiful young woman – just as I was then. I was very vain, why deny it? I was a teenage girl drunk on my own beauty, in love with my own body. They played on that vanity so cleverly to make me feel I would be doing something magnificent.

Yes, I thought the idea was noble. The way they phrased it made so much sense to me. Why should the lame, the idiots, the inferior be allowed to breed? Why not breed for strength and beauty? I never questioned what would happen to those who were not lucky enough to be born Aryan. I just wanted to be a ruler in the new world order. I wanted to be one of the founders of a racially pure aristocracy. It made sense to me. It exalted me. I felt like Mary in those old paintings of the Annunciation. Not that I have ever believed in all that Bible rubbish.

Do you want tea? Coffee? A glass of water perhaps? You look pale. Have you eaten today? I have these cookies. They're very good. I order them from Oslo. Nobody in Berlevåg will sell me anything. Nobody speaks to me. They are poisonous gnomes, all of them, sucking on fishbones here at the end of the world. You will have seen that already.

Where was I?

Yes, Lebensborn. I knew that if I waited in my village, I would wait forever. So I went to Lebensborn myself, as I was. I told no one I was going. I packed, and I went.

There were ten such houses, I think, perhaps more. The house I chose was far from my village, on a magnificent private country estate in western Norway, among woods and meadows, a piece of heaven. It was called Heim Jorundarholt. I simply walked up to the door with my suitcase.

They were surprised to see me. The German nurses asked, 'Are you pregnant?'

I replied, 'No, I am a virgin.'

They asked, 'Then why are you here? This place is for mothers.'

I said, 'I want to be a mother. I want to give you a child. I want to give you *children*.'

They were suspicious at first. I think they suspected my motives. But they took me in and examined me.

Oh, how they examined me! They measured my nose and my ears and my lips. They compared my eyes to a colour chart. They checked my hair to see if I had bleached it. They weighed my breasts and checked the breadth of my hips. They listened to my heart. Then they made me exercise, and listened again. They took my blood and my urine for analysis.

They asked whether there were any Jews in my family. Any Jewish blood in either of my parents. My grandparents. My great-grandparents. My great-great-grandparents. Until I was dizzy with it.

They tried to test if I was really a virgin, of course, but they found nothing to the contrary. Virginity tests are a lot of nonsense, anyway. There's no way to tell by looking at the body. Virginity is in the mind, not down there. So, I made them all think I was untouched, because it was important to be perfect. That's what men want. At least, that kind of man did.

They filled out an 'R' Card for me. A Race Card. There were four categories. Number one was Racially Desirable. Number four was Racially Undesirable. Of course, I scored the highest marks.

When they had done all that, they asked me about Hitler and his book, *Mein Kampf*. There, I was not so sure.

I remember how the nurse with the questionnaire grew

impatient with my answers. She said, 'This one has a wooden head. She is a political blank page.'

But the SS doctor – his name was Ackermann – laughed, and replied, 'With scores like these, she does not need to be able to sing the Horst Wessel Song. She is a virgin in mind as well as body. We can do something with this one. We will write something good on this blank page.' He turned to me and smiled. 'Don't worry, *Liebchen*. We'll find a good father for your babies.'

He reached out to chuck me under the chin, but I did not permit such liberties, and I struck his hand away. 'I am not a fool,' I said sharply, 'and I am not a wooden head or a blank page. I am not educated. But I can learn.'

Dr Ackermann looked at the nurse, and his eyes were bright. 'You see?' he said. 'We will find someone special for this Liv Christiansen. She is worthy.'

I think that was the best day of my life.

How old was I? I was eighteen. A dangerous age. The age at which men find it easiest to kill. The age at which women begin to have their highest levels of hormones.

But not old enough to know what I was doing.

Don't misunderstand me. I am not making excuses. I made my own decisions, and I took my own path. It was not the right path. But once I had set my foot upon it, there was no turning back. My father had been right, after all. My brains had been addled.

I waited a long time for that *someone special*. They had already decided, but they wouldn't tell me who he was, only that he was a brilliant soldier, and fighting somewhere in the world for race and fatherland. They told me to be patient.

In the meantime, I was an intern at the Lebensborn home. They gave me a small room, which I shared with a nurse named Ilse, and in exchange, I helped out. There were always at least two dozen mothers there, often far more. They came for many reasons. Some had been thrown out by their families, and had nowhere else to go. Others had come voluntarily, like me. The majority had been recruited from maternity homes all over Norway. When I say *maternity homes*, I mean those places reluctantly set up by a disapproving state for unmarried mothers. There was a great deal of prejudice against illegitimate birth at that time. There still is, absurdly. The Germans scoured those places. They were very efficient at everything they did, the Germans, very efficient.

The only requirement was that the mothers must be Aryan, and the fathers too. Whoever was granted a Category One 'R' Card was eligible. Of course, it was not difficult to persuade young mothers to leave those bitter penitentiaries, where every dry crumb was begrudged, to Lebensborn houses, where there was beauty and joy.

Yes, beauty. And yes, joy. Can you imagine a great house, set in the most wonderful scenery, filled with healthy, beautiful, happy, blonde women and their babies? It was like seeing the future. It was like heaven. Even now, I have dreams of it. Sometimes I wake crying for what was, what could have been. At Heim Jorundarholt there was no talk of the darkness that lay just behind the painted screen. We did not learn about that until it was all over. In fact, I understood very little about the war, or how it had affected Norway, until the Nazis left, and I had to face my fellow Norwegians.

One didn't have time to get to know the mothers well. They came and went. Most wanted to get back to their lives immediately after the birth. They lacked the vision to want to stay. They took the help that Lebensborn gave them, and then they left. But the babies stayed.

I helped with the babies. I learned a great deal about the care of infants in that time. But I never grew to like them. They were interesting because of the future that they were going to bring. But in themselves – it was just endless feeding, changing, washing. My God! So many babies! I dream of that, too. Strange dreams, in which I am in a room piled with broken dolls that are somehow alive. They say now that twelve thousand or more children were born in Lebensborn houses in Norway just like Heim Jorundarholt. Think of it. And that was only the beginning. Given time, there would have been a million. Two million. A whole new nation.

And all the while, I devoured every newspaper, every magazine, everything I could find about the war. The German army was sweeping across the world, irresistible, triumphant. Each week, it seemed, some new country had fallen. Poland, Denmark, Belgium, Holland, Greece, Yugoslavia. Even France. We drank champagne that night, and promised each other we would go on a shopping trip to Paris.

Of course, I wasn't interested in the war itself. I was trying to identify the man who was going to be the father of my children. They wouldn't tell me anything about him, so I had to try and guess. I knew he was a German hero, but there were so many German heroes. The Nazi magazines were full of them and their exploits. Some were like film stars. I hoped he would be one of these, and not some scar-faced general, old enough to be my father.

I knew that many of these men were married. That didn't matter to me. It certainly didn't matter to Lebensborn. Illegitimacy was not a concept they cared about. They cared only about life. Abundant, healthy life.

At first, I cut the photographs of my favourites out of the magazines, and pinned them above my bed. The nurse I shared the room with teased me about it, which I didn't like. So I started pasting them in a scrapbook, instead. I kept it up to date with their careers, their exploits. I had that scrapbook for years, until they took it away from me and burned it.

\* \* \*

My family found out where I was and what I was doing. They were horrified. My father came to take me home.

I can still see him now, with his hat in his hands, his face all slobbered with his tears. 'Please come back with me, *min vakre datter*, come back to us in Berlevåg!'

But I was unmoved. He had not the slightest idea how committed I was. I said, 'Now I am your beautiful daughter? Remember the ugly names you called me before? Remember how you beat me with your belt? What do I have to go back to? To be a fisherman's wife? You see how I live here! You see how they value me!'

He had to leave with his tail between his legs. And from that day to this, I have never spoken to any of my family. Some of them still live here in Berlevåg, but they loathe me. I don't care. I never think of them. I advise you strongly not to go and find them. You will not be enriched by the experience, I assure you. They are narrow-minded bigots who are best left to their fish guts.

Then, the following spring, Dr Ackermann told me I would soon receive a visit from my mate. He used the phrase '*Dein Schatz*,' your sweetheart. I thought that was silly, but I was secretly pleased, because it implied that he already knew all about me and was eager to meet me.

From that moment on, I felt holy.

I'm not a religious person. I believe that all religions are rubbish. But there is such a thing as holiness. I was consecrated to my mate.

They gave me a photograph of him at last, to prepare me. And they told me his name.

He was not one of the famous officers whose pictures I had pasted in my scrapbook. But I had read about him here and there. He was one of those who did the fighting, not one of those who posed for the photographers.

'Isn't he so handsome?' the matron gushed. 'His name is Ulrich von Breda. A *von*! He commands a tank regiment. An *Oberstleutnant* with medals. A real hero of the Third Reich!'

To tell you the truth, I did not think he was attractive in that photograph. It was not a sweetheart photograph that he had sent. He wore his black uniform, with the SS lightning bolts on the collar, and his cap, with the skull and crossbones over the peak. He was unsmiling, stern. He did not gaze into the camera, but away from it, as though he had more urgent business elsewhere.

But he was unmarried. And he was young. That was a relief to me, although I would not have refused an older man, or a married man.

When the matron had left, I studied the photograph again. I thought he looked like an angel. Not one of your Christian angels, made of pink sugar. A pagan angel. An angel of death.

He came in the spring. The leaves were budding in the forest, and the snow was melting away from the mountains.

There was great excitement when he arrived at Jorundarholt. The nurses were so excited that they fluttered like pigeons. Even Dr Ackermann took off his white coat and put on an SS uniform, and wore his Blood Order medal, which Himmler had given him, as well as his Iron Cross from the First World War.

They made a festival of it. A pagan festival. The dining hall was decorated with greenery, and there were white lilies everywhere. The nurses had a little choir, and they sang something, a Germanic folk song, I think. The babies were all in ribbons and bows. There was roast goose and spring vegetables for lunch, but I couldn't eat a thing, and I don't think he touched his food either. I hardly dared look at him.

He had come in full uniform, just as in the photograph. All black and silver, with shiny boots and a pistol at his side. He was very tall, taller than me, and you see that I am not short. He made little conversation at lunch, barely answering the questions they were all asking him. I remember that one of the midwives asked him if the war would be over that year. He replied quietly, 'Not this year, nor next year.'

I saw only his profile. I thought his face looked as though chiselled from marble, pale and hard. He was not blonde like me; his hair was dark. But his eyes were an electric blue. They pierced through me, and I could not meet them at first.

After lunch, he asked me to go for a walk with him. There was a waterfall not far from the house, a famous beauty spot where people used to go, before Lebensborn commandeered the area. He wanted to see it. So I went with him.

We walked side by side. I had still not yet looked him full in the face. I kept my eyes on the ground.

He asked, 'What are you thinking?'

The question surprised me. I told him the truth. 'I feel like a princess in a fairy tale, who has been locked up in a tower all her life, and whose perfect knight has come to rescue her at last.'

As soon as the words left my mouth, I felt I'd spoken like a fool. My face was flaming. I expected him to laugh at such silly words. But he spoke gently.

'It makes me very happy to hear you say that, Liv. You have a beautiful mind.'

I was overcome with pleasure. He asked me questions as we walked, about my family, my childhood. I told him how my father had beaten me.

'He had better not try that again,' he said quietly, 'or he will have me to reckon with.'

He had a calm manner of talking. He didn't bark or raise his voice. But you could see that he was used to being obeyed. He had an effortless way of commanding others. When he asked you a question, you answered. You would not try to lie to him, or be flirtatious, as was the custom of some young women at the time.

My heart was beating so fast that I was short of breath, and had to find excuses to stop now and then, and pick *blåweiss*, the little blue flowers of spring. Except that my hands were trembling so much that I kept dropping the flowers, like a fool. But he stooped and picked them up for me. I saw how beautiful his hands were, strong and sure.

We reached the waterfall after twenty minutes. The melting snow had swollen the stream and made it all the more dramatic. A torrent came gushing from a rocky ledge high above, and hurtled down into the abyss below, wreathed in mist. All around the place, the stones glistened with moisture. Ferns, moss and other water-loving plants grew luxuriantly everywhere, dripping silver, nodding as the drops fell. It was truly a magical place. A temple of the old gods.

Ulrich said something to me. But the pounding of the waterfall drowned out his quiet voice, and I was forced to raise my eyes to decipher what he was saying.

It was the first time I'd had the courage to look him full in the face. How can I explain how I felt at that moment? My heart, which had been racing, suddenly stood still. A great calm came over me. A great certainty. He was so very handsome. Far more handsome than that lifeless photograph had suggested. His eyes were deep blue, like the sea, and they stared into mine as though he knew everything about me, knew all my secret pain, all my secret hope. There was nothing I needed to tell him, because he had seen it all.

Later, I heard others describe Ulrich as boyish. I am not sure if that adequately captures his beauty. I think he had the secret of eternal youth. His face had no marks of age, despite everything he went through. He was a perfect physical specimen. And he had a wonderful smile. That was the first time he showed it to me. I took a step forward. It was quite involuntary, as iron cannot help being pulled by a magnet. He bent down and kissed me – not on the lips, but here, on my brow. It was like a seal on our pact.

I can't remember how long we stayed there by the cascading water. We certainly didn't speak. The noise of the water was too loud. We just gazed into each other's faces. If there were words, they passed between us without sound, mind to mind, heart to heart.

When we eventually walked back, we found we were both wet with the mist. His beautiful uniform was soaked, and my flimsy spring dress was clinging to my skin. I felt his eyes on my body. I wanted him to look. I wanted him to desire me.

I was shivering, both with the cold and with emotion. They had lit a fire in one of the sitting rooms, guessing, I suppose, that we would come back cold and wet. Everybody vanished, leaving us alone. We sat by the fire to dry off, and he told me a little about himself. He was born into a military family, Prussians, who had been fighting in German wars for generations. He was not boastful, but as he talked, I began to realise that he had achieved a great deal in his young life.

He'd excelled at school, in both academics and sports. He'd joined the SS at eighteen, and had been given command of a Waffen-SS tank platoon at twenty-three. He'd taken part in the invasion of Luxembourg, which surrendered within a day. Then the Netherlands. Next Belgium. They'd deployed secretly into the woods, raced around the battle lines, and surrounded the British, driving them into the sea.

Not pausing to rest, they'd cut through Belgium and bypassed the famous Maginot line. He had taken part in the staggering conquest of France, leading his tank group in a lightning race to Paris. The French had capitulated with their army almost intact. Hitler had compelled them to sign the surrender in a railway carriage in the Forest of Compiègne, exactly the same location where Germany had surrendered at the end of the First World War. Ulrich regarded this as the pinnacle of his career so far, avenging the humiliation of his father and uncles in 1918.

He'd met the Führer, who had personally given him the Knight's Cross, which he wore at his throat. He had just been promoted to Lieutenant-Colonel. And now he was here in Norway.

I felt a fierce pride in all his accomplishments. Can you imagine how honoured I was to be chosen to bear his children? To mate with this warrior, this knight? This superman?

He'd been given a fortnight's leave to be with me, on the personal orders of Himmler, the head of the SS and the architect of the Lebensborn programme. It was queer to think that someone as powerful as Heinrich Himmler was involved in the conception of my child. I should have been flattered, I suppose. But the truth was that it made me uneasy.

It made me feel like a marionette, who danced on strings held by vast and shadowy hands behind the painted scenery. But I put such thoughts out of my mind. Only Ulrich mattered to me.

Dr Ackermann had ordered the staff to prepare quarters for us away from the main house. They chose a gamekeeper's lodge on the estate, at the edge of the woods. It was a highly ornamented nineteenth-century cottage, with rows of antlers on the walls, bearskins on the floor and all kinds of hunting rifles in racks. There was a big kitchen with an iron stove in the middle, an upstairs with a balcony overlooking a meadow of spring flowers, and most importantly, an enormous bed carved like a sleigh. It was there that you were conceived.

We made love every day and every night. And I can tell you, it was not a difficult task. We were ravenous for each other. We knew that the difficult part was going to be saying goodbye at the end of this fortnight in heaven.

Yes, I told Ulrich that he was the first. I knew it would matter to him. Honour was his soul, the breath of his life. It was the only time I lied to him, and I never deceived him in anything else ever again.

Nor was it far from the truth. Before him there had been my Uncle Oluf, drunk on aquavit, and later on, a boy hiking in the mountains, who'd lodged with us for a few days one summer. Neither of those experiences had made much impression on me.

But Ulrich was different. He made love to me with tenderness and passion that I never knew were possible.

That first time was a revelation. Afterwards, I lay in his arms, floating.

'I never knew it could be like this,' I whispered.

'For me it was the same,' he replied, stroking my hair. 'You are so beautiful. I expected—'

'What did you expect?' I asked, smiling.

'Somebody cold. A Nordic ice maiden.'

'And what did you find?'

'I found you,' he said simply. He was not given to making romantic speeches. But I took it as a compliment, and did not make the mistake of trying to make him say more.

'I only want to please you,' I said.

'You succeed.'

Later, I prepared a meal for him in the kitchen, with the food they had stored there. He watched me as I cooked, with those blue, blue eyes. I had never been so happy before. I felt that, for the first time in my life, I had found my equal. My mate.

'What are you thinking?' I asked him.

'I am wondering whether you believe in all this,' he replied.

'In all what?'

'Racial hygiene. Lebensborn.'

I paused in my work, surprised. 'Don't you?'

'Himmler is asking all of us in the SS to have as many children as possible. Most of us are ignoring him.'

'Why?'

'We are men, not farm animals. Besides, it's somewhat absurd. Have you seen Himmler, that grubby little chicken farmer? And what about Goebbels, with his club foot and snake eyes? Hardly an Aryan. And *he* has six children.'

'But his wife is a true Aryan. She is lovely.'

'That has not stopped Goebbels from having an affair with a Czechoslovakian actress.'

I was taken aback. But of course, he knew all the gossip about the top Nazis. 'Well, at least their children are beautiful,' I said. 'You should not be saying these things.' He smiled at me, and I was piqued. 'Why are you laughing?'

'You are funny.'

'Thank you so much,' I said acidly.

'To tell you the truth,' he replied, 'I've been dreading this. But you are a breath of fresh air, Liv.'

'Dreading it!'

'You don't think I *wanted* to come here?'

I was so upset that the tears of humiliation and anger came to my eyes. I thought of the months I had dreamed of this, of the joy I had just felt in his arms. 'And it means nothing to you!'

'You misunderstand me,' he said in his calm way. 'It means a great deal to me. To be ordered to leave the front and travel to Norway to mate with a stranger, solely in order to breed children for Heinrich Himmler – that was an imposition. But to meet you and know you and make love to you has been nothing short of wonderful.'

I was still angry, and very disappointed by his attitude. 'Preserving the Aryan bloodline is vital. You should not be flippant about that.'

'I would rather you came to bed with me for my own sake,' he replied, 'than for my Aryan blood.'

'You and your blood are the same thing,' I retorted.

His eyes were suddenly sad. 'Ah, Liv. When you have seen as much blood as I have, you will realise that one man's blood is very much like another's. When it is in, you are alive. When it is out, you are dead. That's all there is to it.'

We agreed to disagree on the subject. It was very strange to me that he had no interest in racial hygiene. He did not care about children, had never thought of having any, until Heinrich Himmler had issued that order. He told me that if he'd had to pay for the upkeep of his child, he would have refused. But Himmler had assured them all that children born in the Lebensborn programme would be cared for by the State. So he had accepted. But he cared very little whether he had offspring or not.

It was as though there was a gap in his understanding of the world. On the other hand, he knew so much about so many other subjects. And he came to care very much for *me*. I had to accept that that was the most important thing. So long as we produced children together, we did not need to discuss it further. He had his thoughts and I had mine.

In the event, I did not become pregnant that time.

It was a bitter disappointment to me, that after those glorious days together, no child grew in my womb.

But by the time he left, I knew two things. One was that we had to meet again. And the other was that I loved him.

Of course, neither of us knew what was going to happen to us later on.

And that was a blessing.

We were both sure of final victory. The war was going so well for Germany. The possibility of defeat – and the consequences of that defeat – didn't even occur to us at that time.

A few years later, he eventually came to see that the end was coming. I never did. I lived in a blissful dream at Heim Jorundarholt. A maiden in an ivory tower, waiting for her knight to return. It was not until the war was over that I began to understand what I had done.

From that time on, the lodge was my home. I never went back to sharing a room with Ilse. And I was no longer merely an intern at Heim Jorundarholt – but a woman marked out by destiny.

The war dragged on. By now, it seemed the whole world was caught up in it. The Japanese had begun sweeping through the Far East. The vast majority of Europe was under German occupation. Our allies the Russians and the Italians were picking up what remained. But the obstinate British held out somehow, despite losing ground in every direction, and despite Goering's efforts to pulverise their cities from the air.

Then Hitler decided to invade Russia in the summer, and Ulrich was to be in the spearhead.

Yes, of course I was afraid for him. Russia was so huge. To capture it would be Hitler's most dazzling coup yet, but the risk of failure was immense, and the personal danger to Ulrich was terrible to contemplate. We all knew it. Everyone at the Lebensborn house was subdued from then on. We read the newspapers anxiously every day.

I was irritable and tense for months and years after that. To tell you the truth, I could never understand why Hitler had taken this decision. He and Stalin had signed a pact just a couple of years before this. With the Russians on our side, the war would have been won easily. Attacking them had opened a vast new front, and created a vast new enemy.

But Hitler was maddened by the lust for destruction. It was then that I began to hate him, for putting my Ulrich's life at risk. If I could have got near him, I would have thrust a knife in his liver and happily watched him die in agony.

It sounds strange to you that I hated Adolf Hitler? It's why I cannot say that I was a true Nazi, because to be a true Nazi meant Hitler-worship. What I worshipped went beyond Hitler.

I didn't see Ulrich again until months later, when the autumn had set in. The autumn comes early in northern Norway.

He arrived unannounced this time. Nobody had been informed that he was on his way. He travelled straight from the Russian front to Norway, and arrived at the gamekeeper's lodge early one frosty morning. I opened the door to find him standing there, dirty, exhausted, and smelling of war. You cannot imagine my joy. I couldn't restrain my tears.

'I didn't know whether you were alive or dead,' I said, holding him in my arms. 'Why didn't you answer my letters?'

'I received none,' he said, stroking my hair with a blackened hand. 'We've been travelling a hundred miles a day sometimes. None of us have had any mail for weeks.'

We pulled off his uniform, which was so stiff with grime and oil as to be like a suit of armour. He lay in the bath, almost too tired to wash himself. I soaped him, checking his body for injuries. There were so many cuts and bruises disfiguring his beauty, most sustained in the cramped confines of his tank, that he looked like an absolute map of war. But none were serious, thank God. Not then.

I made food for him, and while we ate, he told me about the fighting. It had been a lightning war, just as in France. The speed and precision of the German Panzers had been used to deadly effect on the great plains and in the marshes of the Soviet Union. In Minsk they had encircled the Soviet 3rd and 10th armies. Barely a day later, in Brody, they had destroyed hundreds of the enemy's tanks in an incredible victory. They'd entered Riga unopposed. Ten days later, they had encircled the Soviet 16th and 20th armies, together with over 300,000 troops, at Smolensk. The swiftness of their progress, and the scale of their victories had shattered the Russians' morale.

They had entered the Ukraine, the breadbasket of Europe. At Kiev, they had encircled over 600,000 Soviet troops, yet another stupefying defeat. Now almost half the Red Army were prisoners of war. Leningrad was in the Germans' sights, and they were marshalling their forces, preparing to lay siege to the city. Ulrich had been granted compassionate leave because of the death of his grandmother. But he had lied to his superiors, and had chosen to come to me instead.

This struck me in the heart like an arrow. I covered my face and burst into sobs all over again.

'What good would I do, standing at her graveside?' he asked wearily. 'I would rather be here, with you.'

It was a token of his great love for me, and I was overwhelmed. How many nights had I lain awake, fearing that he had forgotten me, that because of my failure to conceive, he had been sent to other women, and that his remembrance of me had been erased by other bodies, other faces.

But not so. He had proved as true as Krupp steel. As I said, honour was his soul, the breath of his life. Where he loved, he loved truly and indivisibly.

He fell asleep in my arms, and lay like the dead all night. But early in the morning, he awoke, and mounted me like a bull. Then I knew that he was mine. I possessed him, as he possessed me. He was a man, a real man.

The next day, we walked in the woods. The leaves were already thick on the ground, and falling all the time like rain. It was very still, very silent. I began to speak against Hitler, calling the invasion of Russia a great folly, an act of madness.

He stopped me. 'Hitler is the greatest military genius the world has ever seen,' he said. 'Don't be seduced by those who doubt him. They have no more substance than these dead leaves, and they will burn like these leaves. Tomorrow, we stand at the gates of Leningrad. By next year, we will have Moscow, and the great Stalin will be hanging from a lamp-post.'

'I'm only afraid for you,' I whispered.

He smiled grimly. 'If I die, I will be happy in Valhalla. I will wait for you there.'

For the rest of the walk, he talked about Hitler's infallibility, and the necessity of utter obedience to the *Führerprinzip*, the leadership principle that took its authority directly from the Führer's will. Before long, he had put his strong arm around my waist, and forgiven me.

I never made that mistake again. It was another thing we had to agree to disagree on. He was blindly loyal to Hitler, as were nearly all in the SS. The difference between us was that he placed his faith in a man, and I placed mine in nature. But I could not say that to him. I simply had to watch while he – together with millions of others – was destroyed.

But at last, joy! I was pregnant. By the time he left for the Russian front again, new life had begun in my belly.

They wanted me to go to Germany for the birth.

It seemed to matter a great deal to them. By now there was a full-time SS race specialist at Heim Jorundarholt. 'You must go to Berlin for your confinement!' he ordered me. 'It will give the baby a special status. A German child should be born in the Reich!'

And at first, the idea was attractive. I would be treated like royalty, and I would have the excitement of travel to a great city. But further details emerged. I would be expected to learn German and undergo indoctrination courses. I would live with Ulrich's relations until the birth, and then I would be sent to live and work on a farm in the country. I might be mated with other men.

I didn't like any of that, so I said no. I refused to change my mind, despite the pressure they put on me. It meant I would have very little time with the baby, but as I told you, I am not fond of babies. I am not a sentimental woman. I have had only two emotions in my life, love of myself, and love of Ulrich.

\* \* \*

The child was born the following summer.

During the nine months of my pregnancy, I saw Ulrich only twice, both for very short visits. We were happy together. We didn't talk about the coming birth, because we both knew what was going to happen.

As for sex, it was better than ever during the first visit. I was a lot more swollen the next time he came, and I was afraid he would find me unattractive. In the event, we were able to please each other in many ways other than intercourse, and it was perhaps more erotic than it had ever been.

The baby was a girl. I was pleased about that. I will not go into the details of the birth, because they are familiar to us all, the pain, the pushing, the mess. If you are lucky – or unlucky, depending – you will go through it yourself one day.

I was only interested in whether the baby had ten fingers and ten toes. The race specialist assured me it was a perfect specimen. I had done a good job, and that pleased me. After that, I let others attend to the child. I knew that the more I had to do with it, the harder it would be to part with it.

I had seen many women come to Heim Jorundarholt, have their babies, and leave dry-eyed a few days later. I told myself to be the same as them. I knew I must not form a sentimental bond with the infant, because my destiny was to bring more Aryan children into the world. As a surgeon cannot be emotional about his patients, so I could not afford to be emotional about my babies. They were my gift to the race. One cannot ask for a gift back, can one? I am trying to tell you the truth, and I do not wish to hide any of my folly. My madness, if you like to call it that.

I was content with what I had done, and I rested. My principal goal was now to recover my figure and my looks, so that when Ulrich returned, he would still find me beautiful.

The child was sent to Germany. Yes, I shed tears when she was taken away. I had not expected to feel such a wrench. It took me by surprise.

Dr Ackermann had anticipated this. He gave me drugs – hormones to alter my mood, amphetamines to quell my depression. He was a very clever doctor. After a few weeks, my emotions were stable.

I never saw the baby again.

# CHAPTER SEVEN

# AGNES

*Norway, 1968*

Agnes had listened for almost two hours, barely speaking, barely moving. The turmoil inside her had made it difficult for her to breathe at times, but she had tried to show no emotion, though her feelings had ranged from revulsion and horror to something like pity. She kept her eyes steadily on the woman who sat opposite her in the stark living room, where the chairs were uncushioned, the walls bare of art, the windows uncurtained, so that Liv Christiansen's voice echoed, unsoftened by any furnishings to absorb it.

It was a clear, hard voice, and the woman to whom it belonged was clear and hard, too. She sat with her back very straight, her slim ankles crossed, self-disciplined and taut. She was still handsome, though there were no efforts to enhance her beauty with cosmetics or the aid of a hairdresser. The strong, long fingers that were clasped in her lap were innocent of rings or nail varnish. The creases that bracketed her mouth and eyes were not yet deep, and there was no grey in the short, blonde hair. The long, elegant neck, of which she was evidently proud, was unlined.

In Agnes's mind, a phrase was echoing, one Liv Christiansen had used – *a perfect physical specimen.* This woman – her mother – personified health and fitness. But there was nothing warm about her. And there was certainly no evidence that she found Agnes's visit a pleasure, or even interesting.

*I was wary of forming a* sentimental *bond with the infant,* she had said. *I was content with what I had done. My principal goal was now to recover my figure and my looks.*

That was all that had mattered to her.

Agnes had no doubt that Liv Christiansen was her mother. The physical resemblance was impossible to miss. It became stronger with certain gestures, certain expressions, and when that happened, Agnes was looking at an image of herself in two decades' time.

'I will make coffee,' Liv said, rising. 'Perhaps you would like to ask some questions when I come back.'

She went into the kitchen, straight-backed, her head held high. Agnes discovered she could breathe again. She was, she knew, in a state of shock; nothing was real. She felt as people must feel during a car crash: that the world was tumbling and collapsing all around her, but it was all a dream.

*This woman is my mother*, she kept thinking blankly. Not buried in St Michael's churchyard, but here, alive, talking to her.

And her father had been an SS officer, in a black uniform, with lightning flashes on his collar and a death's head on his cap. Her mind shied away from the thought, not wanting to visualise it. But the image loomed out of her imagination, nevertheless. A cold sweat broke out on Agnes's skin. Her lungs felt paralysed again. Panic was very close. She stood up, her legs shaky, and went to the window. *Now I know who I am. They warned me not to look for the truth.*

The view didn't help. It was alien, that pale blue sky, that deep blue sea, the emptiness of this world – none of it was soothing.

She heard the clink of glass from the kitchen. Looking over

her shoulder, she glimpsed Liv gulping a glass of water down, and saw her rinse the glass at the sink. But when Liv came back into the room, carrying a tray, she brought a strong smell of alcohol with her.

On the tray was a coffee pot and two plain white cups. No milk or sugar, just a plate of the biscuits that came from Oslo, because nobody here wanted her in their shops.

She cocked her head. 'It looks so peaceful out there now, yes? But in the winter, the sea is a monster, trying to devour the land. You have questions?'

Agnes found her voice. 'So I was sent to Germany as a baby?'

Liv had been pouring coffee. She looked up at Agnes in surprise. 'You? No, of course not.'

'But you said—'

'You are confused. The first child was sent to Germany in 1942. By the time you were born, in 1945, the war was over. You stayed in Norway with me.' She straightened. 'Are you all right? You had better sit down. You are very pale.'

Agnes groped her way back to the hard, flat chair and sat down. 'I was your second child?'

'Yes, of course.'

'With the same father?'

'With Ulrich, of course.' She passed Agnes the cup of coffee. 'I would have accepted nobody else.'

Agnes was too shaky to take the cup. 'Then I have a sister.'

Liv's tone was impatient as she put the cup down on a side table. 'Yes, of course.'

'Where is she now?'

'I don't know,' Liv replied flatly.

'Is she alive?'

Liv shrugged slightly. 'One can hope. But perhaps it would be better if she was not.'

'But you said she was sent to Germany! You must know who took her!'

'Perhaps I knew once. But small details escape me. The electroconvulsive therapy saw to that. It was intended to make me forget everything. So I obliged.'

'Wasn't there any paperwork?'

'There were a few documents, once. They were lost years ago.'

'Don't you *care*?' Agnes cried.

'I stopped caring in 1945,' Liv replied dispassionately. 'Perhaps you will let me finish my story? I will try not to be too tedious.'

'You aren't tedious. You are . . .' Agnes couldn't find the word.

Liv nodded. 'You think me a wolf mother. Cruel. Heartless. Perhaps you are right. But it doesn't matter to me in the slightest what you think of me, so you can scream at me if you wish. You would not be the first.'

'I don't want to scream at you. I just want to know the truth.'

'Very well. I will be brief.' She sat down, crossing her ankles, holding the coffee cup as though she wanted to warm her hands. 'You were conceived in September, 1944. It was the last time I saw Ulrich. By then, the campaign against Russia had turned into a debacle. He was lucky to escape with his life, and to be sent back to Germany for the final defence of the Reich.

'I remained at Jorundarholt until you were born. At that time, the whole Lebensborn apparatus was being dismantled. They all went back to Germany – Ackermann, the nurses, the race experts, the last of the mothers, the lot. Heim Jorundarholt was closed, and I was left to face my fellow Norwegians alone.

'The German forces surrendered to the Allies in May, 1945. By the time you were three months old, the King and the government had returned from exile, and the purge had begun. Vidkun Quisling, the prime minister whom the Nazis had put in power, was on trial for his life.' Liv's face twisted, as though the coffee were unbearably bitter. 'And little Liv Christiansen was chased through the streets of Oslo by a mob of patriots.' She had spoken the last word with biting contempt. 'Men who had not dared to say boo to the Nazis for four years, men who had obeyed their every command with *Jawohl*, and *Zu Befehl*, those same poltroons were suddenly heroes.' She fell silent for a long time.

'What happened to you?' Agnes asked at last.

'I knew my fellow Norwegians. I knew how they would behave. I had gone to Oslo to have my baby because I was hoping to lose myself in the city. But I had bad luck. A woman who had worked at Heim Jorundarholt as a cleaner recognised me. She screamed at me in the street. A mob formed, and they chased me. I had my baby in my arms, and I couldn't get away.

'They cornered me in a back alley. They tore you from my arms. You were crying, but I didn't make a sound. I didn't give them that satisfaction. They ripped off my clothes and they raped me there, in the street.'

'I'm so sorry,' Agnes whispered.

'I don't know how many of them did it. Perhaps five or six. But I remember that there were women watching, laughing, encouraging them. That stayed in my mind for a long time. Yes.' She sipped from the cup. 'They were not very nice to me, my fellow Norwegians.'

'You didn't deserve that.'

'Kind of you to say so,' Liv replied ironically. 'But it didn't end there. They shaved my head. And they took you away.' She was dry-eyed, calm, but Agnes felt there was a scream somewhere inside Liv, a scream that she refused to let out. 'It was the last time I saw you.'

'What do you mean?' Agnes asked.

'They turned me over to the authorities. I was arrested and sent to a concentration camp outside Oslo, with hundreds of other women, *Nazi whores*, they called us, because we had been in love with German soldiers. They told us we would be deported to Germany. I was there for two months, waiting. They wouldn't tell me what had happened to you. I begged them to tell me, but they refused. You had just vanished. Then, one day, a nurse came to the camp and informed me that you had died in an orphanage. For a long time, I believed you were dead. For more than twenty years.'

'But I wasn't.'

'No. Evidently not,' Liv said dryly. 'My world took on a new shape from then on. They decided not to deport me to Germany in the end, because I had not actually married Ulrich. As if that mattered! But to such narrow minds, such things assume great importance. After they told me you were dead, I broke into pieces. They examined me – just as the Nazis had examined me – and decided that I must be crazy. Crazy to have wanted the child of a German. Crazy to have accepted help from Lebensborn. So I was transferred from the camp and committed to a psychiatric institution.'

A sudden loud thud at the window made Agnes jump in shock. She looked up. A clod of earth had struck the glass, spattering like a fat spider.

'Children,' Liv said laconically. 'Or perhaps adults. Your arrival has awakened memories. Although such memories seldom sleep.'

'After all these years!'

'After all these years,' Liv said, nodding.

'I'm so sorry if I've brought you trouble.'

Liv shrugged. 'I accepted long ago that I would never escape. After the insane asylum, I was shattered. They used drugs, electric shocks. On and on. For two years. They said it was therapy, to put me right, but I believe it was merely refined torture. Punishment. It was so easy for them to be cruel, when they had such a good excuse.

'I must tell you that those years burned out whatever compassion I had left in me. Compassion for others, I mean. The idealism that I had felt, my dreams of bettering humanity, all that was gone. It was all I could do to survive.

'I tried to rebuild my life when at last they discharged me, but wherever I went, there was more punishment. If I was lucky, a cold stare, a vicious word, the refusal of a job. If I was unlucky, a kick in the stomach, or my hair torn out.' She pointed to her head. 'I have learned to wear it short, as you see.'

'I came to the end of my tether in the 1950s. I planned to kill myself. Then, my mother died. And although she had disowned me in life, in death she had been kind. She left me money, enough to give me a decent existence. I came back to Berlevåg. I hoped I could live out my life quietly, with a kind of peace. But of course, they eventually found me out. And since they did, they do not speak to me, and I go on the bus to Kirkenes to shop, and order my cookies from Oslo.'

Agnes found her voice. 'When did you learn I was alive?'

'Last year. A woman wrote to me from Tromsø. A retired nurse, one Birgit Halvorsen, the one who had come to me in the camp. She said she wanted to confess something that had been on her mind for a long time. She had given my baby to a British officer in the occupation force in the autumn of 1945. You must have been six months old at the time. You were in an orphanage with other children of *German whores*. He had offered to adopt you.' Liv smiled tightly. 'She was only too happy to oblige. Getting rid of unwanted German babies was a priority for such people. There was nothing legal about it, of course. He smuggled you out of Norway, and I was told you had died of diphtheria. It was all I deserved, so they thought.'

'I'm sorry,' Agnes said sadly. 'So sorry.'

'You knew none of this. You have nothing to be sorry about.' She paused. 'It was particularly hard for me. The first child – I knew she would be sent away. So I deliberately avoided forming a bond with her. Do you understand?'

'Not exactly,' Agnes said hesitantly.

'She went straight on the bottle,' Liv said impatiently. 'Formula. The nurses made it. They fed her. I was given drugs to stop the milk. But by the time you were born, Lebensborn was no more. I had to give birth alone. I was hiding in an apartment in Oslo. An old crone came in when she heard me crying out. She helped me through the last stages. She cut the cord and cleaned you up. Then she put you in my arms. And I breastfed you. From the day you were born. You understand now?'

Agnes could not speak for the lump in her throat. She nodded.

Liv went on. 'Breastfeeding, of course, creates a union between mother and child. If I could have avoided it, I would have done. But I could get no formula. And I could not let you die. So there was no choice. The bond was formed, whether I liked it or not. There are hormones—' She gestured with one hand, as though waving away something that bothered her. 'Physical processes. They change one. When they took you away from me, the bond was torn. All that time in the camp, I made milk. For weeks. I begged them to let me have you, but they refused. I tried to find another baby to give it to, but there were no babies allowed in the camp. I was still making milk when they sent me to the asylum. It dried up there.'

She rose, and cleared the coffee things away. Agnes was struggling to keep her emotions in check, a choking mixture of compassion and revulsion. Again, she heard the chink of a bottle from the kitchen, and when Liv returned, the alcohol aura around her was even stronger.

'That nurse from Tromsø,' Agnes said. 'Do you have her address?'

'Ah. You intend to seek her out?'

'If she will see me.'

'Perhaps she may. She is a mealy-mouthed penitent, trying to atone for the unatonable. Such people are either at your feet or at your throat. But I will give you the letter she sent me. Make what you want of it.'

'What about my sister?' Agnes pressed. 'Where was she sent? You must remember *something*!'

Liv thought for a while, her eyes absent. 'They told me she had gone to a Nazi family who wanted children.'

'Nothing more than that?'

'Nothing more than that. I purposefully did not ask for any details. I did not want to be haunted in later life. What else do you want from me?'

'My father. Is he dead?'

'Ulrich? No. He's alive.' She saw Agnes's jolt of shock and smiled dryly. 'A strange day for you. You have come to Berlevåg an orphan, and will leave with a handful of strange new relations. But do not make the mistake of thinking we are a family. We aren't.'

Agnes caught her breath. 'Do you know where he is?'

'Ulrich was put on trial for war crimes after the Germans capitulated. As though all war is not a crime! He was accused of having shot American prisoners. The prosecutors asked for the death sentence. He spent fifteen years on death row, waiting to be executed. In the end, his sentence was commuted, and he was released. He tried to make a new life in Germany, but like me, he failed. He was persecuted by the Marxists and the other Bolsheviks. They hounded him wherever he went. They prevented him from getting any work. They even tried to kill him. He was forced to disappear. I have no idea where he is now.'

'So you never communicate with him?'

'There would be nothing to say. Too much has happened to us both. I imagine that fifteen years in a death cell, and two years of electric shock treatment would have approximately the same effect. Let me advise you strongly against trying to find him. Shall we walk outside? The weather is fine today.'

Liv led Agnes up the hill from her house, following a footpath through the moss and Arctic poppies. There was nobody around. The sunlight, bright and clear, gave everything a crystalline glow. As they walked, Liv continued talking. Out in the open air, her voice seemed less hard, more feminine.

'That woman gave me the British officer's name. Wing Commander Louis Tolliver. *A war hero.*' She said the words with bitter contempt. 'It was not difficult to find out where he lived. For a few months, I didn't know what to do. But eventually, I wrote to him. When he didn't reply, I assumed he was ignoring me.'

'He wasn't ignoring you. He was trying to write a confession – perhaps a plea for forgiveness. I think the strain killed him.'

Liv nodded grimly. 'Then he was punished at last.'

'He was a good man!' Agnes said defensively.

'A *good man?* Who stole my child and ran away with her for more than twenty years? You cannot be so naïve.'

'I'm not naïve. But I try to understand what he did.'

'Yes?' Liv replied scornfully. 'And what is it that you understand?'

'He had fought against the Nazis for six years. And in the last months of the war, he lost his son to the German bombs. Perhaps he felt justified.'

'Men always feel justified in their cruelty,' Liv retorted. 'Don't speak to me any more about him. You make me angry.'

Agnes hesitated, then asked in a low voice, 'When my letter came, were you – glad?'

'It was strange.'

'Is that all? Just strange?'

'I don't know what you want me to say.'

'You must have felt *something*,' Agnes tried, 'or you wouldn't have written to my grandfather in the first place.'

'When one believes for twenty-three years that one's child is dead, and then finds out that she is alive, one is naturally curious.'

'Curious,' Agnes repeated. 'But not interested.'

'What is the difference?'

'You can be *curious* about a scientific fact. To be *interested* in someone means you feel some emotion.'

'What emotion do you want me to feel?'

'You are unnatural,' Agnes said in despair.

'Agnes.' Liv spoke her name for the first time, as though trying it out. 'Agnes is not the name I gave you. I called you something else. But Agnes will do. Agnes, they strapped me to a board twice a month and applied electrodes to my temples. There was no anaesthetic, no tranquilliser. Only the electricity that went through my brain until I had a violent seizure. I would wake up having emptied my bowels and bladder on myself, alone in a cell, not knowing my name, or where I was, or what had been done to me. I would be left to clean myself, to claw back my memories, to try and remember my past, and why I was there. It would take me a fortnight to make that terrible journey back to who I was. And then they would be ready to do it again.'

'I'm so sorry!'

'Two years of that – and everything else they did to me. I don't ask you to imagine it, because you cannot. I don't have what you call "emotions" anymore. I could not afford them, even if I had any left. And you have not come here for a touching reunion with a long-lost mother. Or if you have, you will be sorely disappointed.'

'But you called me to come to you!' Agnes couldn't help crying out. 'Why did you do that if you feel nothing for me?'

'I told you to come because writing it all down would have been very tedious,' Liv replied flatly. 'And because I knew that you would eventually find your way to me. I wanted to get it over with. And now it is over with. After today, we will not meet again. I can do nothing for you. And you can do nothing for me. We can only bring one another sorrow.'

'You are very hard!'

'I am as I am. I have always refused to lie or pretend. Perhaps that is the only good quality I have.'

'You haven't asked me about my life, my childhood, my work. Nothing about my dreams or ambitions. Nothing at all.'

She did not respond to that. 'This is my world. Look.'

They had reached the rocky outcrop at the top of the hillock. They turned and took in the view of Berlevåg's painted wooden houses, the fishing harbour, and the dark sea beyond. It was a beautiful but bleak landscape. There was nothing soft about it. This was a place where life was a struggle, bounded by the sea, shaped by the sea, defined by its power to arbitrarily give and take life.

'This is where I was born,' Liv said. 'This is where I will die. Nobody cared when I arrived, and nobody will care when I depart.'

'*I* will care!' Agnes couldn't help saying.

Liv looked at her quickly, as though surprised. 'Why should you care? I am nothing to you.'

'You're not nothing! You're my mother. Whatever you say, you can't have erased me from your life.'

'Other people erased you from my life, for twenty-three years. You cannot fill those years, Agnes.'

'But there will be years to come.'

Liv made no reply to that. She put on a pair of dark glasses, and Agnes couldn't see her eyes anymore. She appeared to be absorbed by the view. Then she stooped and picked up a stone. She threw it with unexpected force in the direction of the town. It clattered over the rocks, bouncing here and there, until it was lost in the grass. 'Every time they throw something at my windows, I come up here and throw a stone at *them*,' she said grimly.

'Can I come back one day?' Agnes asked.

'I don't want to see you.'

'Why not?'

'I can't bear to look at you.'

Agnes gasped. 'Why not?'

Liv kept her face resolutely turned away from Agnes. 'Because you left me and went with *him*.'

'But – I didn't make that decision! I was a baby! You can't blame me for that!'

Liv turned to Agnes at last. The sunglasses veiled her eyes. 'When I look at you, I see the life I could have had. The life I *should* have had. The happiness that was stripped away from me. To think of that happiness kills me now. It is better that you go, and we forget each other.'

Agnes felt that she had been shaken and emptied. 'Can I at least write?' she whispered.

'Write if you want. I don't promise to read.' She glanced at the steel watch on her slim wrist. 'Your bus leaves in fifteen minutes. You have just time to get to the bus station. You cannot stay here.'

Agnes knew there was no point in arguing. Or talking further. She held her hand out. 'Thank you for seeing me.'

Liv's handshake was firm, her breath overlaid with aquavit. 'Don't come back.' As Agnes turned unseeingly to walk back down to Berlevåg, Liv spoke once more. 'You may think very badly of me, Agnes Tolliver. Do you know what my name means in Norwegian? It means Life. Perhaps you will remember that.'

Agnes stumbled several times on the way down the hill to the little town. She didn't know she was crying until her eyes were so blinded by tears that she could no longer see where she was going.

She had to stop to recover, but she was trembling all over, as though an electric current had been driven through her body.

When she reached the bus stop, a woman was standing there, waiting. She came towards Agnes, and spoke in Norwegian.

'I'm sorry,' Agnes said blearily, 'I don't understand.'

The woman leaned forward and spat, calmly but forcefully, in Agnes's face. Then she walked away with the air of someone who had done their duty.

Agnes wiped the spittle off her cheek numbly. The Kirkenes

bus came rumbling around the corner. It stopped with a pneumatic hiss of brakes, and Agnes climbed back on board.

It took her another two days to get to Tromsø by ferry, bus and train. The complex coastal geography of Norway made travel a singularly drawn-out affair. There was plenty of time to dwell on the horror of being the daughter of two committed Nazis. But she doubted whether she would ever get used to the idea.

She'd been brought up, like so many British children of her generation, to think of the Nazis as the ultimate evil. The crimes they'd committed were so vast that they defied understanding. One couldn't even contemplate them without being overwhelmed.

But it had also provided a profound comfort that being British meant being on the side of the angels. It meant being part of the forces of light and good. Waving the bright Union Jack in the sunlight of moral superiority had been a way of coping with the wickedness of human nature. You were part of the great alliance that had stopped Hitler and dismantled the hideous empire he had tried to build.

It was crushing to find that, after all, she was deeply stained with that darkness.

Barbar had been a war hero. It had always been so clear in her mind. He had fought the Nazis, and he had won. Black and white, night and day, good and evil.

But Liv's pain and anger had shown her something she hadn't wanted to look at before now. Barbar had done something wrong, something terribly cruel. Something that wasn't noble at all – even if you took into account that he'd lost his own son, and meant the best for an innocent child.

Now there was another vision of Barbar, something much murkier. He'd connived at stealing a baby from a powerless, vulnerable mother, and had allowed Liv to think her child was dead for over twenty years. That wasn't very heroic. It was a picture that had to be clarified if she was to keep sane. And some of the answers lay in Tromsø.

She reached Tromsø on the overnight train. She had spent much of the journey between uneasy waking and nightmarish sleep, her emotions drained by the long journey to Berlevåg and her meeting with Liv.

Liv. Life. Her mother. A woman who had transgressed. But who was in the end, perhaps, more sinned against than sinning. Liv had said that Barbar had been punished at last. That had shocked Agnes. But she was starting to see that in this turbulent story, everybody was punished, one way or another – the innocent along with the guilty.

She found Tromsø to be yet another Norwegian city hemmed in between deep blue water and stark mountains. It was bigger than she had expected, a mixture of modern glass monoliths and quaint, painted wooden houses, set on a large island. She found a taxi to take her across the huge bridge that connected the island to the other side of the city, to her destination, the home of a retired nurse named Birgit Halvorsen.

It was a wooden house like the others in the quiet street on the hillside, but any claim to quaintness had long since been stripped away by neglect. The paint was peeling off the boards, revealing the grey wood underneath, and the stained shutters hung crooked on corroded hinges. The place almost seemed deserted, and Agnes's heart sank. Had she made this long journey for nothing?

She knocked on the door. She was half expecting that there would be no answer. But then she heard a slow shuffling from inside the house, and the door creaked open.

The woman standing in the dark corridor was wearing a grotesque mask, and dragging something behind her on a trolley. Agnes was shocked at first, and then realised that the thing on her face was an antiquated rubber breathing mask, and the object on the trolley was a heavy oxygen bottle.

'Fru Birgit Halvorsen?' Agnes asked.

The woman raised her hand slowly and pulled the mask away from her mouth so that she could answer. '*Hvem er du?*'

'My name is Agnes Tolliver. I got your address from Liv Christiansen.'

'Liv Christiansen?' The woman searched Agnes's face. Then there was a sudden flare of some emotion, almost too powerful for the frail body. The filmy grey eyes closed for a long moment, then opened slowly. The woman was trembling, now. 'I know who you are,' she said in a papery voice. 'You had better come in.'

# CHAPTER EIGHT

# BIRGIT

*Norway, 1945*

Yes. It's true. I was in charge of those babies in 1945. It was technically an orphanage. But there were only German children there. The authorities ordered us to keep them apart from Norwegian children, foundlings, orphans of war and so on. They considered it unseemly to mix them with the children of patriots. They were the children of our enemies.

I'll make a confession, and maybe you won't understand: I could hardly bear to look at them.

Babies call to us. Especially to us women. We're supposed to respond. It's in our nature, they say.

But when I looked at those babies, I saw in them everything that was horrible in the Nazis. And worse, everything that was horrible in ourselves.

I saw our dishonour, in having capitulated to the Germans in only three months. I saw the shame of having the traitor Vidkun Quisling as our leader. I saw the disgrace of our Norwegian women, who spread their legs for the conqueror, and bore his tainted seed.

You never had the Nazis on top of you. You have grown up

in a free world. We had them as our masters. For five years. None of us will ever forget it. That particular flavour remains in the mouth forever.

Five years. They knew we hated them, and they treated us badly. They were angry with us because they thought we were the same as them. But we weren't. No matter how much they tried to make us become like them, they could not succeed.

And *this* child . . .

This child was even more disgusting. You know about Lebensborn. Himmler's plan to populate the world with so-called Aryans? As if he were breeding dogs or cattle? So.

And *this* Norwegian woman had volunteered for the programme. The paperwork was all there to show what she had done. She was proud of it. One could understand a woman who had fallen pregnant against her wishes, and who wanted to get rid of the baby discreetly. But here we had a woman who had offered herself to the Nazi breeding machine. The same machine that was crushing us. The same machine that killed my husband.

Yes, it is strange to be talking about *that baby*, with you before me. I don't wish to give you offence. I am simply telling you how I felt. How we all felt.

You remind me of Liv Christiansen. You look like she did, then, in 1945. The hair, the eyes, the face. You are tall, too, like her.

Don't flinch. Nature makes us alike in body to our parents, but leaves us to create our own souls. You're different from your mother. You are quiet, refined. Your gaze is gentle. You've been brought up to be a lady. An English lady.

Liv Christiansen, excuse me when I say this, was an arrogant bitch. If you could have heard the way she *swore* at us. The foul language, insults that only Nazis used.

Oh yes, she was a true Nazi. No different from the vile SS monsters in the camps, the ones who murdered my husband.

My husband was arrested simply because he was a socialist. They took him away in the first weeks of the occupation. He was sent to a camp in Germany. A year later, they told me he was dead. They said he had died of typhus. But someone who was in the camp with him told me that the guards beat him to death with clubs.

They beat him to death – that gentle man who wanted only good for others. That poet, that scholar. That man who dedicated his life to the community.

Well. That is how they were, the Nazis. Whatever was beautiful, they trampled on it. As for their own culture – you know what *that* was. Your father was a war criminal. You know that. But I never met him, and we do not need to speak of him here.

And all that is why we detested those babies.

They were a legacy that we had to bear, whether we liked it or not. But I tell you this now: I was afraid of myself. Afraid that I would do something terrible. Rid our country of those abominations, erase them from the world.

It would be so easy. No need for violence. A gentle pressure here, a push there, and it would be done.

And I will tell you something else: sometimes I withheld your bottle, and left you to cry with hunger. Until I could not stand your crying any longer. And then I picked you up, and thrust the rubber teat in your mouth, just to stop myself from—

Well, you understand.

And there were others who felt the same way. Many of us.

We had been given the task of nursing these German children, and we did it. But not willingly. No, not willingly.

It was as though the Nazis were still set over us. Babies are little tyrants, you know. They command, they bawl orders, they get their way. There is no disobeying them.

I see the look in your eyes. You are thinking that I was not very womanlike. Not worthy of the name of nurse.

Perhaps I wasn't.

I had no child of my own. They took my husband from me before we could have one. While *she* was producing babies for Hitler, I was a childless widow.

And I have never had a child since. I could have had one. My second husband was willing. But I said no.

And perhaps it was that experience – the German babies, on top of the war, the loss of my husband, and all of it – that decided me finally to never bear a child. Whenever I thought of the idea, I was repelled. Perhaps my desire to be a mother was burned out of me then. Or perhaps I never had it to start with. And that is why I was the way I was.

I tell you all this so that you can try to understand. If you are willing. But you are not interested in me. It is your part of the story that you have come to hear, not mine.

So. Here it is.

I met him in The Ritz bar in Skillebekk. During the war, it had been a place where German officers and Norwegian fascists went to drink. Now the British went there instead. And we more refined Norwegian women went there to thank them.

I used to see him sitting in the same place at the bar, the same stool every time. The same drink – whisky and soda. He drank alone. The other British officers drank together. But he was always on his own. He would drink until he could drink no more. Then his military driver would come and help him to his car, and take him away.

Don't misunderstand me. He was a *Herre*. An aristocrat. A real English gentleman. Always courteous, always dignified. Yes, you remind me of him, too. I can see how he brought you up. You have some of his mannerisms. You listen well, as he did. That is a rare talent.

I could see that he was a sad man. Very sad.

One night – and I don't know why I did it, except that I'd had too much to drink myself – I sat next to him at the bar. I asked him, 'Why are you so sad? Have you lost somebody?'

He replied, 'My son is dead.'

I don't think either of us would have said these things usually, but drink makes us talk to strangers. I told him, 'My husband is dead, too.' I thought at first he hadn't heard, but then he reached out and he put his hand over mine. Just like that. And he looked into my eyes.

Now, in my village, when I was a child, there was a deep well. We were forbidden to play near it, but one day a little boy fell in the well. They tried to get him out, but he was too weak to hold onto the rope. I looked down at him and caught a glimpse of his face looking up, before they pulled me away. And your grandfather had the same expression in his eyes. Lost. I just started to cry. I couldn't help it.

In this way we met. And later, had drinks together. He taught me to like whisky and soda.

He was very distinguished, Wing Commander Louis Tolliver. He had medals for bravery. A handsome man. When you looked into his face, you saw goodness. He did not smile much, but when he did, you felt warm, as though the sun had come from behind a cloud. There was grey in his hair. I suppose he was around fifty-five then. Old for that war, for it was a war of young men. There were lines in his face and there was grief in his eyes.

I took him to my house one night. We undressed and we got into the bed together. But neither of us could make love. We were not looking for sex, you see. We were broken and angry, and wanting comfort. So we lay in each other's arms for a long time, in silence, until we fell asleep. And in the morning, he dressed and went to work.

But before he left the house, he kissed me. And I thought, 'This is a good man.'

He was lost and alone, and so was I. We didn't know what to do with our lives.

All those years of war, and for what? To have torn away from us what we held most precious? It was very cruel. His only son and his daughter-in-law had been killed by Hitler's rockets. He felt that his future and his past had both been cut off from him.

'I longed for grandchildren,' he told me. 'I will never have them now.'

I said, 'You can marry again, you are not so old,' but he shook his head.

'My heart is broken,' he said. 'I have nothing left to give a woman.'

'Come to the orphanage,' I replied. 'You can have your pick of grandchildren there.' I don't know what prompted me to say it. I laughed, and added, 'But they are all little Nazi bastards.'

He said, 'I would like to see them.'

So I took him to the orphanage.

Now, you must remember that all these children – the oldest were around a year, the youngest, including you, were just a few months old – all these children were born into privilege. The German fathers made sure that their whores were fat as butter, while the rest of us went hungry. The mothers got the best of everything. They were well-fed, lived in clean places, had doctors, whatever they wanted. They lacked for nothing.

And the same applied to the children. I was a nurse, so I took down all the details. The birth weight of the German babies was far higher than the rest of the population. They were healthier. They had no vitamin deficiencies. While the Nazis were in charge, even in the last days of the war, when everything was scarce, these women and their brats lived in luxury. The rest of the population starved.

Can you wonder that they chased these women in the streets?

Can you wonder that we hated those children?

But your grandfather saw none of that. All he saw was that the children were innocent and beautiful.

It was summer, and the weather in Oslo is fine at that time of year. The skies were clear, day after day. We put the children out in the sun morning and afternoon. That was the time he liked to come. He wanted to simply watch the children in the sun. I think he found it healing in some way. Really, it was like a cure of some kind for him. I noticed that he was drinking less.

We started to talk about giving him one of the German babies, at first not very seriously, but then later with some urgency, when it grew likely that he would be posted back to his own country soon.

You were his favourite among the children. One could see that right away. You were just the kind of baby that people like. You were always smiling, always placid. And of course, very pretty. A little golden angel.

I think he had chosen you from the very first moment.

The daughter of Liv Christiansen! If he had chosen any one of the other children, it would have been more straightforward, because their mothers were nowhere to be found. They were true orphans. Nobody wanted them. We could have done what we wanted with them.

But your mother was very much alive, under arrest in a prison camp for traitors. She was a public scandal. And she wanted you back.

Oh, yes. That Nazi wanted her Nazi child back.

There were some who were saying, 'Give the bitch her whelp, what does it matter?' But I stood in the way. I hated her, I can say that now. I wanted her to suffer. In my mind, she had come to stand for everything – the war, the occupation, my Ernst's death, all of it. So keeping her away from her child was my revenge.

You think me cruel. As bad as the Germans.

But there was something else in my mind, and that was the future. What were we to do with these children as they grew, and entered our society? The doctors told us that these German children would be mentally defective. They would carry genetic diseases, they said. They would continue to pollute the Norwegian race. And the Lutheran ministers said they would be morally contaminated, and perhaps would grow up to be Nazis, and bring Hitlerism back to Norway.

It was not so easy to know what to do, I can tell you. I said to myself, 'If we can get rid of one child, that is one problem less.'

And he wanted *you*, Commander Tolliver. He was obstinate.

I said, 'This is the child of your enemies, Louis – the ones who killed your son, and killed half Europe.'

He replied, 'All the more reason why I should choose her.'

I said, 'Remember, her mother is still alive.'

He replied, 'I will remember it, but she will never know. I am rescuing her from a life of shame. She will grow up free.'

I understood what he meant. 'Then this is a good thing,' I said.

He told me, 'I need a child to care for, and she needs someone to care for her. I can never replace my son, but I have the love and the resources to give this creature a good home.' He said, 'She has the sweetest smile I have ever seen.'

And so we did it.

There was not much difficulty. I asked one of the doctors to issue a death certificate, and just like that, you were dead.

I never knew what name he gave you. Until now. He took all your papers with him, but those papers were meaningless. Scraps of Nazi filth. Officially, you were nameless. You had no identity. All that was to come, in your new homeland.

The day that he took you away from the orphanage was the day Vidkun Quisling was executed by firing squad at Akershus. It was a day of justice in Norway. How we loathed him. His very name has become a synonym for betrayal in all the world: a very special kind of betrayal – a fawning, grovelling, backstabbing kind of treachery. I felt it was a day of purification.

And then we had to tell Liv Christiansen that her child was dead.

\* \* \*

I volunteered to go to the camp to inform her. She was not living in good conditions there, dressed in a prison shift of grey burlap and made to sleep with twenty others in an unheated hut. A great descent from her former heights!

They had shaved her head in the street, and by now it had begun to grow back in tufts and patches. She looked like a scarecrow. She was thin, too, with dark circles around those bright blue eyes. She looked ill. And I was glad to see her like that.

I was never beautiful, like her, not even then, when I was young. Her beauty made me angry. Like her arrogance, it was a kick in the stomach for me. I was jealous, yes. I wanted to see her humbled. I wanted to see her brought low.

I am telling you the absolute truth, as you see. I want to hide nothing. There is no point. Not anymore.

I brought her the news, and I was thinking, 'This will break her, this will be the end of her.' I felt a certain thrill, yes. I wanted to see her cry. I wanted that satisfaction.

But I was not prepared.

She fell to her knees and screamed like an animal. Screams that pierced me, and made me run away from her to fetch the guards.

It was then that I asked myself for the first time, 'What have I done?'

But it was too late by then to change things. You had gone with your grandfather, the death certificate had been issued. To admit what we had done would have caused trouble, because it had been done illegally.

The guards came. They had to restrain her, because it seemed she wanted to claw her own eyes out. They injected her with a sedative, but even that didn't stop her screaming.

Those screams haunted me. They haunt me still. Whatever she was, she was a mother. And I took her baby away and gave it to a stranger. I broke her heart.

They said that she had accepted the loss of the first child, which had been sent to Germany. But that the loss of the second child was unbearable to her. Why? Who knows? Because the war, *her* war, had been lost? Because the man she loved had been lost? Because now that the Germans had left, she was finally alone? Nobody can know the human heart. Still less the heart of a woman.

They sent her to an insane asylum.

And many times, over the years since then, I have asked myself again and again, 'What did I do?'

It weighed on me. I would wake at night in a sweat, wishing I could undo what I had done. But of course, I never could. There was no atonement for me. The only sacrament for me was confession. And I had no one to whom I could confess.

The years went by, as fast as seagulls flying home from the ocean. And at the age of fifty-six, I was diagnosed with cancer. Of the womb. Is that not ironic? One could almost believe in a vengeful Jehovah. I retired from work, and went on a disability pension. The cancer creeps around inside me, from organ to organ. They have warned me that I may not have more than a few months. I'm not religious, but I did not want to leave this life with that on my conscience.

So I took the decision. I found out where Liv Christiansen had gone. She had hidden herself in Berlevåg, away up there in the Barents Sea, where she was born. I found out her address, and I wrote to her.

I confessed what I had done. I asked her to come and see me, if she wanted to know more. I am too sick to travel such a long way, you see.

I don't know what I was expecting. A reply of some kind. But there was none. Just silence. Until you knocked on my door. You tell me she is indifferent. Perhaps that is the wrong diagnosis. Perhaps she is resigned, rather. After twenty-three years, one's grief fossilises. No mourning lasts that long.

Or perhaps it is her turn to punish me.

To withhold absolution, and let me die with my sin on my head. Who knows?

Do I regret anything else? I regret the pettiness. What I did, I did out of spite. I could tell myself that I wanted to give you a better future than the one in store for you here in Norway, as the daughter of a Nazi collaborator. But I don't know if that would be true.

I just wanted to hurt another woman, who had things I didn't have. That was it. That was all.

# CHAPTER NINE

## AGNES

*England, 1968*

During the long journey back to England, Agnes thought constantly about her meetings with Birgit Halvorsen and Liv Christiansen. Each in her way had filled in the dark gaps. But it was Liv who haunted her emotions. The woman who had borne her, who had breastfed her, and who she had been torn away from.

A Nazi child.

That's what Birgit Halvorsen had called her.

Was it possible that in her baby mind, some memory lingered of those traumatic months, when she was suddenly bereft of a mother, at the mercy of strangers who hated her? If there were such memories, they were buried very deep.

She couldn't bring herself to call Liv Christiansen her mother. And yet, Liv *was* her mother. And there was no way to get around that fact, or ignore it, or resolve it in any comfortable way.

The life that Liv had led was unfathomable to Agnes. There was much to pity. She'd been abused all her life, one way or another. Yet Birgit had been right: there was an arrogance in her that was hateful. Was it arrogance? Or a kind of madness? And if it was a personality disorder, was it hereditary? Had she inherited Liv Christiansen's delusions of grandeur, her bigoted ideas about race?

Barbar had raised her to be patriotic, and to love England. Glyndebourne, Wimbledon, the Henley regatta, Royal Ascot, the Chelsea Flower Show. And, of course, Gilbert and Sullivan.

But surely that wasn't the same as believing that all other races were inferior? Looking at herself now, she could see that perhaps there *was* bias in her, even if it was unconscious. There *were* prejudices, feelings of superiority. She'd never thought of the Second World War as having been about race. But it had been. It had been attitudes like Liv's that had enabled the conquest, enslavement and extermination of millions, because the aggressors had thought them inferior. It was a terrible thought.

And she had been born to two people who'd fully believed in that dreadful philosophy.

The day she'd spent with Liv had changed the way Agnes saw herself. Changed? No. It had shattered her self-image, like a hammer thrown through a mirror.

She'd always been pleased with herself. Pleased with her graceful figure, her blonde hair and blue eyes, her quick intelligence. Being told she was 'perfect' by admiring men like Bill Dawlish. Those little vanities were now burdens that bowed her down. She'd believed her parents to be dead, and she hadn't ever bothered her head about who she looked like, who she took after. Barbar had been vague about the subject. And she'd never bothered to question why there were so few photos of her parents at Dowdeswell Hall. Not even photo albums. As though Barbar had hidden or destroyed everything that might have raised difficult questions. As though Barbar's life before 1945 had been deliberately erased.

Birgit Halvorsen had helped her to understand that Barbar himself had been destroyed by the death of his only son and his daughter-in-law. He'd started a new life with the baby he'd stolen in Norway, and had drawn a veil over the past, never lifting it until the day he'd died. She had replaced the dead. She had been essential to his emotional survival.

And his secrecy about her true origins hadn't just been guilt over the theft of a baby.

It had also been to protect her from the shattering knowledge that her parents had been Nazis, one an SS murderer, the other a woman so obsessed with grandiose racial dreams that she was willing to be a breeding machine for the Nazi state. And growing up with that knowledge might have crippled her.

It had already had a devastating effect on her. Her mind was filled with the pitiful black-and-white images she'd seen of the war: the crushed cities, the emaciated victims of the camps, the vast landscapes of mass murder. She felt implicated in that somehow. And there was no way she could escape it.

She'd been warned about seeking the truth. She'd ignored the warnings, and now she was paying the price.

Could she undo any of it? Would she make it all disappear with a wave of a magic wand, if she could? She felt like someone who had waded into a raging river, and found herself being overwhelmed; to turn back now would be as difficult as to go on. She had to continue through it to the other side, and face the knowledge that would come to her on the far bank.

When she got back to Dowdeswell Hall, the first thing she did was write a letter of resignation to Kennard Coleridge at the *Evening News*. She needed to face whatever was going to come single-minded and undistracted. She would go into the office later in the week and say goodbye in person to everybody.

131

The second thing she did was make an appointment with Mr Nethercott, Barbar's lawyer.

She saw him in his chambers in Cirencester, the pretty market town that was the centre of the Cotswolds. It was a day of alternating clouds and sun, and from time to time a shaft of sunlight slanted through the mullioned windows of Mr Nethercott's room, making the dust motes glow as they drifted slowly in the air, then faded swiftly away.

'You lied to me,' Agnes said bluntly.

Mr Nethercott did not blush, or even have the grace to look shamefaced. 'I was acting under instructions from my client. I followed his wishes.'

'You knew the truth about where I came from.'

He spread his plump hands. 'I knew the little that your grandfather decided to share with me. No more than that.'

'My father was an officer in the SS. One of the wickedest organisations ever to exist.'

'That much I knew.'

'Birgit Halvorsen told me that she gave all my papers to my grandfather. I know he wouldn't have destroyed them – that wasn't in his nature. But he wouldn't have kept them at Dowdeswell Hall, either. I think he gave them to you. And I think you still have them.'

Mr Nethercott had been having a biscuit with his cup of tea. He sat in silence for long moment, brushing crumbs off his waistcoat. 'Your grandfather entrusted some documents to me in 1945,' he said at length. 'He instructed me to keep them safe, and to destroy them in the event of his death. This puts me in something of a quandary. There is no doubting that your grandfather broke the law – indeed, broke several laws both here and in Norway – when he brought you into Britain in 1945. This introduces – shall we say a *tension* – between on the one hand, my obligation to uphold the law as a solicitor and, on the other hand, my obligation to protect my client's rights. Now in the case—'

'Are you going to give me the documents or not?' Agnes cut in, impatient with the legal debate.

He sighed, rose from his chair and went to a metal filing cabinet. He took out a grey folder and passed it to Agnes. He resumed his tea and biscuit while she opened it.

It contained two old sheets of paper and an enamelled badge. The first document was a typewritten letter in German, which she could not read. But the SS logo at the top of the page was unmistakeable.

The second document was some kind of certificate, also in German. It also bore a runic symbol at the top, a split 'Y' like a woman's cleft. Beside it was the word 'Lebensborn'.

'That one is your birth certificate,' Mr Nethercott said, indicating it with his biscuit.

Agnes stared at the quarter-of-a-century-old document, thinking of everything it represented. 'What does it say?'

'Well, for some reason the line for date of birth is blank.'

'That's because they issued it before I was born. My mother told me I was born in April, 1945 – not September, 1944, which is the date Barbar made up.'

'Well, you're six months younger than you thought. That's a good thing, isn't it?' Mr Nethercott said. She glared at him, and he hurried on, 'Of course, your grandfather had to supply a birthdate that was prior to your parents' death. The next lines give your mother's name, Liv Christiansen, your father's name and rank, one *Oberstleutnant Waffen-SS* Ulrich von Breda – and lastly, the name you were christened with.'

Agnes deciphered the black-letter script with difficulty. 'Friedelinde,' she said quietly.

'Something of a mouthful, I agree. Apparently it means "gentle peace". Not too bad, all things considered.' He took a bite of the biscuit. 'Could have been a lot worse. But as your grandfather said, "That will never do in Gloucestershire."'

Agnes remembered Liv's words. *Agnes is not the name I gave you. I called you something else.* She picked up the badge. It was enamelled in the Nazi colours of red, white and black. The same cleft Y symbol was in the centre, flanked by the SS runes. Around the rim was written, *Heilig soll uns sein, jede Mutter guten Blutes.* She looked up at Mr Nethercott for an explanation.

'Apparently,' he said diffidently, 'it means "Sacred to us shall be every mother of good blood." If you look carefully, there's a little "H.H." for Heinrich Himmler. His words, it seems.'

Agnes shuddered as she put the thing down. 'It was very wrong of you not to answer my questions before now!'

'I wanted to dissuade you from digging into the past,' he replied in a gentler voice. 'I believed that no good could come of it. I still believe that.'

She held up the other document. 'What does this one say?'

'It seems to be a letter to a family in Germany, telling them of your birth. My German's not good enough to translate it. Arrangements were being made to send you to be adopted by them. But history intervened, as it so often does. After your birth, you were stuck in Norway. And you know the rest.'

'Who else was told about all this?'

'Here in England? I don't think anybody knows.'

'People have said things to me that I didn't understand before. Dr Dobbie, for example. And Mrs Cawthorne. I'm sure they know.'

'Well, they were the people closest to your grandfather. And they would have been here when you were brought back as a baby. So I imagine your grandfather gave them some explanation. Perhaps not all the—' He waved his biscuit.

'All the stuff about my Nazi parents,' she supplied bitterly. Agnes sat in silence for a long time. Mr Nethercott waited politely. At last, she looked up at him. 'You were my grandfather's lawyer. Now I want you to be mine.'

He looked cautious. 'Miss Tolliver, I was your grandfather's friend. But I am about to retire. I'm afraid—'

'You didn't just lie to me,' she said, her voice steely. 'You lied again and again. And you lied to my face. You owe me some truth, now.'

He winced. She had penetrated the armour of his complacency at last. 'Whatever I can do to be of service, of course.'

'Firstly, I want you to get these documents translated into English for me.'

'Very well.'

'Secondly, I want you to engage an investigator.'

'An investigator?'

'A private eye, someone like that. Someone who can trace people and find things out.'

Mr Nethercott scratched his fat chin. 'If you are planning what I think you are planning, may I advise most strongly against digging any further into ancient history. At the risk of repeating myself, no good can come of such a proceeding.'

She ignored that. 'I want the best you can find.'

'Miss Tolliver, this is most unwise.'

'The unwisdom or otherwise doesn't come into it,' she retorted. 'This is something I have to do. If you won't help me, I'll go elsewhere.'

'If you insist,' he said with a sigh, 'I will endeavour to engage someone. But I warn you, this kind of investigation is not cheap.'

'I'm happy to pay for results. Which brings me to the third point. I'm going to sell Dowdeswell Hall. And all the contents. I want you to find me a buyer and handle the sale.'

'Sell it?' He looked astonished. 'My dear Miss Tolliver, Dowdeswell Hall has been in your family for—' The words died on his lips as he saw the look in her eyes.

'Not *my* family, Mr Nethercott. *My* family stamped around in jackboots.'

He sighed. 'You have absolutely nothing to do with those terrible people.'

'I'm afraid that I do. I loved Barbar, but I don't belong in his house any longer. I want to find out where I *do* belong. And I will take it from there.'

He lowered his head. 'Very well. Leave it with me.'

She drove back to Dowdeswell in her Mini, along the familiar country roads that in places were overhung with trees, in others bounded by hedgerows or drystone walls, winding between the gently swelling hills that gave the Cotswolds their name. The farmers' fields were golden, ready for the harvest. Here and there, hayricks were already being erected, churches of dried grass set up in the stubble.

Her emotions were complex. And they went far deeper than learning she was an Aries, and not a Virgo.

There was only one other person in the world who might be able to understand what she was going through. The sister she had never known. The sister who had been stolen from her.

That sister, a few years older than she, was the only human being she could talk to about the pain she felt, the questions that haunted her. If she couldn't find her sister, if she was lost forever, then she would be truly bereft. She had to find her.

The old house was looking particularly beautiful today. The intermittent sunlight was tender on the golden stones. Barbar's Rolls-Royce gleamed on the gravelled drive. It was a perfect picture of an English way of life, elegant, tranquil, privileged. She recalled her childhood belief that it was always sunny here. And perhaps it would always be sunny at Dowdeswell, at least in her memories.

But entering the house and walking through the rooms she'd grown up in, she felt like an impostor. This was not her home any longer. The portraits of seventeenth-century Tolliver ancestors stared down at her with stony disapproval. The fine old furniture, which Mrs Cawthorne had polished for decades, was looking dusty and unwelcoming. The very life in the place seemed to have died along with Barbar.

And, she was starting to realise, the world exemplified by Dowdeswell Hall was also dead.

It was 1968. In an age when civilisation could be consumed by thermonuclear war at any moment, it seemed absurd to cling to an Edwardian way of life, with servants and great houses and vintage Rolls-Royces. If you were Roger Daltrey or Mick Jagger, perhaps you could splurge your cash. But ordinary people couldn't afford it anymore. Trying to keep it up had ruined Barbar.

Life was too fast, taxes were too high, changes came too quickly. To own a house like Dowdeswell meant being tied irrevocably to an era and a place – and life nowadays was all about freedom, mobility, keeping up with the times.

The difference between her busy weeks in London and her peaceful weekends at Dowdeswell had always been marked, though enjoyable; now she saw the gulf between the two life-styles as a chasm which could no longer be bridged. Without Barbar here to welcome her, and knowing what she now knew about herself, she wanted to get away from here.

Barbar had left her all this, with characteristic generosity. He'd treated her like a real granddaughter, right up to his death. But she was not his granddaughter, and she couldn't make herself believe that she was any longer.

She went into Barbar's study and looked at the broad leather desk which had always been piled with books and papers in his lifetime, now tidied bare by Mrs Cawthorne.

A complex mixture of emotions rose up in her, choking her for a moment. Most of all, there was regret that he'd never told her the truth. He'd left her to find out on her own, without him there to explain anything.

She thought of a phrase Birgit Halvorsen had used.

'Oh, Barbar,' she said to the empty chair, 'what did you do?'

* * *

Other thoughts came to her in the days that followed. Barbar might have done something illegal, cruel. But he had also saved her from what would almost certainly have been a grim life in Norway.

She now knew that the children of German soldiers and Norwegian women were treated badly in Norway, almost as badly as their mothers. To be spat on in the street – as she had been in Berlevåg – was just one of the ordeals they had to endure. Heartlessly unfair as it was, they were paying for the sins of their mothers, made to feel shame, turned into outcasts. Many of them had even been forcibly deported to Germany after the war, to take their chances there.

Barbar must have foreseen what her life in Norway would have been like, and perhaps mercy had formed part of his decision. He had saved her from that life, and she would be eternally grateful for that.

The translated documents arrived in the post a few days later.

As she already knew, the birth certificate was stark, giving only the place of her birth, her mother's and father's names, and the name which she had been given at an SS 'naming ritual', Friedelinde.

The letter, however, was more informative:

*18th December 1944*
*To: Herr Generalmajor Heinrich Ozerki*
*Mariensberg in Ostpreußen*
*Elbingstraße 4*
*R IV / I - A. E. - 023 - Hei / MHW*
*Subject: Placement of Child*

*Dear Herr Generalmajor Ozerki,*
*    I am delighted to inform you that we will soon have another girl to join your family. The parents*

*are the same as in the case of the first child.*
*You already know how excellent this bloodline*
*is. They will be full sisters. I am sure you will*
*approve.*

*The birth will take place in April, 1945, in*
*Lebensborn Heim Jorundarholt, in Norway, as*
*before.*

*If you accept to receive this second child, con-*
*firm with me and I will arrange transport to you*
*when the child comes.*

*It will not be necessary for you and your wife to*
*complete the proofs of racial health, since these are*
*already on record with the SS.*

*I hope that my news to you has given you and*
*your wife special Christmas joy.*

*Heil Hitler!*
*(signed on behalf)*
*Ackermann, RuHA Lebensborn Norway*

She read the lines with her heart beating fast. *Another girl to join your family.* That meant her older sister had been sent to this family in 1942! She had a name, and she had an address. With that, she could do much.

# CHAPTER TEN

## AGNES

*Munich, 1968*

It was a shiny, post-war, glass building, one of the few in a city that was defined by beautiful old palaces, soaring church towers and what appeared to be a resolute effort to rebuild the skyline exactly as it had been before the carpet bombing of 1944.

When Agnes mentioned this impression to Karlheinz Ozerki, he agreed.

'There was a lot of opposition when we submitted the plans five years ago. People said, "We don't need modern buildings. It's just not München." This is a very conservative city, as you perhaps can tell, *ja?*'

This plump, good-looking man with the aristocratic profile had once been Karolina's stepbrother.

He was in his mid-thirties, and dressed with exquisite care to bridge the gap between conservatism and modernity – a traditionally tailored three-piece suit enlivened by a mauve silk shirt open at the collar and shiny Chelsea boots with Cuban heels in the style made popular by the Beatles.

The arched nostrils and sculpted lips went with the curly hair (long enough to fall over his collar) to suggest an actor suited to romantic roles – albeit perhaps one who lived a little too well – rather than the head of a successful manufacturing business that he was.

'Other people,' he went on, 'said, "If you don't want to see modern buildings, go and live in the Black Forest." What *we* said was, "Modern buildings are essential to create office space and living space without losing the green areas that make Munich beautiful. Let us join the economic miracle that is taking place." Of course, we won the argument.'

A light was winking on the console on his desk. He pressed a button and murmured in German. Satisfied with the reply he received, he leaned back in his chair, which was made of chromed steel and black leather, and considered Agnes with his fingers steepled over his burgeoning belly. 'But you have not travelled all this way to discuss the urban planning of Upper Bavaria.'

'No,' Agnes agreed. 'I know you're busy, and I'm grateful that you've made time for me.'

'Yours is a very interesting story.' His eyes flattered her, suggesting that his interest didn't end with the story. 'I'm fascinated.'

'It means a great deal to me.'

'Of course. But sadly, I don't think I will be able to help you much in your quest.'

'Why not?' she asked in dismay.

'Please don't imagine that this means I am being obstructive. My generation of Germans are committed to righting the wrongs of our parents in any way we can. We believe in transparency and accountability. You need have no fears on that score.'

'Thank you, Herr Ozerki.'

'Call me Karlheinz, please.' A sleek young secretary brought in Italian-style espressos in fashionably thick coffee-bar cups. Agnes followed Ozerki's example, and drank the boiling mud in one mouthful, resisting the impulse to wince at its bitterness.

'I remember your sister very well, of course,' he went on. He raised a manicured hand as he saw her expression. 'That is to say, I remember her arrival. I was a boy of eleven or twelve when she came from Norway. She was only a few months old.

'My parents were deeply committed to National Socialism. Especially my father. My stepmother also – though she was more than twenty years younger than he was, and had not gone through what my father had been through. I mean the disgrace of military defeat in 1918, the humiliation of the Treaty of Versailles, the long battle to keep Germany from falling into the hands of the communists, the hard-won victory of 1933 which put Hitler in power. He went through all that, and he was a dyed-in-the-wool Nazi. I say this with shame. But it is the truth.'

Agnes nodded. 'It's understandable,' she said diplomatically. His English was excellent, with a slight accent, and marked by a habit of adding *ja* to the end of sentences.

'I brought this into the office. You may be interested.' He took a concertina photograph album from a drawer and put it on the desk in front of Agnes, opening it to a black-and-white studio photograph of an attractive young woman dressed in the fashions of the 1940s.

'That is my stepmother. She was a very pretty woman, as you see. My mother had died young, and my father remarried in haste, so as to give me and my sisters stability, as he saw it. Sadly, it seemed that my stepmother could not have children. After five years, when the war had already started, they took the decision to adopt. Children were arriving in the Reich from Poland. Orphans, they said. Others said they had been stolen because they looked Aryan. After the parents had been shot, of course.'

'Oh, my God,' Agnes said in horror.

'But my father, as in all things, insisted on *das Beste vom Besten*. A top-quality Aryan infant.' He smiled dryly. 'His close relationship with the high-up Nazis entitled him to claim the best of the best, and to receive it. Himmler took a special interest in the case, as he always did in other people's marriages. And that was how Karolina entered our lives.'

'Karolina!' Agnes repeated.

'That was the name they gave her. You didn't know this?'

'No.'

He turned the page. 'Here she is.'

Agnes leaned forward eagerly. The double album page was stuck with a dozen small snaps of a baby in an absurdly long and frilly pinafore outfit. The sleepy little face gazed back at the camera from various poses, mostly prone on a rug. Agnes stared from photograph to photograph, hunting for some kind of recognition. But they were just baby photographs from a quarter of a century ago, taken by a doting mother with no regard to the cost of film. All she could tell from the monochrome prints was that the baby's hair was blonde, her eyes light. The inheritance of Liv Christiansen.

On the next fold was a larger photo, taken professionally, of the same baby, propped up on a cushion, surrounded by toys. Agnes searched for some family trait in the small, round, solemn face. But again, it was just a studio photograph of a long-ago baby. These were the first photographs she had seen of her sister, yet they had little impact on her.

'Have you got any other pictures?' she asked.

Ozerki shook his head. 'Regretfully, no. The family albums were all destroyed in the air raids. And Karolina didn't stay with us for very long, in any case.'

Agnes tensed. 'Why not?'

'The Allies were stepping up their bombing campaign. They struck Berlin. Then followed Hamburg.' He grimaced. 'Thousands died. It was decided that we children were to be moved to the countryside for safety. My sisters and I were sent to Denmark with Constanze. Karolina was sent to stay with my grandparents on their farm in Ostpreußen – Eastern Prussia. Both of these areas were considered safe. Far enough from England to be out of reach of the Lancasters.' He spread his hands. 'But like so many calculations made during those years, it was mistaken.' He glanced at the square gold watch on his wrist. 'It is nearly twelve thirty. Will you join me for lunch? I generally have a light meal just down the street.'

'That's very kind of you,' Agnes said, reflecting that she didn't have much choice, if she wanted to hear the rest of the story.

The restaurant he took her to sustained the theme of ancient and modern. The décor was trendy, with brightly glazed Italian tiles and oversized orange lamps hanging low over each table, but the menu was heavy, and traditionally Bavarian. The lightest thing she could find on it was a *Schnitzel*. He tucked into two fat *Weisswürst* with creamy mashed potato and sweet mustard, expertly skinning them while she toyed with her *Schnitzel*. There was no conversation during lunch. He ate in silence, with great seriousness, drinking a Paulaner; and after the main courses, suggested they share a *Kaiserschmarrn*. The rich pancake, smothered in plum jam, reminded her of nursery puddings at Dowdeswell. She had little appetite for any of the food. Her stomach was far too stressed.

She had made another long journey to meet Karlheinz Ozerki. Mr Nethercott had engaged a painstaking investigator on her behalf, who had tracked down the Ozerki family through German military records. Karlheinz's father, the major general mentioned in the Lebensborn letter, had been a Nazi party member and an associate of Heinrich Himmler. He had played a heroic role in the First World War, and during the Second had served as an instructor at the military academy in Potsdam.

He had gone into business after the war, supplying parts for a large German car manufacturer, and had died in 1958, leaving the business to his son, Karlheinz, now spooning up *Kaiserschmarrn* across the table from Agnes. She had written to Karlheinz and had received an encouraging reply. She had travelled by train from St Pancras, a ten-hour journey. But if there was paydirt among the *Kaiserschmarrn* and *Weisswürst*, she had yet to strike it.

At last, the 'light lunch' was over. Karlheinz lit a slim cheroot, after carefully asking her permission, and resumed the narrative, wreathed in smoke.

'Of my time with my sisters and stepmother in Copenhagen, I will say little. We saw some bombing towards the end of the war, but nothing like what was done to Germany. The hardship we suffered was minimal by comparison. East Prussia, however, was a different story. The Russians were approaching through Poland and Hungary, and there was no way of stopping them. The *Gauleiter* of the region, Erich Koch, hid the truth from the civilian population, feeding them a constant diet of propaganda until the last minute. When he finally ordered the evacuation, it was already too late. The Red Army overran them in a matter of days.' He paused, puffing reflectively on his cheroot.

'What happened to your grandparents?' Agnes asked.

'They were killed,' Karlheinz replied. 'I am sorry to tell you this. Sorry for you and sorry for myself. They did not survive. We lost our beloved Oma and Opa.'

'And Karolina?'

His voice was gentle. 'You must accept that your sister is dead.'

The word hit her like a lead bullet. 'You don't know that,' Agnes exclaimed tautly. The little candle of hope could not have been extinguished so soon!

'If Oma and Opa did not survive, it's impossible that your sister could have survived, either.'

'Why do you say that?' Agnes demanded. 'If you don't know what became of them? Surely there must be some records?'

'What happened in East Prussia has not been recorded,' he replied quietly. 'Not in the official history books. Do you know a painting called *Dulle Griet*, made by Pieter Bruegel the

Elder? No? Go and see it sometime. It's in Antwerp. It gives you an idea.'

'An idea of what?'

'The mouth of hell opening. The atrocities. The massacres. The mass violations of women and girls. The burning and looting. When the Red Army reached German civilians, they exacted a terrible revenge.'

Agnes was silent, her heart sinking into the pit of her stomach. Karlheinz studied the ash on his cigar reflectively. 'And after the slaughter,' he went on, 'came the famine. Food production collapsed. The Russians took everything. Hundreds of thousands died through starvation.'

She felt cold. 'Has anyone ever been back there to look for the family?'

His expression was pitying. 'We did our best, Agnes, believe me. After the war, we tried for years to find out what had happened. We learned that Opa and Oma were murdered. Their neighbours were all dead or missing, too. But there was no trace of Karolina. She was so young, you see. Just a little child. She could not have lived without Opa and Oma. As for going to look for her, Germans are not welcome there. East Prussia was divided between Poland and the Soviet Union by the Potsdam Conference. The Iron Curtain has been drawn right across what used to be Greater Germany. The Soviets don't allow visitors from the West. And they don't welcome family enquiries, either. Besides, any ethnic Germans who survived the war were expelled in 1946 and 1947. There just aren't any East Prussian Germans left. As the Bible says, *In der Hölle ist keine Hoffnung.* In Hell there is no hope.'

'I see,' she said dully.

'It's better you accept this now than cling to a dream,' he said. 'The truth is best. I could have written it all down in a letter, but I wanted to meet you. We are, after all, relations of a sort.'

Agnes felt as though an iron gate had been slammed in her

face. She sagged in her chair. 'I appreciate you being frank with me,' she said in a hollow voice.

'I remember the Nazi era well,' he went on conversationally. 'I can't deny that it was a great time to be a German. The unity, the patriotism, the national pride. It was intoxicating. Soul-stirring. Of course,' he added smoothly, 'one didn't know about the dark side.'

'You mean the systematic murder of non-German millions,' she couldn't help saying.

He frowned. 'You are right to rebuke me. I should not have spoken like that.'

Agnes shrugged. 'The truth is best.'

'I agree.' His eyes glinted slyly. 'But do not forget, my dear Agnes, that you yourself are German. And that your father was one of those who committed the systematic murders, *ja*?'

'I don't forget that,' she replied sourly.

'There is another side to being German, which is eternal. Schiller, Goethe, Bach, Beethoven, Brahms. You like music?'

'Yes.'

'You should stay a few nights in Munich. It is the concert season. We can go to some performances together. Music written by Germans, played by Germans, for Germans. You will understand your heritage a great deal better.'

Agnes was too filled with despair to be attracted by this prospect. 'I have to get my train home,' she said in a bleak voice.

'You are grieving for the sister you never knew?' Karlheinz said ironically, but not without compassion. 'I wish I could help you with that. But it is a form of grief unknown to psychologists.'

'I'm not grieving. I was just so hopeful of finding a connection.'

'I understand. You are not married? No children?'

'No to both questions.'

'Me neither. Well, *um genau zu sein*, I have been married, but am no longer married. The experience was not good. So. What can I tell you about little Karolina that will help?' he asked rhetorically. 'That she was *ein süßes Baby*, very cute. That our stepmother was besotted with her, and would not let her out of her arms. That she grew into a sturdy little toddler. As the eldest, and the only son, of course I was not so interested in babies and their doings. I wanted to join the army as soon as possible, and be like *Vati*, with a sabre and a chest full of medals. But my sisters also found her irresistible. They played with her like a doll.'

'That doesn't help, I'm afraid,' Agnes said sadly. She glanced at her watch. 'I've taken up so much of your time. I'm very grateful to you, Karlheinz. I should get back to the station now.'

He stubbed out his cheroot. 'But you must meet Constanze before you go!'

'Constanze?' she asked.

'My stepmother. She may be able to tell you some amusing anecdotes about your sister.'

Agnes hesitated. She just wanted to get back to Dowdeswell and lick her wounds. But the thought of meeting someone who had actually held her sister in her arms struck some kind of chord in her heart. 'Wouldn't it be an imposition on her?'

Karlheinz laughed. 'You make her sound like a frail old lady. Constanze is only forty-nine, and in better shape than I am, I assure you. She insists on meeting you. I will be in serious trouble if I do not bring you to her. She lives just fifteen minutes from here, in Nymphenburg.'

'Where the china comes from?'

'*Stimmt!* The exquisite porcelain milkmaids with the peaches and cream complexions, just like you. I will call Constanze to tell her we're coming. You will still be in time to get the overnight train back to London.' He slapped the table. '*Komm!* I will take you now.'

His car was a butter-yellow Mercedes convertible. As she sank into the soft leather seats, he told her proudly, 'It's a 250 SL.

Six cylinder engine, disc brakes. Two hundred kilometres per hour on the autobahn. What do you drive?'

'A Mini Minor,' she said, and when he didn't look impressed, she added, 'but I've inherited an old Rolls-Royce from my grandfather.'

He pricked up his ears. 'What model?' he asked, pulling out of the shadowy underground garage into the sunlight of the street.

'A Phantom.'

'What year?'

'1930, I think.'

'What are you going to do with it?'

'I'm selling it.'

'I will buy it,' Karlheinz said decisively. 'I will fly to England, we will haggle over the price, I will pay twenty per cent more than it is worth, and I will drive it back to Munich.'

Agnes smiled, despite her sore heart. 'I like the part about paying more than it's worth.'

He put his foot down to accelerate. 'Then we have a deal.'

Nymphenburg turned out to be a quiet but obviously wealthy suburb, where self-consciously pretty houses sat complacently behind pocket-handkerchief-sized front gardens. 'Much of this area was flattened by bombs in 1944,' he told her. 'Rebuilt now, better than before.'

After skirting the royal parks, Karlheinz drove down a quiet avenue lined with stately old firs and pines, and stopped in front of a handsome, pink-stuccoed villa with green shutters and curvaceously ornamented gables.

'Constanze is very excited to meet you,' he told Agnes before opening the doors of the car. 'But I warn you, we don't exactly get on, she and I. We are too close in age. And I am afraid that when my father married her, I cast her in the role of wicked stepmother. Perhaps there was some sexual attraction on both sides,' he added casually, 'which produced tension. Who knows? *Kom!*'

The door was opened by a housemaid in a grey tunic. Somewhere in the house a small dog was yapping shrilly. The maid led them through rooms furnished in a rather flashy, opulent style to an elaborate glass conservatory which looked out onto the immaculate back garden. The woman who was sitting there rose to meet them. She was unmistakeably the same person from the wartime photograph, a little sharper-featured now, but still striking. She wore a pleated silk dress in peacock blue, and had evidently made her face up carefully for this meeting. She reached both hands out to Agnes.

'My dear! Thank you for coming to see me!' She kissed Agnes on both cheeks, careful not to smudge her lipstick, then led her to the window. 'Let me look at you.' The china-blue eyes devoured her. 'This is what my Karolina would be like now. How wonderful to see it! What a gift!' She half-closed her eyes and breathed in deeply. 'Ah. That magical scent of youth. *Wunderschön, wunderschön.*' Finally, she condescended to notice Karlheinz. 'Hallo, Monster,' she greeted him disdainfully.

'Hallo, Constanze. Do you have any of that cream cake from Erbshäuser?'

'He is a greedy pig,' Constanze remarked confidentially to Agnes, as though Karlheinz were not there. 'He always was. A little fat boy, and now, as you see, a big fat man. As soon as he sees me, he wants to eat.' She gave Karlheinz a saccharine smile. 'Of course, Monster. I sent Hilde to buy it fresh this morning. She will bring it in shortly.' She drew Agnes to the wicker sofa, with its garish pattern of oversized poppies. 'Sit with me, my dear, and tell me all about yourself.'

'There isn't much to tell,' Agnes replied. 'I'm still finding out "all about myself". And putting the pieces together isn't easy.'

'But that is the story of all our lives,' Constanze said, patting her hand. 'Just begin at the beginning.'

It took a surprisingly long time to tell Constanze the story, starting with Barbar's death and the half-burned letter in the fireplace. Constanze listened intently. Karlheinz ate two slices of a cream cake with cherries, watching the women with velvety brown eyes.

'But this is most admirable,' Constanze said at last, pouring tea for Agnes. 'You are a very special young lady. Of course, one expects something special from the daughter of a true Aryan and an officer in the SS. What a pedigree! You must be so proud, my dear.'

'I don't think that having a father in the SS is a source of pride,' Agnes said dryly.

'Nonsense. The SS were the elite of the elite. They still are.' She waved a hand wearing a glittering diamond. 'Some of the top companies in this town are run by ex-SS officers.'

'Constanze,' Karlheinz said warningly.

'They are the only ones who know how to get things done,' Constanze retorted.

'Like mass murder,' he scoffed.

'*Ach*, nonsense. Grotesque exaggeration.'

'I'm afraid my stepmother is a little backward in her thinking, Agnes,' Karlheinz said through a mouthful of cream cake.

Constanze ignored him again. 'And now you are searching for your sister? *Ausgezeichnet!*'

'Karlheinz says that she couldn't have survived the invasion.'

'Nonsense,' Constanze retorted. It was evidently one of her favourite words. 'She is alive.'

'How do you know?' Agnes demanded eagerly.

Constanze laid both hands on her breast. 'Because I feel it *here*. If she was dead, I would know.'

Agnes glanced at Karlheinz, who rolled his eyes. 'Oh, I see,' she said flatly.

'Never underestimate a mother's instincts,' Constanze replied in a sharp voice. 'Yes, I regard myself as Karolina's mother, and Karolina as my child. My only child.' She shot a cold blue look at Karlheinz. 'Monster hated me on sight, and taught his ugly sisters to hate me too. But with Karolina, I felt an instant, eternal connection.'

'This happens,' Karlheinz commented ironically, 'when two babies meet.'

Constanze dabbed – or pretended to dab – a tear from her eye. 'You see how he still despises me? He loves to wound me. His father was a great man. But *he* . . .' – She let her expression convey her opinion of her stepson.

Feeling uncomfortable, Agnes looked at her watch. 'I should be heading to the station.'

Constanze rose. 'Come and meet my Fritzi before you go. He has been calling for you all this time. Monster can stay here and eat more *Schlag*,' she added pointedly. 'Fritzi will bite him if he sees him. Fritzi hates Monster. Dogs can always tell a person's true character.'

Karlheinz produced a horrible smile, and reached for a third slice of cake.

Uncertainly, Agnes allowed herself to be led upstairs to what was evidently Constanze's bedroom, a pastel-pink boudoir crowded with frills and flounces. Fritzi turned out to be a liver-coloured miniature dachshund who had already left a small sausage of excrement on the pile carpet. He dashed around their feet, shrieking and snapping somewhat alarmingly. Constanze was suddenly businesslike. She produced a notepad from her bedside and gave it to Agnes. 'Write down your address,' she commanded over the dog's yaps. 'I know some of the ex-SS. I will ask them to help.'

Agnes was taken aback. 'To help?'

'To find out what happened to Karolina. They have many contacts. A network, you understand. I have often thought of it. But now I will do it.'

Agnes gasped. 'Can they really help?'

'We will see. You have made me ashamed of myself,' Constanze said. Away from Karlheinz, she had dropped the little-girl manner, and had become older, tougher. 'Whatever Monster told you, we made no effort to search for your sister.'

Agnes was startled. 'Why not?'

'It wasn't appropriate, my dear. The war had ended. We were all trying to cover up the things that had been done. Children stolen from the occupied lands, Lebensborn, all that.' She dabbed her eyes. The tears seemed real this time. 'We were warned to admit nothing about it. It was taboo. You understand? We had to hide the truth to stay out of trouble. My husband was a friend of Himmler. He was lucky to escape being put on trial. My baby had disappeared, and Monster and my husband said it was for the best. For the best! How *could* they say that? But I had to go along with it. Now you force me to face the truth. The SS are the only ones who remember what really happened.'

Agnes hesitated. 'Are they still Nazis?'

'They are what they are,' Constanze said brusquely. 'Everybody knows who they are, but nobody talks about it. *Alles klar?* Write down your address and telephone number.'

Agnes found that her hands were shaking as she wrote down the details. 'Here.'

Constanze took the paper and folded it. Her tears had gone now, and her mascara was undamaged. 'Don't tell Karlheinz about this. He is so concerned to be uncontaminated, above reproach. As though they didn't make their fortune with the Nazis. Unfortunately, he holds the purse strings. If I annoy him too much, he will find ways to make me uncomfortable. Delay my allowance, and so forth.'

'I won't say anything,' Agnes promised. There was a nauseous worm squirming in her stomach now, a feeling compounded of uneasy hope and active horror.

Constanze leaned forward and kissed her cheek – a proper kiss this time, which left a red lipstick imprint. 'You are a good girl. It has been a privilege to meet you. I will be in touch if I hear anything.'

\* \* \*

Driving away from the villa, Karlheinz asked Agnes, 'What did she say to you upstairs?'

'Nothing, really. She just wanted to show me the dog.'

'It's a horrible little animal, isn't it?'

'I'm quite fond of dachshunds, actually.'

'Had it crapped on the carpet?'

'Yes,' Agnes conceded. 'It had crapped on the carpet.'

'It always does when it's excited,' he said. 'That's one of the reasons I hate it. You'd better check under your shoes. Now, let's arrange for me to come and buy your grandfather's Phantom.'

As he chattered on, Agnes fell silent. In his shallow, uncaring way, Karlheinz Ozerki had blown out her candle of hope. His stepmother had relighted it.

On the surface, Constanze Ozerki was a pampered, selfish woman whom Agnes had found shocking, with her open admiration of the Nazis and her description of their atrocities as 'grotesque exaggeration'. But Agnes had sensed a steely core beneath the frothy lace. And when Constanze had spoken of knowing ex-members of the SS, Agnes had believed her.

If, as Constanze said, the SS were the only ones who 'knew what really happened', then perhaps – just perhaps – there was a thread that could link her to her lost sister.

There was only one problem. And the problem was that she had just made a pact with the Devil.

Or perhaps, that pact had been made for her, at her birth.

She was the daughter of Nazis. So was Karolina – if she was alive. Not Nazis in history books. Real Nazis, still alive almost a quarter of a century after the war. A father who had been imprisoned as a war criminal. A mother reviled by her own people.

How could she escape that taint? All roads were leading

her to the most sinister philosophy of the twentieth century, a philosophy that had caused the death of millions. A philosophy that had brought her and her sister to life.

She had no choice but to follow that road, until she discovered the truth.

# CHAPTER ELEVEN

## KAROLINA

*East Prussia, 1944*

It is the autumn of 1944. Karolina is too young to have much concept of time, but she has spent three months with the Lithuanian family.

Their farm is near a village she has never learned the name of. They took her in when they found her in their barn. The other children fled, but Karolina was too weak to walk any further.

There is a name for them – people call them *Die Wolfskinder*, the wolf children. They live by begging, stealing, scavenging and foraging. If they're lucky, knocking at a stranger's door will yield a morsel of food. If they aren't, dogs will be set on them, or they will get a thrashing.

In bad times, they comb through garbage, or live on what they find in the woods: ferns, sorrel, fungi, thistles. If desperate, they boil leaves and bark into a bitter broth, which sometimes makes them terribly sick.

For the time being, she has a home.

The Lithuanians burn her clothes, which are full of lice, and give her new ones – dungarees too big for her, so that she has to keep the trouser cuffs rolled up, and a jersey that is more patches than wool. She wears these clothes every day.

They take the precious oilskin wallet with her identity papers in it, and put it away, and tell her she must consider herself Lithuanian now. Nobody ever admits they are German.

They give her a new name.

'Your name is Stanislava,' the mother tells her. 'Say it.'

'Stanislava,' Karolina whispers.

'You sound German. Speak it properly,' the woman says angrily. 'Say, *my name is Stanislava.*'

'My name is Stanislava,' Karolina repeats.

'Again!'

Karolina struggles to get it right. Lithuanian is a difficult language, though she's picked up a few words in her wanderings. After a while, she learns to think of herself as Stanislava, and the farm as her new home.

Food is very scarce. But the family feed her enough to claw her back from the starving, emaciated state she has got into. She has shelter, and doesn't need to sleep in barns or burned houses anymore.

But there is a high price to pay for this kindness. Weak and small as she is, she's expected to work from dawn to dark. She fetches wood for the stove and draws water from the well. She can only carry one log at a time, or half a bucketful of water, so she works all day, staggering under the burden. Her reward is enough food to keep her alive.

The Lithuanian family is large. There are five adults and four children of varying ages. The ruler of the house is the father, whom they call Vilkas. He is ferocious if she flags.

'Lazy brat!' he shouts. 'Idle devil. I'll boil you in the stew pot. I'll feed you to the wolves!'

Most frighteningly, he threatens to show her papers, which he keeps locked in a drawer, to the Russians. That's a threat worse than being boiled or fed to the wolves, because it's real.

She knows he doesn't want her there. He's angry with his wife for taking in an extra mouth to feed.

If his wife is around, she calms Vilkas. But she isn't always there. Vilkas is very strong, his hands knotted with sinew and muscle. He can lift huge stones from the fields and carry them in his arms. Karolina knows he could crack her bones if he wanted.

The other children ignore her at first. She is just another farm animal. The mother tells Karolina she can sleep with the youngsters, in the huge feather bed that all four children share; but as they would have done with any presumptuous animal, they indignantly push her off onto the floor.

The floor is hard and cold. She learns that if she waits until the early hours, she can creep back onto the bed without waking them, and steal some warmth and comfort. But she has to make sure she gets up before they do, and slip away, or they will attack her with hard fists and heels.

The two boys are particularly disdainful of her. The middle girl, a redhead, can be spiteful. But the youngest, Eglė, who is about Karolina's age, is curious about her, as she might have been about a pig or a sheep that could talk.

'Where do you come from?' she asks Karolina.

Karolina waves her hand. 'Over there.'

Eglė accepts this. To her, the world ends at the boundaries of the farm. Karolina knows that the world is a far vaster and darker place. 'What happened to your family?' Eglė asks. 'Did they die in the war?'

Karolina doesn't want to think about what happened to Oma, but the memory is always there, no matter how carefully she tries to skirt round it: Oma lying on the bed after the Russians had finished with her, the wide, dark pool on the floor, Oma's head stuck on the dressing table.

She never knew what happened to Opa. He vanished, along with all the animals and everything of value.

Karolina can't talk to Eglė about any of that, so she tells her about the good things instead. About how Opa and Oma had cows, pigs, rabbits, ducks and geese. About how there were always generous family meals, with food piled on your plate.

Eglė loves to hear about the food. So Karolina tells Eglė about how Oma went to the miller every week with meat or milk, and came back with a sack of flour, and baked bread for the whole farm, domed loaves of *Bauernbrot*, fragrant with caraway, anise, fennel and coriander. On holidays, there was always cake – honey cake, marzipan cake or *Gugelhupf* with a hole in the middle, snowy with powdered sugar.

She had loved to help Oma in the kitchen, even if all she did was stick her fingers in the sweet dough, or sit on a stool, chattering. Oma's love was expressed through food and huge, floury hugs. The kitchen was always warm. It was where Karolina had felt most loved and cared for. Where she had last been safe.

Eglė wants to know how the cakes had smelled and tasted. Every detail. She makes Karolina recite everything again and again, closing her eyes and flaring her little nostrils to capture the imaginary scents of dough and sugar and spices.

But, of course, all that is gone forever. It ended the day the Russian soldiers came.

It was Elke, the red-faced, rough-palmed Silesian milkmaid, who hid Karolina under the empty flour sacks, and told her not to move or make a sound. And it was Elke, later, who packed Karolina's satchel and ran off with her into the woods. She'd been crying because of what the Russians had done to her, but at least they hadn't chopped her head off. She hadn't fought them. Oma had fought like a tiger, Elke said, and they'd grown angry, and had tried to cut her throat. But she kept struggling, so they'd taken her head right off, and put it on the dressing table to watch what they did with the rest of her.

But Elke was too fat and old to get very far, and she had

fallen in a canal and drowned. Karolina couldn't remember whether she threw herself in, or someone had thrown her in. All she knew was that she was alone after that.

The satchel had contained some food and a few clothes, but they hadn't lasted long, either. The only thing she had left was the oilskin pouch that Elke told her never to lose, never *ever* to lose, because it contained her papers, and without her papers, nobody would ever know who she was, or where she came from. Identity was the last thing you gave up. Even if it was an ephemeral, dangerous treasure.

She had lost everything else. Her home, her family, security, even her country. She had only her courage to see her through. And the fragile support of other children. The lost ones. The wolf children.

She had roamed with the other wolf children in the woods, fields and bombed cities until the Lithuanian family took her in.

But Vilkas's attacks grow worse. He takes to hitting her until her thin body is covered in bruises. It seems as though in his mind, everything that he fears and hates is concentrated in Karolina. He blames her for the war, young as she is. 'The Nazi viper,' he shouts. 'It's her fault. All her fault.'

Then, one awful day, he catches her alone in the kitchen, and beats her so savagely that she thinks he will kill her. She curls up in a ball as the stick rains blows on her. She doesn't cry out. She just tries to survive. There is nobody else in the house, so nobody comes to stop him. He only stops when he grows tired. Then he drinks half a bottle of the fiery horseradish schnapps that he brews himself, and goes to sleep in the chair next to the stove.

When she can move again, Karolina gets up off the floor. She takes a knife from the counter, and limps silently to Vilkas's room. With what little strength she has left, she opens the drawer, and gets her oilskin wallet, with its precious papers inside, and tucks it into her jersey.

Then she creeps back to the kitchen, holding her breath in case she wakes Vilkas, who is snoring by the warm stove. If he wakes, she decides, she will stab him in the heart with the knife. But though he grunts and shuffles in the creaking chair, he does not wake.

She snatches some food from the larder, bits of bacon fat, some stale bread, some withered fruit. She stuffs these in a sack.

Then she slips out of the kitchen door, and hobbles as fast as she can for the trees.

By the time darkness falls, she is deep in the woods. Karolina has been in the woods at night so many times. She isn't afraid. But she is very lonely until she can find the other wolf children. She misses them. She misses Eglė. But she knows that if she hadn't run away, Vilkas would have killed her. Her body aches from head to foot, a tight suit of pain.

She knows better than to make a fire. The Russians watch for those thin plumes of smoke among the trees, and come looking. So she makes a nest of dried leaves and burrows into it. She gnaws some of the bacon fat and the dried bread, putting the rest away. She might have to live on this meagre store for a long time.

The full moon comes up, escaping from the branches that claw at it, growing smaller and colder and brighter as it rises in the sky. Karolina keeps very still. She's learned how to do that. She knows how to become part of the forest. She covers herself with dried leaves, and sleeps.

The next morning, she starts walking. She has to find the other children. Alone, she will be dead in a few days. But it's months since they passed this way. They could be anywhere by now. The only way she'll survive is to find them.

She stays near the roads, but never ventures on them. That's far too dangerous. The Russians ride around in jeeps, travelling fast, looking for stray Germans and Lithuanian partisans. They can be on you in a flash, before you have time to dive into the ditches.

The landscape is changing. Green leaves are turning to orange, yellow and brown. It is becoming cold. Karolina thinks longingly of Oma's stove. But that's just a dream, now.

The next evening, she comes across a fence that blocks her way. She would have climbed over the fence, but hanging on it is a sign. It is painted yellow, and bears a skull and crossbones. That means a minefield lies ahead, and she can't go any further.

It's close to nightfall. She turns back from the fence and goes among the trees to find somewhere to sleep. It isn't a good place. There are brambles everywhere, hooking in her clothes and hair, scratching blood from her hands and ankles. But she can't stay out in the open overnight. She finds a bank with a little overhang, and tries to make a shelter there for her aching limbs.

When she looks in her bag, there is nothing left in there, only a few crumbs. Dismayed, she thinks she must have dropped her little store of food along the way. Then she remembers that she has already eaten it, nibbling, gnawing all day to stave off the ache of hunger in her belly.

Somehow, she manages to go to sleep, despite the grinding of her empty belly.

When she wakes, there are children standing around her. They have found her. She is saved.

Benno, at fourteen, is the oldest of the children. Karolina is weak, so he carries her on his back. They plod through the mud and patches of snow. Then the shots ring out.

Karolina sees the soldiers coming across the field towards

them. They are Russians. You can tell by their greatcoats and their fur caps with the red star.

Benno drags her with him as he runs towards a coppice, almost yanking her arm out of its socket. Bullets howl after them, cutting through the snow. They plunge into the thicket, oblivious of the branches that claw at their clothes and faces.

The thicket is mainly made up of hornbeams, their dried leaves still clinging on stubbornly despite the winter. Benno hauls her as far as they can go among the trunks, and then down into a hollow. Karolina is gasping in the icy air. He lays his finger on her lips, his eyes warning her to be as quiet as a little mouse. She holds her breath, despite the stabbing pain in her chest and the pounding of her heart.

They can hear the Russians on the road, walking up and down, shouting at them to come out. Two of them stop just twenty yards away, so close that they hear the scrape of a match, and smell the acrid tobacco smoke. The men mutter to each other for a while. The children hear the gurgle of a bottle, catch the whiff of vodka.

A thin scream comes from further up the road. The voice of a child, begging not to be hurt. The two soldiers run off to join their comrades, heavy boots thumping in the snow. More confused Russian voices drift on the wind. The child's screams rise in pitch, piercing. Then there are two shots. The screaming stops.

Benno and Karolina lie motionless, listening. At last, the Russians leave. Two or three of them are singing together in harmony, voices strangely melodious, fading on the wind.

When complete silence falls at last, Benno whispers, 'They got somebody. Stay here. I'll go and see who it is.'

Karolina huddles down. Her stomach hurts with hunger. She makes a ball of snow and eats it slowly. The ice numbs your stomach for a while.

The dried leaves rustle, and Benno wriggles back beside

her on his knees and elbows. There is a smear of blood on his cheek now. 'It was Jonas,' he whispers. 'They shot him. He's breathing, but he's bleeding a lot. The Russians haven't gone far. We'll have to wait until they leave.'

Karolina starts shivering violently. Benno opens his coat and pulls her against his body. He wraps the coat around them both. It had belonged to a dead man they'd found, and it is capacious, but it still smells of what oozed out of the dead man.

When it is nearly dark, they creep out of the thicket. The burning farm is a red glow in the twilight. They can hear the Russians shouting and singing, and occasionally, firing their guns.

They make their way along the road. Every now and then, Benno gives a low whistle. He can imitate the calls of lots of different birds. Most of the real birds have flown away by now, but the Russians wouldn't know that.

And one by one, the other children come out of hiding and join them. There are fewer than before. Some have fled. Others have been less lucky. They find Jonas in a slushy pool of blood, and roll his body into a ditch, and cover it with snow and earth as best they can. But dogs and other animals will soon find it, all the same. They are starving, too.

Benno leads them towards the burning farm. Some of the children don't want to go. But Benno knows the farm, and says it is the only place they will find food and shelter for the night. He knows where they can hide.

Benno leads them to a barn. The roof has been blown off in an air attack, but there is some protection from the wind. They huddle together. They can hear the Russians clearly, triumphant voices loud in the night. Benno leaves them to find food. They wait for an hour, wondering if he will ever come back. But eventually he creeps into the barn with an armful of stale bread that he has managed to scavenge. They share the food carefully, not letting a crumb go to waste. They share everything equally. It is their law. Then they settle down.

But it is hard to sleep. All night they hear the sound of women screaming and begging for mercy while the Russians whoop and laugh and sing. Benno, who knows the family, cries. He seldom cries. But today has been a bad day.

By the spring of 1945, Karolina is still living wild in the marshes, fields and forests of East Prussia.

She is a year older. But a century has passed inside her. Benno is no longer with her. She can't remember when he disappeared, or how. But he has gone. Others carry her now, taking turns to hoist her on their backs, when her legs can go no further.

She is still roaming with bands of other lost children.

Of the original group, none remain. Indeed, the children have changed time and again, some dead, some vanished, a lucky few finding homes that would take them in.

Another bitterly hard winter is beginning. The wolf children walk for miles from village to village, farm to farm, door to door.

Each time a stranger gives her kindness is a little miracle. She is grateful beyond words. Each time she is turned away is another rejection, another piece torn off her tattered sense of self-worth.

There is nothing she yearns for more than to be loved again, to find people who will care for her, to go back to what she has lost.

She looks for that lost love everywhere.

She thinks she has found it one day, when an old man sees her sitting at the roadside and comes over to her. He looks a little bit like Opa Ozerki, but thinner and balder. But he greets her warmly, as though he knows her. He has a brown paper bag in his pocket, and in the brown paper bag are *Schnecken* – sticky, coiled cinnamon buns.

Karolina hasn't seen *Schnecken* for years. Her eyes grow very wide. Are they for her?

Before long, she is sitting on the old man's knee, devouring a bun. He tells her to call him Opa. He talks to her lovingly, strokes her tangled hair, just as Opa used to.

He sees the bruises on her arms and legs, and clicks his tongue sympathetically, kissing the sore places to make them better. He picks the leaves and straw off her filthy dress and out of her hair.

She is overwhelmed by his kindness. She feels as though her heart will burst with gratitude. The sweetness of the bun; the sticky mouthfuls slipping into her empty little belly; the security of Opa's arms around her.

He gives her lots of kisses. His chin is very bristly and scratchy, but Opa Ozerki's was too, except on Sundays, when he shaved for church. She doesn't mind the prickles, because the kisses are what she has dreamed of. Only, she doesn't like being kissed on the mouth.

'You are so pretty,' the new Opa murmurs. 'Such a little *Schnecke*.' She giggles because it means a snail, like the bun he has given her. 'Such a sweet little *Schnecke*. Such a precious little pearl.'

She squirms and he laughs. His face is brown and wrinkled like a walnut, but his teeth are amazingly white, like china. She can smell schnapps on his breath.

'Where are your parents?' he asks.

'I don't know,' she replies.

'Not here?'

'No.'

He points up with a gnarled forefinger. 'In heaven, maybe?'

'Maybe,' she agrees.

'They are better there,' he smiles, showing those china teeth. 'Much better up there than down here. So you are all alone? Poor little *Schnecke*. Opa will take care of you.'

Karolina can't eat any more of the bun. She is starting to feel sick. The rich, lardy confection is too much for her digestive system.

But the Opa is holding her very tight, and his fingers are roaming all over her, investigating her lean ribs, her hollow belly.

'Hush, little one,' he mutters, 'be still, now. Be still!'

She doesn't want to offend him, when he is being so kind and loving to her. But she doesn't like what he is doing. She has a sense of privacy. Whatever squalor the children are in, they always respect that in one another.

This Opa is invading part of her that belongs only to her, to nobody else in the world. His fingers are wandering up her bedraggled dress, trying to find a way under her knicker elastic. His other arm is pinioning her with surprising strength, stopping her from escaping.

She knows that this isn't right. This is what the Russians do to women.

She fights to get away from him, fights the way Oma fought the Russians, like a tiger. But he has fastened her arms against her body, and his face has changed now, no longer smiling, but glaring at her.

The struggle is too much for her stomach.

With a wrench of her guts, the *Schnecken* mush surges up her gullet and out of her mouth, and splashes all over Opa.

Cursing, he lets her go and jumps up.

Freed, Karolina doesn't hesitate. She takes to her heels and runs like the wind. Down the road, towards where the other wolf children are gathering burdocks. She looks over her shoulder, but the Opa isn't trying to follow her. He's too busy trying to wipe vomit off his clothes.

By the time she reaches the other children, he has vanished. The sickly grease of the *Schnecken* is still coating her gullet. She spits and spits, and chews a rank burdock leaf to get the taste away.

The betrayal of that experience will stay with her for years, a nauseating feeling in her stomach that will come to warn her when others offer sweet things and smile with too-white teeth.

She decides to stop believing in God. God is clearly an adult, and you can never trust adults.

There is bad luck.

Karolina is captured by the Russians, along with a large group of the wolf children.

The soldiers have prepared this carefully. The children are camped in a clearing in the forest. The weather is mild, but they need a campfire to cook their food. The smoke of their fire gives them away. The Russians come silently through the trees and surround them, so there is no escape.

There are some older children in the group, thirteen and fourteen. They are taken away in the evening, into the forest. Soon the sound of the girls screaming is heard. It goes on for hours. There are shots, too. And the drinking songs that the Russians sing so well.

Karolina is too small to interest them. But a passing soldier, for no reason, kicks her in the side with his boot as she sits huddled and shivering. Everything goes black before her eyes. At last, somehow, she manages to start breathing again. But she has to breathe very slowly, shallowly. Every breath is agony.

In the morning, some of the older children return. The girls are vacant-eyed. They don't speak about what was done to them.

None of the boys return. They are never seen again.

Now the Russians tell the children they must march with them. They are making their way to a town sixty miles to the north.

The march is eight hours a day, at the pace of grown men. It is hard on the younger children. Harder still on Karolina, who can barely put one foot in front of the other without gasping in pain. She soon falls behind, to the end of the tatterdemalion column.

The Russians only stop to set fire to houses and farms they pass on the road. They are expert at this. Some of the soldiers carry flamethrowers. There are tanks of oil on their backs, and their guns shoot a jet of flame a long way. They use these to good effect, burning buildings, crops in the fields, and sometimes people. One of the soldiers likes to point his weapon at the children, which makes them scream in dread and cover their eyes. He is entertained, and repeats the joke several times a day.

They walk for miles each day. Every night, unless they manage to flush German women out of the burning farmhouses, they take the same girls away. The girls scream less and less each time, and every morning fewer of them stagger back to the group.

The men they encounter on the road are shot without mercy, whether old or young. Their bodies are left where they fall.

The children's shoes, already old and broken, disintegrate under the hours of walking. Many end up with feet that are bare, or if they are lucky, bound in strips of bloody rag.

Karolina is very weak now. She can no longer keep up, even with the stragglers. She is terrified they will shoot her. She tries with every ounce of strength in her small body. But her ribs hurt so terribly that she cannot breathe properly.

At last they notice how far behind she has fallen. They shout orders at her, but she cannot obey, not even to save her life.

One of the soldiers comes back for her. It is the man who likes to threaten the children with the flamethrower. He points his weapon at her, grinning. He issues a command in Russian. Karolina does not understand. She stands apathetically, unable to move. She stares at the tattered wildflowers that grow in the ditch beside her. She has reached the end of her road.

She has seen the flamethrowers used many times, men and women turned into human torches. She knows there is a loud bang when the fuel is ignited. She hears the bang now, and waits for the flames to engulf her.

But there are no flames. The soldier curses, fiddling with his weapon. But he cannot get it to work. After a while, he loses interest in her. He turns and leaves, not looking back. He breaks into a trot to rejoin his comrades.

Karolina looks up at the heavens. There is a ragged hole in the clouds, and a patch of blue sky is visible. She wonders whether there really is a God, after all, and He is looking down at her through the ragged hole.

And if He is, she wonders what He has in store for her next.

She is with a new group. She never sees any of the last group again. The pain of her broken ribs slowly heals, as do her torn feet. The new group is made up of older, stronger children, experts in survival. They know lots of tricks. They can steal the eyes right out of your head. They even steal from the Russians.

They reach the outskirts of Königsberg, which has been reduced to ruins by air raids, and which is a city of desolation. They shelter in a cellar, where rats scuttle over them, biting and squealing all night.

At daylight, they hear boots crunching down the stairs. They try to hide behind the jagged heaps of rubble. It is too late for that. Four Russian soldiers come into the cellar, holding machine guns. The children scream hysterically.

But instead of shooting them, the Russians laugh. '*Krieg kaputt*,' they say in their bad German, '*Krieg vorbei*.'

Eventually they understand what the Russians are saying. The war is over.

The soldiers drive the children out into the daylight. Seeing their wretched condition, one of the Russians spits.

'*Rattenkinder*,' he says. Rat children. But he gives them half a loaf of black bread and a piece of sausage.

They devour the food, blinking in the cold spring light. When the shooting starts, they scatter, desperately hunting for cover. But for once, the Russians aren't shooting at people. They are firing into the air, deafening volleys of triumph.

Slowly, the children pick themselves out of the gutter, staring in wonder at the soldiers who dance like crazy men and empty their magazines into the sky, as though they want to kill God.

The shooting lasts well into the night. Then the raping starts again. The children are slowly drawn into a feeling of exhausted hope. If the war is over, then surely things are going to get better from now on.

But they aren't.

Another two years are to pass, another twenty-four months of hunger, wandering, fear and loneliness.

Finding food is critical. A day without food means you are weaker and colder the next day, which makes it harder to find more food. It is a downward slope that ends in death.

With the countryside laid to waste, the only food is to be found in the garbage piles in the towns.

Karolina learns a new trick from some older children: they jump trains.

Passenger trains are few and far between. But freight trains chug through the countryside, sometimes loaded with goods, other times almost empty. If you manage to get on one of these, you can travel from one town to the next in a few hours, instead of walking for days, which will kill you sooner or later, one way or another.

There are different ways to get on a train. The worst and most dangerous way is to climb onto the couplings between carriages. It is freezing cold out there, and if your arms and legs get numb, you will fall under the iron wheels. And if you let your legs dangle, they might get between the buffers, which will pinch off your legs as easily as you pinch off lice.

You can climb onto the roof of a carriage, and lie flat, and try to hold on. If the train goes slowly, it can work. But if it picks up speed, you risk being swept off to broken bones or death.

The best way is to sneak into the railway yard at night, avoiding the night watchman and his flashlight, and keep trying the doors of the cattle trucks until you find an empty one open. Then you slip inside and curl up in a corner under whatever filth you find in there. If the guards notice you, they might beat you unconscious. But if you don't steal anything, they might take pity on you, and pretend they didn't see you.

In fact, it is through riding a train that Karolina's time as a wolf child comes to an end at last, in 1947.

The *Kommissarin* watches Karolina with cold eyes from across her desk. She wears a grey uniform. She is Russian, but she speaks German.

'Your name is Karolina Ozerki?'

Karolina nods.

'Speak,' the woman snaps. 'Don't nod your head at me like a puppet.'

'Yes,' Karolina whispers.

The *Kommissarin* has Karolina's oilskin wallet in her hands. She studies the wrinkled, stained papers. 'Do you know what these documents say?'

Karolina shakes her head, and when the *Kommissarin* opens her mouth to shout, quickly adds, 'No.'

'Can't you read?'

'No.'

'At your age, you cannot read!' The woman doesn't hide

her contempt. She holds up one of the papers, and points to a symbol stamped at the top. 'Do you know what this means?'

Karolina has seen it a thousand times before. 'It means Germany,' she says in a small voice.

The *Kommissarin* slams her broad hand on the desk so loudly that Karolina jumps. 'It does *not* mean Germany! It is the swastika, the symbol of the defeated fascist regime of Adolf Hitler!'

Karolina sits very still, looking at the ground. She knows without a shadow of a doubt that her life has reached another turning point. Two days ago, she had climbed into the baggage-car of a train with some other children, and had concealed herself behind the trunks and suitcases.

They'd thought the train was heading to Kaunas, where there is more food, and often kinder people. But they'd made a mistake, and the train was travelling in the opposite direction. After eighteen hours, the door of the baggage car crashed open, and rough hands had dragged them out onto a platform in Berlin.

The railway police had turned them over to the Russian Ministry for Internal Affairs, the dreaded MVD.

The *Kommissarin* holds up another sheet of paper. She points to another symbol. 'Do you know what this means?'

Karolina stares at it. It looks like a twig, or a tree without any leaves. She whispers, 'No.'

'It means you were born in shame. It means you are an enemy of the people. Your parents are criminals.'

Karolina is about to be sick. Elke had told her that the papers in the oilskin were precious, and would save her life one day. Instead of that, they have enraged this uniformed Russian, and have put her in mortal danger. The *Kommissarin* rises from her chair and stalks out of the room. Karolina sits very still, her heart thumping. She can hear the woman talking to a man out in the corridor.

'What do you want to do with her?' the man asks. He is a German.

The woman's reply is low and unintelligible.

The man sighs. 'She is just a child.'

The woman's voice rises. 'A fascist child, Bergmann!'

'But a child, nevertheless. And – respectfully – that would be tantamount to a death sentence.'

'She deserves no pity. She is an abomination. *Lebensborn!* My God!'

'Yes. Incredible.'

'Can't you smell her? She is stinking up the whole office.'

'She's been living like a wild thing for more than three years,' the man says mildly. 'If she deserved punishment for the mere fact of having been born, then I humbly submit that she has already been punished sufficiently.'

The woman makes a spitting sound. 'We must get rid of her.'

'That is not so easy.'

'Why not?'

'She is already in the system. There is paperwork.'

The woman gives a bitter bark of laughter. 'You Germans and your paperwork! You have a system for everything, from gas chambers to wiping your arses.'

'It's in our culture,' the man replies equably. 'To be German is to be systematic and orderly. We will take her off your hands.'

'And do what with her?'

'Put her in an orphanage. Educate her. Teach her right from wrong.'

'The Nazis sent you to a concentration camp for being a socialist, Bergmann. They nearly killed you. And you have pity on this creature?'

'We will take her. We can make something of her.'

'What can you do with a little monster like that?' the woman demands.

'If she survived the war, then she has something special inside her. May I speak to her?' the man asks.

'Be my guest. But hold your nose.'

Karolina hears the man come in. She can hear that he walks oddly, with a bad limp. She hunches in the chair, tucking her chin into her chest, waiting for a blow.

'Look at me, girl,' the man says gently.

Slowly, she looks up. Herr Bergmann is a gaunt man, wearing steel-rimmed glasses. His face has been severely damaged. One side has been crushed in like a tin can that has been kicked down the road. The eye on that side is sunken deep into his skull, and peers out dully, like a wet, red pebble. He has perched one buttock on the *Kommissarin*'s desk, his knobbly hands clasped together. He wears a drab suit and a fawn coat, which are both far too big for him, as though he has lost weight. Some of his fingers are missing. He examines her with his good eye.

'Do you know what you look like?' he asks.

Karolina shakes her head.

'Perhaps that's just as well. Don't worry. I looked just like you, not so long ago. Tell me something. Are you a good girl?'

Karolina thinks. 'Oma and Opa—' She stops.

'What?'

'Oma and Opa said I'm a good girl.'

'Those people were not your grandparents,' the man replies calmly. 'They are dead. So are your mother and father. But you have a new family, now. A socialist family, who will care for you. Your name will no longer be Ozerki. We will allocate you a new name. You will be a German again. But a very different kind of German. A clean German. A decent German. A good German. Would you like that?'

Karolina nods. Any family sounds wonderful to her. Any country that will have her sounds wonderful. It has come at last.

Sanctuary.

'There, there,' the one-eyed man says gently. 'Don't cry, Karolina.'

She hadn't even known she was crying. But now that she has started, she can't stop.

# CHAPTER TWELVE

# AGNES

*West Berlin, 1968*

Agnes was back in Germany, just two weeks after her visit to Munich. But this time, she was in Berlin. And Berlin was a very different city from Munich.

Where Munich had been tranquil and traditional, Berlin was in a ferment. The atmosphere was gritty, electric. Yet somehow, it suited her feverish state of mind.

She had flown into Berlin-Tempelhof in one of BEA's new Super One-Elevens, because she wanted speed – the call was far too urgent to take the train, even though she was running short of money. From the moment she reached the terminal building, she was aware of the noisy protests. Students were greeting arriving passengers with chants and placards at the bus ranks. She walked past them to get her bus into the city.

Near her hotel in Spandau, the demonstrations were larger and the message more explicit. The students were marching with large portraits. She recognised Ho Chi Minh, Che Guevara, Lenin and Marx. There were other faces she didn't know, but she got the general idea. A powerful left-wing movement had galvanised the young people of the city.

Her hotel, apparently one frequented by Americans, was the subject of a protest all to itself – a row of young people holding placards comparing Lyndon Johnson to Adolf Hitler. There were also North Vietnamese flags, and a bearded young man with a loudhailer, ranting about the Vietnam War, watched by a stolid group of sour-faced police.

She checked in at the desk. This was an expensive hotel, but Constanze had insisted she use it and no other. In fact, it was an expensive trip all round for an unemployed young woman, and she didn't want to waste a day more than she had to. She shared the elevator going up to her floor with a middle-aged American couple, who had been bitterly offended by the placards.

'Those kids wouldn't know a Nazi if one bit them in the ass,' the man said angrily. He glared at Agnes, as though suspecting her of communist inclinations too. 'Last time I was here I was in uniform, and we had real Nazis to deal with.'

The irony didn't escape her.

Her room was small but comfortable. The first thing she did, before she unpacked, was to work out how the bedside phone connected to an outside line, and then make a call to Constanze Ozerki in Munich.

'I've arrived,' she said.

Constanze was in conspiratorial mode. 'Good. They will make the appointment. You will be contacted. Be ready. Stay in the hotel. Don't go out. And draw no attention to yourself.'

'Okay.' Agnes put the phone down, her stomach tightening with nerves.

She'd brought a large suitcase, one of Barbar's, because she had no idea how long she would be staying in Germany. It was a vintage Papworth officer's suitcase, perhaps the very one Barbar had travelled back from Norway with in 1945. She put her clothes away neatly in the cupboard, and finding herself at a loose end, went back down to the foyer to see about a cup of coffee, and study the protestors with a journalist's eye.

They were well-organised. Though muted by the window in the hotel's café, the chants, led by the boy with the loudhailer, were synchronised. Agnes estimated that at least a quarter of the demonstrators were girls. A few had young children with them. Every now and then, the chanting would pause, and someone would take the loudhailer and make a short, impassioned speech, which was greeted with cheers and pumping clenched fists. This was a lot more serious than the anti-war protests she'd seen in London.

The coffee was served with whipped cream, which she hadn't asked for and didn't like. Most of the people around her, middle-class and middle-aged, were ignoring the protests, their noses buried in newspapers. She asked the waiter for a copy of the *Evening News,* just to see if it was surviving in her absence. Apologetically, all he could offer were copies of *Der Spiegel* and *The Economist*. She chose the latter. Even the usually unflappable *Economist* was speculating about a radical leftward turn in European politics. De Gaulle in France and Kiesinger in Germany, old-style right-wing political leaders, were both beleaguered by radical movements. After two decades of peace, street-war had returned to the ancient capitals of Europe. The boulevards of Paris were being dug up for cobblestones to hurl at the police. In Berlin, firehoses were being turned on the demonstrators. In Italy, neo-fascists and far-leftists were rioting on the campuses.

It was a long, lonely afternoon. It started to rain towards five o'clock. The demonstrators pulled on plastic ponchos, but as the rain grew heavier, they started to drift away. Soon the street reverted to a capitalist stream of taxis and limousines. It was dinner time.

At seven thirty, more for something to do than because she was very hungry, Agnes wandered into the hotel's restaurant. It was crowded, and she was squeezed onto a small table in one corner. She spent a long time reading through the menu to kill time, and finally settled on a bowl of potato soup and a glass of *Gewürztraminer*.

She'd wanted a light supper, but when the *Kartoffelsuppe* arrived, it turned out to be a very substantial basin of garden vegetables, sausage, bacon and potatoes in a rich broth thickened with cream. It was delicious, however, and she appreciated the comfort it brought. Lately, she had spent a lot of time alone in foreign cities.

When she could eat no more, she pushed the bowl away. The waiter who came to take it back to the kitchen bent down confidentially. 'The gentleman at the table over there asks if he may join you for coffee,' he murmured. She looked up. The waiter had been careful not to point, but she saw a middle-aged man a few tables away, looking fixedly at her. She was about to automatically refuse when it occurred to her that this might be the contact promised by Constanze. She nodded. 'All right.'

The man came over and bowed formally to her. 'Dr Markus Kurz.'

'Agnes Tolliver.'

'How do you do?' He took the chair opposite her. He was wearing a dark suit and a grey silk tie that matched his silky grey hair. She estimated his age at around sixty.

'Are you a doctor of medicine?' she asked.

'Organic chemistry,' he replied, unsmiling. 'And you, I am told, are a journalist?'

'Not at present. I've resigned from my job.'

'*Ach so*. Then you are not in Berlin for journalistic reasons?'

'I'm here for family reasons.'

'That would be much better. If you are here for journalistic reasons, then you must tell me the truth.' His voice was as silky as his hair and tie. 'If you are looking for a sensational story, you will not be welcomed.'

Her heart was beating faster. 'I'm not here to write about anybody, Dr Kurz. I'm here to find out whether my sister is alive.'

'*Ja, ja*, good, good.' He raised an eyebrow to summon the waiter. 'You will join me in a coffee? Perhaps a *digestif*?'

She deemed it polite to accept. 'Thank you.'

The digestif came in two small glasses, and was heavily flavoured with caraway. '*Kümmel schnapps*,' Dr Kurz said, smacking his lips after he'd tossed it off. 'Very beneficial after a restaurant meal.'

'As an organic chemist, you would know.'

He did not catch her light irony. 'Oh yes, I can vouch for this,' he said seriously. He lit a cigarette. Germans smoked a lot, she reflected. The upper air in the restaurant was wreathed in blue smoke. He leaned forward, lowering his voice. 'Forgive me for insisting. I must be certain that you have no intention of writing about your visit to Berlin. This could be very dangerous. Both for the persons involved . . .' – he met her eyes coldly – 'and for yourself.'

'You don't need to threaten me, Dr Kurz. I have no intention of making anything public. I'm looking for information for myself.'

'May I ask, are you a Jewess?'

'No.'

'No Jewish blood?'

'If you know anything about me, Dr Kurz,' she said dryly, 'then you must know that I come from pure Aryan stock.'

'So we hear. Is it true?'

'Yes.'

Despite his silvery hair, his eyebrows were very dark, and somewhat satanic. His hooded eyes searched her face from under them. He nodded at last. 'I hope we understand each other.'

She was tired of the rigmarole. 'I hope so. Now, can you give me the information I need?'

'I will give you a time and an address. I want you to understand that nobody lives at this address. It is only a meeting place. There you will find the person who can help you.' He raised a warning finger. 'Tell no one where you are going. And check that you are not followed. Use a taxi. After he has delivered you, send him away. He must not wait. You understand? This is how we operate.' He rose and made her another little bow. 'You will find the details in your room. Good night, Fräulein Tolliver.'

Before she could ask any more questions, he was already walking away.

She signed for the meal and hurried up to her room. But there was no sign of any message. Tense and disappointed, she sat in front of the television set, watching the news on *Deutsche Welle*. It was largely about the day's protests in Berlin, which had turned violent in parts of the city. Batons and tear gas had been brought out. Several young people, either unconscious or deploying passive resistance, were carried limply to police vans.

Depressed, she got ready for bed. Then she noticed the slip of paper that had appeared under her door somehow, without her hearing anything. She picked it up. The address meant nothing to her, but there was a time and a date: four o'clock in the afternoon the next day.

She called Constanze again. 'I've got an appointment.'

'I told you that you would be given one,' Constanze said smugly.

'A man came to my table. He was rather threatening.'

'Of course. That is how they stay safe. They do not play games, my dear. And neither should you. Do exactly what they tell you, and everything will be fine.'

\* \* \*

Obediently, she got into a taxi that passed in front of the hotel the next afternoon. She gave the driver the address. He nodded and set off without speaking. He was foreign, a *Gastarbeiter*, probably Turkish. She looked out of the window at the city. From a building, a banner crudely signed *Jetzt ist der Teufel los* fluttered in the mizzling rain that continued to fall. It struck her as a rather sinister omen – 'Now the Devil has been let loose.'

It was a long drive, and the route took them into an industrial area. It was not merely drab; many of the buildings still bore the scars of war, brick walls pockmarked with bullet holes, in some cases, just ruins. This was a part of Greater Berlin that had not yet been rebuilt, and had the air that it never would be.

At length, the taxi arrived at a large factory block. It was one of those structures that had been damaged in the war, and it appeared deserted, the windows bricked up.

'Are you sure this is the place?' she asked the driver.

'Sure,' he replied, peering at the brooding grey walls. 'Maybe I wait for you? No taxis here.'

'It's okay,' she said, remembering her instructions. 'But thank you.'

She paid him, and watched him drive away, her heart filled with misgivings. The street was empty.

Huddled in her mackintosh and carrying her briefcase, she picked her way cautiously to the entrance. Yellow tape was tied along the fence, the printing on it faded and all but illegible, no doubt warning of an unstable structure. A rusty iron gate blocked the way, but it wasn't locked. Heaving it with all her strength, Agnes managed to get it just wide enough to squeeze through. Beyond was a metal rolling door, severely dented by explosions. It, too, was open just wide enough to admit her. She entered the dark, echoing space.

Machines hulked in the gloom. They had been stripped of anything removable, and were just carcases, evidently unused for decades.

'Is anybody there?' she called. Only the echo of her own voice and a faint flutter of wings answered her.

The floor was littered with rubbish. She picked her way deeper into the structure, passing what must once have been a production line where workers assembled some industrial product on long benches. Cobwebs hung in festoons from hoists and lifts.

Immense pipes led from one section to the next. She had to duck under them to keep going forward. A few birds, or perhaps they were bats, fussed among the roof trusses, disturbed by her approach.

At last, the chambers opened out into a wide, empty space that was bare of all equipment. The darkness was lit by a large hole, high up in the roof. In the shaft of watery, grey light that came down was a man in a felt hat and a long raincoat. He was standing next to a big, dull metal tank, like a boiler, that was half-buried in the floor.

'Hello?' she called uneasily.

He looked over his shoulder, revealing a thin, bony face. 'Come.'

She approached him. He appeared to be in his fifties, tall and lean, standing with military uprightness, his hands behind his back. 'I'm Agnes Tolliver,' she said.

'You may call me Baldur.' It was a thin-lipped, ascetic face with a curved nose and sharp cheekbones. His eyes surveyed her coldly from the shade of his hat's brim. He didn't offer his hand. 'You claim to be the daughter of Ulrich von Breda?' he said without preamble.

'That's what I've been told.'

'Show me,' he commanded.

She'd been emphatically instructed by Constanze to bring

her documents with her to Berlin – the originals, not under any circumstances copies. She took them out of her briefcase and handed them to him. He held them up to the light, checking the quality of the paper. 'There is no watermark,' he said curtly. 'Authentic Lebensborn documents have a watermark.'

'Those papers have been in a lawyer's safe since 1945,' she retorted. 'They came directly from my mother. There's no chance that they could be forgeries, watermark or no watermark.'

'You defend the documents with vigour,' he commented sourly. 'Are you so eager to be the daughter of Ulrich von Breda?'

'No,' she replied shortly. 'I would be far happier if I'd never found those documents. But I did find them. And now, I just want the truth.'

He grunted. 'In the last year of the war, luxuries such as handmade paper were dispensed with.' He handed them back to her. 'Your documents are in order.'

'Then can you tell me what I want to know?' Agnes demanded.

'That depends upon what you want to know.' His voice was clipped, his German accent sharply pronounced. 'Knowledge can be dangerous.' He indicated the huge metal cylinder half-buried at their feet. 'Take this object, for instance.'

'What is it?' she asked.

'A ten-thousand-kilogram bomb.'

Agnes's skin went cold. She took an involuntary step back. 'Are you serious?'

'Oh, yes.' He pointed a finger at the hole in the roof up above them. 'Dropped by a specially strengthened RAF Lancaster in February, 1945. The British called them "earthquake bombs". They were designed to bury themselves in the ground and to collapse everything for hundreds of metres around them when they exploded. Nothing more powerful was known until Hiroshima.'

'Can it still explode?' Agnes asked, suddenly dry-mouthed.

'Yes, at any moment.'

'You should tell the bomb disposal people!'

'If I do, they will detonate it with a controlled explosion,' he replied. 'That will be the end of this structure, which was built by my father when I was a child. The bomb reminds me of him. It makes me feel that he is still alive in some way, just sleeping in the ground. I like having it here.'

'You're mad.'

'I have been told so.' He cocked his head at her with sly irony. 'Are you afraid?'

She'd been about to beg him to move away from the horrible thing, but it suddenly occurred to her that this was some kind of test – of her courage, or her resolution. 'No,' she said flatly. 'I'm not afraid.'

'Why not? Are you suicidal?'

'It's been here for more than twenty years. And if it chooses to explode now, neither of us will know anything about it.'

Baldur kicked the dull steel casing with the toe of his boot. Agnes didn't flinch. 'The Allies dropped over a million tons of bombs on Germany,' he said in a calm voice. 'Ten per cent of those failed to detonate. Every year, thousands of tons of unexploded munitions are dug up from German soil. Before any construction project begins in our country, whether it is for a skyscraper or a family porch, the ground must be surveyed and certified as cleared of unexploded ordnance.'

'Germany started the war.'

He ignored that, staring at the bomb. 'Germany is asleep. Like this bomb. You saw the young longhairs throwing stones on the television?'

'Yes.'

'They are paid by Moscow to promote communism. And the fat poltroons who now run Germany allow them to spread their poison unopposed.'

'Not exactly unopposed,' Agnes said, reluctantly drawn into the man's diatribe. 'The police arrested a lot of them.'

'Those are not *police*,' he retorted. 'They are packets of lard in uniform. Soft. And the agitators will be out of their cells by teatime, freed by their Jew lawyers. But like this bomb, Germany can come to life again. It is our task to stand guard until the moment is ripe.'

The man was even crazier than she had thought. She forced herself to stay on track. 'I was told you could give me information about my sister. Whether she's alive or dead.'

'Why should I be in possession of such information?'

'Constanze Ozerki told me you know everything that happens in East Berlin.'

He showed a gleam of pride. 'We have agents on the other side of the Wall, yes. Men loyal to Germany, the real Germany. We have penetrated their organisations. The communists are not supermen.'

'Then can you tell me whether she's alive?'

His pale eyes turned back to her. 'Your sister is alive.'

Agnes's heart jolted. She forgot all about the huge bomb under their feet. 'Is that true?' she gasped.

'They gave her a new name. One of the most commonplace names in Germany. To take away her individuality, of course. She is called Karolina Schmidt.'

Agnes was breathless. 'Where is she?'

'A few kilometres from where you stand. On the other side of the Wall.'

She had started trembling. She couldn't help it. 'Have you got an address?'

'It will be sent to you before you leave Berlin.'

She forced herself to remain calm, keep still, not raise her voice. 'I've come a long way, Herr Baldur. *I need her address.*'

He held up his hand to silence her. 'You are not in a position to make demands,' he said icily. 'I repeat – it will be sent to you before you leave Berlin. You need not concern yourself with anything more.'

Was he just saying this to get rid of her? Was there any truth in it? She wanted so desperately to believe; but how could she trust anything that came out of the mouth of this self-proclaimed Nazi? If the Devil gave you an assurance, what was it worth?

'I *am* concerned,' she said. 'I can't help being concerned. Surely you must understand that?'

'For a third time, I repeat – you will receive the information before you leave Berlin.'

She had no choice but to accept that, and pray that it wasn't a cruel lie. 'There's something more,' she said tersely. 'My father. Do you know where he is now?'

His face was forbidding. 'Why do you ask this?'

'I want to meet him.'

'You will never meet him. You are nothing to him.'

'But he is something to me. Tell him I want to speak to him.'

'I have no communication with him.'

'I don't believe you. If you are ex-SS, then you'll know where he is. And you probably contacted him before I was told to come to Berlin.'

His eyes narrowed. 'You are very sure of yourself.'

'I'm just not a fool, Herr Baldur. He knows who I am, doesn't he?'

'He shares the opinion we all have of your generation. You are weak. Pampered. Overindulged. You have never had to fight for anything since your birth, but you are ready to spit on your parents because you think we did everything wrong.'

Agnes was angered. 'It sounds as though you have a very bad relationship with your own children.'

'The man you call your father does not regard you as his daughter.'

'It doesn't matter what he thinks. I *am* his daughter, whether he likes it or not. And so is my sister. He fathered us deliberately. It was not an accident. He intended to bring us into the world. We're his blood. Isn't that what you people care about most? *Blood?* Good, Aryan blood?'

'You talk of sharing his blood, but you do not even speak German. You are British. And it was the British who kept von Breda on death row for fifteen years, punishing him for actions which your people and the Americans allowed yourselves in the name of war.'

'He can't refuse to help us,' Agnes said obstinately, 'at least once.'

His eyes were hard. 'What are you talking about?'

'Your organisation is active on the other side of the Wall, you've just told me that. If you have the resources you claim to have, you could get Karolina out.'

'You are mad.'

'Ask Ulrich von Breda,' Agnes said sharply. 'Ask him to help me get his daughter to the West.'

'There is nothing he or you can do for your sister,' Baldur said grimly. 'The communists will never let her go. They do not forget and they do not forgive. Be content knowing that she is alive. It's the best you can do.'

'I think you underestimate my generation,' Agnes said. 'You certainly underestimate *me*.'

'I doubt it,' he retorted. He looked at his watch. 'It is time for you to leave. A car is waiting for you outside the factory. It will take you to your hotel.'

'Tell him I'm prepared to do anything. Tell him that even if he cares nothing for us, it will be a blow against the communists.'

'Enough,' he snapped. 'Great risks have already been taken on your behalf, Fräulein. Great efforts have been made. A network has been compromised to satisfy your curiosity. What has been done, has been done to oblige those who asked on your behalf. Not for you. Be warned – if you speak one word of this to anyone, if you put any of us in danger, you will pay a heavy price. Now go.'

There was no point in outstaying her welcome. 'I'll wait to hear from you, Herr Baldur.'

She didn't get a reply. She turned and walked away, leaving the man and his unexploded bomb. She looked back once, just before exiting the huge, empty chamber. Baldur was still standing in the shaft of light, staring after her. She couldn't see his expression.

The car waiting outside was driven by an elderly man who neither looked at her nor spoke to her on the way back to the hotel. The rain was clearing. In the gaps, blue sky could be seen. The edges of the clouds were dazzling white, appearing almost solid.

Her name was Karolina Schmidt.

And she was alive.

She played her conversation with Baldur back in her mind. She had planned it so carefully, had painstakingly rehearsed what she would say – but it hadn't turned out the way she'd hoped. Not at all. Had she said the right things? Would he really pass the message on to her father – a man who avowedly cared nothing for her? A notorious war criminal, a Nazi? A ghost?

She didn't have the answer yet. But she knew that Ulrich von Breda was the key to getting her sister out of East Berlin, and that she would not rest until she had achieved that.

There was an ominous ache in her belly. Yet again, she had offered to make a deal with the Devil. She had put herself on the line. Whether the Devil accepted or not, she stood to lose her soul.

But perhaps she had lost her soul already.

Her world had been shattered. War, politics and ideology had dislocated everything she had thought true, and had scattered all the pieces across Europe. It was a jigsaw she was determined to reassemble.

And first, she had to find Karolina Schmidt.

# CHAPTER THIRTEEN

# KAROLINA

*East Berlin, 1968*

'Do you remember how you cried when I told you there was a place for you in the new Germany?'

Twenty years had not changed Herr Bergmann much. The close-cropped hair around his ruined skull was whiter. And the remnant of an eyeball in the deep socket, which had once gleamed red, was now a dead grey coal. But there was no glass eye to take its place, and the dingy suit and grubby coat that hung on his gaunt frame might have been the same ones she saw in 1947.

He had even adopted the same position, perched on a desk in front of the chair where she sat, looking down at her through steel-rimmed glasses.

'You cried as though you would never stop,' he went on conversationally. 'We'd seen many orphans, but you were the most degraded of them all. Starved almost to death, smelling of rotten garbage. But it wasn't just your papers which made you different. Do you remember the KGB officer who wanted to send you to a labour camp in Siberia? But I said, "No". I said, "I can make something of this child. I see something special in her". Do you remember?'

'Yes,' Karolina muttered.

'I remember it as though it were yesterday.' He laced his mutilated fingers around one bony knee. 'I remember placing you in the newest of the orphanages. I remember telling the teachers to give you special attention, extra lessons, extra food. "This one is special," I told them. And they treated you well, didn't they?'

'Yes.'

'We gave you a new name. A new life. We planted the acorn, and waited for the oak to grow. Your supervisors sent me a report on your progress every year. I read each one carefully. And sometimes I would come to watch you – in the classroom, in the gymnasium, in the swimming pool. Perhaps you didn't notice me.'

'I saw you.'

He nodded. 'You have eyes like a hawk, don't you, Karolina? The instincts of a wolf.'

His voice was quiet as always. But she knew that Herr Bergmann had become a powerful man over the last twenty-one years. His presence here, on the top floor of this vast Stasi complex in Berlin-Lichtenberg, known with universal dread after its street address simply as 'Normannenstrasse,' was proof of that. Quiet as he was, there was a remorseless quality in his calmness, and she knew that he could extinguish her life with a word.

'You grew into a beautiful young woman,' he went on. 'An athlete, a fine student, a brilliant linguist. As I knew you would. Nobody would recognise you as the filthy waif who was begging for scraps in 1947.'

'I worked hard,' she said defiantly.

'Oh yes, I know you did. But something, somewhere, went wrong. Didn't it? I had great plans for you. But the reports took a strange turn. "Karolina shows signs of aggression towards her teachers. Karolina is becoming antisocial in her behaviour. Karolina takes vodka into the classroom. Karolina listens to decadent Western music. Karolina is hostile towards the apparatus of the State." Do you know what I replied?'

Karolina shook her head silently.

'I said, "Leave her be. She is a young wolf. Young wolves bite and snap at the adults. But they grow up. Let her run with the other young wolves. She will return.'''

Herr Bergmann hoisted himself off the desk and limped to the window. The room overlooked a courtyard far below, certainly a fatal fall should Herr Bergmann ever choose to throw himself out. But the window was securely barred against any such attempt.

'Then,' he said, looking at the grey sky, 'when you started at the university they told me you were mixing with dissidents. Showing contempt for the rules of the socialist state. Taking drugs. And at last, they brought me the inevitable news. "Karolina has tried to escape to the West. She actually reached the Death Strip itself before any of the guards spotted her." I didn't know whether to be proud or angry. In fact, I was both. Proud of my protégée for running circles around the oafish guards. Angry that she had shown such lamentable lack of judgement.

'I had to take a decision: to protect you yet again, or let the judicial system deal with you. I could have saved you from Stauberg. But that would have been the wrong decision. It would have given you the idea that you were free to do what you wanted.' He looked over his shoulder at her with his one good eye. 'And you are not free to do what you want, Karolina. Frau Hedwig made that clear, didn't she?'

'Yes,' Karolina said wearily, remembering the hard palm slamming across her mouth.

'You betrayed us. What do we do to people who betray us?'

'You crush them,' she said in a low voice.

'Yes,' he said calmly. 'But I did not want you crushed. You needed a lesson. I wanted you punished. But not broken. Because I still believed in you. They wanted to sentence you to twelve years in Stauberg. I said, three will be enough. When you were released, they said, now ten years in a factory. I said, five. They were very angry.'

There was no doubt who *they* were. Karolina glanced up at the bear-like face of Leonid Brezhnev, the Russian leader, who glowered from the official portrait over Bergmann's desk. Bergmann nodded. 'No doubt you listened to Comrade Brezhnev's speech at the Warsaw Pact meeting?'

'I am not allowed a radio or a television,' Karolina replied dryly.

'A pity. He spoke of the international responsibilities of socialist countries. He reminded us that all Warsaw Pact countries have an obligation to defend socialist gains. Do you understand what that means? It means that three weeks ago, Russian tanks rolled into Prague and occupied Czecho-slovakia because a handful of students put on miniskirts and began talking about freedom. You heard about *that*, I am sure.'

'Yes.'

'We do not want to see Russian tanks rolling down Unter den Linden.' He came away from the window. 'The Russians do not trust us fully. Not after five years of war, in which millions died on both sides. Not after we starved them in Stalingrad. They watch us constantly. Why do I remind you of all this? Because on that day in 1947, when I saved you from being sent to a gulag, I made a commitment to the Russians – that I could turn you, a daughter of Nazis, into a loyal communist. Do you understand?'

She was sullen. '*You* made the commitment, not me.'

'But you are a test case,' he snapped, with sudden sharp-ness. 'You are the proof that a German can be trusted. The proof that we can behave decently without a gun pointed at our heads.'

'I don't do any harm. I just want to be left alone.'

He was angry now behind the cold façade. 'You are too old to be spouting teenage clichés like *I want to be left alone*. You've been thrown into the garbage can of history, which is precisely where I found you in 1947. Look at me, Karolina!'

Reluctantly, Karolina raised her eyes to Bergmann's ravaged face.

'Do you know what is done to human beings in the basements of this building?' he demanded. 'The same things the Nazis did to me. Every day I wake up in pain. Is that what you want for yourself? Don't you know what your life can be like? You can have it all. Leisure, books, a nice apartment, a radio, a television. A place among the elite of our society. You can even travel to the West. A different life! A future!'

'By turning myself into a prostitute?'

'By serving the State,' he said with a steely note. 'We are all called upon to serve in different ways. You might have had a glittering career, once. If you had only learned discipline. This is what you have left. And believe me, you are lucky to have it. Very lucky. Seize this opportunity with both hands. It's your lifebelt.'

He must have touched some electric bell, because the door of the office opened, and Hedwig came in. Her thickset body was encased in a tight suit. The square-heeled shoes and the grotesque beehive hairdo were clearly designed to give her height. But she didn't need it. Her aura of menacing authority was palpable.

'Yes, Herr Bergmann?'

'I think Karolina is ready to start her training.'

'Yes, Herr Bergmann.'

'Perhaps we can begin with the preliminary introduction.'

'Of course.' Hedwig turned to Karolina and snapped her fingers. 'Come.'

The projection room was small and dark. It had a strange smell, of stale cigarette smoke and unclean bodies, which seemed to emanate from the shabby cushions on the chairs. The projectionist was a wizened old man in a brown coat. Karolina was put in front of the screen. Hedwig sat behind her. Hedwig's heavy perfume mingled with the grimy odour of the seats to produce an unpleasant mixture of enforced intimacy.

The projector whirred into life. Flickering numbers on the screen turned into a grainy colour film of a couple on a bed in what looked like an expensive hotel room in the West. Both were naked.

The woman was young, her smooth body endowed with ample curves. The man was much older, his limbs skinny, his head bald. He was having difficulty with the sex act. The woman was encouraging him with startlingly explicit murmurs which were faithfully recorded on the soundtrack. She was speaking English.

'The microphones are in the bedside lamps,' Hedwig said behind Karolina. 'The cameras are in the ceiling light and the television.'

The cameras were pitiless, shameless. They spared no detail, missed no salacious angle. Karolina could not watch the spectacle. She dropped her eyes to the blank notebook and pencil Hedwig had given her.

Hedwig's strong fingers and thumb bit into her neck. 'What, are you, the Virgin Mary? *Look*,' she commanded harshly.

Karolina forced herself to obey. The scene was completely without eroticism, like the crudest kind of pornography. But it was replete with ugliness.

After it was over, they lay together, the woman pillowing her partner's head on her breast. The camera, evidently operated remotely, zoomed in on their faces. The woman stroked his sweaty cheek. He was breathless. The soundtrack was clear and loud:

*Do I ask too much from you, my love?*

*No, no. I'm just not as young as I was.*

*Oh, darling, nonsense. You are a bull! My bull! I dream of these moments, when you fill me so completely. Are you like this with your wife?*

*You must be joking. My wife's cold as ice. She doesn't have what you've got, baby. We sleep in separate bedrooms. If she wasn't my boss's cousin, I'd have divorced her years ago. You know that.*

*But you're tense today. I can feel it.*

*Maybe a little.*

*Let me get you a drink. You've earned it.*

*You're an angel.*

The camera zoomed out to follow her as she went to the cocktail cabinet. While her back was turned, the man glanced at his watch and sat up, arranging the pillows. He appeared pleased with himself. She returned with two drinks and two lit cigarettes. She slid into the bed beside him. He gulped gratefully at the drink and inhaled deeply on the cigarette. She resumed the conversation casually.

*Is work still so stressful? Is that why you're tense?*

*The East Germans are tough negotiators. They don't give an inch.*

*But you're tough, too, darling.*

*I'd like to be. But Harold is so spineless. He's prepared to bend over backwards. He'll give them everything they want to secure the deal. All the specifications, early delivery, easy payment terms. Everything. I wish he'd just get out of the way and let me do my job.*

*Poor darling. So frustrating.*

*I can't even complain to my wife, because the fat cow tells him every word I say. I can't talk to anybody.*

*You can always talk to me.*

*This is boring stuff for you, kid.*

*Not at all! I find everything you say so fascinating!*

The man rambled on for a few minutes, talking about the product he was marketing, encouraged by the woman, who murmured sympathetically, asking just enough questions to keep him talking.

At last the man looked at his watch again.

*Got to go, sweetie. I was due back at the office half an hour ago.*

*Just once more, darling. Please. For me.*

*I'm late as it is. Anyway, I don't think I can manage.*

*I bet you can.*

Karolina tried not to watch as the woman serviced him, moaning and pretending to enjoy the act. But it was hard to look away when Hedwig's fingers once again clamped around the back of her neck.

At length it was done. The man dressed quickly and left the hotel room. The young woman lay on the bed for a while, stretching. Then she got up and went to the bathroom, where she could be seen brushing her teeth. The film clattered to an end. The old man in the brown coat turned up the room lights.

Hedwig came round to sit opposite Karolina. Karolina could still feel the pressure of the other woman's fingers on her neck. 'Did you find that arousing?'

'No,' Karolina said tightly.

Hedwig glared. 'I told you not to play the plaster virgin with me. Do you think your whore mother didn't do the same thing? Tell the truth. Did you find it sexy?'

'No.'

'I did. I always find it arousing to watch others make love.

No matter who they are. Soon, I will be watching you on a bed just like that one. I will enjoy that very much, Fräulein Schmidt.'

Karolina said nothing, trying to hide her nausea.

Hedwig lit a cigarette. She had applied so much of the dark lipstick she favoured that her lips clung to the filter. 'So. What did you learn from that little home movie?'

'Nothing.'

'Try harder,' Hedwig said, narrowing her hard, black eyes threateningly.

'I learned that your agent is a bad actress.'

'Very good,' Hedwig replied. 'Then you will be able to do much better in her place. I will hold you to that, little Nazi. What else?'

'The man must know she's just pretending.'

'You think so?'

'She was so crude.'

'You think he was a sophisticated man?'

'Of course not. He was a pig.'

'Then she matched his expectations.' Hedwig blew smoke into Karolina's face. 'More.'

Karolina forced herself to speak. 'It was a lot of effort to get a few details of a business transaction.'

'The transaction is not the important thing. The film itself is the prize. What would happen to that pig of a man if the film – or even a few stills from it – were to be sent to his wife? His boss? A Western gossip magazine? He would be destroyed. When he is shown the evidence, he will understand that. So that old man is ours for life. You understand?'

Karolina grimaced. 'Yes.'

'And that girl is Irina, one of our best Juliets. You can learn a lot from her, believe me. We will watch the film again shortly. This time, you will take notes in your little book. You will use these notes to write a report for me. This time, you will notice everything Agent Irina does. With her body, with her mind. You will miss nothing. You will observe how careful the agent is to flatter the target, to praise his manhood, even though he is obviously a sexual weakling. You will observe how sympathetic she is to his selfish complaints. How delicately she gets him to talk about his work, without awakening his suspicions in any way. You will notice the perfect balance she maintains between the roles of mother and whore. These are the two roles you will learn to combine. Mother and whore.'

'I'll take notes,' Karolina said dryly.

'Don't use that insolent tone to me.' Hedwig reached out and pinched Karolina's inner thigh hard enough to make her gasp. She had the cruel fingers of a provincial schoolmistress. She studied Karolina with a sharp gaze. 'You're pretty enough,' she said grudgingly, 'if you get rid of that sour expression. It makes you look like a bowl of curdled cream. And you speak languages. How many?'

'English, French and Russian.'

'Oh la la. What a little genius. Let's see if you can learn how to fuck.' She snapped her fingers at the silent old man, who had been rewinding the reel. 'Again.'

It was evening by the time Karolina reached her apartment block. The sun had just set, leaving the sky lurid. She was exhausted, still nauseated. It had been a day of gritting her teeth, while being forced to study a new pseudo-science invented by the Stasi, the psychology of seduction. The corruption of married men began with small things, apparently, designed to indicate that you were sexually available. How to dress (not too slutty), how to sit in a bar (a dangled shoe on one foot was a potent symbol), how to smoke (women who smoked were considered by men to be more available), a catalogue of enticements. She'd found it absurd, but utterly crushing in its banality.

And this week had been the thin end of the wedge that was being driven into her soul. The week to come would be far worse. They called it 'conditioning'. It meant accustoming her mind to what it was going to have to endure.

She desperately wanted a shower to wash away what she had seen at Normannenstrasse, and by this time the swimming pool was closed.

She took the single towel she owned, and went as quietly as she could to the bathroom. The section was in darkness. All the lights in the corridors and ablution area were off. There were frequent electrical problems in this building, despite its newness: it had been built so carelessly that it was already starting to fall apart.

But to her intense relief, the bathroom was empty. There were usually a couple of dubious men hanging around hoping for an eyeful of a female body, and something more, if they could get it.

She stripped naked, and slipped into the shower cubicle. She turned the taps, but no water came out. She cursed in despair.

It was then that they grabbed her.

There were two of them. They were strong, experienced. They dragged her out of the shower cubicle and slammed her against the tiled wall, cracking her head and rattling her teeth.

One had a flashlight. He played the beam over her nakedness and whistled.

'There was more than meets the eye, eh? Not bad!'

The gleam of the flashlight reflected from the tiled walls lit their faces in a ghostly glow. She saw who they were: the two Stasi men who had confiscated her apples and her copy of *Buddenbrooks*.

'What do you want?' she asked shakily.

'We're here to help you, Juliet,' one said. It was the thinner of the two.

The fatter one laughed. 'Yes. We're here to give you a little practice for your new job. Did they teach you any new tricks at Normannenstrasse today? You can show them to us.'

'We'll tell you how well you've learned them,' the thin one grinned. He was unbuttoning his trousers. 'We're good judges. Call it an object lesson. For free.'

Karolina let her body go completely limp. She sagged like a broken marionette. The fatter man, who had been holding her by one arm and her throat, was taken by surprise. 'Shit,' he muttered, trying to hold her up.

She tensed and swung her free arm, driving her fist into the fat man's nose. He reeled back, blood instantly bubbling at his nostrils. She swung her fist again at the thin man, but he jumped back out of her reach. 'You little snake,' he grunted. 'You'll regret that.'

He moved in on her, clawed hands held at shoulder height, wrestler style, ready to grapple. Karolina was panting for breath already, her heart pounding in her ears. The thin man lunged at her. She managed to twist away and evade him. If she could just get to the bathroom door and out into the corridor, she could outrun them, naked as she was.

But the fat man's nose had already started to pour, and her bare feet slipped in a splash of warm blood on the tiles. She lost her balance. A strong hand clamped on her wrist, jerking her around, forcing her arm up her back, making her scream in pain. She had taken them by surprise for a moment, but she didn't stand a chance any longer.

'How do you want to do this?' the thin man asked his partner.

The fat man was trying to staunch the blood pouring down his face. 'Hold her still,' he bubbled. 'She broke my nose. I'm going to break hers. Then she's ours all night.' He groped at her body clumsily.

She fought with silent ferocity, trying to kick at them with her heels. But they were Stasi, trained to do this. They crowded her against a basin, pushing her back over it until she thought her spine would break. A knee thrust between her thighs, forcing them apart.

*No*, she thought in a silent scream. *Not this.*

The lights suddenly came on, dazzling them all. 'That's enough.'

The two men whipped round. Someone had come into the bathroom, a broad, stocky figure. It was old Herr Möller, the handyman.

'Let her go,' he said in his rasping voice.

'Fuck off, Opa,' the thin Stasi man said furiously, 'or you'll get hurt. This is none of your business.'

'Yes?' Herr Möller lifted something. He was holding his spade, the one he used at his allotment. 'Let her go and get out.'

'You're making a big mistake,' the fat man said thickly. But he was eyeing the spade cautiously.

'No mistake,' the old man said contemptuously. 'I'm not afraid of the likes of you bastards. I was killing Russians when you two slobs were shitting in your diapers.' He hefted the spade like an axe. 'One more warning. Then you'll both leave without heads.'

There was no question that the old man meant what he said. He was a formidable opponent, and Karolina suddenly realised that although she'd always thought of him as 'old Herr Möller', he was probably not yet sixty. And that the oddly shaped spade he invariably carried was a military entrenching tool, the blade shiny and sharp with use.

The Stasi agents sullenly let Karolina go. They edged warily around Herr Möller. 'We'll be back to settle this,' one of them spat.

'No, you won't,' Karolina panted, 'because the first thing I'm going to do tomorrow morning is report this to Herr Bergmann. You're both finished.'

The threat made the two men flinch. The fat one wiped blood off his lips. 'It was only a bit of fun, you crazy bitch,' he muttered. 'We wouldn't have done anything to you.'

'Get out,' Herr Möller said tersely. 'Don't let me see you around here again.'

'Keep your hair on, Opa.' But they slunk out. Herr Möller didn't lower the spade until they heard a car start in the street outside, and drive away into the night.

He put the weapon down. The experience had left him as unmoved as if he'd stepped on a couple of beetles. He didn't look at her nakedness. 'You all right?' he asked.

She nodded, suddenly drained. 'Thank you, Herr Möller.'

'I was in the Brandenburgers during the war,' he grunted. 'I've always hated communists.' He found the stopcock on the wall, and twisted it back on. The shower burst into life, making damp clouds of steam. Hot water was one of the few compensations for living in East Berlin. 'Have your shower, *Mädchen*. I'll stand guard outside.'

She nodded, too close to tears to risk saying anything more.

When he'd left, she stumbled back into the shower cubicle, and tried to wash herself. She was almost too shaken to manage. The assault had stirred up terrible memories from her earliest childhood. Monsters that she dared not name were awakening in her deep memories, filling her with terror. When that dark sediment was stirred, she faced the despairing question: why was her life like this? What had she done wrong?

She tried to let the hot water soothe away the horrors of the day.

The Stasi hoodlums who'd attacked her had known that she was being enrolled as a Juliet. Someone had been careful to tell them. And the same someone had urged them to come round and casually rape her. They would never have dared interfere with one of Bergmann's protégées unless encouraged by a powerful someone.

There wasn't much doubt in her mind as to who that someone was: the woman who enjoyed mauling her physically, who called her *das kleine Nazi-Mädchen* or *Die Jungfrau Maria*, who took pleasure in humiliating her in any way possible. Hedwig.

She had threatened to report the attack to Bergmann, but she knew it would do no good. He had judged her a failure. She would never win back his respect. He no longer saw her as a protégée. That was gone forever.

And the next time the Stasi came round, Herr Möller would not be there with his spade. She had no way of defending herself.

When she got back to her room, she felt emptier than she had felt since prison. How long could she continue to live like this? They had done their best to break her. She hadn't broken yet, but she had come close. Too close.

Was it worth going on? Behind her lay years of pain and misery. Ahead of her lay years of degradation. Rafael's picture of her eventually retiring to some quiet town in ten years, where she would have a quiet life, a quiet job and 'a couple of kids' was a vacuous lie. If she survived the next ten years, she would be destroyed in body and mind.

Wasn't it better to end it all now?

She'd once read some philosopher who had said that there was only one door into life, but there were a thousand doors out. She could surely find one of them. She'd seen so much death, since early childhood. It no longer frightened her. Life was only worth clinging to if there was a modicum of hope for better things. A shred of dignity one could cling to. She no longer had those gleams of light. Wherever she looked, there was darkness.

She had made up her mind. She would start looking for one of those thousand doors out of life.

# CHAPTER FOURTEEN

# ULRICH

*Spain, 1968*

The man who had told Agnes Tolliver to call him Baldur drove slowly and carefully towards the old Spanish *masia*. His rental car, a white Renault 4, struggled on the rough, pot-holed farm track. Not for the first time, he cursed Ulrich von Breda for having chosen this part of rural Catalonia. There were far more accessible regions of Spain where a man could live a quiet life and be happy. But von Breda had his own way of doing things, and was as obstinate as a mule.

He reached the old stone farmhouse, which was set on a steep hillside, against a magnificent vista of the distant Pyrenees, which even in summer were inlaid with snow. Von Breda's dogs, two trained German Shepherd bitches, raced towards his car, barking fiercely. He got out cautiously, and allowed the animals to sniff him, checking him against their memories of who was allowed on the property and who wasn't. He was not fond of dogs. The SS-Junker School had given him a puppy to raise at the beginning of his training; two years later, to prove how effective the training had been, he'd been ordered to cut its throat before qualifying for a commission. Since then, he'd avoided forming bonds with dogs. But von Breda had no such qualms.

The dogs followed him, eyes watchful, tongues lolling, as he walked to the *masia*. Von Breda himself was at the side of the building, splitting logs with an axe. He had stripped to the waist. His lean, tanned torso looked like the body of a much younger man. Only his face bore the lines made by fifty-two years, and perhaps something more than time. He kept his hair cut very short. It was grizzled at the temples now. But the muscles of his arms and shoulders were smooth and quick as he brought the axe down on the log in front of him, splitting it easily despite its girth. There were already some three tons of wood, stacked with meticulous precision against the wall. It was a long, cold winter in these parts.

'Heil Hitler,' Baldur greeted von Breda.

'If you mention that swine's name to me again, I'll bury this axe in your head.'

So it was going to be one of those days. Baldur watched as von Breda split the halves into quarters. Finally, von Breda turned to look at his visitor with deep blue eyes. 'What is it this week? Odin? Loki?'

'Baldur.'

'If you used your own name, Gottfried, it would be less confusing.'

'You may call me what you choose.' Gottfried surveyed the denuded slopes around the *masia*. 'Soon you won't have a tree left around here.'

'I like a clear field of fire.' Von Breda stacked the wood he'd just cut, and carefully wiped the axe. 'And I don't like people creeping up on me.'

'Nobody is creeping up on you, Ulrich.'

'One of the dogs got sick three days ago.'

'You think it was poison? Maybe she just found a dead sheep.'

Von Breda dried the light sheen of sweat off his body with a rag, and pulled on his shirt. 'You want a beer?'

'After driving up this damned mountainside, yes.' As he followed von Breda into the house, he added, 'You should get a lad to help you with this sort of thing. If you hit your leg with that axe, you'd bleed to death, and nobody would find you for weeks.'

'At least the dogs would have something to eat,' von Breda replied laconically.

The interior of the *masia* was stark and neat. There was no attempt to soften the stone walls, just the bare necessities of von Breda's existence – a primitive kitchen, a few chairs, a rack of shotguns and hunting rifles, and of course, the chessboard by the window, with a game halfway in progress.

'As a matter of interest, Ulrich,' Gottfried asked, 'who do you play against?'

'Ghosts.'

'Do you win?'

'Invariably.' Von Breda took two bottles of Bock from the fridge and opened them. The men settled into armchairs opposite each other. They drank the dark beer in silence for a while, the dogs lying on the cool slate floor at their feet.

'I gave them a little help,' Gottfried said at last. 'I told the Englishwoman where to find her sister.'

Von Breda's anger was instantly ignited. 'Why the devil did you do that?' he demanded harshly.

'She would have found out anyway, sooner or later. And it seemed churlish to refuse such a simple request.'

'Sentimentality will get you killed,' von Breda said, pointing the neck of the bottle at Gottfried. It looked uncomfortably like the barrel of a gun. 'More importantly, it will get *me* killed.'

'Nobody knows where you are, Ulrich.'

'What about the supervisor in her building?'

'Möller? He watches over her like Cerberus. He'll never say a word.'

'Unless someone shoves a fistful of deutschmarks in his face. Or threatens to cut his balls off.'

'He's a Brandenburger. Tough as old boots.' Gottfried finished the bottle in a long swallow. 'She wants to meet you.'

'Which one?'

'The Britisher.'

'I hope you told her that was impossible,' von Breda said grimly.

'I'm still thirsty.' Gottfried swirled the lees in the bottle meaningfully.

'I'm not a waiter,' von Breda said, jerking his head in the direction of the fridge. 'Get it yourself.'

When Gottfried returned with a fresh bottle, he asked von Breda, 'Aren't you curious about them in any way?'

'No.'

'Strange. I detest my children, but I still like to know what they get up to.'

'I have no children.'

'That's disingenuous, if I may say so.'

'The difference between you and me,' von Breda said shortly, 'is that you have a television. I do not. So my brain is not addled by watching tele-romances.'

'She's not motivated by sentimentality.'

'By what, then?'

'She thinks we can get her sister out of the DDR.'

'"We?"'

'Our organisation.'

'You're mad.'

'She pointed out that it would be a blow against the communists. A small retaliation for what they've done to our fatherland.'

'The *children*, as you call them, can do it for themselves.

They don't need us. They can simply put the girl in the trunk of a car and drive out of Berlin.'

'And if they are caught?'

'It's not my concern,' von Breda said, his eyes glinting dangerously now. 'I trust you didn't give the Britisher any grounds to hope we would intercede?'

'I spoke as you told me to speak,' Gottfried retorted. 'I'm not soft-headed.'

'Sometimes I wonder.'

'Nevertheless,' Gottfried said reflectively, 'the Britisher has pluck. I couldn't help being impressed.'

'She is not by any chance pretty?' von Breda asked dryly.

'She is prettier than *you*.'

'The bar is not very high in my case.'

'She reminds me of you in other ways, however,' Gottfried said, looking at his comrade slyly.

Von Breda clenched his jaw ominously. 'In what ways would that be?'

'She's resourceful. Intelligent. Courageous.'

'And this is your pathetic attempt to flatter me?'

'Those are qualities you *once* had.' Von Breda's big hands were clenching and unclenching. Gottfried saw that they were strengthened and roughened with manual work, and reflected complacently that his own manicured ones were far more elegant. 'But now you are turning into an anchorite. Sour. Desiccated. With neither imagination nor emotions.'

'I can do without emotions, Gottfried. Of the past twenty-three years, I have spent fifteen in the shadow of the gallows. It's enough for me just to be alive. And to stay alive.'

Gottfried looked around. His bony face was contemptuous. 'This is not exactly life.'

'Compared to your luxury villa overlooking the yacht basin in Marbella, perhaps not. But let me tell you, it is still better than the death cell in Landsberg Prison.'

'Better to live one day as a lion than a hundred years as a sheep.'

Von Breda tensed in outrage. 'You quote Mussolini at me? That's worse than Heil Hitlering me. They lost the war for us, those amateur, meddling bastards, and wasted the lives of our comrades, and turned our achievements into shit.'

There was a long list of people whom Ulrich von Breda had never forgiven. It began with Adolf Hitler, whose interference in the running of the war he blamed for Germany's defeat; and year by year, it seemed to extend to the entire human race. 'Yes,' Gottfried said imperturbably. 'We know all that. But it's 1968, Ulrich.'

'I know what's going on in 1968!' von Breda snapped. 'Even if I don't have a television. Which seems to be more than you do. Franco is losing his grip on this country. Strutting little popinjay! Why isn't he in Hell with the other two swine?'

Gottfried shrugged. 'What can you do? Franco is a religious fanatic.'

'There are other kinds of fanatics in Spain, Gottfried. The communists are getting the upper hand. Students are marching, workers are striking. The Basques are murdering whomever they please. Even here in Catalonia, they're screaming for independence. The country is falling apart. The whole of Europe is falling apart, just as it did when you and I were in short pants.' Von Breda's voice was rising. 'The Reds tried to assassinate me in France, and then again in Portugal. And you want me to get involved in some crazy scheme that will inevitably expose me? Why don't you just take a shotgun off that rack and blow my head off?'

'I thought you could dispense with emotions,' Gottfried said ironically. 'Keep your temper, Ulrich.' He calmly drained his second bottle of Bock. But in truth, he was always afraid of Ulrich von Breda. Especially when the anger seized him. Then the man seemed to be about to erupt like a volcano. Everything around him vibrated, even the air. You felt the heat radiate from his soul.

During the war, von Breda had been famous for his cool exploits. But perhaps even then there had been rage, deep in the man's core. Perhaps that explained the things he'd done. The extraordinary military achievements. The killings. Perhaps in those days he'd been able to cloak the furnace with a mantle of ice. But fifteen years of waiting daily to be hanged had worn away the crust, leaving the hot core perilously close to the surface.

Not many Waffen-SS commanders had survived the war. Most of those who did had unobtrusively melted back into civilian life in Germany, Austria and other countries, slipping into well-paid business careers and raising families. Von Breda was not like these.

Of course, the war-crimes trial and the subsequent sentence had been hard on him. But even there, he had been lucky – considering the things he'd done. The reason that his execution had been delayed for so long was that the prosecutors had spent years searching for hard evidence of other massacres in Russia, France and Italy. That evidence had not been forthcoming, for the very good reason that it was all buried in the ground. The killing of the Americans in the Ardennes was the only one they'd been able to pin on him, and that was chiefly because there had been a survivor, an enlisted man who had given evidence at the trial. A single man's evidence; but clear as a bell, and given the requirements of the tribunal, more than enough to convict von Breda.

'Have you recovered your temper?' Gottfried enquired after a long silence. 'If you have, then listen to me. We need to do something about these daughters of yours. Because they're going to attempt an escape whether we help them or not. And if they get caught, which they will, your name will soon come out. And if that happens, people will remember your exploits. And they'll start looking for you again.'

Von Breda's fists clenched. The look he gave Gottfried was frankly terrifying. 'If you hadn't stuck your damned fingers in—' he said in a grating voice.

'Don't blame me,' Gottfried retorted. 'If you didn't want children, why did you have them?'

'Get out,' von Breda rasped. 'I've had enough of you.'

Gottfried knew that tone, and didn't hesitate. He stood up. 'I'll come back when you're in a better mood. Think about what I said, Ulrich. There isn't much time.'

Driving away from the *masia*, he half-expected a bullet from the hunting rifle to come through the rear window. They had once been friends, but those days were long gone. What they were now, he wasn't sure. Just men tied together by common sins, perhaps.

He would have to report this conversation, of course. Nobody would be pleased. Many in the organisation actively hated von Breda these days. It was not hard to see why. It wasn't just the anti-Hitler rants, which were blasphemy to most of them. It was more serious than that. He endangered them all.

But nor would they authorise assistance to the girls unless von Breda begged for it.

He managed to get out of sight of the old house without being shot, and within half an hour, he was on the road to Barcelona.

After the sound of Gottfried's car had faded away, von Breda sat immobile for a while, his mind churning. The dogs, sensing his mood, watched him cautiously, their noses between their paws on the slates. Then, in a swift movement, he surged to his feet and kicked the chessboard hard. The board split in half and the carefully laid schemes of Alekhine and Capablanca flew into the air, pawns, kings and queens spinning. The dogs leaped up, barking excitedly.

'Hold your tongues,' von Breda growled. They immediately fell silent, tails sweeping from side to side, their eyes intent on his face. He picked up his alpenstock and stamped off for a walk outside.

His land was steep. The compensation was panoramic views all around, essential for a fortress. He climbed uphill, because if they ever came for him, they would approach from above, not below. He liked to see things from his enemy's point of view. A stream ran through the property, close to the house, its deep bed all but lost in ferns. The dogs burrowed into the undergrowth to drink, then followed at his heels, mouths dripping. They did not gambol or deviate. They were unquestioningly devoted to their master.

He needed to purge the anger from his blood, or it would fester. Many things about Gottfried enraged him, not least the schoolboy conceit of adopting the names of old Germanic gods. As if *that* would shield his identity.

Von Breda slashed at the brushwood with his alpenstock. *These daughters of yours.* How dare Gottfried use that language to him? As if he was expected to be responsible for two bastards he had fathered in another life, another time, another world.

Damn him for his meddling. What right did he have to intercede?

Von Breda was a fit man, but the climb was very steep, and he moved fast; and after half an hour, he was panting, sweat stinging his eyes. He had reached the boundary of his property. He turned and looked across the valley. The air seemed to swim in the summer heat. From here, you could see all the way to the Mediterranean, a distant smear of cobalt. The dogs sat panting on either side of him. One licked his hand, and he stroked her ears absently. His anger had drained away.

'Good girls,' he said quietly. 'Good girls.' The dogs swept the ground with their tails, joyful to be back in favour.

He hadn't thought of Liv Christiansen for years. It was not a memory he wanted to revisit. His meetings with her had been interludes in war. And like all such interludes, they had entered deep into his heart. Too deeply and too painfully to want to examine the wound.

She had loved him in her mad way, he was sure of that. He had passed over his grandmother's funeral to be with her. Had that been mad love, too? Or simply lust? The desperate, Darwinian impulse to mate of a creature threatened with death?

He had never wanted children, had never thought of them. She had her own ludicrous ideas of perfecting the race and so forth.

The last time he'd seen her had been a few weeks before the Ardennes campaign. They'd rutted frantically at Jorundarholt, wanting to lose themselves in each other. She'd seemed oblivious to the fact that the war was lost. He hadn't wanted to disillusion her. Her bright dreams of a glorious Aryan future were in tatters, like the wings of a butterfly at the end of summer. And she didn't know it.

They had been everything to each other for a few brief days – barely knowing each other. They had become parents – barely knowing each other. How strange that he had not set eyes on either child they had produced. Strange, and yet fitting. What child would benefit from having him as a father? He would be nothing but a curse. A man sentenced to hang for war crimes. A member of an organisation, the SS, which would soon be declared criminal.

He had done frightful things, and he had not yet paid for what he had done.

Far better never to think of Liv, or of the lives they had brought into this world.

Far better to compose himself for death, alone. He had sought it often enough. One day, it would be handed to him free.

# CHAPTER FIFTEEN

# KAROLINA

*East Berlin, 1968*

The water at the high-diving board end of the pool was very deep. Karolina sank slowly towards the bottom, seeing the light grow bluer and darker. She let a stream of silver bubbles escape from between her lips, and watched them make their way to the surface, carrying with them her breath. Her life.

As she emptied her lungs, the negative buoyancy of her body increased. She descended more surely, no longer needing to propel herself. She reached the smooth white tiles at the bottom, and lay there, inert. High above her, the surface was a sheet of liquid platinum. On the other side was the world, with all its suffering. Down here, in the depths, it was just her. Alone.

The pressure of the water was powerful at this depth, hurting her ears, trying to crush her. All she had to do was open her mouth and draw in a great lungful.

She'd heard that doing that killed you surely and swiftly. Just a few seconds of pain, they said. The shock disabled your central nervous system. Your lungs stopped working in an instant.

Oxygen stopped being delivered to the heart, the brain. Your body shut down. If you were very slim, as she was, you wouldn't float back up. You would stay down here, in the cool, dark, blue depths. Nobody would even notice you down here. Nobody would try and save you until it was far too late.

It was the traditional way hopeless women killed themselves, wasn't it? Throwing themselves into rivers and lakes. You read about it. At least the swimming pool was clean. Convenient.

Anyway, it was the way she had chosen to go. She had no access to pills. Spilling her own blood was messy and uncertain. The other ways didn't bear thinking about. And she'd always loved the water. It was her element.

She'd decided to wait until she started to feel the effects of oxygen deprivation. That would make everything quicker. She knew from her training that she could hold her breath for three minutes. After that, everything started to hurt. She would breathe water in at that point, and it would all be over.

She felt the slow, dull thud of her heart. The tingling of the blood seeking oxygen in her veins. There was a great sadness in her soul. Sadness that it was all over so soon. She wasn't even twenty-eight. It hadn't been much of a life.

But there was also relief. And peace.

That was all she wanted. Peace

She had been underwater for two minutes now. Only a minute left. She wondered whether her life would flash before her, as some people said it did.

She hoped not. She got ready to draw the water into her lungs.

She felt something touch her arm, and opened her eyes slowly.

Astonishingly, there was someone beside her. A woman who had swum down to her, whose pale face peered at her anxiously in the dim light.

Karolina felt a wave of bitterness rush through her. Even in this last moment of her life, she was being frustrated.

She could hardly drown herself now. This interfering busy-body would raise the alarm. There would be the indignity of having her lungs emptied, some lifeguard's mouth on hers in the kiss of life, artificial respiration, all that fuss. And then back to the desolation.

The stranger was jerking her thumb upwards urgently, her eyes wide. When Karolina, numb with despair, did not respond, she grabbed Karolina's arm and hauled her off the bottom clumsily.

It had taken Karolina so much effort to reach this point. She was limp with defeat. She allowed the other woman to pull her up to the light.

They broke the surface together. Karolina drew in a deep lungful of air, staring up at the sky she'd hoped never to see again.

'I'm sorry, so sorry,' the other woman said. Surprisingly, she spoke in English. 'I know you were probably fine, I just got so worried when you didn't come up.'

Breathing shakily, feeling the oxygen feed her lungs again, Karolina at last looked at the woman who'd thwarted her plan. Her oval face, beaded with water, was youthful and unblemished. 'You *were* fine?' the Englishwoman asked. 'Weren't you? Are you unwell?'

Karolina was incapable of responding. The power of speech had left her. Coming so close to death, and then being pulled up had stunned her, leaving her weak.

'Let's get out of the water,' the Englishwoman said, concerned by Karolina's unresponsiveness. 'Come. Please!' Like an anxious collie with an errant lamb, she cajoled Karolina to the edge of the pool. They hauled themselves out, water streaming down their flanks. The chatter of voices drifted into Karolina's consciousness. It was Saturday, family day, and people were starting to arrive, spreading blankets on the grass and reserving places on the wooden spectator tiers.

The Englishwoman handed Karolina a towel, and led her to a seat. Karolina dropped her chin, and tried to let the hot sun massage away the misery that knotted itself around her neck and shoulders. She just wanted to vanish, to float away. The shrieks of children all around were like a chorus of seagulls, and she could imagine herself on a beach somewhere far away, alone, with no troubles. She drifted in her fantasy.

'I speak very little German,' she heard the other woman say. 'I'm English. Do you understand what I'm saying?'

'Yes,' Karolina said in a low voice.

'I was watching you. I saw you go down to the bottom. And I waited for you to come up. And – well – when you didn't, I panicked. I'm so sorry.'

'It's okay.'

'It's Karolina, isn't it?' the woman asked.

Surprised to hear her name spoken, Karolina looked up. The woman who'd rescued her was wearing a one-piece bathing suit of the type that were rented out by the pool authorities. She had a full, squarish mouth, a straight nose with delicate nostrils, and eyes of a deep blue, like Karolina's own. Her brow was high, framed by waves of wet hair that was a white-gold colour. It was such a familiar face that she struggled for a moment to identify it, before conceding that she had never seen it before.

'Who are you?' she demanded.

'My name is Agnes Tolliver.' The woman paused, as though wondering whether the name meant anything to Karolina. When it evidently didn't, she went on talking, quietly but quickly. 'You're the daughter of Liv Christiansen and Ulrich von Breda, aren't you?'

Karolina was even more disturbed. She drew back instinctively. 'How do you know that?'

'You were born in Norway, and sent to a family named Ozerki, in East Prussia. Is that right?'

Her mouth was dry. 'Yes.'

'There's something you need to know. In 1945, Liv Christiansen and Ulrich von Breda had a second daughter. She ended up in England.' The woman paused.

A sudden blazing light dawned on Karolina. 'You?' she whispered.

'Yes.' The deep blue eyes were so clear, so candid that Karolina knew they couldn't lie to her. 'Me. They christened me Friedelinde, but the man who adopted me called me Agnes. I'm related to you. Very closely related.' She paused, drawing a deep breath. 'I'm your younger sister.'

Karolina couldn't speak. She was immobilised, as though she'd been injected with some nerve-toxin that had turned all her muscles to stone. Was this yet another Stasi trap? Another cruel refinement of torture? She stared at the intense face, with its faint blush of pink under the smooth cheeks, the thick eyelashes that were so much darker than the hair. 'It's impossible,' she whispered at last.

'But it's true. I wouldn't have broken it to you this way, but I didn't have any choice. I'm only in East Berlin for the weekend.' Agnes hurried on. 'I have a two-day visa to visit the Pergamon Museum. I've told them I'm a student of Greek antiquities, writing a book. I've come to see the new exhibits that were sent from the Hermitage in Russia.' She touched Karolina's hand. 'Look,' she said, 'I know this is a lot to take in. And I know there's nothing you can say now. I'm going to leave in a moment. In case they're watching us. But is there somewhere we can meet, where we can be private?'

Somehow, Karolina managed to form the words. 'There is nowhere,' she said.

'Your apartment?'

'Impossible.'

'Then can you come to the Pergamon tomorrow morning? Entrance is free on Sundays. There's an exhibit called The Ishtar Gate. I'll be there from opening time, ten in the morning. I'll wait for you.'

Karolina nodded dumbly.

'Please don't go under the water again.'

'Okay.'

'Promise me!'

'I promise.'

Agnes lifted Karolina's numb hands to her mouth and kissed them both. She got to her feet. 'Our world is broken,' she said. 'We're going to put it together again.'

Then she was walking away down the stairs, without looking back.

Karolina took the tram to the Pergamon Museum on Sunday morning. Her heart was pounding in rhythm with the clattering of the iron wheels. She hadn't slept at all last night. She hadn't even gone to bed. Her mind was too vividly filled with Agnes Tolliver's face, her voice, the extraordinary import of her words.

A sister.

If it was true, then she was not alone in the world.

That was an astonishing concept. A fairytale. Like a poor waif learning she was a princess. But *was* it true? She had thought about it for hours through the darkness. What the Englishwoman had said was possible. If one child had been born through the Lebensborn programme, then why shouldn't the same couple have produced a second child a few years later?

She knew little about the man and woman who had created her other than their names and that they were Nazis. That was the worst thing anybody could be in the DDR's eyes. On top of that, the man was a war criminal, the woman a bawd. That was what they had told her. *You were born in degradation*, as Hedwig had succinctly put it. She'd been told never to even think about them, and she had obeyed.

But she'd fought all her life to shake off the stigma of her birth. And looking into Agnes Tolliver's bright face, she had seen the possibility of another existence. Freedom. An uncursed life.

But what if it was a trap of some kind? You couldn't live in the

DDR without suspecting a trap in everything. A wasp behind every spoon of honey, fangs behind every smile.

Or even worse – what if she'd finally lost her reason, and had conjured up Agnes Tolliver and the entire episode in her mind? What if she arrived at the museum to find it had all been a fever dream? Or a hallucination produced by some drug the Stasi were experimenting on her?

She was approaching this meeting with an almost unbearable mixture of emotions – hope, dread, suspicion, excitement. She could hardly sit still on the hard wooden seat. Her hands were trembling and her legs felt like jelly.

Despite living in Berlin, Karolina had never been to the Pergamon Museum. It had been partially closed for over a decade, its fabric damaged by Allied bombing, its treasures looted by the Red Army. It had only reopened in the last few years, and the last few years of Karolina's life had not included museum visits.

It was a stupendously grand building, approached through a colonnade of giant pillars. It was a vision of a Germany that had once been glorious, not the degraded squalor of modern East Berlin. If this was a trap, then it was a spectacular one. She entered the museum, looking for signs to the Ishtar Gate exhibit. The arrows directed her through a long passageway, lined with striding lions cast in ancient blue-glazed bricks.

Impressive as that was, it was nothing to the impact made by the Ishtar Gate itself, which occupied a whole wing of the museum: a vast archway supported by two massive towers, fifty feet high and a hundred feet wide, the entire structure built from turquoise glazed bricks and studded with golden bas-reliefs of lions, bulls and dragons.

She couldn't help staring up at it in awe as she approached.

Then she heard Agnes's quiet voice beside her. 'It was the gate of Babylon, built by Nebuchadnezzar, two thousand five hundred years ago. Isn't that incredible?'

Karolina closed her eyes. She dared not turn her head. 'I still don't believe you're real,' she whispered.

Agnes's warm hand closed around her arm. 'I feel the same. But we're both real.' Karolina opened her eyes slowly. Agnes was gazing at her with that strange intensity in her eyes. 'I just want to stare at you all day long,' Agnes went on, 'but we have to pretend to be sightseers. Shall we walk?'

'I can't,' Karolina said. 'My legs are shaking too much.'

'Mine, too. Let's sit on that bench over there for a while.'

The great hall was crowded. This was a popular exhibit. The bench already had people sitting on it, but they found a space to huddle close together. Agnes turned to Karolina and took both her hands in her own. She spoke in a low voice. 'This is like a dream. I want to laugh and cry at the same time.'

They stared at each other in silence, each drinking in the other. Karolina struggled to find something to say. 'Please don't disappear,' she said at last. 'It would kill me.'

'I'm here. I promise I'm here.'

'I've been so alone.'

'So have I. I just didn't know it. I didn't even know you existed until a few weeks ago.'

'How did you find out about me?'

'I met our mother.'

Karolina became very still. 'She's alive?'

'Yes.'

'Where?'

'In Norway. She lives in the remotest place you can imagine, at the edge of the world. I'll explain everything later, when there's time.'

There was only one question in Karolina's mind. 'Why did she abandon us?'

The quiet pain in Karolina's voice was so intense that Agnes's own eyes filled with tears. 'She didn't abandon us. She gave us away. I don't know how to describe her. She's so strange.

Difficult. Driven half-crazy by suffering. Or maybe she was half-crazy to start with. I can't say.'

'Who would deliberately have children and then give them away?'

'I don't think she had anything else in her life. She's very proud of her looks, her physique. Her *blood*. She wanted to make copies of herself, but she was too damaged to look after them.'

'I don't understand that.'

'Nor do I. She was a Nazi. She gave you to a Nazi family in Munich. She was going to give me away too, but the war ended, and she was forced to keep me. The Norwegians took me away from her and gave me to Barbar. The man I thought was my grandfather.'

'And he gave you a good life?'

'Yes, a good life.'

'My life has been not so good,' Karolina said quietly. 'And the man? Have you met him?'

'Our father? No. Nobody knows where he is. He was in the Waffen-SS. Commander of a tank regiment. He was convicted of war crimes. Shooting prisoners of war. He spent fifteen years in a military prison, but he's free now. You know all that?'

'Yes,' Karolina said bitterly, 'I was told about it every day for years.'

'They won't tell me where he is now. In hiding somewhere.'

'Are we cursed because of them?'

'No!' Agnes said urgently. 'Don't ever think that! We're our own people.'

Karolina searched the face that was so familiar, and yet so new to her. 'Do I look like *her*?'

'She's tall and blonde. There is a resemblance. But not a close one.'

'And you?'

'I don't think I look like her very much.'

Karolina reached out, almost timidly, and touched the other woman's smooth face. 'You're twenty-three.'

Agnes tilted her head to caress Karolina's hand with her cheek. 'Yes. And you're twenty-seven.'

'Do we look like each other?'

'Maybe a little.' Agnes lowered her voice. 'There's only one thing I can think of. Getting you out of the DDR to the West.'

Karolina dropped her hand back in her lap. 'That will never happen.'

'It *will*,' Agnes said fiercely. 'We're going to make it happen.'

'How?'

'I'm going to ask our father's people to help us.'

'The *Nazis?*'

Agnes grimaced. 'Ex-Nazis. I had to ask them for help to find you. And I'm going to ask them to help me get you out of here.'

Karolina shook her head. 'We can't take help from those people.'

'Why not?'

'You know why not. You know what the SS did in the war.'

'Who else can get you out of here?'

'Are you a Nazi?'

'Of course not! Are you a communist?'

'I don't know anything else,' Karolina said quietly. 'I was brought up to be a communist. But they say I betrayed the system. I tried to get over the Wall when I was nineteen. They caught me, of course. I was sent to prison for three years. That's where they broke my tooth. And I have scars from beatings. I was lucky. It could have been fifteen years. I might never have come out alive. But since I was released, I have to do exactly what they tell me. I had to drop my university degree. I have to work night shift on a production line. I can't have friends.' She stopped, surprised by the tears that were sliding down Agnes's cheeks. 'Please don't cry. If you cry, I'll have to cry, too.'

'I'm so sorry, Karolina.' The blue of the Babylonian tiles was reflected in Agnes's wet eyes. 'I don't care who they are or what they did, so long as they can get you out of this terrible place. I know we can do this. As for asking for help from ex-Nazis – their mad schemes brought us into the world. The least they can do is help us now.'

'Have they said they would help?'

'No. Not yet. But I can be very persuasive. Especially now that I've met you. You wait and see.'

'I'm watched by the Stasi all the time.'

'There are friends close to you as well, Karolina.'

'Who?'

'There's a man in your building. He's in touch with the people I spoke to. He was the one who told me where to find you yesterday.'

'Herr Möller,' Karolina guessed. 'I am sure *he's* a Nazi.'

'Möller is willing to help, Karolina. What else matters?'

Karolina stared at this extraordinary sister who had suddenly appeared in her life, so positive, so dazzlingly full of determination and energy. She was like a creature from another world, another planet. 'You're amazing,' Karolina sighed. 'You're radiant.'

'So are you.'

'No. I'm not like you. You were brought up in the light. I was brought up in the darkness.'

'Don't say that!'

'It's true. You think anything's possible. I know it isn't. We'll always be different.'

'We're yin and yang. That's a good thing, isn't it?' Impulsively, Agnes put her arms around her sister's neck and hugged her tight. 'How can I have missed you all my life, when I didn't even know you existed?'

'I don't know,' Karolina whispered. 'But it was the same for me.'

Agnes drew back, looking into Karolina's eyes. 'Together, we can do anything. Please believe that.'

'There is something else you have to know. The Stasi have

enrolled me. They've told me I have to work for them from now on.'

'Work for them?'

'I have to sleep with Westerners. Politicians, important business people in Bonn. It will be filmed secretly. And then they can be blackmailed into giving information.'

Agnes's face changed in one second from tenderness into fury. '*What?* Never! I'll never let them do that to you!'

She'd raised her voice, causing people to turn around and look at her. Karolina hushed her. 'Shhh. You can't stop it.'

Agnes was vibrating with rage. 'How *dare* they?' she hissed.

'That's life in the DDR. They tell you what you're going to do, and you do it.'

'How can you be so passive about it?' Agnes demanded. Her eyes, still wet with tears, were blazing.

'Agnes, I've lived a little longer than you. And I've seen things that I hope you'll never see. I know that people with power can do anything they want to anyone.'

'You're going to let the communists do *that* to you – but you won't accept help from former Nazis? That's mad, Karolina.'

'Perhaps I am mad,' Karolina said with quiet dignity. 'Everyone is mad on this side of the Wall. But then, we don't have the expensive psychiatrists that you Westerners have.'

'I can't believe that we're already fighting, ten minutes after finding each other.'

'We're not fighting. But I'm a realist.'

'There has to be a way out!'

'Oh, there is.'

Agnes's face changed at Karolina's tone. A realisation was dawning on her. 'Is *that* what you were doing at the pool yesterday?' she asked slowly. '*Drowning yourself?*'

'Something like that.'

Agnes sagged as though she'd been punched in the stomach. 'Oh, my God. Oh, Karolina!'

'It's okay,' Karolina said lightly. 'You came along just in time.'

'You mean, if I hadn't been there, you'd be dead right now?'

'I might not have gone through with it.'

'I know enough about you to know that you would.' Agnes dragged her eyes away from Karolina, and looked up at the majestic structure that towered over them. 'Look at it. It's called the Ishtar Gate because it's dedicated to Ishtar, the goddess of fertility, love and war. Don't you think that makes her the right goddess for us? Fertility, love and war. That's how we came about.'

'It's also the gateway to a city that no longer exists,' Karolina said gently. 'The city of a dream.'

'I'm not just a dreamer, Karolina. There's so much to talk about, but now isn't the time. I have to go.'

'No!'

'I have to.' Agnes's eyes were full of tears again. 'We've been together too long already. But I'll come back. And we'll have a plan to get you out. Believe that.'

She kissed Karolina quickly, and rose. A minute later, she was lost in the crowd.

'You have been broadening your horizons, *Nazichen*,' Hedwig greeted Karolina on Monday. 'A visit to the museum, no less. Why?'

'So that I can have something cultural to talk to my targets about,' Karolina temporised.

Hedwig's eyes were hard as black glass. 'Oh, really? And who was the sexy girl who was hugging you?'

Karolina's heart jolted into her mouth. She kept her expression relaxed. 'An old friend. We called her Bunny at school. I forget her real name.'

'You forget the name of an old schoolfriend who hugs and kisses you when you meet?'

'I forget it as far as *you're* concerned,' Karolina retorted.

'Don't worry. We'll soon find out who she is.'

'I don't want any trouble for her. She's a decent person.'

Hedwig sneered. 'We're all decent people, *Nazichen*. Except you.'

Karolina said nothing.

Hedwig looked her up and down contemptuously. 'You could learn a lot from a girl like that. She knows how to dress, how to make herself look good. In fact, you can tell her there's a job for her here if she wants it. No blue movies for you today. You're going to the dentist. He's going to take impressions. We're going to fix your teeth. Get ready.'

# CHAPTER SIXTEEN

# ULRICH

*Munich, 1968*

The *Konditorei* was one of Constanze's favourites. Not only were the pastries and coffee excellent, but the booths at the back of the shop were perfect for a private conversation. Not that she minded being seen with a companion as distinguished looking as Gottfried Reichensperger, even if he was calling himself Baldur something or other these days. But caution was necessary; and being clandestine was almost as entertaining as being thought to be having a little *Liebesaffäre*.

'I'm so glad you could see me,' she said to Gottfried. 'I wouldn't have asked. Only, this can't wait.'

'It's always a delight to see you, Constanze,' Gottfried said gallantly. He picked up his fork and addressed his plate. He had asked for a strudel. It was deliciously light, the pastry leaves almost floating off the melting apple slices. 'How can I help you?'

'It's about the girls.'

He concealed his discomfort. 'Ah, yes.'

'Agnes has come to see me again.'

'Has she?'

'I don't mind telling you, I'm getting very fond of that child. You were impressed, too.'

'Yes, yes.'

She frowned. 'Don't keep repeating "Yes, yes" in that dubious tone, Gottfried. This is very urgent. Thanks to your help, she met Karolina on the other side of the Wall.'

'Good, good.'

'Not good. Do you know what she found out? Those communist bastards are planning to turn Karolina into a prostitute.'

Gottfried was startled. 'What?'

Constanze nodded grimly. She had worn dark glasses in the interests of discretion. Now she took them off. Her eyes, heavily made up but nevertheless penetrating, bored into Gottfried's. 'Whoring for the Stasi. Getting important men into bed so they can be filmed and then blackmailed into spying. My daughter, Gottfried. *My daughter.*'

'I've heard of this kind of thing,' he muttered, thinking fast.

'The filthy swine. There is nothing they won't stoop to. Agnes is in a terrible state. So am I!'

'You're right to be.'

'Something has to be done,' she said sharply. 'I won't allow this, you know. You have to get my daughter out of there.'

It hadn't taken Constanze long, he reflected, to start referring to Karolina as *my daughter*, despite a quarter-century hiatus in parenthood. 'I've raised the issue with the girls' father,' he said cautiously. 'He's very reluctant to get involved.'

'Perhaps he'll change his opinion,' she replied succinctly, 'when he hears his daughter is fucking for the Stasi.'

'I don't know about that.'

'Don't your people want the child freed?'

'In principle, yes. But they won't act without the father's approval.'

'You mean none of them will risk their arses, so he has to do something himself?'

She was a perceptive woman. He nodded. 'Effectively, yes.'

'You'll speak to him again, then – this von Breda?'

'It will do no good,' Gottfried said unhappily. 'He's not interested.'

'Then make him listen! I want my daughter back, even if he doesn't. What kind of man is he, anyway, who refuses to help a child in trouble?'

*A very strange kind of man*, Gottfried thought, but didn't articulate the words. 'He has had difficulties since his release from prison, Constanze. He managed to get a decent job with a large company in Frankfurt but the unions got to hear about it. They're all communists, of course. They threatened to bring production to a standstill if he wasn't sacked. The management had no option but to comply.'

'Spineless pants-shitters.'

'A similar problem occurred with his next job. Then he left Germany altogether and moved to France, but the local newspaper identified him there. Someone fired a shot through his kitchen window. So he tried Portugal next. He hadn't been there six months when a young radical tried to knife him in the street.'

Constanze grimaced. 'He's obviously a popular fellow.'

'Unfortunately, he refuses to change his name.'

'Unlike you,' she remarked sweetly.

'We must all take precautions, dear lady,' he replied, unfazed. 'It would help greatly if he made some effort to mask his identity. But he is too arrogant, Or perhaps too foolhardy.'

'Where is he now?'

'I'm not at liberty to tell you that, but he's found some peace. He gets by with help from his old comrades, and doing a little translation work. Understandably, he doesn't want to incur any more unwanted attention.'

'What if his "old comrades" suspend their contributions, Gottfried?' Constanze was a very handsome woman, but her face was like a Gorgon's as she said the words. 'Put pressure on him, damn it. He can't cower in some hole, shirking his responsibilities as a father and a German.'

'That is a possibility,' he admitted carefully.

'If your organisation won't help, I'll go across to the East and bring her back myself.'

'Don't try that.'

'It's a pity my husband isn't alive. He would know what to do.'

'No doubt.' Gottfried toyed unhappily with his strudel. He had lost his appetite. 'I'll speak to the others. And then to him.'

'Good. And do it quickly, please. There isn't much time.'

Making his way to the airport, Gottfried did not relish the prospect of another trip to the *masia* in Catalonia. No, it was too isolated there. If von Breda became unpleasant, he would be at a disadvantage. And there were those damned dogs to contend with. No! Better to round up some of the others, and summon him to Marbella.

He was bitterly regretting the invitation he and the others had extended to von Breda to come to Spain. They'd thought they were doing the wretched man a favour. And look where it had got them.

And it was always problematic when the women got involved. Especially a woman like Constanze Ozerki, selfish, self-absorbed, and with plenty of friends. After years of indifference to the fate of this wretched girl, she was suddenly claiming to experience maternal feelings. A joke. Really, a joke. But it would be unwise to ignore her.

As for applying pressure on von Breda, that was going to be like tying a knot in a tiger's tail.

The damned communists! They had a low, crude kind of cunning. The disgusting scheme was a provocation, of course. They knew exactly who the girl's father was. What was their intention? Simply to inflict a brutal punishment on an old enemy? Or something more elaborate?

Either way, getting the girl out of East Berlin was not going to be easy if the Stasi had their claws into her. They would be watching her like hawks hovering over a mouse.

The organisation that he and von Breda both belonged to was extensive and powerful. But the truth was that they were all getting old. These wartime skeletons rattled in many of their closets, but some were growing weary of confronting them. They were now grandfathers in many cases, whatever they had been during the war.

They could be very effective, of course. But not without good cause. And the unpopularity of Ulrich von Breda was an obstacle. He had made himself odious to many of the senior members. Insulting the Führer was not the way to win such hearts and minds as theirs. He was regarded as a problem, not an asset, to people who'd spent two decades patiently building new lives for themselves. His long incarceration, and the furore that had erupted when he'd been released instead of being strung up, had made him a very hot potato.

Notoriety was exactly what the organisation tried to avoid. And trouble followed Ulrich von Breda wherever he went – strikes, violence, journalists raking up the war in uncomfortable ways.

Yes, von Breda had spent fifteen years on death row. But there was still a strong feeling in certain quarters that he had not yet begun to pay for his crimes. What had possessed von Breda to shoot American prisoners of war? They'd all felt no qualms about the things that had to be done during the war. Jews, Slavs, partisans, *Untermenschen,* yes. But Americans? With the war all but lost? That alone had made von Breda *persona non grata* to the senior members. It had been an act of insanity; and as a former *Gruppenführer* had said to him recently, 'There is only one way to deal with a mad dog.'

Lastly, there was the issue that Constanze had raised: money. Unable to work in any public role, von Breda now depended heavily on charity from the organisation. They'd voted him a monthly stipend which covered his costs. A trickle of income from his translating work supplied his beer money. The organisation was wealthy; but it did not like to throw its cash away. And getting the payments funnelled to von Breda without revealing their source was a complicated task which someone had to undertake every month. The fact that he was not remotely grateful for this assistance – indeed, complained constantly that it was too little – irritated members even further.

These thoughts circulated in Gottfried's mind as he boarded his flight back to Spain. He was a ruthless and dangerous man, and it had occurred to him several times over the past few years that putting a bullet in his old comrade's head would draw a line under the whole problem. He might indeed suggest that solution to the group shortly.

Ulrich von Breda was in a veterinary clinic on the Costa Brava with Kaiserin, one of his German shepherds. The dog was lying on the veterinarian's stainless steel table, panting heavily, and evidently in distress. The vet himself was listening to the animal's heart and lungs through a stethoscope.

'Is it poison?' von Breda demanded impatiently.

'I'll take samples,' the vet said. 'But I doubt it.'

'This is the second time in a month!'

The man shrugged. 'During the hot weather, dogs can pick up these things. They eat rubbish they find, drink dirty water and so forth.'

'My dogs do *not* eat rubbish or drink dirty water,' von Breda said sharply. His tone made the vet look up warily for a moment. He had served in the Waffen-SS Veterinarian Corps on the Russian front, with the rank of *Oberfeldwebel*, although he was now ostensibly an innocuous Belgian named Schubert. The two men had a low opinion of one another. Von Breda considered Schubert an ignorant horse-doctor, while Schubert considered the other a paranoiac as unstable as a nuclear isotope. It was only their shared military history which bound them together.

'As I said, I will take samples,' Schubert said coolly. 'As soon as I get the results back from the laboratory, I'll let you know. In the meantime, you had better leave her here with me for a day or two.'

'I don't like to be without her,' von Breda growled. 'I need security.'

'You have the other animal. And this one is not much use to you as a guard dog in her present condition.'

'I still want her with me.'

'You are welcome to take her, of course. But if she dies in your care, please don't put the blame on me.'

'Dies?'

'She is strong, but you see how unwell she is. Dogs can deteriorate very fast. Listen to reason.'

In a cold rage, von Breda paid the man and left without Kaiserin. Those in the waiting room, with parakeets and cats on their knees, stared curiously as he passed, having heard angry German spoken in the consulting room. He caught the word *Nazi* whispered by a woman, and glared at her savagely. Spain had once been a country where fascists, domestic and foreign, were a ruling class. Things were changing fast. Disintegrating every day.

He strode along the waterfront, past the white yachts of the rich and the shabby *mallorquinas* of the fishermen. His emotions were churning, muddying his thoughts. He'd been summoned by Gottfried Reichensperger to a meeting within a few days. He knew what it would be about. He knew what they were going to say.

Was it his duty to take responsibility for two girls he'd fathered a quarter of a century ago? He'd been ordered to do the fathering by Reichsführer Himmler. Let the self-appointed heirs of the defunct Nazi state take care of the result.

He'd never so much as set eyes on the girls. They were nothing to him. He cared infinitely more for his dogs than for them. Dogs and daughters. Daughters and dogs. One daughter imprisoned, one daughter free. One dog in a cage at the vet's, another waiting at home. The symmetry was disturbing.

And there was the question of poison.

If someone was poisoning his dogs, it could only mean one thing: that they were preparing to come for him. That fool of an *Oberfeldwebel* understood nothing. A man who'd spent the war drenching pack horses! What did he know about noble creatures like dogs?

Von Breda avoided any contact with his neighbours, Catalan farming folk who kept themselves to themselves. But there was always the chance that someone would notice something, someone would say something. Someone would guess something. Someone would recognise his face. And then they would come for him.

The meeting was held in Marbella, at Gottfried's villa. The town, and the Costa del Sol in general, had been favourite retreats for senior SS officers since well before the war. The assistance given by Hitler to Franco from 1936, enabling him to grasp power during the Spanish Civil War, had not been forgotten; and when the war had ended to the disadvantage of Germany, a warm (if discreet) welcome had been extended to such ex-military gentlemen as now needed a safe haven.

Gottfried's villa was set on a cypress-studded hillside with views of the harbour basin of Puerto Banús. It boasted an immense swimming pool, Moorish towers, extensive gardens and accommodation for twenty people or more. Possession of the place guaranteed Gottfried a certain status. It was a popular venue for reunions, and Gottfried was a popular host. Members, some of whom had to fly considerable distances to attend these meetings, enjoyed the luxuries he provided.

Von Breda, who was too poor to have flown in from Catalonia, and who had instead taken a fifteen-hour bus journey to get here, regarded the place with undisguised disgust. It revolted him.

And just before he'd set off, the cursed horse-doctor had telephoned him to say that Kaiserin had died. The cause of death was still being determined. He'd thought himself incapable of grief, but he'd burst into tears at the news. He was still heartsore.

Nor did it improve his mood when he was greeted with formality but little warmth by the dozen men who had already arrived. He could sense their distrust and dislike all too well.

The afternoon was spent around the pool, in reminiscences, exchanges of news and mild to moderate sunburn. In the evening, Gottfried brought in a trusted neighbour who had prepared a hog roast. The fragrant smoke rose to heaven. The pig was perfectly cooked by nine o'clock, the succulent meat falling off the gleaming bones in heavy platefuls. The members feasted and drank in the sunset, and then relaxed in the soft Mediterranean twilight, prone on loungers.

It was left to Gottfried, as host, to open the discussion.

'Gentlemen, we all know why we are here. A situation has arisen with regard to the children of Ulrich von Breda.'

'Do not call them my children,' von Breda cut in harshly. 'I strongly object to that term.'

'What term would you like us to use, von Breda?' a former *Sturmhauptführer* asked laconically.

'I don't care. These girls have no connection to me whatsoever.'

'Let us say then,' Gottfried resumed, 'that a situation has arisen with regard to these girls who have no connection to Ulrich von Breda whatsoever, other than being his children.'

There was a ripple of laughter.

Furious, von Breda rose to his feet. He had eaten nothing, while watching the others glut themselves, fat bellies hanging over their shorts, jowls shining with grease. 'I refuse to discuss the issue on these terms,' he barked.

'You misunderstand the occasion,' Gottfried said silkily. 'This is not a discussion, Ulrich. The discussion has already taken place without you. You are here to receive orders. Sit down.'

Grimly, von Breda sank into his chair again.

'We are all agreed that the situation is intolerable. The East German secret police have chosen the elder of the girls to train as a state prostitute. A *hetaera*, for those of you who benefited from a classical education. Needless to say, it's totally against her will. This is a clear provocation. Our organisation does not usually involve itself in family affairs, as you know. But Europe is at a tipping point. Communism is once again a palpable threat.'

He drank from his beer glass. There was absolute silence now.

'Had the Americans followed our urging in 1945,' he continued, 'and joined with us in crushing the Russians, we would all now be living in a very different world. But that did not happen. And so, I repeat, the spectre of revolution is once again a reality. You have all seen what is happening in the countries where you currently reside. And what is happening in our own beloved fatherland. Subversion. Insurrection. Destabilisation.'

'The damned unions,' someone grunted.

Gottfried shook his silvered head. 'It is of no use to blame the unions, the workers, the students, or any single group. This is a malignant movement that has its roots in Moscow, and nowhere else.'

'Hear, hear,' someone else muttered.

'Against this Marxist tide, gentlemen, we ourselves are an important bulwark. For many of us, the war against communism began right here in Spain, in 1936. We waged a wider war from 1939 onwards. Unfortunately, the world ranged itself against us, and we were able to wound the snake, but not kill it. And now it is poised to strike again. We have a clear duty to act. That duty stands before us.'

Von Breda had not eaten, but he had drunk abundantly and perhaps unwisely. His head was swimming and his heart was pounding. 'Arrogant rubbish,' he said roughly. 'As if a gaggle of old women like you could do anything against the Soviets.'

'We are all soldiers!' someone said.

'Soldiers?' he retorted. 'What did any of you do in the war? None of you ever faced a real enemy. No, you crept around behind the front line, far from the battlefield, keeping your uniforms clean, killing women and children. Do you think that made you soldiers? Butchering defenceless Jews? Shooting old people and babies? It just made you bloodsucking, cowardly murderers. And now you talk to me as though I am responsible for your misdeeds. I fought for Germany, not out of blood lust!'

There was a silence. The former *Sturmhauptführer* who had spoken earlier broke it. 'You are your own worst enemy, von Breda,' he said quietly. 'We invited you to Spain when you had nowhere else to go. We've paid your way ever since. For once in your life, keep your mouth shut and your ears open.'

Gottfried followed this swiftly. 'The resolution of this caucus is that Ulrich von Breda must take responsibility for his daughter. How he does this is up to him. But he must either remove her from harm's way. Or he must eliminate her with his own hands.'

Von Breda gripped the arms of his chair convulsively. '*What?*'

'The organisation will take no part in this operation,' Gottfried went on implacably, 'and will make no financial contribution. False papers and intelligence will be supplied. Nothing more. Should Ulrich von Breda fail to accomplish the task he has been set, the monthly payments that have been made to him for the past several years will permanently cease. And he will no longer benefit from the protection of the brotherhood.'

'You're insane,' von Breda gasped. 'You're asking me to kill my own daughters?'

'*Now* they're your daughters?' the *Sturmhauptführer* said ironically.

'That is one of two options,' Gottfried said in the same calm way. 'Ending the girl's life will forestall the shame of having a flower of the Reich besmirched by dirty communist hands. They are throwing shit in our faces, Ulrich. We will not tolerate that. It would be a humiliation that would damage our prestige enormously. If you choose this option, then what you do with the other girl is up to you. But there is the second option. Get the girl out of East Berlin.'

'How?' von Breda demanded in despair.

'That is up to you. You tell us that you were once a soldier. An SS officer. And there is no higher standard than that. Draw upon what you were. But' – Gottfried's voice grew even silkier – 'do not fail, either way. The price for failure will be high.'

# CHAPTER SEVENTEEN

# AGNES

*Berlin, 1968*

Agnes was burningly aware that there were twenty-three years of catching up to do. Karolina filled her every waking thought. All she wanted to do was rush back through Checkpoint Charlie and be at her sister's side.

But Constanze had told Agnes to wait and do nothing. It was hard to obey that commandment.

So she paced along the course of the Wall for hours, through some of the roughest parts of the city, like a deranged woman, trying to find places where she could look over to East Berlin. As though there was some remote chance of catching a glimpse of her sister.

Of course, there was no chance of that. The East Germans hadn't just built a huge concrete wall; they'd stuck up screens and billboards with anti-American messages in any place you could get high enough to look across. People in the East weren't allowed to even look at the West, let alone go there.

And that meant people in the West couldn't look at the East.

But she'd learned of a couple of spots where West Berliners

went, especially on weekends – gaps where there weren't billboards yet. People climbed onto ladders to be able to see friends and relations on the other side – too far to talk, but you could wave, and they would wave back. Agnes found these waving places inexpressibly pathetic. The insanity of dividing a great city in half, ruthlessly separating neighbours, families, friends, had never seemed clearer than when you saw men and women crying as they waved handkerchiefs to someone a hundred yards away, yet forever out of reach.

Not knowing what was happening to Karolina was a constant torture. She was worried by Karolina's fatalism. Karolina's life had been very different from her own, she knew that, although she was yet to learn the full extent of her sister's suffering. Hardship seemed to have crushed hope in her – or at least, crippled it. Agnes hated to see her accept her fate. *That's life in the DDR*, Karolina had said. *They tell you what you're going to do, and you do it.* And when Agnes had protested, she'd said, *I've seen things that I hope you'll never see. I know that people with power can do anything they want to anyone.*

That had been hard for Agnes to hear. She desperately wanted to give Karolina hope. But right at this moment, it was hard to find, even for herself.

For a moment, despondency overcame her. Then she squared her shoulders. She might be the daughter of an SS officer – but she had been brought up by a Royal Air Force wing commander. If she had inherited anything from either of them, it was tenacity. She would not let herself be intimidated. She would fight to the end.

She summoned up her courage. There had to be a way. And she would find it.

She went back to her hostel room in the early evening. She'd been staying at a much cheaper place than the last time, half a mile or so from Checkpoint Charlie. It was an old schoolhouse that had somehow been spared in the bombing, and had been converted into a spartan guest house for travellers on the cheap. It was run by a religious organisation, with Bibles in all the rooms, framed religious prints on the walls, and regular prayer groups downstairs, which she avoided. There were few comforts, but the location was good, and her room was large, part of an old classroom that had been divided with partitions. Even the furniture consisted of school desks and hard wooden chairs, and the school smell of carbolic, chalk and wax polish hung over everything.

Her room was on the first floor, and she could just see the Wall from her windows, which gave her some small sense of being close to Karolina. She unlocked the door and went in.

For a second, she felt that there was something wrong, without quite knowing what. And then she saw that someone had got into her room – a big man in jeans and a leather jacket, who was seated at the desk. He rose quickly, showing a grim, intent face. Her heart lurched violently. She dashed for the door, but he was upon her like a panther. She screamed once, and then his hand clamped over her mouth, silencing her.

She struggled violently to get free. He was very strong, lifting her easily off her feet and carrying her across the room. He slammed her onto the bed, keeping his hand over her mouth. Fierce blue eyes stared down at her.

'Don't make another sound,' he said in a low growl. 'I'm going to take my hand away, but you will remain silent. Do you understand?' His accent was German, his English fluent. 'Do you understand?'

Panic-stricken, Agnes struggled all the harder, trying to claw at his face.

'I'm not going to hurt you, damn you. Be still!' He released her suddenly and stood back. The swiftness of the release took

Agnes by surprise. She was gasping for breath, her heart racing. 'Not a sound!' he commanded.

'Who are you?' she whispered.

A strange expression crossed his face, weary and angry. 'You demanded that I come to you. So here I am.'

It took a moment for her to register his words. She sat up. 'You're—'

'My name is Ulrich von Breda,' he said curtly, when the right word evaded her. 'You may call me Ulrich, or Herr von Breda, as you choose. Please refrain from using any familial terms.'

She swung her legs over the edge of the bed, and stood up shakily. 'How did you get in here?'

He jerked his head at the old iron fire escape that passed by one of her windows.

'You broke into my room? Couldn't you have knocked on the door?'

'You're going to have to learn caution,' he replied. 'I didn't know who would be in your room.'

To her mortification, Agnes felt tears pressing behind her eyes. She tried to fight down a sob.

'What are you crying for?' he demanded impatiently.

'It's been a shock,' she said in a choked voice. 'And I wanted to prepare.'

'Prepare for what?'

'For meeting you. Not like this!'

'Please,' he said tiredly, 'no sentimental performances.'

She walked away from him to the basin in the corner of the room, and washed her face. She found that her hands were shaking as she dried herself. Was this a dream? 'I'm not sentimental,' she said, turning back to him. 'And I'm not performing. You attacked me.'

'You should not have screamed.'

'You should not have burgled my room!'

He shrugged indifferently. 'The worst is over now.'

'What does that mean? The worst is over?'

He didn't answer the question, but looked around the room dispassionately, taking in the religious prints, the schoolroom furniture. 'This is the best you could afford?'

'I'm on a budget.'

'I was led to believe that you were a rich woman.'

Her heart rate was refusing to return to normal. Somehow, she couldn't catch her breath. She was still afraid of him, unsure of what he would do, wondering if he was going to hurt her. 'Sorry to disappoint you.'

'You have no money?' he asked.

'Not right now.'

'Nor do I. That makes our situation difficult. We're going to need money.'

'To do what?'

'To do anything,' he said impatiently. 'What have you got to eat?'

'Nothing.'

He completed his survey of the room. 'You're going to have to ask them to put another bed in here,' he said.

'Oh, no,' she jerked out. 'You're not staying with me!'

'I'm not spending money on a room,' he retorted. 'I've already spent a fortune on the airfare getting here.'

'My God,' she said. 'I didn't expect a saint. But I didn't expect you to be such a bastard, either.'

'Technically, you are the bastard,' he said coldly.

'Thank you for that.'

'I have made sacrifices to be here. I had to leave my dogs.' He corrected himself. 'My dog.'

'Your dog?'

His mouth twisted. 'You would not understand.'

'I understand dog,' Agnes retorted. 'A canine pet. A lot higher up the scale than a bastard daughter.'

'Is there somewhere around here we can eat?' he asked.

She tried to recover her poise. 'Waldeckpark is not far away. There's a stall that sells currywurst.'

'What the devil is that?'

'It's a long time since you've been in Berlin, isn't it?' she said dryly. 'Come, I'll show you.'

They sat on a park bench, eating the spicy frankfurters and thick-cut potato fries from paper cartons. Currywurst was the universal fast food of streets and parks in Berlin, and there was a queue of people at the stall. In the sandpit close by, parents home from work tiredly pushed children on swings or down slides. The cries of the children sounded like tropical birds against the evening hum of the city.

'We missed all that, didn't we?' she said.

'What are you talking about?'

'It's a joke. How's the currywurst?'

He shrugged. He was obviously hungry, but he ate slowly, his eyes watchful. She had a chance to observe him properly for the first time. After twenty-three years, she had a father. Surely there should be some sense of a rebirth? It was so hard to analyse her own feelings.

He looked older than she had expected. She had worked out earlier that he must be fifty-four or fifty-five. His short hair was grizzled at the temples. By contrast, his brows were dark. Deep lines made furrows on either side of a tightly compressed mouth. His nose jutted like the prow of a battleship, a feature she was glad not to have inherited. His eyes were the most striking thing about him, an electric blue made all the more piercing by his dark, heavy brows. She realised that their colour was almost the same as Karolina's. Her own eyes were a milder, softer shade.

She was still in shock from his sudden arrival. It all felt surreal. She had anticipated this meeting in so many ways, emotional, dramatic or painful, but none of them had been like this. The long journey that had begun in Barbar's fireplace had ended up in a rather seedy park in West Berlin with a tough stranger who was in no sense fatherly. She didn't know what tone to take, what to say.

'I met Liv Christiansen in Norway,' she blurted out.

He tensed. 'I don't want to talk about her.'

'She talked about you.' He made no reply. That line of conversation was evidently closed. She would try again later. 'I wish you had warned me you were coming,' she said, 'instead of jumping out of the scenery like the Demon King in a pantomime.'

'There are people who would try to harm me if they knew I was here. I need to be careful.'

'I've read about the trial . . .' she began unwisely.

'I do not intend to discuss any of my life with you,' he cut in sharply. 'And it's better you don't read anything that has been written about me.'

'That's a tall order. You're my father, after all.'

He turned to her. 'You may believe that there is some mystical connection between us, that you inherited some of my faults or virtues. But you need to understand that my crimes are not your crimes. My life is not your life. You were better off without me, but since you chose to insist, I am here now. But I owe you no explanations, and you owe me none. Let's keep it that way.'

Over the past weeks, she had prepared a long list of questions for when they met, constantly editing the list, adding or deleting questions as she thought about them. The impact of his appearance had blown the list completely out of her mind. She could barely remember the main questions that had been on it. And now, his stony refusal to share anything with her had crushed the few that remained. It was, she felt, tragic.

It was lucky that she'd only had a few weeks of knowing that she had a father at all. If this had been something she'd been looking forward to her whole life, it would have been a crushing disappointment. As it was, she felt wounded in a way she could not even define. There was an ache in her heart for a sentimental reunion that she should have known was never going to happen.

It was hard not to be intimidated by him. His physique was rangy; he was obviously physically fit and strong. But more than that, the most powerful impression he gave was of anger, anger that was unpredictable and barely contained. That was what made him alarming. 'Is there any topic,' she asked ironically, 'that we can discuss?'

'Your sister.'

'All right. Is your organisation going to help?'

His face was bitter. 'My organisation, as you call it, will do nothing.'

'I thought—'

'There is no organisation. A handful of rich, fat, lazy old men, nothing more. I am here on my own, to achieve what I can.'

Agnes felt her heart sinking. 'No help at all?'

'None. And there is no guarantee that your sister can be taken out of East Berlin.'

'But people have escaped!'

'Yes, people have escaped. And each time, the communists close another route. Tunnels under the Wall, swimming across the Spree, it's all been done, and is now blocked, impossible to repeat.'

'Then how are we going to get her out?'

'There are only two options. One is *Häftlingsfreikauf.*'

'What's that?'

'Ransom money,' he said shortly. 'The DDR is in a state of near financial collapse. They will sometimes free prisoners for hard currency.'

'How much?'

'Twenty to fifty thousand Deutsche Marks.'

It sounded a huge amount. Agnes did a swift calculation in her mind. 'I'm selling my grandfather's house in England. I should get enough to cover that. But there's no time.'

'In any case,' he said, 'they may not accept money.'

'Why not?'

'Because what they're doing to your sister is a punishment,' he said grimly.

'She's done nothing to deserve it!'

'She tried to escape. However, the punishment isn't for her.'

'For whom, then?'

'Who do you think?'

Agnes gasped. 'You mean they're doing this to get at you?'

'Me, and people like me. Brezhnev is trying to keep his empire together. He has to keep raking up the war, telling his people that on the other side of the Iron Curtain, fascist neo-Nazi hordes are waiting to invade.'

'That's crazy.'

'It works for Brezhnev,' he said succinctly. 'He's still fighting Hitler, and getting credit for it from his people.'

'What's the second option?' she asked.

'The second option is the simplest. It works for a few hundred East Berliners every year. Someone drives into the Eastern zone in a car. The escapee is put in the trunk. The car drives back to the West. Voilà.'

'Through Checkpoint Charlie?' she said. 'Impossible. I've been through it. The guards search every vehicle.'

'Not through Checkpoint Charlie,' he replied, shaking his head. 'Through Waltersdorf Chaussee, approaching along the expressway from Potsdam to Schönefeld. It's a busy road. There are lots of exits and entrances, as well as rural roads through the woods. It's far harder for them to control.'

'How do you know all this?' Agnes demanded.

He gave her a dry look. 'I fought in the Battle of Berlin in 1945. I know this city like the back of my hand. Even if this is the first currywurst I've come across.' He hadn't finished the meal, but now he wrapped the remainder in its paper, and took it to the trashcan. When he came back, he said, 'I never want to eat that muck again.'

Agnes felt a nervous thrill of excitement. She had no idea whether to trust him or not. He seemed purposeful. But what did she really know about him? 'Do you think that will work? Getting Karolina out in a car?'

'It's our best option,' he said bluntly.

'What are our chances of success?'

'Slim.'

Agnes winced. 'We have to talk to Karolina. I don't know if she'll risk it. She doesn't believe we can get her out.'

He grunted. 'That's the way they want people to think. How do you get into East Berlin?'

'With my press credentials. I'm supposed to be writing a book about classical art, and I visit the Pergamon Museum.'

'No problems?'

'None so far. I don't think they know that I'm Karolina's sister. I'm very careful when I go.'

'Keep it that way.'

She looked at the peaceful cityscape all around them, myriads of lights coming on against a violet sky. She knew what a ruined wasteland it had been a quarter of a century ago. 'You fought in the Battle of Berlin?'

'To the end,' he replied. 'That's how I was captured. My comrades all either died, or made arrangements to be elsewhere.'

'You mean the rich, fat, lazy old men you talked about?'

'Yes.'

'You must have been very loyal to Hitler.'

'I detested Hitler,' he replied. 'But I had a mother and two sisters in the city.'

She realised with a start that he was talking about her grandmother and her aunts. 'What happened to them?'

He didn't answer, and she dared not press the question. 'Why won't they help you – these rich old men?'

'That's too long a story.' He stretched. 'I need to sleep, Agnes.'

'I need to eat. I need to sleep. You're used to having your commands obeyed,' she said mordantly. 'Aren't you, Oberstleutnant von Breda?'

'Do not refer to my rank,' he snapped.

'Okay, Dad.'

'I told you not to use familial terms!'

'It was another joke,' she replied wearily.

They walked back to the hostel. She went to Gabi, the young woman at reception and asked for a second bed for her father. She was expecting the Christian ethos of the place to be a problem, but Gabi didn't turn a hair. 'That will be an extra sixty-five Deutsche Marks per night,' she said. Agnes paid from her diminishing store of traveller's cheques.

The bed was sent up shortly. It turned out to be a military-style camp stretcher with a pile of cheap bed linen folded on it. He refused her offer of her own bed, or even to allow her to make the camp bed up for him. He took it to the area next to the fire escape, where he had entered.

'Planning a quick exit?' she enquired.

'If they come for us, they'll come through this window,' he replied calmly.

'Who's going to come for us? Leonid Brezhnev?'

They lay in the dark at opposite ends of the room, without speaking. After a long while, she asked quietly, 'What kind of dog is it?'

She thought he wouldn't reply. Then he said, 'A German Shepherd.'

'You said "dogs" and then corrected yourself.'

He was silent for another long while. 'Her sister died last week.'

'I'm sorry. What are their names?'

'Go to sleep.'

'*Jawohl*, Herr Oberstleutnant.'

Uncharacteristically, he let her have the last word.

She had a dream that it had all been a dream, that Ulrich von Breda didn't exist. Her sense of loss and panic woke her up. It was very early. But when she opened her eyes, he had made his bed, and was sitting at the desk, writing in a notebook. He was wearing faded denim overalls.

'You're real,' she said.

He looked up. 'We're going to East Berlin this morning.'

'Together?'

He shook his head. 'You're going for another visit to the Pergamon Museum. You'll make your way to your sister's place, as before. Don't go to her room. Go straight to Elias Möller's room and wait there.'

'The old handyman?'

'He's not much older than I am,' von Breda said dryly.

'Oh, he looks ancient compared to you,' she said diplomatically.

'We're not going to be able to do this without Möller's help. I'll meet you there later in the day.'

'How are you going to get into the East?'

'As an electrician.' He indicated his overalls. 'They're rebuilding Alexanderplatz. Workers come in from the West in special buses. I have a pass.'

'Where did you get that?'

'The rich old men are useful for some things.'

They breakfasted on coffee and berliners at a *Konditorei*.

Agnes noticed that people around them all looked at von Breda in a certain way, and treated him with cautious respect. Perhaps they recognised what he had been, or perhaps it was just his size and bearing. When they'd eaten, they parted. She went to the bus station to join the queues of Western tourists eager to see what communist East Berlin was really like.

In the bus, she reflected that it was a very strange feeling to have a father in her life, even a father as remote as Ulrich von Breda. It was a bit like swallowing a hard stone, that got stuck somewhere between your mouth and your belly, and wouldn't go either up or down.

Oddly what bothered her almost more than his cold- ness was her inability to see any family resemblance. Why was that so powerful a disappointment? She could detect no similarities between him and herself, except blue eyes, and they were common features, anyway. She'd inherited her hair and skin, in fact almost all her looks, from Liv Christiansen. As the waiter had said to her in Stavanger, she looked Norwegian more than anything else. Von Breda had black hair – well, greying now – and his skin was tanned. No similarities there; Agnes burned bright red after half an hour in the sun.

Almost as hard to understand was that he showed her no warmth, did not even seem interested in her or her life. Clearly, his dogs mattered far more to him. And just as clearly, he was here under sufferance, wanting only to get back to whatever life he had in hiding. Liv hadn't been any warmer, but at least she had an excuse – years of shock treatment, ostracism and probably alcoholism had erased her emotions. Von Breda had made a conscious choice not to allow any bond to form.

She had to remember that he had been an SS officer. A Nazi.

A convicted war criminal. Whatever he said about detesting Hitler, he had fought for the Third Reich for six years of war. He was not by any stretch of the imagination an ideal father figure.

Was all this going to have a destructive emotional impact on her? Was she going to need years of psychoanalysis later on?

But he was big, strong and capable, and his very presence had filled her with optimism and excitement. Perhaps together they really could get Karolina to the West. And perhaps that mattered more than forming a bond with a father she'd only just met.

Going through Checkpoint Charlie was always like entering another dimension, similar to, but weirdly different from, her own. Great efforts had clearly been lavished on making East Berlin attractive, especially along the bigger roads; flower beds had been planted, new buildings had been raised. But just behind the glossy façade, a dreary alternative reality existed. The city was grey, and marked by austerity. Shops appeared half empty. Down side roads you glimpsed blocks of shattered buildings that had yet to be cleared away. If you looked closely at the busy traffic, you saw that most of the cars were not like the shiny vehicles on the other side, but were odd-looking Trabants, Wartburgs and Ladas. And people were dressed in drab clothes that seemed twenty years behind snappy West Berlin.

The bus skirted Alexanderplatz. As von Breda had said, the square was a vast construction site, a moonscape of raw earth and new concrete, studded with cranes, bulldozers, scaffolding and thousands of workers in hard hats. It was clearly an attempt to make a showpiece, and counteract the shabbiness of the rest of East Berlin. She got off at the museum and went in for appearance's sake, before slipping out again, and making her way to Karolina's.

They had relegated Karolina to one of the worst parts of the city, close to a power station that burned lignite coal, blanketing the neighbourhood with sulphurous yellow smog. The housing blocks where she lived were so badly built that they were already starting to fall apart. Bombsites still hadn't been cleared. Weeds were thriving among the rubble. It cut Agnes to her heart to think of her sister living in this urban wilderness, while she had enjoyed so much comfort in her life.

She stole unobtrusively into the building, which smelled of blocked drains and boiled cabbage. Herr Möller answered his door. He spoke very little English, but he made her a cup of ersatz coffee while she waited. He had several wartime photographs on the walls of his workplace, showing uniformed German soldiers in the field. He saw her looking at the pictures, and tapped one with a ferocious grin, jerking his thumb at his own chest. '*Das bin ich*,' he said. She looked closer, and saw that one of the laughing soldiers was a much younger Herr Möller with a large machine gun.

He tapped other photos, shot in various locations, snowy or grassy. '*Polen*,' he told her. '*Der Kaukasus. Der Balkan. Russland. Die Ostfront.*' He opened a drawer to show her several medals including an Iron Cross. She thought of Barbar's medals, arranged on his coffin. The drawer beneath had various mementoes – a dagger, bits of Allied uniforms, what looked alarmingly like a live hand grenade. Herr Möller was obviously proud of his part in Hitler's war, and didn't bother to hide it. Which was probably, Agnes thought, why he had been relegated to the same accommodation as Karolina. Blocks like these were evidently reserved for those at the bottom of the communist dung heap.

An hour later, von Breda arrived. Möller opened two bottles of beer, and the men went into the kitchen to talk quietly in German. Agnes had no idea what they were saying, but the two old soldiers clearly got on with one another instinctively. Soon there was some quiet laughter, and the clink of two more bottles.

At six o'clock, Karolina at last returned from Normannenstrasse. Herr Möller went up to call her.

# CHAPTER EIGHTEEN

# KAROLINA

*East Berlin, 1968*

Karolina had had to hide things inside all her life. She was an expert at concealment. It had become part of her nature to play this game of poker with life, keeping her face blank, never showing her hand, never revealing her secrets.

But she'd never had a secret as big as this to hide. *She had a sister.*

That was something she was sure they didn't know. Not yet, anyway. If they had known, they would have used it against her already.

It was exactly the sort of thing the Stasi loved to have in your file. If they ever found out, they would use it to exert pressure on her, to blackmail her, even to harm Agnes. She couldn't let that happen, so they must never find out. She had to hide it deep, deep inside, and not let them know by a flicker of an eyelid that something had changed in her.

And something *had* changed in her. It was the biggest thing that had ever happened to her, and she couldn't stop thinking about it. There were a thousand questions she needed to ask Agnes. A thousand stories to share, good and bad. She would be able to talk to Agnes about things she'd never revealed to anyone – because nobody knew what she'd been through, not really. Not about her childhood, not about prison, or any of that. She was a closed book to the world; but she would open that book for her sister. The relief – the joy – would be incredible.

Thinking about Agnes had helped through horrible days at Normannenstrasse. Today, Hedwig had been particularly aggressive. There had been several covertly filmed videos, this time illustrating the more extreme sexual requests that Stasi Juliets were asked to fulfil. These, as Hedwig pointed out, were very useful, as they meant that extra pressure could be applied on the target. But when Karolina had unwisely shown distaste at the things she was forced to watch, Hedwig had flown into a rage, and had slapped her face, threatening her with a real beating if she did not concentrate.

And the visit to the dentist had been depressing. Hedwig had decided that Karolina's broken front tooth was going to be replaced with a gold one.

In Hedwig's coarse aesthetic vision, this was going to be a great enhancement. She herself had several gold teeth. She opened her mouth proudly to show Karolina. Gold teeth in the DDR were a status symbol of the very highest sort. An unmistakeable sign of privilege. The proletariat got steel replacement teeth if they were lucky. Most went with no replacement teeth at all, and put up with gaps instead.

'A gold tooth will make you so sexy,' she had crooned. 'You will look like a rich woman! Men will find you irresistible.'

Faced with Hedwig's own gold teeth, Karolina had felt unable to say that a gold tooth would be worse than a broken one, making her look old-fashioned, and moreover, unmistakeably Eastern European. She felt vandalised by the idea. But there was nothing she could say to stop them. The tooth was being made, and would be fitted in a week.

\* \* \*

Karolina reached home weary and drained, wondering when she was going to see Agnes again. There had been silence from the other side of the Wall for two days now. She was starting to have misgivings. Had the Stasi found out, after all? Were they keeping Agnes away? Her mind filled with images she would rather not see. She needed to swim and cleanse herself. But when she reached her door, Herr Möller appeared.

'Come down to my place,' he muttered.

'Why?' she asked.

He laid a stubby finger on his lips to warn her not to say anything. 'Come,' he mouthed.

Uncertainly, she followed him down to his little office next to the building's boilers and pipes.

To Karolina's joy, Agnes was in the room. But before she could speak, she saw that there was a second person there. A tall, middle-aged man in jeans and a leather jacket. She had never seen him before, yet somehow, without any shadow of a doubt, she recognised him. She stared at him, feeling that the spinning world had suddenly stopped its journey, that everything around her had come to a standstill.

'I know who you are,' she heard herself say.

He nodded, showing no emotion. 'We need to talk,' he said, his voice quiet and emotionless. 'And we don't have much time. Sit down.'

They sat at the kitchen table. Karolina took the chair next to Agnes. Herr Möller made a pot of his bitter, black, sugarless coffee. Karolina couldn't take her eyes away from her father's face. It was a hard face, with flinty blue eyes. She'd known of this man's existence all her life. She'd been told that he was a Nazi, a war criminal, a monster. She'd always wondered what she would say to him if they ever met. As a young girl, she'd had a fantasy that he would come to her, begging for forgiveness. Sometimes, she'd imagined herself haughtily confronting him with his crimes, telling him to begone and never to darken her doorstep again. At other times, she'd thought she would throw her arms around his neck and press her face against his chest. She would feel his arms encircle her, holding her tight, and she would forgive him for having abandoned her, for all his sins.

Neither of those two options were viable now that he had finally appeared in her life.

He was sitting across the table from her; but there was a vast gulf between them, an abyss torn by time, distance, ideology, the lives lived apart. She didn't know how it could ever be bridged. She didn't know whether she wanted to bridge it.

He was talking, in the clipped tones of a soldier. 'The sooner we do this, the better. We're going to keep things simple. In my experience, that is always best, in war and peace.'

'Agreed,' Möller said.

'We will do it this coming weekend. On Friday, Karolina will tell the Stasi that she is getting the flu. She will use white pepper to inflame her eyes and nose. She will make sure to sneeze and blow her nose a lot. She will tell them that she intends to spend the weekend resting in bed. That will make it less likely that they will disturb her. Nobody will want to catch her flu. Can you do that?'

Karolina met his eyes. 'I can do that.'

'Good. Very early on Monday morning, Herr Möller will take Karolina to Potsdam, and then onto some roads that go through the forest. They will wait at a prearranged spot, hidden from view. Agnes and I will meet them there with a car. Karolina will hide in the trunk of the car. Then we will drive to the border crossing near Schönefeld airfield. That crossing is not used by East Berliners. It's for West Berliners and diplomats, so they don't usually search the cars. I will obtain a car with diplomatic plates. I will have papers showing that I'm an embassy functionary of a state friendly to East Germany.

Agnes will be my secretary. If we are lucky, and they do not check with the embassy, it will all pass without incident.'

'What if they do search the car?' Agnes asked.

'We have to take a risk,' he replied bluntly. 'This is the lowest-risk scenario. The expressway is very busy early on Monday morning. It's rush hour. So our chances are good.'

'What about Herr Möller?' Karolina asked.

Möller shrugged. 'Don't worry about me,' he said. 'I will ride back on the bike, and be in my bed by dawn.'

'They will know it was you.'

'I've faced worse than these bastards,' he said.

'Elias was in the Brandenburg Division during the war,' von Breda said to Karolina. 'Reconnaissance and sabotage behind enemy lines. If you knew the things he did then, you wouldn't worry about him now.'

'*You* owe us something,' Karolina said with sudden anger. 'Herr Möller doesn't. Yet you're forcing him to take a terrible risk.'

Her father's face had become even stonier. 'Let us be clear – nobody in this room owes anybody else anything. Any one of us is free to walk out at any time.'

'We know that *you* can walk out,' Karolina shot back bitterly. 'You've done that before, haven't you?'

'Hush, *Mädchen*,' Herr Möller said. 'Nobody is forcing me to do this. I lost my daughter in the war. I would have done the same for her.'

Karolina's eyes were suddenly hot with unshed tears. 'You could come to the West, too.'

He indicated the photos on the wall. 'With my war mementoes and my photographs?' He shook his head. 'There, I would be just another old Nazi bastard. Here, at least they are used to me, even if they hate me, and I hate them. And I have a few old comrades on this side whom I should not like to lose. I'll take my chances here. Listen to your father.'

The word grated unexpectedly on Karolina's nerves. She felt Agnes take her hand, as though she guessed Karolina's emotions. Their fingers twined together tightly.

The two men settled down next to the boiler to talk in low voices, out of earshot.

'Do you have any faith in this plan?' Karolina demanded of Agnes. 'It sounds very rudimentary.'

'He said that simple is best.'

'But this is too simple.'

'I think we have to trust our father,' Agnes replied.

'You think of him as our father?'

'He's all we have,' Agnes replied gently.

'God help us.'

Agnes was troubled by Karolina's caustic tone. 'But he *is* our father, after all. He wouldn't wish us any harm.'

'I think you're being a bit naïve,' Karolina retorted. 'He's never seen either of us in his life before. Why should he care about us?'

'Of course he doesn't know us, and we don't know him. But he's here, now!'

'I don't know how you got him to come here, but I don't trust him an inch. He's willing to stuff me in the trunk of a car, and hope the border police don't find me!'

'He'll be in the car, too,' Agnes pointed out. 'He's taking the same risk you are.'

Karolina pulled her hand out of Agnes's. 'So he's convinced you already?'

'I wouldn't say that. But I will also be in the car, remember.'

'That means your life will be at risk, too. I've learned not to trust anybody,' Karolina said grimly. 'Especially not someone like him. He's a Nazi. Look at his face.'

'I screamed when I saw him,' Agnes confessed. 'I went back to my hotel room, and he jumped out like the Demon King in a pantomime.'

Karolina looked at von Breda over her shoulder. 'Exactly. A *Dämonenkönig*.'

Agnes half-smiled. 'But you know, he is *our* Demon King.'

Karolina frowned. 'You don't expect us to be a family if we ever get out of here, do you?'

'Hardly. He doesn't want *us*. He just wants to get back to his dog.'

'Dog?'

'Yes. The night he arrived, he wasn't remotely interested in me. He was worried about leaving his dog.'

Karolina rolled her eyes. 'My God.'

'I felt a bit sorry for him. Being so attached to his dog shows how lonely he is.'

'Good. I hope his life is miserable!'

'I'm pretty sure it is. But strangely, I feel that he's determined to help us.'

Karolina took Agnes's hand again. 'We have each other, Agnes,' she said, 'but the sad truth is that our parents never wanted either of us.'

'They still don't want us,' Agnes agreed wryly. 'All our mother feels is anger. The last thing she said to me was, "Don't come back." It's crazy, but she blames me for being taken away from her when I was a baby!'

Karolina was quiet for a while. At last she said, 'I understand how she feels.'

'Do you?'

'You had your grandfather. I've been alone all my life. One day, I will tell you a little about my childhood. It was hard. I longed for a father to protect me. But I also hated him for not being there. I think I still do.'

Agnes sighed. 'Perhaps it's enough that we saw him at all.'

'Yes. I never thought I would. It answers a few questions, at least. To see him once in my life is enough.'

'Well, he'll disappear back to Spain as soon as this is over, and we'll never see him again.'

'I will never forget meeting him, whatever happens next. And if the Stasi capture us – well, I would rather be back in Stauberg than do the things they want me to do.'

'Stauberg?'

'The women's prison. They'll put you in there, too.'

'I don't care,' Agnes said fiercely. 'And that won't happen. We'll make this work. Together.'

They had to get back to the West before the checkpoint closed for the night. Agnes hated leaving Karolina in the East. It tore at her heart strings. In the past days, she had grown a powerful sense of responsibility for her sister. Oddly, it was as though she were the elder, and Karolina the younger in some ways. In others, she felt that Karolina knew things that she never would. She had a deep wisdom, almost fatalism, that Agnes found hard to understand. Karolina was what Barbar would have called an old soul.

Agnes had already decided, though she hadn't said this to Karolina, that if they couldn't get Karolina out, then she would go and live with Karolina in East Germany. That would be better than living separated. The idea of having to go through Checkpoint Charlie every time, or of waving to her sister over a minefield for the rest of their lives, was too terrible to contemplate.

She and von Breda travelled separately, and met up in Agnes's room around eight in the evening. Agnes was still jittery about the plan von Breda had outlined.

'Where are you going to get a diplomatic car from?' she demanded.

'A diplomatic car is not required,' he replied calmly. 'Only diplomatic plates. The car can be obtained without difficulty.'

'And who will supply the diplomatic plates?' she pressed. 'Your mysterious friends?'

'They are not my friends,' von Breda retorted, 'and I still

have useful contacts of my own in this country. Please don't interrogate me. I have it all in hand.'

'I'm not interrogating you,' Agnes snapped. 'I just want to be treated like an adult, not a child.'

'Then perhaps you could begin behaving like an adult,' he replied coolly.

'You are really insufferable,' she said.

'So I have been told. You are not the first to make this important discovery. I am going to get something to eat. You may come if you choose.'

She was too hungry to refuse. They walked through the busy streets to a small Vietnamese restaurant that Gabi at the reception desk had recommended. At night, this part of Berlin was lively, young people coming in and out of bars, the sound of music and laughter all around. How different, she thought, from life in the communist zone.

They were offered a window table, which von Breda refused. She had noticed how circumspect he was, cautious in all his behaviour. It was not reassuring. He clearly had something to be afraid of. They sat in a back corner instead, and ordered the cheapest dishes on the menu. The restaurant was small and crowded, the air filled with the smells of cooking, incense and what she strongly suspected was hashish.

'Constanze Ozerki told me that they had to put pressure on you to come,' she said. 'Is that true?'

He gave her a smouldering glance. 'I told you, it was not easy for me to come here.'

'So without that pressure – whatever it was – you wouldn't have come to help us?'

'No.'

'Well, at least you are honest.' Their beers arrived, and she took a long drink of hers. 'You saw the way my sister reacted to you today. Didn't that make you ashamed?'

'Ashamed of what?'

'Of refusing to help until someone put a gun to your head.'

'Agnes, you are wasting your time if you think you can make me feel guilty. I already told you – I owe you no explanations, and you owe me none.'

'That's such an easy cop-out,' she said angrily. 'You slept with our mother, and you think it just ended there. That's like pulling the trigger and saying you're not responsible for where the bullet goes.'

'I think I know a little more about pulling triggers than you do,' he replied ironically.

'Oh, I'm sure you do. Incidentally, do you have any other bastard children out there? Ones we don't know about yet?'

His face was impassive, but she could tell from his eyes that she was getting under his skin, and that gave her a fierce satisfaction. 'No,' he replied shortly.

'How can you be sure – with all the triggers you've pulled?'

'I went to Norway on direct orders from the Reichsführer,' he said. 'So you have a distinguished pedigree. Your existence was planned by Heinrich Himmler himself. I am sure he would have been charmed to see the product of his inspired racial planning. Unfortunately, he poisoned himself in Lüneburg prison in 1945, and was deprived of that pleasure.'

Tears of hurt had filled Agnes's eyes while he was speaking. 'You don't have to say things like that to me!'

'Nor do you have to be so offensive to me.' He drained his beer, and went on tersely, 'I myself was occupied with war between 1939 and 1945. I was captured by the Americans during the Battle of Berlin, and sentenced to death. I spent the next fifteen years in solitary confinement, waiting to be hanged. I have been a free man for only seven years, three months and five days. So yes – I can be sure that although I pulled the trigger on a variety of weapons many times, I did not produce any more children.'

Their food arrived. The lump in her throat prevented her from eating more than a single mouthful. 'Do you have any idea what sort of life Liv Christiansen has had since the war?' she asked shakily.

'The Romans had a saying: vae victis. Woe to the defeated. As the defeated, she and I were both at the mercy of our conquerors. Had we won the war, we would all be living very different lives today.'

'Yes, under the Nazi jackboot.'

'Not you, Agnes. With Himmler's stamp of approval, you would have had a very privileged life.'

'Please stop saying that! It's disgusting!'

'Then let us leave this distasteful topic of conversation for good.' He plied his chopsticks, his appetite evidently unspoiled. 'Please eat. Or you will be hungry later.'

She swallowed. 'That's the first thing you've said to me that sounds like a father.'

'If you want to pretend that I am your father, then treat me like one,' he retorted.

The food was tasty and filling. She managed to eat enough to keep body and soul together. The alcohol also helped. But conversation between them had ground to a halt for the time being, and she didn't feel like renewing it. Conversation with Ulrich von Breda left her feeling bruised.

'There's something I want to tell you,' Agnes forced herself to say at last.

He raised one dark eyebrow. 'Is this more sarcasm?'

'No. It's about Karolina. When I first met her—' She stopped.

'What?' he demanded.

'She was about to kill herself.'

His expression changed. 'How?'

'She went to the bottom of the deep end of the pool where she swims. She was down there for over two minutes. She was going to drown herself. Actually, I jumped in and swam down to her, and made her come up.'

'Would she have done it?'

'Yes, I think so. She's a very good swimmer. She knew what she was doing. She had it all planned. The point is, she wanted to kill herself. That shows the depth of her despair. When I talked to her about getting out of East Berlin, she was apathetic. She said it was impossible, that the Stasi were too powerful. We need to give her back the determination to try. And that won't be easy.'

He said nothing, but she could see he was disturbed by what she'd told him. After they'd eaten, they walked back to the hostel.

They settled down at opposite ends of the room. Agnes took out her diary, and started filling it in. Von Breda got something out of his bag and appeared to be concentrating on it. At last, she noticed what it was – a small travelling chess set. He was evidently playing through the permutations of a famous match, something she had seen Barbar do countless times while he'd been alive.

She cleared her throat. 'Would you like a game?' she asked diffidently.

He looked up at her with sceptical blue eyes. 'Do you play?'

'A little.'

He considered. 'It's not good on this tiny board. Some other time, perhaps.'

She wasn't letting him get away with that one. 'Hold on. I'll see if they've got a full-size set at reception.'

He sighed heavily. Ignoring that, she went down to the reception desk, and returned triumphantly with a nice old wooden set that Gabi had produced.

Barely hiding his weary displeasure, von Breda pulled chairs up to the table, and they set out the board. He was obviously impatient, and wanting to get back to the game he'd been studying on his travelling set. With luck, she thought, he would be off guard and distracted, and she could get an early advantage. Defeating him at chess – or at least knocking him back a little – would be very satisfying.

He played white, and opened fast, not seeming to be thinking about his moves. She kept hers conservative, not showing any hint of the aggression she was capable of. The game moved easily ahead, until all the pieces were in attack or defence positions, and battle could be commenced.

'You prefer Karolina to me, don't you?' she said.

'Why would you say that?' he grunted, eyes fixed on the board.

'You treat her differently. More kindly.'

He was silent while he thought of his next move. 'She has suffered,' he said at last, moving his queen up the board.

'And I haven't?'

'Not in the same way.'

'You don't know what sort of life I've had, Ulrich.'

'I can see it in your eyes,' he retorted. 'You haven't been hurt as your sister has been hurt.'

'Does that make me less worthy of your respect?'

'It makes her more deserving of my compassion.'

'Are you admitting that you feel guilt, after all?'

'I feel sympathy. That's a bad move, by the way. You may take it back.'

'Oh, you're right. Thanks, but I'll leave it. It will teach me to be more careful in future.'

He took the piece she had just moved. 'You have had a good life so far, Agnes. Something that the rest of us haven't had.'

'It was a good life, but it was based on lies. When the lies came out, my "good life" disappeared. I'm not the person I was before all this started. I've changed. Grown. And perhaps it hasn't occurred to you, but I'm the reason we're all here. If I hadn't started looking for the truth, we would all still be scattered.'

He took another of her pieces, which she had apparently neglected to defend. 'That might have been the best thing for all concerned.'

'Except for Karolina. She is all I care about. Getting her out of East Germany. Saving her.'

'That is certainly more important than satisfying your childish curiosity,' he replied.

'Another slap in the face for Agnes,' she responded ironically.

'You English have a saying, "curiosity killed the cat". Unfortunately, curiosity also kills other cats.'

He moved his queen again. She could barely hide her glee; he was falling into the trap she had set. She had to keep him talking, to prevent him noticing. 'Speaking of cats, you never told me the names of your dogs.'

'Kaiserin and Beatrix.'

'Which one died?'

'Kaiserin.'

'How did she die?'

He raised one dark eyebrow at her. 'What does it matter?'

'I'm just curious. What about Beatrix?'

'She is waiting for me in a boarding kennels.'

She noted that *waiting for me*. 'Karolina thinks your attachment to your dogs means that you're lonely.'

'Dogs are more faithful than human beings. They cannot lie, they ask nothing, and they give everything they have.'

'I never had a dog. My grandfather wouldn't get one, even though I begged him.'

'That is very un-English.' He was frowning now as he studied the board. He was starting to suspect that something was wrong.

'Oh, Barbar was extremely English,' she said quickly. 'In the pirate tradition, though. He stole me, you know.'

'Stole you?'

'While my mother was in an internment camp. He'd lost

his own son in the bombing. He took me back to Britain as a baby. She never knew what happened to me. I think it broke her heart.'

'Is that true?'

'Yes.'

'Unlucky for her. Lucky for you.' He moved his queen again.

'You're right.' Agnes could now spring her trap. She brought in the bishop who had been lurking on the other side of the board, and set it down, attacking his king.

He stared at the pieces for a moment, then whispered, *'Du kleine Teufelin.'*

'Is something wrong?' she asked innocently.

'You little devil. You have checkmate in three!'

'Yes, I think I do.'

He raised his eyes to hers. Oddly, he wasn't angry. He seemed almost to be smiling. 'You are very good. But you will not beat me again.'

'Probably not,' she agreed. 'It was enough to beat you once.'

'Your grandfather taught you to play?'

'Yes. He was a county champion.'

'And he was the one who brought you up?'

'Yes.'

Von Breda nodded. 'He did a better job than I could have done.' He toppled his king. *'Gut gemacht.'*

'Do you want another game?'

'No. Enjoy your victory.'

He seemed more relaxed than she'd yet seen her. 'Can I ask you something?'

'If you must.'

'Why did you kill those American prisoners of war?'

He was silent for a long time, and she thought that she had gone too far. But he spoke at last. 'The war took away my humanity. The only emotion I had left was rage. That is not an excuse. But that is the reason. I regretted it later. I had fifteen years to think about what I did that day. But it was too late. They should have hanged me. I never understood why they didn't.'

'Were you a Nazi?'

'You ask that as though "Nazi" meant only one thing. I was not an admirer of the party leaders. That fat swine Goering, the murderous chicken farmer Himmler, the poisonous gnome Goebbels. They disgusted me. But I respected Hitler, at least at first – until I realised he was a raving lunatic. And I was a good German. And I did what I was told. There were many of us like that. I had no hatred of the Jews, but I said nothing when they were taken away. I had no hatred of Russians, but I killed them all the same.' He packed the chess pieces back in their battered wooden box. 'I was a soldier. My job was war, and I did it as best I could. Long before the end, we all knew that Hitler had turned us into criminals. That is why my so-called comrades all disappeared. I could have followed them – to Spain, Argentina, South Africa. But I allowed myself to be captured because I no longer wanted to live with myself.'

He had never spoken about himself at such length, and she was not sure how to respond. 'Thank you for telling me.'

He looked into her eyes. 'I am not a good man, Agnes. If I am harsh to you, it's because I don't want you to form any kind of attachment. Don't get any sentimental ideas about me. There are many people who would be alive today, but for me pulling the trigger. That is not the sort of man you want for a father.'

'Maybe you should let us be the judges of that.'

He rose to his feet, stretching. 'I'm going out for a walk. I need to think.'

Agnes nodded. 'Okay.'

'I have to start early tomorrow if we're going to get everything ready by Monday. I might not come back tonight. Don't wait up for me. Goodnight, Agnes.'

'Goodnight, Ulrich.'

\* \* \*

He walked the streets alone for hours.

How strange it was to be back in Berlin after twenty-three years! The city of his childhood and youth had changed. Sometimes the alleys, garishly lit and crowded, seemed to him like the pleasure quarter in some remote foreign capital, redolent with the spice of exotic cooking, pulsing to the beat of strange music, crowded with people who sang and shouted in unfamiliar languages. At other times he found himself in dark and silent places, where the past hung heavy. The moon had risen, almost full. His mother and his sisters were pale ghosts that whispered to him, *Where have you been? Why did you never come back to us?*

The Brandenburg Gate, floodlit against the night sky, drew him. Peace and majesty radiated from it. But he could not help recalling how Berlin had been in those last weeks of the war – the canyons of ruins so shattered that it seemed human hands could never rebuild them, the flame and oily smoke all around, the dead sprawled in the streets, soldiers and civilians alike. And the endless thunder of the Soviet artillery that drew closer, an approaching *Götterdämmerung* in which the ancient gods themselves were doomed to die.

Once again he was enveloped in that unique stink of war. His ears reverberated with the explosions, the screams of the wounded, the hoarse commands he himself had used to squeeze the last efforts from his exhausted men.

Not far from here, his mother and two sisters had died. The Russians had reached this part of Berlin before the Americans did. That had been bad luck. The fate that had overtaken so many German women now faced them, too. Rather than endure it, the three of them had taken cyanide in the garden of their house. They'd picked bouquets of spring flowers first. He'd found their bodies, together with the dead flowers, on the garden bench where he had played as a child.

His family were gone. He'd seen the city of his birth laid waste. Everything was lost, even honour. He'd no longer wanted to live. Others had fled. He'd allowed himself to be captured.

The war crimes trial had been brief. The Americans had assigned him an American lawyer. Von Breda had been prepared to plead guilty, to get it all over with.

His lawyer had taken a liking to him, for what reason von Breda could not fathom. The earnest young man, who'd never fired a shot in the war, but who'd been put in a major's uniform straight from law school, had made a plea for mitigation, based on the premise, as he expressed it, 'that von Breda's actions were produced by the desperate situation his command was in, and were not altogether from criminal intent.' He'd gone over the losses sustained by von Breda's group, the horrendous injuries, the deaths, the confusion, the close friends who'd died. He'd also begun to mention the bombing of Berlin, the suicide of von Breda's family.

The leader of the tribunal had responded that personal misfortunes were not an excuse for military crimes. A British judge had pointed out that countless civilians had died in Luftwaffe bombing of British cities. And that had been that.

He'd been sentenced along with dozens of others on the same day.

All had numbers hung on large placards around their necks. They'd removed all signs of rank, all decorations, and even all divisional insignia from the men's uniforms. They were all in motley clothing, von Breda in a plain tunic which was far too light for the freezing conditions. He'd tried not to shiver, in case it was mistaken for fear.

The verdicts had all been guilty, the punishments a litany of death sentences, a few life sentences, one or two ten-year terms. Each man had been taken away between two Polish military policemen in American uniforms. Almost to a man, the German officers had been silent and expressionless during sentencing.

Von Breda's name was called. He marched to the bench where the judges were seated, and stood to attention. The Judge Advocate glanced at him briefly before reading the verdict and sentence. The first words were all a blur to von Breda, but he focused slowly as the preamble came to an end:

'... sentences you to death by hanging at such time and place as higher authority may direct.'

The vision faded slowly away, leaving him light-headed. He had reached the Wall.

It cut across the city, a sword of concrete blocks and barbed wire. The Russians had violated Germany, and their final deed was to violate Berlin with this act of crude, brutal, possession. It filled von Breda with fury. He could see the searchlights of the border guards on the other side, relentlessly probing, searching for those who were madly enough in love with freedom to risk an escape. They all ended up hanging on the barbed wire.

He stood with his fists clenched in his pockets, his teeth clenched. All those mistakes that had led to this. Those dreadful, dreadful mistakes. If he could have undone them now! But he could never undo any of it.

He turned away and walked on, his head down, thinking. *Why did you kill those American prisoners of war?* she had asked him. Because emotion had seized him by the throat. That was why. Emotion had turned him from a soldier into a beast.

Emotion had got the better of him too many times in his life. It was a monster that lived in some dark cell deep inside him, waiting for its moment to get out and wreak havoc. He was best with a game of chess, where logic ruled. And she had beaten him even there, the little devil.

He recalled the dancing blue light in her eyes as she'd grinned at him in impish triumph over the trap she'd laid for him. *Die kleine Teufelin!*

It had been so easy to think of them as cyphers, abstracts

that had no connection to him – until he'd met them, touched them, heard their voices. Then they had suddenly, with terrible power, become overwhelmingly real. Agnes, the cool English-woman with the sweet face and the will of steel that was so like his own. Karolina, a wild bird like her mother, wounded and brave, surviving horrors with an inner strength that came from God knew where. From him? From Liv?

What she had told him about Karolina's attempted suicide had unsettled him deeply. He'd firmly rejected any guilt about the girls. He'd refused to acknowledge responsibility. But all that had changed somehow, almost overnight.

Where did this frightening new emotion come from, this new, fatal mistake?

What was this visceral tie that pulled him to them? It had infected his blood. He was not the same anymore. He would never be the same again. He should never have come to Berlin! And yet he could not refuse. It hadn't been Gottfried and his vulgar threats that had brought him here. It had been something else. A cry for help that had crossed the decades and the voids and had reached a heart that he'd thought dead: the stone heart in his breast that now pounded like a fist, heavy and purposeful.

He had come here to fulfil a destiny that had been laid down for him long ago and far away.

He had been very good at killing between 1939 and 1945. He'd shown an aptitude for war and death. Now he had to learn how to protect life. How to care for his children.

He thought of their faces, so different, and yet so alike. Sisters. Agnes and Karolina. Karolina and Agnes. The two lives that he and Liv had created, and then abandoned.

Well, those birds had come home to roost.

He knew now that he was irrevocably committed to them. And he also knew that he was not going to emerge from this unscathed.

Yes, he could walk to the railway station now and get the first train out of Berlin, go to earth in some unknown corner of the world and never think of the girls again.

But that was as impossible as sprouting wings and taking to the air. He was tied to them now, and they were tied to him. Blood to blood. Blood had made them. Only blood could set them free.

It was just a question of how much, and upon what altar, it was to be spilled.

# CHAPTER NINETEEN

# THE SISTERS

*West Berlin, 1968*

True to his word, von Breda didn't come back that night. He had disappeared, and did not return during the next day, either.

Having been strictly instructed by him not to cross over to the East, Agnes found herself at a loose end. She had little to do but think about Karolina – and the few details about his past life that von Breda had told her. As far as parents went, she thought wryly, she and Karolina had not won the lottery.

Her father was not back by the time she went to bed on Thursday night. Nor did he return during Friday. She had started to get intensely worried. Had he abandoned them, and disappeared back into the void? If his instruction to stay in the West had not been so emphatic, she would not have been able to resist going across to see her sister.

On Saturday afternoon, Gabi from reception came up to her room. 'There's a call for you downstairs.'

Agnes hurried down. The hostel was too basic to have telephones in the rooms, but there was a pay phone in the lobby that guests used. She was expecting the call to be from Ulrich, but it was Constanze Ozerki's voice that came through.

'Hallo, *Liebchen*. Is there any news?'

Ulrich had told her not to discuss details of the escape plan with anyone else, so she didn't mention them. 'No news, Constanze. We're still hoping to find a way out.'

'This is disappointing,' Constanze said sharply. 'I would have thought that by now he would have something in hand. After all, the man was an SS officer.'

'Constanze,' Agnes said in alarm, glancing to see whether Gabi could listen in to the call, 'this is a public telephone. You don't know who's listening!'

'*Ach*, nobody cares anymore,' Constanze retorted. 'The SS were supposed to be the perfect soldiers. The ones who got things done. Why is he so slow? If he doesn't do something soon, those swines will have my daughter in a brothel!'

'Constanze!'

'I want to speak to him myself. Put him on.'

'He's not here.'

'Well, where is he?'

'I don't know,' she confessed.

'You don't *know?*'

'I haven't seen him for a couple of days.'

'*Mein Gott.* The scoundrel has run away from his responsibilities yet again!'

This coincided uncomfortably with Agnes's own fears and suspicions, but she tried to soothe Constanze. 'I don't think that's the case at all. I'm sure he's working on it. But we should not be discussing this on a public telephone. It isn't safe.'

'You are right. I will come to Berlin and speak to him myself.'

Agnes's heart sank. 'I really don't think that's a good idea—'

'Nonsense. You are too soft with him. Of course, the man is your father. But men need to be managed, even fathers!'

'Please don't come to Berlin, Constanze. The situation is very delicate.'

'*Natürlich*, one understands that,' Constanze said indignantly.

'What do you think I am? We are talking about my daughter here. My only child.' Her voice almost broke. 'My lost child!'

Agnes felt panic rising. If Constanze came to Berlin, things would get extremely complicated. 'We're expecting a resolution very soon,' she said, choosing her words carefully. 'Imminently, in fact. I can't talk about it on the phone. But it's much better if you stay in Munich for the time being. I promise I will call you with any news.'

There was a brief silence while Constance considered this. 'No,' she said decisively. 'I must be there. I will get the train tomorrow.'

The line clicked dead in Agnes's ear.

At last, late that evening, Ulrich reappeared, coming into her room unannounced. He looked tired and scruffy, his lean jaw stubbled, his hands dirty with oil.

'You look like hell,' she said unkindly.

He shrugged. 'I've been busy.'

She looked at his oily hands. 'Doing what? Working on a tractor?'

'Something like that.'

'I've had a call from Constanze Ozerki.' She told him about Constanze's intention to arrive the next day. She'd expected him to hit the roof, but he seemed unperturbed.

'It's good,' he said. 'When she arrives, tell her all about the plan. Keep her happy. You can even discuss the details.'

Agnes narrowed her eyes. 'Aren't you being a little incautious? She's not exactly discreet.'

'I think we can trust her,' he replied coolly. 'After all, she has the fantasy that she is Karolina's mother.'

'She wants to give you a piece of her mind.'

'Unluckily, I won't be here.'

'You're going back?'

'Early tomorrow.'

'There isn't much time left, Ulrich.'

He met her eyes with a hard glint. 'I am aware of how much time there is left, Agnes.'

'Well?' she asked impatiently. 'Is everything going according to plan?'

'There are a few details to iron out.'

'Is it going to work?' she asked in a low voice.

'There is no reason why it shouldn't.'

'There must be at least a hundred reasons why it shouldn't,' she retorted.

'Everything will be all right if each person does their duty. Don't lose your nerve, child.'

She stared at him with her eyebrows raised.

'What's the matter?' he asked, frowning.

'You called me "child".'

'You object to the word?'

'No. But it's suspiciously like a term of endearment. Or at least, a familial one.'

'Don't get your hopes up.'

'What are you going to do when this is all over, Ulrich?' she asked gently. 'Go back to your solitude in Spain? Never see me or Karolina again?'

'I told you, having me close by will not enhance either of your lives.'

'And I told you – we are the best judges of that.'

'No,' he replied shortly, 'you are not. Leave all this, now. It's irrelevant.'

'All right. Tell me what you want me to do. When do you want me to go across to the East?'

'I will send you a message,' he replied. 'You may not recognise the voice or the messenger. But it will be identified by a codeword. The name of one of my dogs. The one which died. You remember it?'

'Yes.'

'If any instruction arrives with that codeword, obey it implicitly. Don't hesitate. Don't question it. That's vital. You understand?'

'Of course.'

'Just obey. That's all. I'm relying on you, Agnes.'

'Got it,' she said.

'Do you want a game of chess?'

The chess game lasted far longer than the last one. As he'd predicted, she wasn't able to win a second time, but she was able to stave off defeat until the end game, where his careful planning made it impossible for her to continue.

'You are strong,' he commented, putting the pieces away, 'but you need more practice.'

'Since my grandfather died, I have nobody to play against.'

Von Breda leaned back in his chair, studying her face. 'You remind me of your mother,' he said unexpectedly. 'But she was a wild bird. You are a garden bird.'

'I'm not sure if that's a compliment or not,' Agnes responded uncomfortably.

'It's just an observation.'

'What's the difference between a wild bird and a garden bird?'

'A wild bird can never live in a garden. The other birds will peck it to death.'

'I think that happened a long time ago,' Agnes said sadly. 'They didn't just take her baby away – they gave her years of shock treatments, amounting to torture. And she's hated wherever she goes, even in the remote village where she lives now. Someone spat on me there, just because they guessed I was her daughter.'

'But I imagine she fights back?' he said quietly.

'She throws stones at them.'

He nodded slowly. 'I can picture that.'

'She's completely alone, Ulrich. There are no curtains on her windows, no pictures on her walls. And she drinks too much. She has to order everything from Oslo because they won't serve her in the village shops. She's an outcast.'

'As am I. If you're asking me to go and see her, forget it. How do you think those people will react if her SS lover comes to join her? They will be out with flaming torches and pitchforks.'

'You could take her to Spain with you.'

'My time in Spain is coming to an end. There will be no safety for her with me.'

'Why do you say that?'

'The action in Belgium was not the only one of its kind. We were ordered to take reprisals in Russia. To shoot partisans in Italy. Other actions that I prefer not to remember. I will never be forgiven. There will always be someone waiting to kill me.' He said the words matter-of-factly, but they sent a chill down her spine, and she shuddered. 'One of these days, I will switch on the ignition in my car, and a bomb will blow me to pieces. Or a sniper will pick me off as I walk on my land. I live under sentence of death, Agnes. I cannot share my life with anyone else.'

She was dry-mouthed. 'I had no idea about any of this.'

'My so-called comrades detest me, because my very existence puts them all in danger. None of them were captured and put on trial, you see. Their names are not known, as mine is known. Their sins are hidden, but mine are not. They will be happy to see me dead. They will probably help my assassins.'

'That's terrible!'

'I committed crimes against the human race. It's not fit that I should still be walking the earth. I refuse to kill myself, because I am a soldier. And I will defend myself. But that is all I have.' He rose to his feet and stretched. 'We will worry about these things later. Put them out of your mind. I need to sleep, now.'

Agnes lay awake for a long time in the darkness before sleep came. She'd played a game of chess with Barbar just before he'd died. The thought that history was about to repeat itself disturbed her.

And when she woke, early the next morning, von Breda was gone.

The tap on the door came at four o'clock on Sunday afternoon. Agnes's heart jumped, and she hurried to open the door. A man she didn't know was standing in the hallway. He was nondescript, but his age and bearing reminded her of Elias Möller.

'Good afternoon,' he greeted her quietly. 'Fräulein von Breda?'

She blinked at the name. 'Uh – yes.'

He handed her a folded slip of paper. 'A message from Kaiserin for you. *Wiedersehn.*' Without waiting for a reply, he gave her a quick salute, and went back down the stairwell.

Agnes read the note quickly. It was an address in Berlin, and beneath it was written, 'Wait here with Constanze and a car tomorrow morning from 0730 hours.'

She hurried after the man, calling, 'Stop, stop! This isn't the plan!' But when she reached the street, he had vanished.

Electrified, she hailed the first cab that passed and made her way to Constanze's hotel.

Karolina woke from a troubled sleep to see a dark figure looming over her. She drew a breath to scream, but a gloved hand gripped her shoulder hard.

'It's me.' The low voice was Elias Möller's. 'Get up. Quietly! We're leaving.'

'What time is it?' Karolina groped for the light switch, but again, Möller's hand stopped her.

'No lights. No noise. No talking. Get dressed. Don't take anything with you.'

Her heart thudding against her ribs, Karolina found clothes and pulled them on. Herr Möller opened the door of her apartment and peered out. It was still night. He jerked his head for her to follow him.

The block was silent as the grave, and almost as dark. Karolina noticed that all the lights in the corridors and hallways were off. As the building's handyman, she guessed, Möller would have shut off the circuits. They went down the stairs like shadows. At the exit of the building, Möller made her wait once again while he checked the street. Then he jerked his head. 'Quickly,' he whispered. 'Follow me.' He set off, shouldering a large knapsack.

The streets of East Berlin were silent and empty at night, so much so that the noise of traffic and the occasional wail of a police or ambulance siren in the West could be heard from across the Wall, miles away. There was nobody about. Nevertheless, they kept under the trees and close to walls, away from the dim pools of light provided by the street lamps, walking quickly but quietly. Herr Möller's stocky figure moved just ahead of her, his cropped head turning now and then to look over his knapsack and check that she was keeping up.

She had no idea where they were going. This was not the plan that they had discussed. According to the plan, they should have left early on Monday morning – that was tomorrow.

'Careful now,' Möller hissed. They had reached a fence made of corrugated iron. He pulled one of the sheets aside and hauled himself up the rubble behind it, reaching back a hand to help her. She clambered over the top and jumped down into wasteland. They were in one of the bombed areas that remained all over this part of the city.

It was very dark here, and the ground was an obstacle course of ditches, rocky heaps of stones and some remaining walls of what had once been houses, their empty windows indifferent to the furtive human passers-by. The whole expanse was waist-high in fireweed, which proliferated in bombsites, feeding on the chemical residues left by high explosives and burning. As they trampled the plants, the aromatic scents filled the night air, herbal and astringent from the leaves, appley from the ripe berries.

Soon, they were lost in a maze of wartime devastation. One vast crater appeared to lead into the next. Under the ceaseless rain of Allied bombs, whole blocks had been destroyed. But Herr Möller was unhesitating. This was a journey he must have made many times before, she realised. At times they had to climb up steep piles of debris, their feet slithering on shattered bricks, their clothes catching on tangles of exposed pipework that were like the entrails of slaughtered beasts.

They reached a half-gutted church, its outline just visible in the darkness. The steeple lay in a long, crooked line across the ground. Both ends of the building were gone, and all the windows were empty of the stained glass that must once have filled them; but the nave remained, and Möller led her into it. Halfway through, he stopped, took off his knapsack, and put his fingers to his lips. Karolina tried to still her panting. The old fellow had set a brisk pace, and she was out of breath.

He listened for several minutes, seeming to cock his ears like an animal. There was no sound. At last he was satisfied. 'The moon is coming up now. It's bad luck, but it can't be helped, so be careful. Stay in the shadows. Okay?'

'Okay.'

He shouldered his knapsack. 'Ready?'

'Yes. But where are we going?'

'You will see.'

They set off again, emerging from the other end of the church. As Möller had said, the moon was rising, an icy disc edging up behind the ruins. Its cold light showed that they were crossing what had once been the churchyard. The ground had been heaved up by an earthquake bomb, the ancient tombstones toppled and scattered, as though the dead had tried desperately to claw their way out of the earth. It was an unearthly sight.

Karolina shuddered as they made their way over cracked stone slabs bearing the names of long-dead Berlin families.

Then it occurred to her that the shattered graves were a sign of some kind of resurrection; and for the first time that night she realised that she herself was moving towards freedom. Her stomach lurched. Dare she hope that this time, she would make it? Here was only imprisonment and pain. On the other side of the Wall, she had a sister, a future, even a father of sorts.

These thoughts had almost brought her to a standstill. Herr Möller hissed at her angrily. She quickened her pace to catch him up.

They emerged from the churchyard and crossed a silent street. Karolina knew where they were, now. They had reached the area allocated by the Soviet occupiers as vegetable patches for East Berliners, in an effort to provide extra food in a city that was perpetually hungry. The little market gardens stretched out under the rising moon, most of them presided over by crazy sheds erected out of whatever scrap materials the gardeners could find, or studded with relics from bombed houses – bath-tubs, rickety chests of drawers, old boilers. It was here that Herr Möller had his allotment.

They made their way through the orderly rows of onions, potatoes and cabbages. Here and there, gardeners were already at work in the pre-dawn hours, dark figures hoeing or watering their precious crops. The city was about to wake up.

Herr Möller's shanty was larger and better built than the others, cobbled together out of clapboards and corrugated sheeting. When he opened the door, Karolina saw why it was so substantial: it housed a motorcycle.

Möller wheeled the machine out. It was an old MZ with a sidecar, its bodywork plentifully dented, but with an engine that gleamed. Möller passed Karolina a helmet and goggles. 'Put these on.'

She obeyed. There was also a scarf to wrap around her lower face, making her effectively unrecognisable. Möller tilted the fairing of the sidecar forward. She climbed into the hard little seat and he brought the fairing down, sealing her in behind the Plexiglas windshield. He stamped on the kick-starter, and the engine rumbled into life.

'*Los*,' he muttered, and they set off.

It was now around 5 a.m. and the sky was starting to lighten. The moon was also high by now. The cloak of darkness was being lifted.

As they rode through the streets, they began to see other vehicles, and occasionally factory workers walking to the early shift. Huddled in the nacelle of the sidecar, Karolina felt surprisingly cold. Möller hadn't let her take anything with her. She thought of what she'd left behind: a few clothes, a few tattered books, some cheap kitchen things. What a pitiful life! How sterile and constrained! It made her want to weep to think of how little a life it had been.

Her thoughts turned to her last escape attempt, so many years ago. How had she had the courage to attempt it, at the age of nineteen? She remembered her determination to get away from the irksome restrictions of life in the DDR, to escape to a life which she could only imagine through pop songs and smuggled magazines. She'd been so naïve! She hadn't dreamed of how much worse her life was to become.

The Wall had only recently been built, then. It had not yet become the fearsome bulwark against capitalism that it was now. But it had already been a deadly obstacle. She'd embarked on it as though it was a Sunday picnic. Weed and schnapps had played a large part. She remembered telling the others that she was going to escape.

'You'll never make it,' one had warned.

'Send us a postcard of the Brandenburg Gate,' Steffi, her best friend at the time, had laughed. She meant the other side of the gate, the side that East Berliners could never see.

'I promise I will,' she'd said, hugging Steffi. That had been the last time she'd seen Steffi. The last time she had hugged any of her friends.

How had she not been torn to pieces by the dogs? Shot by the guards? Blown up by the mines?

She remembered the lights dazzling her, the hoarse klaxons screaming, the metallic voice of the loud hailers booming *'Halt! Halt! Don't move! Stay where you are!'*

She remembered the cold realisation washing through her that it was all over. That she could never again be the golden girl of the socialist state. That from this point on, her life was forever shattered.

She'd been too dazed to cry or protest as they'd seized her and dragged her back from the minefield. But she had kept her eyes on the other side of the Wall, on the West, on the forever lost what-might-have-been, until they had thrown her to the ground and locked her hands behind her back.

Prison had been dreadful. The day she'd arrived, four female guards had taken her to the shower rooms and had held her under water until her lungs filled, and she was at the brink of death. They'd let her cough it agonisingly up and claw her way back to life. Then they'd repeated the performance four times more.

After that, they'd beaten her with rubber truncheons, concentrating on the places that would bring the most lasting pain – her kidneys, breasts and legs. Then they had dragged her to her cell. Solitary confinement for three months to begin her sentence.

That had been her introduction to Stauberg. The passage to a world of brutality.

The next two years and nine months had been a long second act. Crushing boredom had been the threnody. But incidents stood out in her memory. The day the guards had broken her teeth in the dining hall because she'd spat a piece of gristle back onto her plate. The day they'd pulled her pants down and bent her over a trestle and whipped her buttocks with electrical cable because she'd been 'insolent'. The times they'd told her she was going to be released, and made her pack her things, only to howl with laughter when they revealed it was just a joke.

She huddled down against the wind. She wasn't going back to prison. The next time a gun was pointed at her, she was going to make sure they shot her.

One way or another, this was her last exit.

# CHAPTER TWENTY

# THE WALL

*Berlin, 1968*

The journey on Herr Möller's motorcycle was a long one. But Karolina soon realised that they were not making their way south-west to Potsdam, but were travelling in the opposite direction, towards the north-east of the city. She was puzzled, then anxious.

'Where are we going?' she shouted to Möller, but he simply shook his head and laid his gloved finger on his lips to silence her.

They were travelling through what had once been new suburbs, streets of endless apartment blocks built cheek by jowl with one another before the war to accommodate city workers and their families. Now, the blocks were rundown and shabby, many so badly damaged by the tank warfare that had taken place here in the winter of 1944–1945 that they were effectively uninhabitable. And every few streets, a gaping hole showed where an Allied bomb had landed.

Möller rode stolidly, obeying all traffic signs, never exceeding the speed limit. It was cold, but the sun was coming up. The sky was at first blood-red, then salmon-pink. On the bigger streets, trams were starting to run. Workers were on the move. This was a part of Berlin that Karolina didn't know well, but a street sign revealed they were heading towards Schönholz, which she knew was a leafy, wooded outskirt, favoured by middle-ranking party *Apparatchiks*. Indeed, the cheap apartment blocks were already giving way to comfortable, middle-class villas.

Compared to the bombed-out industrial suburb where she had been exiled, it was very pleasant. Here, repairs to war damage were evidently a higher priority. New roads were being built, bombsites were being cleared. They passed a large construction area where rows of bulldozers, diggers and mobile cranes were waiting to spring into life. Clearly, being in the party brought benefits which were denied to humbler folk, who had to put up year after year with environments degraded by war.

They passed Schönholz railway station, where commuters were starting to assemble, some reading books as they walked, others still half asleep on their feet. A mile or so past the station, Möller took a smaller road, leaving the traffic behind. It led through sandy, low, unbuilt hills, covered with bushes and weeds, beside the tracks of the S-Bahn railway. And after a mile or so, he turned into a forested area where there were no houses to be seen.

It was extraordinary, Karolina thought, how quickly the urban landscape of Berlin gave way to woodland or expanses of water. They could have been buried in the country, and not in the suburbs of a great city. The trees hung over the road, making a green tunnel. She was baffled. Why had Herr Möller brought her to this rather remote part of Berlin? Had something gone terribly wrong with the plan?

He slowed the motorcycle and turned off again, this time into the woods. The tarmac gave way to earth. Möller's motorcycle bumped uneasily over the ruts. This track was so overgrown that branches snatched at them as they passed, forcing Karolina to duck.

At last, the jarring journey ended. Möller switched off the

engine, dismounted, and opened the hatch of the sidecar to release Karolina. Stiff with being cramped so long, she clambered out and arched her back, looking around her. They were deep in the woods. The silence was deafening after the constant rumble of the MZ.

'What now?' she asked Möller anxiously.

'Now we walk,' he replied. 'But first—' He put their helmets into the sidecar and then covered the motorcycle with branches, which he'd evidently prepared in the past couple of days, as Karolina noticed the cuts were fresh and the leaves still green.

'So we're not going on the expressway?' she asked as he worked.

He shook his grizzled head. 'No.'

'But what about the plan?'

Möller arranged the cut branches to his satisfaction, camouflaging the machine as best he could, and turned to her. 'That was never the plan, *Mädchen*. They listen to everything we say in that building. They think I don't know they have microphones hidden in the ceilings. We had to throw them off the scent. They'll be waiting for us at the Schönefeld crossing.' He smiled grimly. 'They'll wait a long time. Come!'

He led her in single file along a narrow track that wound between the trees. Doves and other woodland birds were singing, and once they startled a hare, which sat up and stared at them with wild brown eyes before dashing away.

After a few hundred yards, they emerged cautiously from the woods to the edge of an expanse of open scrubland. Then she saw it, fifty yards away, a grey, ugly, concrete barrier that blocked the way, extending to the right and left as far as the eye could see.

The Wall.

Möller stopped her from leaving the cover of the trees. They hunkered down together among the yarrow and the elders that grew wild all around.

'The guards don't patrol here because it's difficult to get to,' he said in a low voice. 'They don't think anyone would come here. But we will keep out of sight, all the same.'

'What are we waiting for?' she whispered.

'Your father. Are you hungry?'

Karolina nodded. Möller disappeared among the brush. She turned her gaze back to the Wall. The vegetation had been cut in a wide strip all along the concrete base. The Wall itself was around ten feet high here, made of sheer concrete slabs, capped with Y-shaped steel brackets which supported a dense coil of barbed wire that stretched all along the top.

Looking at it now, she felt a spasm of revulsion that was like nausea. How she hated it! It embodied all the cruelty, all the narrowness, all the obsessive paranoia of the communist system. Even as a *Wolfskind*, she'd been free to wander with the others across a landscape that was devastated by war and bristling with mortal dangers, but nevertheless open.

The Wall had placed limits on every life. It had blotted out the horizon. It was the murder of a city, a country. It was where every hope perished. It was where growth ceased. It turned Berlin into a prison.

If she could have torn it down with her bare hands, she would have done it right now.

With a smooth rustle, Elias Möller was beside her again. For a burly, middle-aged man, he moved silently through the brush. He had collected a handkerchief full of late blueberries, which he held out to her. They were sweet and juicy. 'Where is Ulrich?' she asked, devouring them gratefully.

'He will be here soon. Patience.'

'But—'

'Patience,' he repeated. 'No talking.'

Karolina fell silent. She stared at the coils of barbed wire and wondered how anyone could ever get over that. It was now seven thirty, and growing warm and humid. The sun was up. The sky was a delicate blue, streaked with cirrus clouds. They stayed hidden from sight. Karolina was a tight bundle of nerves, her heart alternately accelerating and sinking. Incredibly, Möller fell asleep, his cap over his eyes, his arms folded on his breast. The old soldier had not forgotten the survival tricks of the battlefield.

The warmth had almost put Karolina in a drowse when her ears caught the indistinct note of an engine. She sat up quickly. It had awoken Möller too, and he produced a small pair of binoculars from his coat pocket, peering cautiously over the tops of the bushes.

'Here he comes,' he muttered with quiet satisfaction. 'Not long now.'

Karolina strained her eyes to see what Möller was looking at. There was a faint, distant smudge of grey smoke in the trembling summer haze. Then she saw the vehicle take shape, crawling towards them like a giant bug. She couldn't identify it at first.

'Get ready,' Möller said. 'This has to be quick. Remember – be brave.'

Now she could make out some kind of construction vehicle, painted a dirty grey. As it drew closer, she saw with astonishment that it was an old Liebherr mobile crane, like the ones they had passed at the construction site near the railway station. The massive wheels supported a platform on which a telescopic tower hoist was mounted. And she could see that Ulrich von Breda was at the wheel, wearing white overalls and a hard hat.

'I'm going over the Wall in *that*?' she gasped.

Möller's face was tense. 'Don't move, yet. Wait until he reaches us.'

The mobile crane rumbled up to them, its bulk like a

prehistoric monster of some kind. Von Breda positioned it close to the Wall. He waved to them.

'Go!' Möller commanded sharply, slapping her on the shoulder. Her legs as shaky as a newborn fawn's, Karolina ran towards the machine, Möller following close behind.

Von Breda jumped down from the driver's seat as she reached it. He put his arms around her, tight enough to squeeze the breath out of her lungs. For a moment, there was nothing in her mind but this embrace. When she'd first met him, such a short time ago, all she felt was anger and distrust. Now, for a split second, she was whole – whole as she had never been before, whole as she might never be again. The rhythmic thudding of the diesel engine was like the beating of a great heart around them.

Then her father pulled her to the front of the crane. Attached by chains to the hook on the front of the hoist was a steel mesh basket, designed to hold building materials. 'You will have to jump the last part,' he said. 'Roll with it. Like a ball. Understand?'

She couldn't reply. Her throat was too choked. He hoisted her into the basket as easily as if she'd been a kitten. Then he climbed back into the driver's seat and grasped the levers. The engine roared, black smoke pumping from the exhaust.

'Hold tight!' he shouted.

The basket swung free, forcing her to grasp the rusty chains for balance. The machine was old but powerful. Slowly, the sections began to extend, telescoping outward and upward. She was being pushed away from the cab, and at the same time lifted alongside the concrete blocks. She saw Elias Möller looking up at her, his hands on his hips. She saw her father pulling on the levers.

As she rose slowly into the sunlight, strange, inchoate memories whirled in her mind, memories of arms that had lifted her long ago, of arms that had held her up to the sun, of voices that had been full of love and laughter. Of a time before sorrow. Of a time of innocence.

Up, up, the tower lifted her, passing the swirls of hooked steel wire. As if in a dream, she could now see over the Wall. She could see the steel tank-traps down below, the electrified fences, the raked gravel in the middle that was the Death Strip, seeded with mines. There was a guard tower, but it was empty.

Then she heard the first shots. She twisted in the steel cage to look back in dread. A military truck was speeding across the mown strip towards the mobile crane, a dozen armed, uniformed border guards in the back.

Von Breda was ignoring them, concentrating on manoeuvring the tower. But Herr Möller had taken shelter on the lee side of the vehicle. He was holding something – a war-era machine pistol. He fired a careful burst at the guards' truck. It swerved abruptly and came to a standstill about thirty yards from the crane. The soldiers jumped down, grasping rifles. One knelt and aimed at the basket Karolina was in. She was frozen with terror. But another burst from Möller's machine pistol forced the marksman to run for shelter before he could loose off a shot. The others followed suit, taking cover behind the truck.

Her father was apparently indifferent to the firing, carefully manoeuvring the Liebherr so that the arm could be extended further across the gap. The basket was inching towards the other side of the Wall, but every now and then, von Breda had to drive the vehicle back to get better clearance. She was swinging high in the air now, with a bird's-eye view of everything – the men shooting at one another on the east side, the brutal layout of the Wall below her, and the suburban houses of West Berlin on the other side. The blue of heaven above.

The border guards had gone on the attack now. Their truck inched forward, the men following behind it, step by step, firing their rifles around the sides. The loudspeaker mounted on the truck was booming. She heard the familiar, harsh, metallic voice, 'Halt! Halt! Remain where you are! Throw down your weapons. Do not move!'

These were the dreaded and hated *Grenztruppen* who each year killed untold numbers of East Germans trying to escape to the West. They were highly trained. They knew what they were doing.

The guards were gaining on the mobile crane, despite Herr Möller's bursts of fire, which had by now starred – but not shattered – the windshield of the truck. The guards' bullets were ricocheting off the crane, whining through the air. The arm of the crane was moving with agonising slowness, but she no longer cared about that. She just wanted her father to stop what he was doing, so they wouldn't kill him.

Then she saw her father hit. He slumped over the steering wheel, his head lolling. The arm of the crane stopped moving, leaving her stranded high above the Death Strip.

'No!' she screamed in horror.

With a slow effort, von Breda hauled himself upright. His white overalls were stained dark red across the chest. But his hands groped for the levers, and the arm began to swing again, jolting into movement.

And Elias Möller broke cover now, coming around the Liebherr with his machine gun, firing short bursts as he walked towards the guard truck. At least two of the *Grenztruppen* had been hit, and lay in the wake of the truck, unmoving. Karolina clung to the chains, high in the sky, frozen with horror as her father inched her towards freedom.

He had known this would happen. Suddenly, she understood. He and Herr Möller had been prepared for all this. They had known they could never survive it. They had both accepted it. For her sake. That had always been the plan.

There was a volley of shots. Möller went down, his machine pistol silenced, and sprawled among the weeds like a broken doll.

She was sobbing, her heart splitting in two. She had just found her father, and now she was losing him forever. Nothing had passed between them except a few harsh words and a rough embrace. And now it was over.

She saw her father hit again, his body jolting with the bullets that pierced him, the crimson stain spreading over his overalls. But he clung doggedly to the controls of the Liebherr. And with a final jerk, he brought the arm of the crane crashing down. It smashed onto the barbed wire and the metal supports, crushing them. But she was dangling just across the Wall, in West Berlin.

She heard someone screaming her name.

'Karolina! Jump! Jump!'

She remembered her father's last words: *You will have to jump the last part. Roll with it.* She opened her eyes. Below her was a grassy bank. And on the bank was her sister, holding out her arms.

'Jump, Karolina!'

She swung herself out of the steel cage. For a moment, she hung in the air, swaying. Then she let go. But she was too close to the barbed wire. She fell into it, the steel thorns seizing her as though they were alive. They tore into her clothing, stopping her descent, clawing at her flesh. She hung there, upside down, unable to move, hearing the gunfire on the other side of the Wall that ordained the death of her father.

Ulrich von Breda clung to the steering wheel of the Liebherr, his hands slippery with blood. He managed to raise his head and look at the arm of the machine which had made a bridge to freedom for his daughter. The plan had worked, as he'd prayed it would. He hadn't deserved that. But *she* had deserved it. And that had saved them both.

The terrible injuries caused by the *Grenztruppen*'s bullets were such that he knew he could not survive them. He had come to the end of his road. It could have been a longer road, a road that led to a peaceful old age, surrounded by love and respect. But he had taken bad decisions in his life, had done terrible things. There was no forgiveness for him. All those dreadful mistakes. He was lucky to have salvaged, at this last moment, some kind of honour. Against all the lives he had ruthlessly taken, this one life he had saved was a tiny candle in a vast darkness.

He had brought his far-flung daughters together. It was something to throw in the balance. It would make no difference to the judgement that awaited him. But it was not nothing.

And at least he was dying like a soldier, on the field of battle. Not cowering in ignominy, murdered by the many people who hated him. He was grateful for that.

He turned his head to look at Elias Möller, who lay next to the crane, staring up at the sky with empty eyes. He, too, had died a soldier's death. They would meet in hell, soon enough.

Dimly, he heard the warning shouts of the border guards approaching, calling on him to surrender. They didn't know he was unarmed. Möller's old Schmeisser, lovingly hidden away for two decades, had been the only weapon they could lay their hands on at such short notice.

There was one last thing he had to do.

Fighting against the choking blood in his torn lungs, he forced himself to rise to his feet and face the *Grenztruppen*. He clenched his fists and bared his teeth, the last defences he had against a hated enemy. He saw the grey-clad men raise their rifles and fire one last volley at him.

One final agony. The *coup de grâce*. And then he was done with it all.

Seeing her sister hooked on the coils of barbed wire was the single worst moment of Agnes's life. The cruelty of fate was never more naked to her. She screamed Karolina's name, trying to help her; but she hung too high, out of reach. At any moment, the guards' bullets would come, killing her as she hung helplessly, a butterfly caught in a steel spiderweb.

The knot of curious passers-by which had formed in the quiet suburban street shouted advice or encouragement. But none of it was any use.

Until Constanze drove the car up the bank, its wheels spinning in the soft earth, and brought it crashing into the Wall, the radiator bursting in an explosive cloud of steam.

'Get on the roof!' she shrieked at Agnes.

Agnes didn't understand at first. Then she scrambled onto the roof of the car and stretched up her arms. Now at last she could reach Karolina. She pulled hard on her sister's shoulders, sobbing for air, again and again. And at last Karolina was free. She fell heavily into Agnes's arms, her clothes ripped, her flesh bleeding. Clinging to each other, they slid off the car and onto the soft green grass, and lay there wrapped in one another, inseparable.

The East German authorities made the most of the 'incident', playing down the embarrassing fact of a successful escape by an East German citizen, and presenting it as a triumph of the ever-vigilant Stasi against 'encroaching capitalism'.

A 'notorious Nazi war criminal' had been shot, along with his accomplice, while engaged in unspecified activities designed to bring serious harm to the DDR. Two brave border police officers had been seriously wounded defending the State, but were expected to survive their injuries, and were being recommended for medals. It was yet another example of the endless attacks on the Warsaw Pact being mounted by the Western imperialist forces of evil, and would lead to increased vigilance, the only way to defend democratic socialism.

This story had the effect, at least, of taking the pressure of publicity away from Agnes and Karolina, although Constanze

Ozerki was more than willing to give interviews to anyone who would listen, explaining that it was solely through her determination that her lost daughter had been found and restored to her. She was the woman who had driven her luxury car like a battering ram into the Berlin Wall, an act of deep symbolism. In a life that had been comfortable but largely dull, it was a personal drama that she would continue to revel in for years to come, long after her contact with – not to mention her interest in – both Karolina and Agnes had faded away.

She'd wanted both girls to move into her opulent hotel with her, but they'd preferred to stay in the hostel, not least to get away from reporters and photographers. And Karolina needed quiet and privacy to recover.

The long nightmare was over. But like all nightmares, it did not leave easily. It kept them in its grasp for a long time, slowly fading, becoming a dream, and then at last, reality.

A few days later, when the fuss had died down, a parcel arrived from East Berlin for Karolina, wrapped in brown paper and neatly tied with string. Agnes was afraid that it was a bomb, some kind of revenge from the Stasi. But the West German police assured them that the package had been examined, and contained nothing harmful.

Karolina opened it with her bandaged fingers. It contained only a book: the copy of Thomas Mann's *The Magic Mountain* that Rafael had given her, and which she had been reading.

There was now a brief inscription on the first page – just the date of her escape. Someone had written it, and the same someone had posted the book to her as – what? A memento? A salute? Had it been Rafael who had done this? Perhaps the only person with the authority to do it was Bergmann himself. It was, perhaps, his farewell to her.

She would never know. But the book was the only thing she had from her life in the East, and it meant much to her.

Karolina had suffered several cuts from the East German

barbed wire, some requiring stitches and a course of tetanus immunoglobulin and antibiotics. But these were not what made her cry from time to time. She, more than her sister, had formed an instinctive, emotional bond with Ulrich von Breda, a bond which went beyond moral questioning. Whatever he had been, whatever he had done, he had freed her at the cost of his own life. She felt that she owed him a debt.

It was Agnes who found a way they might repay it. The same stranger who had delivered von Breda's note on the eve of the escape returned with a second message some days later. As before, he disappeared as soon as he had delivered it. And as before, the note was brief and cryptic. It was an address in northern Spain, and beneath it a name – Beatrix.

'I think he wanted us to look after his dog,' Agnes said, stroking her sister's golden hair.

'His dog?'

'A German Shepherd called Beatrix. She's in a boarding kennels in Spain. He had two dogs, but one died. I don't think he had anyone else in his life. And if she's not taken out of there, she'll probably be put down in the end. He left us this.' She passed the note to Karolina. 'What do you think?'

Karolina's face lit up. 'Of course! We can't let them put her down. Let's go and get her!'

'All right. Agreed. I've never been to Spain.'

'I've never been anywhere,' Karolina said wistfully.

'We've got the whole world to explore,' Agnes said, smiling into Karolina's eyes. 'Where do you want to go?'

Karolina picked up the Bible which lay beside the bed. 'I used to have one of these,' she said. 'Officially, there's religious tolerance, but they still confiscated it. I enjoyed reading it. There's a passage that I always thought was so beautiful.' She leafed through the pages, found the passage she wanted, and read it to her sister:

'"Entreat me not to leave thee, or to return from following after thee; for whither thou goest, I will go, and where thou lodgest, I will lodge.'" She closed the book and looked into Agnes's eyes. 'That's the answer to your question, my sister.'

# EPILOGUE

*Norway, 1969*

It was winter now, and an icy wind was blowing. The harbour had been whipped into yeasty foam around the boats, which strained at their moorings. Snow lined the streets. But Berlevåg was just as Agnes had left it, a remote fishing village at the top of the world, the sky crowded with screaming, swooping gulls.

The last time she had come here, a stranger had spat in her face. But today she had her sister walking by her side, and although the few people in the streets stared at them, nobody spat. Of course, there was also the German Shepherd dog that went with them. It was a beautiful animal, but it looked as though trying to harm its owners might be a bad idea.

The path up to Liv Christiansen's house was steep, made slippery by ice. They had to walk carefully. The Arctic poppies were long gone. They left the gaily painted village houses behind, and climbed up into a frozen realm. Liv's house stood stark and alone, as before, white as bone against a leaden sky. That there were no flowers in the garden to be shrivelled by the cold meant that the place never changed, winter and summer.

'Oh,' Karolina said, with a catch in her voice. 'How lonely!'

'Yes,' Agnes said, squeezing her sister's hand. 'So lonely.'

Karolina stared at the dark windows. 'How can she live like this?'

'I don't think she had much choice. Are you sure you want to go on?'

'Yes,' Karolina said after a pause. 'I'm sure.'

'I warn you, she's half-crazy.'

'But so am I,' Karolina smiled. 'Maybe the craziness will cancel itself out?'

Agnes opened the gate, and they climbed the steps to the front door. She knocked. The silence was broken only by the mournful sound of the icy wind that came off the Barents Sea. Were they too late? Had their mother left this place? Would she open the door, even if she was here? Was she perhaps dead?

And then they heard footsteps from within. The locks rattled and the door opened. The woman in the doorway was unchanged since Agnes had last seen her. Her eyes, the blue of cornflowers, surveyed them both. She did not speak.

'You told me not to come back,' Agnes said. 'Don't be angry. I wanted you to meet my sister.'

'I am not angry,' Liv said. 'I read of his death. I knew you would bring her to me.' She stepped back. 'Come in.'

Karolina went first, as befitted the elder, and Agnes followed. They entered their mother's house. There was a fire burning in a stove somewhere in the interior, and it was unexpectedly warm.

Liv hesitated for a moment, like someone preparing to dive from a great height. Her eyes swam with tears.

Then she put her arms slowly around her two daughters and drew them close.

# ACKNOWLEDGEMENTS

My heartfelt thanks go to Emilie Marneur, Cara Chimirri, Laura Gerrard, Kay Coleman and the wonderful team at Embla.

# ABOUT THE AUTHOR

According to *Cosmopolitan*, Marius Gabriel 'keeps you reading while your dinner burns.' He is the author of a number of historical novels, including *The Girls in the Attic*, *Goodnight, Vienna* and *The Parisians.*

His novel set in wartime Paris, *The Designer*, won the Romantic Novelists' Association Prize for Historical Romance.

# ABOUT EMBLA BOOKS

Embla Books is a digital-first publisher of standout commercial adult fiction. Passionate about storytelling, the team at Embla publish books that will make you 'laugh, love, look over your shoulder and lose sleep'. Launched by Bonnier Books UK in 2021, the imprint is named after the first woman from the creation myth in Norse mythology, who was carved by the gods from a tree trunk found on the seashore – an image of the kind of creative work and crafting that writers do, and a symbol of how stories shape our lives.

Find out about some of our other books and stay in touch:

X, Facebook, Instagram: @emblabooks
Newsletter: https://bit.ly/emblanewsletter

Printed in Great Britain
by Amazon